The Secret Cure
SUE WOOLFE

The Secret Cure
SUE WOOLFE

PICADOR
Pan Macmillan Australia

First published 2003 in Picador by Pan Macmillan Australia Pty Limited
St Martins Tower, 31 Market Street, Sydney

National Library of Australia
cataloguing-in-publication data:

Woolfe, Sue.
The secret cure.

ISBN 0 330 36436 7.

I. Title.

A823.3

Set in 10.8/14.2 pt Sabon by Post Pre-press Group
Printed in Australia by McPherson's Printing Group

To a brother I never knew

I, with my melancholy, I, who often look upon myself as a despicable being, a good for nothing creature who should make his exit from life – I shall be upheld for ever by the thought that I am bound to Rousseau.

From *The Private Papers of James Boswell*, quoted in *The New Confessions* by William Boyd, Penguin, London, 1987.

Dear Professor Mueller

Here is the memoir and the letter that I told you about. I have
included in the letter some extracts from the investigation. They
will be familiar to you but because of the letter, I hope you will
read them in a new light, and change your mind. – T.

Part One
THE MEMOIR

CHAPTER 1
During which I walk into the world 7

CHAPTER 2
I take that fateful first step 17

CHAPTER 3
I consider my silence 23

CHAPTER 4
Despite my mother's warning, I find my love 31

CHAPTER 5
An accident affects my destiny 38

CHAPTER 6
So I become a spy 46

CHAPTER 7
During which I acquire a rival 56

CHAPTER 8
I resolve to know the meaning of love 66

CHAPTER 9
My rival becomes strangely burdened 71

CHAPTER 10
My rival's troubles are hinted at 80

CHAPTER 11
My rival reveals a fatal flaw 86

CHAPTER 12
I fall into the Slough of Despond, but so does my rival 91

CHAPTER 13
During which my rival makes an enemy and I make a plan 94

CHAPTER 14
My rival makes many enemies 99

CHAPTER 15
I begin to understand his fatal flaw 105

CHAPTER 16
I make my love a home 123

CHAPTER 17
A painful lesson 126

CHAPTER 18
My rival begins to decline 140

CHAPTER 19
During which, despite it all, my plan begins to work 155

CHAPTER 20
During which my plan founders 160

CHAPTER 21
I briefly contemplate poison 169

CHAPTER 22
An awful silence prevails 183

CHAPTER 23
I find a way to bear this torment 191

CHAPTER 24
Sandy uses my love as a bait for my rival 195

CHAPTER 25
During which my rival becomes an object of general suspicion 201

CHAPTER 26
I am plunged into an unbearable history 218

CHAPTER 27
I become a welcome visitor 230

CHAPTER 28
I hold new hope that my love will come to her senses 239

CHAPTER 29
Marconi changes my destiny 245

CHAPTER 30
I give up my love but begin to speak 252

CHAPTER 31
Sandy strikes again 257

CHAPTER 32
I am not invited to a party, but I am fatefully inspired 273

CHAPTER 1
During which I walk into the world

I KNEW RIGHT FROM THE START that my love was impossible. My mother had given me many warnings about human nature, but the one I heard most was to expect nothing from this tiny and pitiable world, especially love.

Despite the tiny and pitiable nature of the world, my mother instructed me that I should behave with honour (my father was oddly silent on this and most matters) so I knew that spying was dishonourable. But the honourable life was invented by people whom nature has smiled on, and made whole. Then there are the rest of us.

That's why I shouldn't have gone out into the world, even for the brief visit I envisaged. It's difficult to visit the world only briefly – though that's no excuse – I scarcely know how to think about what I've done. But now that I never intend to return to it, I will write up the shambling notes I made on bits of paper of all sizes and shapes – notebooks, the backs of envelopes, on cards and even on the occasional receipt, whatever was handy at the time in my shed near the statue of Samuel Craven Sudlow. I collected all the bits and pieces in two commodious cardboard boxes which now sit beside my favourite armchair (the blue velvet one, pushed near the window light). I've spent many weeks ordering the notes in the way they should appear in this memoir.* Order will teach me the import of what I've done. And what I failed to do.

Though how can I keep to order when my pen is bursting out of my hand with the memory of my first sighting of my love?

It was early in 1980 when I began to take these notes, and I remember it as a summer of the wildest winds in our country's short recorded history. They came from the west and swept across our desert, down the craggy mountains white and scented with flowering gum trees, and roared into Sudlow. They smelled of the places I wished I'd been to, the ideas I'd never quite understood, the conversations I felt doomed never to have and the woman my mother said I should never search for.

Late on the first day of those winds, I'd been leaning out the window gazing at nothing in particular in my street with its rows of morose Victorian buildings, their stone walls stained with a century's soot from the mines, their windows blank-eyed and grimy, their arched doors permanently locked, though Sudlow's central square was only a block away. But I wasn't thinking about Sudlow. I was troubled with a dream from the night before that kept poking at me.

I have the note to hand somewhere – to fill my empty days I'd taken to writing down lists of my dreams.

Here it is!

'Dream 27th February 1980 – a woman with her face turned away, lying on blood. She leaps up, like the flames of a fire.'

....

* He must have put together this memoir after all the years he spent in the lab taking notes. So I would date the notes from the year he mentions, 1980, through till about 1985. At all events, he must have finished the memoir before 1997. – T.

It came true! The dream came true!
But order, order.

I needed distraction that day – anyone or anything would do, an old lady heading for the church where I'd sung when I was a boy in the choir, or a man coming to kick impatiently against the kerb as he waited for the brothel to open. The church is below me but opposite, an ugly grey structure with pillars like animal claws knuckling into the footpath, and the brothel is off to the left on the top storey of one of the disused office blocks. It was, as far back as I remember, almost hidden from my view by the giant star-shaped leaves of a plane tree, and certainly it's still hidden from the ken of the old parishioners and the young priest whose jeans used to stick out beguilingly from under his cassock as he peered up the street for the organist, always late and puffing, his hair in damp, apologetic tendrils.

On that fateful day when my memoir begins, it was too late for church, and too early for the brothel. Buses regularly rumble down my street as they go through to the highway and out of Sudlow, but there was not even a bus in sight to distract me. I was alone under the sky.

There was nothing new in that. I'd been alone for seven years since my mother's death. I'd wanted nothing to change after she was gone. At first that was easy. My mother must've guessed her end was coming, and she'd set up a trustee to manage me. Two days after the funeral (thank God she'd organised it – I couldn't have), a young lawyer came knocking on the door. I'd glimpsed his smooth, self-assured face through my peephole and recognised him as the only other mourner at the crematorium. I'd panicked – I'm always panicking, I see in my notes, but I must admit to it – I panicked at what he might expect of me. So I didn't open the door, I hid instead.

His expensive shoes (with toe-caps) scratched the hall floor for a long time while he waited. At last he pushed something under my door and I heard him clump down the stairwell. Only when his car started in the car park did I open the door. He'd left a clutch of cream business cards full of scribble – no, here they are, and there's no scribble at all, in fact it's a painstaking copperplate done in studious black ink, though I notice he'd twice misspelled apartment, adding an unnecessary second p.

He'd written that my late mother (how her name still brought the tears welling in my eyes!) had told him of my incapacity, so he was surprised not to find me in. She had asked him to see to my every comfort. He was to select and deliver to my apartment a six-monthly package of what he called personal items, which turned out to be bulk packets of disposable razors and toothbrushes with stiff bristles. (He would only oversee the selection and the delivery, of course, because a lawyer cannot be an errand boy.)

More importantly, and again according to my mother's instruc- tions, he was also to deliver a weekly supply of my regular diet (the handwriting now wavered somewhat disapprovingly across a sec- ond business card), stated by my mother to be chocolate biscuits, tomato soup, ham off the bone, blackcurrant jam and Vegemite. If my diet changed (there is a slight crossing out and the beginning of a word that could once have been 'improved') I could contact him in writing, and to this end my mother had left a box of postage stamps in the second drawer on the right of the dining room bureau. (I already knew this, I knew every item in this apartment – I had just discovered she'd even packed into the spare wardrobe a job lot of navy trousers and blue shirts from a bankrupt factory so I wouldn't have to shop for clothes but would always be colour coordinated.) As postage charges increased, he was to present me with new stamps. Perhaps I didn't know that my mother had also sent a long-standing order to the milkman, who would bill him.

Of course, the copperplate smoothly continued on another cream card, I could contact him in a crisis about extra matters – for an extra fee. He would administer the basics – the deliveries and the apartments – for one half of the rent of one of our apart- ments, which he would extract (said the fourth card) before banking the remainder in the account set up by my mother.

There the copperplate communication ended.

So for my whole life I'd never have to think about the world or speak to it. My mother had believed that I'd never want to, or be able to.

She'd also left me the apartments – even as I write, still noisy with tenants, thanks to our work after my father's death – the books and the Handel recordings she'd inherited, as well as an automatic navy Hillman Hunter.

My mother had learned to drive the Hillman Hunter as soon as my father died, while I would cower beside her, passing notes that she couldn't read because she was speeding too fast – here's one in my childish handwriting:

'Dear Mum,

That was a red light.'

It was her one joy in the tiny and pitiable world, to screech through it in the Hillman Hunter, shouting out the wound-down windows:

I'll show you!

My mother had considered the car her friend, her only friend, in fact a boyfriend. A good man for climbing hills, she'd say, making me hot with jealousy. She even had a driving outfit, a rather stern rose-pink jacket and skirt with lace-edged sleeves (she was never seen without lace), which she'd wear whether we headed off to the sea or into the grey–green bushland that ranged like a wild animal nipping at the edges of Sudlow, threatening to devour us all. Sometimes she'd drive off without me, spinning down the street in her rose-pink suit with her hair whipping out of its pins and streaming behind her like a russet scarf. I'd crouch over a book to escape from the fear that she'd never return. But at last she'd burst through our front door so wind-burnt and bright-faced that I knew she'd shown them, whoever they were.

(A note here – ah, the disorderliness of memories. Once, when she'd reluctantly accepted my company on a spin in the bush and we'd stopped at a service station – hundreds of miles from any-where except the desert – she'd gone off to powder her nose in the ladies, leaving the engine running and the transmission in drive. I was twelve at the time and there beat, under my grey jumper rather impatiently and unevenly knitted by my mother, a heart growling with tiny rebellions. I simply couldn't stop myself – I slipped into her seat, eased the handbrake off and gave the accelerator an exploratory poke. The Hillman Hunter slid away, to my horror, and stopped, to my relief, outside the garage restaurant. I trembled for what she might say, but just as she'd angrily opened the Hillman Hunter door, a wolf whistle cut through the air. We both swung around. A man in the kitchen of the restaurant was bowing to my mother. She started, blushed, flounced her rose-pink skirt into her seat, all arms and legs (as I remember the moment now, I realise that she was trying to keep her left side, her birthmarked side, away from him – vain, adorable and secretly hopeful creature that she was), and she said:

Goodness knows where we'll end up today!

We only ended up at home.)

Ah, if only the pitiable world had bowed more often to her, how different her history and mine might have been.

Now there was only me, the books and the music. Once a month I had a small diversion, going down the stairs to our garage (scuttling like a cockroach past my tenants' open front doors in the hope no one would recognise me and ask me about the mice in the stairwell or the worn patch in the lobby carpet – those questions which require more than a silent nod in answer. Indeed, this fear made me a conscientious landlord, and much correspondence passed between me and the young lawyer about mice and carpets). In the garage, I'd lock the door behind me and turn the ignition key to let the Hillman Hunter tick over, give each tyre a bit of air with a footpump, check the oil level (it was always the same), check the water in the battery and the radiator (it never evaporated much), and dust and polish the navy duco. If I linger on this memory, it was because I felt strangely powerful in that garage. I'd pretend that she was sitting beside me, a passenger now, but her red hair, I imagined, was still flapping with defiance at our city.

Once I started to think that I should actually drive it – in her memory of course – especially when I came across a book by a racing driver (maybe *The Technique of Motor Racing* by Pierro Taruffi? Read when at lab, so try shelves dining room to living room).* I managed to back the Hillman Hunter out of the garage with Taruffi propped up companionably on the passenger seat. But Taruffi's interest in how to do a four-wheel drift at 150 miles per hour at Le Mans didn't help a lot when I was trying to steer while reversing down the driveway. I didn't get any further than the letterboxes. I wasn't meant to do this, I thought. I put the Hillman Hunter away, went upstairs, made another pot of tea and opened another book.

Apart from these visits to the car, I had only the company of the goings-on in the church and the goings-on in the brothel. The church didn't have many goings-on – not even a choir now – and from the brothel I didn't hear much either. I'd encountered brothels in literature, so I knew that from brothels there should be light-hearted sounds of drinking and merriment, perhaps a piano tinkling, gusts of laughter, and soaring cries of passion. My brothel wasn't like that. Only on hot nights did I hear anything – girls leaning out into the street from the windows, telling each other to come and catch the breeze. The only one I knew was called Charlene by the other girls.

Look at the moon, Charlene, a girl's voice might call out, and Charlene would come and lean out. That's how I remember her – round-cheeked, snub-nosed, with wavy silver hair in the moonlight.

Can that be true? Could a young woman have waves of moonlight-coloured hair?

The moon's as bright as the sun, Charlene called once back into the room, but her voice drifted between the leaves of the plane tree and across to me.

I wish we could see the moon on the ocean, she said. Imagine it – like a pathway to somewhere we've never been!

....

* He never got around to checking the accuracy of the references he makes. I think it was too daunting to try, because of the bewildering system, if I may call it that, of his family's vast library. – T.

Charlene had waved to me when I was twelve, when I was first losing my voice, and she'd shown me that under her pink satin slip, her fawn nipples were shaped like the leaves of the plane tree. I'd tried to hide my surprise and wave back politely but ever since, when she came to gaze out the window, she'd ignored me. Nevertheless, I loved her dearly and every afternoon I looked for her. Then one dreadful day, in my twentieth year, while I was still in mourning for my mother, I'd seen the flash of an engagement ring on her finger as she reached for the window catch. Perhaps she was marrying one of the kerb kickers, though which one I never knew.

After Charlene left, I fell into a melancholy, the sort of melancholy the great poets wrote about when they were pining for love. I'd find myself weeping over silly things for no reason at all, the rising of the moon, for example, now that Charlene was no longer sharing it with me. I'd spend fourteen, fifteen hours a day in sleep, and wake exhausted, I'd grind my teeth in fury at the earnest way the priest clasped the hands of his stooped congregation (by now he'd moved on from denim jeans to corduroy ones) and at the blind, uncomprehending way the new prostitutes' breasts nuzzled against the windowpanes when their owners watched for customers between jobs (Charlene's breasts hadn't seemed blind and uncomprehending at all). The problem was, I had nothing to believe in, nothing to yearn for. It wasn't that I expected happiness. I would have welcomed heartbreak as I spat grape pips towards the pink scalps of the parishioners so they looked up and spoke of rain. Everyone except me seemed to believe that things had a shape, a pattern, that if their lives hadn't moved into a shape yet, they would soon, but for me there would never be a shape at all. I'd grown impatient with singing along to my records, and impatient with the books. For a start, by this time I'd read my way around the apartment from the front door as far as the living room. What if the books ran out before my life did? And worse, books were too accommodating – even when they argued for preposterous action they were like adoring dogs which I could shut outside in the cold.

Then came the days of the wild summer westerlies that slammed doors all through my apartment as if everything was finished, as if doors would be slammed forever.

The world is a tiny, pitiable thing, I said, just as my mother had taught me. I have no wish to know it.

But my voice echoed mockingly among those slamming doors. How did I know what the world was? Since I was a boy, when my father had pulled me out of school so I wouldn't shame him anymore, I'd only glimpsed the world from a speeding Hillman Hunter.

And my mother – am I setting this down in the right order? – my mother had said something very odd on the last day of her life, something that contradicted all she'd taught me.

No – later. I'll set it down later.

I should've returned to my book. If I had, then nothing would've happened. But I didn't. Instead I paced around my apartment, past the huge grandfather clock, past all the books my mother had placed tearfully in their serried rows, and past the ever-diminishing unread books, past my piano with all the sheets of music I'd already sung, my stereo with all the music I knew by heart, past my tidy, narrow bed where I would toss alone for the rest of my life, and then I paced back to the window.

A wild plan came to me. I could leave my apartment – how the thought thundered in my mind! – go down into the street and see all the people I'd never seen since childhood. I could be like my favourite character (what was his name?) in a book by Dostoyevsky (read before my mother died, so check between the front door and my bedroom), an endearing, melancholy, apparent simpleton who was both honourable and wise as he lurched unarmed over the battlefields of Russia to learn about the human heart. I'd only have Sudlow to wander in, but surely I'd become wiser (I thought I was already unimpeachably honourable) as I rubbed shoulders with the bustling populace, and stood at shop windows fingering the change in my pockets to encourage the toils of shopkeepers – one hand behind my back, the other leaning perhaps on a furled umbrella like that hero in . . . *War and Peace*! I could saunter out soon – tomorrow, after breakfast even – perhaps I could handwrite a note for the shop assistant, who I imagined as a girl with rosy cheeks and a gingham apron:

'A pot of tea for one, please.'

I could smile at passers-by and give lollies to their children, if that is what one does these days, but certainly I could give meaty bones to their dogs.

(Here's a note I never sent – 'Write to my lawyer to add meaty dog bones to my weekly delivery.')

I could sit in parks, my arms looped casually on the back of a bench, in fact I could be quite urbane in parks, my shirt collar open, my benign glances taking in the boys bowling cricket balls and the lonely mothers sunning their babies. I could ride on public buses – could I get on a bus without speaking? I could sit in a hotel lobby and pretend I had a traveller to wait for, and watch the ardent gazing of lovers before they ascended to their rooms. I could be seen by the grateful populace appreciating the ornate buildings and squares our nineteenth-century forefathers had devised in the hope they were building a thriving and prosperous city. I could wait underneath the timetable at the train station and check my watch anxiously against the station clock, I could hurry with the crowds through the subway under the station, I could be part of it all, and learn about the human heart, though what I'd certainly learn is what my mother said, that the entire scurrying world is a tiny, pitiable thing, that to be part of it is nothing, merely nothing.

Surely that last breathless, contradictory pronouncement of hers was the result of the appalling heat, and the ghostly hand of death.

I could visit the world, I thought, for – a week? How my heart pounded, but a week out of an entire lifetime seemed rather miserly. A year? A year was too extravagant. A month! I could with fortitude manage a month, and then return to my apartment and my books and my music and know that when I'm old (in those days I considered forty to be old), when I lie on the white sheets of my deathbed alone, I'll be able to say that, for a month, I knew the world and my mother had spoken truthfully – it was indeed nothing.

CHAPTER 2

I take that fateful first step

I RAN AROUND THIS APARTMENT, finding my walking shoes, almost new though long mouldy with disuse and humidity, and a jacket, fearful that my courage would shuffle off me like an unbuttoned garment sliding down to slump at my ankles. I grabbed an umbrella to go with my rather bookish picture of myself, and put it down – who could hold an umbrella against this wind? I remembered to take a notebook and pen, for it came to me that I should note down fragments from the world, because sometimes fragments are like lopped-off columns, making the eye reach beyond to see what might have been more clearly than what is.

Until then I hadn't noticed that in my loneliness I'd made the things in my apartment into companions. So the workbenches had gleamed in a smiling way while I made my first cup of tea in the morning, and the shadows, lengthening into the same shapes every day and then receding, had become like friends who apologetically must step outside for a while to run an errand but they'd be back the next day. The water in my pipes had seemed to whinny like an animal begging for a pat, and the roof had ticked in a chatty way as it cooled in the evening. Even the wooden windowsill had thrown a friendly warmth onto my sleeveless arm. Only the heavy, dark wood furniture bought by my parents for their wedding seemed disappointed, reproachful even, as if they'd given it expectations of a more purposeful life and now it had to settle for my petty one.

As I ran downstairs, each step jarred me into an embarrassed awareness of all these contrivances devised in my isolation. But I would leave such foolishness behind, and return in a month a wise man of the world.

I burst out into the street, and the heat and wind of the great outside hit me like a wave. Nevertheless, I walked calmly round to the square, but everyone was right at that moment getting on buses, wind-cowed, fumbling for their change, or huddling darkly in shop doorways. It seemed that they hated the wind. I wanted to shout: Smell it! Feel it! Think of the promises it makes! But of course I have no voice. I halted, foolish, confused, and a bus blew grey exhaust fumes over me as it revved past. I felt from the windows only the blank circles of watching faces. Scraps of newspaper blew towards me, to wrap around my legs like washing. Down a side street, I glimpsed a goods train laden with coal. The sudden shriek of its horn sounded like a dying animal. I looked up at the buildings for help but they were covered with graffiti.

Nevertheless I had come to exile myself into the world for a month and surely, surely the world would notice. I was dizzy with hope that someone would hail me from a passing car, to ask the time or the way, not that I could answer, of course, but perhaps they would laugh if I bent about like a lashing tree to mime the power of the wind or if I flopped sideways to show that I was suffering in the heat. Instead, what I heard was scornful laughter, just like in my childhood. I wheeled around, but naturally it was only the buffeting of the wind in my ears, carrying old echoes from my schoolyard taunters. Those taunts never go away completely, they are still in the molecules of air, the way that everyone's breath is, even molecules of the actual air once breathed in and out by Julius Caesar. So mockery lasts forever.

I wanted to dash back upstairs but I must appear to be taking the air, I thought, even though it was scorching my throat as I breathed. I must not retreat until I have walked through a decent passing of time, perhaps ten minutes, that would do, no one would question a young gentleman taking a turn around the streets for ten minutes, I thought. Then I will return upstairs and reconsider.

And so I allowed myself to blow up the hill towards the district hospital, my shirt billowing, and I hoped I looked like a medieval explorer, Vasco da Gama, perhaps, heading towards China, stalwart, determined, never thinking of stopping to cavort with the singing mermaids nearby, should there be mermaids. Like da Gama, all that filled my view, I pretended, was the windswept horizon.

In this bereft and clownish state I reached the entrance of the hospital, a sprawling, hilltop nineteenth-century building whose gates are still grand like a portal and flanked on either side by giant gold sandstone columns. It comforted me that they had been carved into the heads of lions by some newly arrived, homesick artisan at least as displaced as me, though lions have never been seen in this remote country. I couldn't resist giving each of them a pat. Perhaps that was my undoing.

I can contain my pen no longer. I will allow it to remember my first glimpse of her, so like my dream!

My love, entering those gates, that portal. My love in her white lab coat with red silk swirling beneath it, just like my dream –

No, I will keep to order, I swear.

Order will save me and inform me.

So, there I was, outwardly confident but inwardly dithering. Patting the lions' heads while I waited for a plan to occur to me. I had to stay in the world for another ten minutes at least. And then I noticed a gleaming new motorised lawnmower abandoned where the ambulances come in, a mower with a scarlet seat. A mischievous impulse came upon me after my years of restraint. I seemed utterly unlike myself at that moment, as if the winds and the heat had created a new me whom the ordinary careful me could only watch. I found this new impulsive me walking up to the mower and sitting on that hot red seat, which curved deliciously into my bottom, and I fiddled with the controls, and the mower started. I'll get off it, I promised my former circumspect self, I'll get off in a minute.

I mowed right across the lawn – of course I knew I should not be doing this, but it was such a pleasure, the wind cutting into me like a knife, cutting into all those dull years of my confinement, so I was giddy with hope and the warm cut grass with its armpit smell and the engine roaring as I've never been able to, not since everything went wrong, and behind me, a long straight wake. It moved me to tears, that wake, as if by making it so straight I was putting things to rights. I'll mow just one minute more, I said, and that will be it. But there was a crop of dandelions wagging insolent yellow messages ahead, and I couldn't stop myself riding on and mowing them down.

Then suddenly I was turning a corner and up loomed a huge shed. I fumbled for the brake – was there a brake? – and I crashed to a stop in front of a man in a uniform.

What the hell are you up to? he shouted. It's the front lawn that they'll see!

So I roared my way to the front lawn. I didn't look up, in case they were all looking down, whoever they were, and I hoped they were admiring the hard-working mower man with the impressive wake. The Australian flag was flying like defiant hair out the window of a speeding car, and streamers attached to the stone walls had begun to tear off in their enthusiasm, and a banner was stretched in tight wrinkles across the door, saying 'Welcome Home'. Of course no one was welcoming me home, but I was thrilled with all my usefulness. When I'd subdued the entire lawn to barely a fuzz, I ran back to the shed with long, proud strides and found a broom and swept all the paths of every single clipping so the faded concrete beamed like a river in the sun.

Still no one told me to leave! I swept so hard that the head of the broom fell off. I ran back to the shed for another, and that's when I overheard what the fuss was, that a senior scientist from the hospital laboratory had been tipped to win a certain Prize, but it had been awarded to another country, whimsically, they said. He'd been travelling overseas and had just come home, but the journalists from *The Sudlow Echo* and the district television news had heard the rumours and were anxious to promote state-wide – even, it was hoped, national – indignation at such a slight to our city.

I went home, eager to see my lawns in close-up on the TV news. I switched it on at the right time and there they were, as smooth as the sea. That's why at first I scarcely noticed what the great scientist was saying.

It was his silence that drew my attention. People in TV interviews are seldom silent. He gazed with a shy intensity over my shoulder straight into my kitchen, directly at my toaster with its little circle of crumbs, as if he hadn't eaten for a while. Then he glanced at the interviewer in a quick, bird-like way, hoping the questions were over, when clearly they had scarcely begun.

Feel? he finally said in answer to some question that the interviewer had asked at least half a minute before. He thought about it further.

I don't know, he concluded unhappily.

Suddenly I believed I was looking at a man who'd never considered his feelings, whether he was in love, whether he was happy, if he liked Mozart or Shostakovich, the mountains or the sea, chocolate cake or vanilla.

He smiled lopsidedly, a sweet, apologetic grin. He had handsome, deeply hooded eyes, a shock of blond hair that stood almost upright from his forehead and seemed paler than his skin, but what I really noticed was his vulnerability. His face was more open than anyone's face I'd ever seen. He seemed a man without guile, and even more careless of his clothes than me. He'd worn a suit to the reception, but it was too short, as if he'd rushed into a shop and grabbed it blindly. His tie had a long and unexpected splotch on it, like oil paint. Yet you felt his intelligence in every movement of his face.

Looking back, I saw even then that he was one of those rare people you might come across once or twice in your lifetime, who alter your perception of everyone else. He made me suddenly marvel that people contain within the thin membrane of their skin a whole tumultuous universe that ends at their toes, at their fingers and at the edges of their face, and this all against a green lawn recently mowed – by me!

Are we finished yet? he asked innocently.

I understand, said the interviewer, a little flustered, that you're in immunology and highly regarded for your work to stop the body rejecting transplanted organs.

The scientist looked relieved at the mention of immunology and took a breath to speak, but a crow cawed in the tree above and he had to wait until it had finished.

The problem with most discoveries is knowing what to make of them, he finally managed to say.

He smiled apologetically again, though there didn't seem anything to smile at. There was a shadow on his front tooth – I suspected it was a star of parsley, perhaps from something he ate at the hospital reception. And I was becoming suspicious that the mark on his tie was a bit of dried egg.

Then unexpectedly he was off, escaping in almost a lope, careless that his trouser legs ended too soon and showed his bare pink legs above his turned-down socks, communing with his own tumultuous universe again and entirely forgetting that we were watching. I had a feeling that if he wanted to, he'd keep running away from the camera, even going as far as the desert whose tiny undulations lapped against our certainties as much as any ocean. The camera followed him across my lawns and I saw that I'd missed one skinny, wagging dandelion.

So right from the first, Professor Gunther Mueller and I were linked.

The next day I woke to a disturbing silence and found that the wind had died along with all its promises. Only a drift of leaves was left on the street below me, and above, there was a glowering, surly sky. The heat had faded into disappointment. The world is nothing, the sky said. I turned my face to the wall and clutched at sleep. But my pact kept scratching away at my peace like a branch on a windowpane, so eventually I got up, dressed, breakfasted and walked back to the hospital to sweep and clip its lawns, and the world was so indifferent that no one told me to leave.

CHAPTER 3

I consider my silence

ON MY THIRD DAY OF SWEEPING, the shadow of a large figure fell over me. I looked around and there was a middle-aged
woman. I stopped sweeping, dreading what was to come. She
didn't look like an authority, but a bunch of keys clanked omi-
nously at her waist.

You're not in a uniform, she said.

I searched her voice for accusation.

She wasn't in a uniform either, just a floral dress, but she had
an air of legitimacy, and I had none. We gazed at each other. A
long moment passed. Muscles moved across her cheeks. I tried to
speak.

I planned to say, 'I'm just helping the hospital'. 'I' used to be a
sound I could sometimes make but this time 'I' got stuck, wedged
between my tonsils. My jaw clamped. I tried to shake it free, the
way a dog shakes a ball, but it wouldn't move. I began to bang my
jaw while she watched.

They haven't employed you, have they? she said.

All I could do was shake my head. The game was up, I believed,
so I turned and headed off towards the gates with their lions'

heads, that portal, a portal no more, to go back to my apartment, to my isolation. But her voice came floating over the lawns.

They often employ the wrong ones, she called.

I turned.

Come on, she added.

She was moving towards the hospital, her swaying skirt as busy as her stout legs. She swept inside and I scuttled behind in her slipstream, past the reception area where a chattering group of office girls eyed me suspiciously but dropped into silence because of her. She turned down a corridor, and I turned behind her. She stopped at a door, unclipped the bunch of keys at her waist, opened up, and nodded impatiently for me to go through.

Goodness, man, are you always so timid? she asked.

I expected a manager's office and to be given a reprimand for trespassing, or at least put up with an interrogation, but all around me were just silent shelves.

I suppose some things are better left unsaid, she said. She spoke thoughtfully as if I'd just taught her that.

She turned to rummage on the shelves, and brought back something folded and grey, a grey uniform.

We wouldn't want you to stand out like a sore thumb, she said.

Then she led me out and locked up the room again.

Go and change – there's the Gents, she said.

I hurried away before she thought better of it, sat down in one of the cubicles, and cried. No one had ever given me a uniform before. A uniform means you're part of something. Since the choir, I'd never been part of anything.

I put it on and checked myself in the mirror. In the echoing of leaky cisterns (which I was to learn to tinker with constantly), an ordinary, solid, hard-working citizen stared out of surprised and slightly bulging eyes.

I shouldn't have dawdled because the woman was outside in the corridor, her arms folded. She nodded approvingly when she saw me.

You've got decency written all over you, she said. I wish I could say that for us all.

So the uniform had made me look like my true self, an unusually honourable person – as I thought then.

She led me to a tearoom where other grey uniformed men were standing in groups, having what I soon learned to call a smoko. Like the women in reception, they fell silent at her approach. She put her hand on my shoulder and announced that I'd been in a terrible accident that had left me mute, but for now I'd be joining them. As she swept out, she added:

Isn't someone going to get him a cuppa?

So a cuppa was got, full of burning hot, sweet milky tea which I tried to sip while the other grey men stared at me with the sort of awe usually felt for people who've returned from the dead. Then someone made a joke about the weather (my note here – 'So windy it would blow a dog off a chain') and everyone burst into loud laughter and I laughed too, though I didn't think that it was funny at all.

In fact, my stutter probably came from my father, an angry man with a dingy little electrical shop full of old washing machines and fridges and TV sets that he never got around to repairing, and dreams that one day a wealthy widow would walk in with an iron that needed fixing, and marry him. He who aims at the stars shoots higher than he who aims at the trees, he told me. He'd begun stuttering when he was eight years old but he didn't take it lying down, he said, and he'd cured himself by the time his voice broke.

No wealthy widow had walked into his shop, but in his thirtieth year when he was called out urgently to fix a blown fuse in the grand house of the wealthiest family in town, who should answer his knock on the tradesman's entrance but their only daughter, Berry. She had six older brothers in the family business, and she was already well into her forties and utterly dominated by her parents who'd named her after the strawberry-shaped birthmark on the left side of her neck. But her right side was pretty, she was dressed in an apron frilled with lace, she had a mane of wavy russet hair that flowed almost to her knees, and my father was a man who'd been waiting a long time.

Charm leapt to his lips, for perhaps the first and last time in his life.

Your hair's like the sea, my father said right there on the doormat, dressed in his overalls, luckily a clean pair that morning.

I have to run my fingers through it. A sea of red flowers. May I?

She was charmed, and held it out for him to stroke, and his hand, though gnarled, seemed softer than anything she'd ever known, so she brazenly did what she'd always longed to do, she held out the right side of her face for him to kiss, the pretty side where there was no strawberry stain.

Berry! You're dawdling again – come inside! called her mother, who was waiting to organise the day's housework.

But my father kept kissing the right side of Berry's face until her mother's footsteps came too close.

My father diagnosed the great house as being dangerously wired, and rewired it slowly and methodically, room by room, day by day. By the time he'd finished, Berry and he had planned a blissful life together. Her parents refused their permission and they didn't come to the wedding. Berry ended up inheriting only this library, this collection of every known recording of Handel, and this block of six flats, at that stage all utterly derelict. My father considered derelict flats a grievous insult after he'd taken their disfigured daughter off their hands, and only ever renovated our apartment, extending it into part of the apartment next door in order to accommodate all the shelves he had to build for all the books. Not that he ever read any, but he liked to be seen as a man of letters.

There's a photo of him wearing his smoking jacket – really just a velvet jacket – with pipe in hand. Behind him are dozens of untouched, unread, very upright books.

I remember when the books were delivered shortly after my grandmother's death. They were stacked in towers in the living room and my mother took the books out, one by one, box by box, and placed them on the new shelves. She started from the left-hand side of the front door and worked around the apartment in a clockwise fashion. My mother was always a dresser, even at home, and I still remember her stocky figure in a silky grey dress and grey high heels as she stood on a little ladder reaching for the upper shelves.

My job was to kick along the floor whatever box she happened to be emptying at the moment, and hand her up armfuls of books, and the occasional dry, lacy handkerchief for her tears. (Why did I leave home? she'd whisper to me and I had no answer to that.) So in this way we worked our way towards, into and out of the bedroom she shared with my father, then along the hall towards, into and out of my bedroom, towards but not into the bathroom, from the bathroom towards but not into the kitchen, then along towards, into and out of the dining room and the lounge room and right around the apartment back towards the right-hand side of the front door. She ran out of shelves and eight boxes have never been unpacked; they've just become part of the furniture I skirt around. The only trouble with this arrangement was that the books had been plonked into the boxes by a careless servant just where they happened to squeeze in, without regard to subject or author, and my grieving mother put them up on the shelves in the same way – as if Dewey had never devised his admirable System. When my mother had filled all the shelves, we were walled in with the great thoughts of the western world, though how to locate any particular thought, I've never been able to work out.

Living in a renovated apartment amongst crumbling ruins was like hiding in a hilltop cave while all around smashed a tormented sea. When my father was out tinkering with someone's Mixmaster, my mother and I would creep around the other apartments to discover another floorboard spongy underfoot from termite damage, another waterstained ceiling, another gutter hanging by a thread of rusty metal, more chunks of plaster fallen off the walls, more rising damp. All around the grounds lantana and privet grew, and we regularly had to chop errant and prickly boughs just to get to our letterbox.

It's not my parents he's avenging, it's me, she'd say. He thinks I tricked him into marriage.

My father spent his time and the money he earned on me instead. I was to make up for his disappointments. Though we ate very little meat and my mother never bought herself a new hat, I was sent off to Latin classes, to elocution lessons, to tennis lessons (my father believed that tennis was played by people as important as I was to become), and to choir in this grey church opposite my window. I hated it all except the choir and I would happily have spent all my time hanging around in his dingy shop fixing fridges. To make some grandmother's old Silent Knight begin to hum was my greatest joy. But my father forbade that. My mother said I was a genius with wiring, just like my father, but she wouldn't have said it to him because everything she said seemed to make him furious.

Shortly after my twelfth birthday, when my father was walking me home from tennis and demanding to hear my score, my voice faltered and stopped.

Say it! shouted my father in the street, careless of other schoolboys staring. Say it! Spit it out like a man!

But losing six–love, six–love just wouldn't be said.

My voice came peeping out after he'd left for work, but it seemed frightened of him and when he returned home, it went away again. It was a stutter more severe than his – it was a silent stutter.

My father told me to get a grip on myself, to get over it like he had, not to take a minor setback like this lying down. But no matter how hard I tried to get a grip, no sound would emerge.

There might have been a moment when I stopped trying to unlock my jaw. Did I just give up? To all intents and purposes, I became a mute. People would ask me a question and I'd writhe, trying to force a sound out, any sound. But they wouldn't even know I was trying to speak. How I longed to have an ordinary, noisy stutter, so that people would say to each other:

Hold on – I think he's trying to say hello!

Most times, I couldn't even grunt.

Strangely, I could still sing in the choir, and how I loved standing in the front row, second from the end, opening my mouth to usher out a voice that rang all the way up to the rafters. The choir master often pointed me out to people, the boy who couldn't speak but could sing like an angel.

One day, after a performance in the town square, the choir was presented to the Sudlow mayor, a man with an imposing stomach and three chins that rippled down towards it. My father was in the crowd and I could hear him clapping longer than anyone else, and people good-naturedly hushing him.

The choir master put his hand on my shoulder and whispered:

The mayor has promised us a cheque, and I want an angel to go up and accept it. You can do it, he added as he saw my horrified face. All you have to do is walk up and stick your hand out. You can do it – go now! he said, and gave me a little push. I still remember the warmth of his well-meaning hand on my back.

I forgot to move my feet, and almost fell. The crowd was silent, even my father's hands had stopped clapping. I thought: All I have to do is walk up and stick my hand out. So I did – almost. I took one step after another, held out my hand, took the cheque and it was nearly over and I could walk back. But then something unto-ward happened. The huge man with his ceremonial chain tugged me over to the microphone and said:

What's your name, young lad?

I couldn't say my name.

From that moment my father took me out of school – there were enough books around our walls for an education, he said – out of the world and, as a punishment, out of the choir. That night, and for the remaining two years of his life, with all the doors and windows shut to muffle the noise of my shrieks and my mother's pleas, as if the wild ocean of our crumbling flats could know or care, my father belted me. His secret cure, he called it. Try! he'd shout. Try!

One day when he was belting me, his heart gave way. He rallied enough to lift his head.

At least have the grace to say goodbye! he cried.

But I didn't, or couldn't, and he died.

———

My mother sold his shop with its flyspotted glass window and all its unrepaired machines, and sent out the invoices he'd never got around to sending. With the money she had one of the apartments, apartment number four, repaired and sold. Then she had the other four repaired, their kitchens and bathrooms and bedrooms and halls. She let me hack away the lantana and the privet, and she planted a garden and made a narrow car park.

I watched the workmen and got in the way, but she gave them strict instructions that I wasn't to hold a hammer in case I lost a thumb. She never knew that I held a hammer many times, I couldn't bear not to, and I wired and soldered and sawed and measured. Each time an apartment was finished and rented to a tenant, we'd celebrate by taking a spin in the country in the navy Hillman Hunter, and at night I'd go to sleep secretly imagining the new tenant family was just at that very moment admiring the taps I'd helped install or the walls I'd helped plaster. I imagined them saying: We must meet this workman and shake his hand!

My mother said we deserved our pleasures, and perhaps we did.

CHAPTER 4

Despite my mother's warning, I find my love

I KEPT GOING TO THE HOSPITAL day after day in my grey
uniform. It was so crisp it fretted my skin, but I didn't mind because
it was keeping me company in my new life.

At first I was terrified of the other grey men, waiting for them
to gang up against me like the boys had at school once my stutter
set in. But day after day, they didn't. At the end of my first week,
Marconi, the most frightening of them all, came up to me and
pointed to my silent mouth.

Keeps you out of trouble, eh? he said and dug me in the ribs.

He had a scar like a purple intestine across his neck. (How did
the other guy look? he was often asked when banter was needed,
and everyone would begin to guffaw. Quiet, was the regular
answer. Corpses usually are.)

We both laughed at his joke and a little squeak of excitement at
such camaraderie came out of my mouth. He was startled but I dug
him in the ribs in return and that went down very well.

In fact, they all seemed eager to laugh at anything, often the
same joke over and over, and they all slapped their thighs and dug
each other in the ribs to emphasise that it was indeed the same

joke, in case anyone hadn't noticed. I rehearsed being fun-loving in front of my mirror, particularly chortling and slapping my thighs. I wished my father had told me about chortling and side-slapping. But perhaps he didn't know.

I learned that the hospital board had recently opened up and refitted the sleepy old laboratories that formed a wing on either side of the hospital, and had employed several research scientists, including the eminent Professor Gunther Mueller I'd seen on TV. They'd headhunted him from a distant university. But the grey men said that their jobs were as important as anyone's, so they called themselves after the world's most famous scientists – there was a Volta, a Rutherford, a Tesla, an Einstein and the scary Marconi, who'd taught me about rib-digging. Since I was new, I got Galileo, which no one else wanted because they all believed he'd been burnt at the stake. (Burnt rare or burnt medium? was one of the jokes, intoned in what was considered an English butler's accent, and gales of laughter followed.) I never got a chance to tell them my real name. I was just Galileo.

I soon discovered tensions. For example, every day the matron and sometimes the nurses wrote up on a chalkboard the problems that the grey men were to fix:

tv in common room on blink
new washing machine no spin
ward 3 fridge froze
laundry stairs chipped – who will break their neck?

We grey men were expected to do the next job on the list, no matter how unpleasant or dull, come back to the board and initial it, and then go on to the next job. On my second day as a grey man, wanting to please everyone, I rushed through the jobs and did them all, but I began to notice that most of the Gs I'd written on the board were rubbed out and a V, R, T or M inserted instead. A mistake, I thought at first, and corrected it, but Marconi came up behind me. He must've been lying in wait.

You trying to prove we're all bludgers? he shouted.

I shook my head so much my teeth almost rattled.

From then on I slowed down and did the same number of jobs as the others. I learned to look busy, especially at shift changes, because then I'd look busy to both the staff coming off duty and the people coming on. I even learned to stagger while I carried an empty bin.

For all my caution, my blood hammered in my ears one afternoon when Marconi stopped me in the corridor just as I was leaving. He was a giant man, and I'm short as well as a little rotund, so he had to bend over to speak to me. Little noises of terror kept coming out of my mouth. Marconi had to repeat the invitation several times before I could take it in.

We've hooked up a closed-circuit TV. Come and perv, it turned out he was saying. My whimpers had scarcely died away when he added:

On Shirley.

I'd noticed Shirley. She was noticeable because she did everything noisily; she even breathed noisily. She was an untrained technician and worked in the 'kitchen' part of one of the big empty labs, Top Lab, I'd heard it called. It linked to the hospital by a long corridor which I'd blundered down one day, for grey men were not supposed to be in the labs unless there was a crisis. I became adept at inventing crises. Now in my mind I am always in Top Lab as it was then, the door leading to the car park – how often my rival lingered at that door – the staircase leading up to his shared rooms, and the tiny area of the 'kitchen', which had no walls like an ordinary kitchen but was open to the rest of the lab. (There was an older scientist, a parasitologist, who worked out the back in what was called the Animal House, and two other women scientists who sometimes visited Top Lab but trooped off down the corridor and through the hospital to disappear into Lab Two, the lab I ransacked in my desperate attempt to copy Lotti's handwriting.

But I am getting ahead of myself again. Order will prove to me that there was a pathway of sense and logic in all that I did, and that I didn't create the catastrophe.)

————

Everything about the hospital was sprawling and cavernous. It meandered across the hill and down the other side. There were staircases that ended in blank walls and courtyards filled with weeds and boarded-up rooms and even a ballroom for the gentry of old Sudlow – now patients played ping-pong in it on rainy days.

The little shed where I went to spy on my love was in another neglected courtyard with lantana and garbage bins no one seemed to empty. It was dominated by a once-proud fountain dedicated to the memory of Samuel Craven Sudlow, after whom our city was named – or at least, renamed. Its original name, Saucepan Creek, wasn't considered a suitable name for a metropolis in the making, but the name of Sudlow, the benefactor of the hospital, gave us a respectable English tone, it was felt. I discovered, under a pile of rotting tea-chests, a bust of Mr Sudlow carved into the bowl of the fountain, a disapproving nineteenth-century gentleman with down-turned lips, a high starched collar, a carefully waxed moustache and a severe chin. Under his pocket chain and over his heart was a blackened brass plate he'd had inscribed with the words of Herbert Spencer: 'The human race is not forever to be mis-ruled by the random dictates of unbridled passion.' I smugly agreed, polished the brass till it shone, and re-stacked the tea-chests.

Sudlow's eyes, trained on my shed, were blind, the way statues are blind. If I'd figured out how to make the fountain play, he would've seemed like someone who, despite all his importance, didn't know to come in from the rain.

Shirley in her little kitchen section in Top Lab looked like an ant, or perhaps, with her golden hair, more like a beetle, and the lab was so barn-like that above her was a brooding immensity of space. There were no knick-knacks in Top Lab, no holiday postcards, no mess or piles of forgotten work, there were only workbenches and official black signs that threatened Sharps, or Danger. Shirley was in her late twenties, with big fashionable shoulder pads under her lab coat. She had chubby hands which she held at shoulder height during conversations, rounding her fingers into goblets for her thoughts, and then sliding her fluttering fingers down their stems, so her thoughts seemed visible, swaying like glinting wine. (Over the time I observed her, she gave up this distracting mannerism and clasped her hands over her stomach instead.)

She'd push her regulation protective glasses up on her crinkly sounding blond hair in a glamorous way, so for a moment she was like a movie star with sunglasses. Though her blond hair was tied back and under a regulation protective cap, it always threatened to stray out, and sometimes it did, falling over her face with an almost audible whoosh – and she only reluctantly fastened it back. She was a woman who went to a lot of trouble with her lipstick, so in that stern, colourless place you were always aware of her crimson lips; in fact, her lips seemed to take up a lot of any room she was in. Beautiful faces seem carved, with deeply set eyes and high cheekbones, but Shirley had an uncarved, shapeless face. You only noticed that when she wasn't smiling, and she was always smiling her crimson smile.

Marconi's invitation put me off going in to my new job for a day. I liked being a man with decency written all over him, and I worried about whether or not it was honourable to perv for the good of my worldly education. But I reasoned that my mother had insisted that I'd never have a wife, so I'd never be able to watch all those little things that women do when they're on their own. Of course, I'd watched my mother, but mothers aren't quite women. In the end, I decided I should accept the invitation because I was only going to be in the world a short time, and I must take every opportunity to see it.

In Top Lab there was a little room under the stairs full of old equipment (including an old-fashioned brass microscope, which a Mrs Bertrand Archibald had donated – it had a brass plate rather like the one over Samuel Craven Sudlow's heart, except that hers was engraved 'To the eager men of science to assist their healthful spirit of enquiry'. Its mechanisms had long ago seized up.). Shirley had shoved the machines aside and hung up a long mirror, so she could use it as her powder room. Often she went there with her make-up case (Marconi explained this to me in a condescending way, while I nodded and tried not to look like a perv). She had no way of knowing that the grey men had somehow acquired a camera and installed it in her powder room with a long lead hidden under the lino all the way down to their smoky, noisy tearoom.

I'd never been so close to a woman before, except, of course, my mother. I even felt a little moved with the sudden intimacy of it all, especially when I saw she'd taken into the room her old white 1950s-style make-up case emblazoned with stars; those golden stars in their white heaven made it such a childish and hopeful little case – but even if I could talk, that wasn't something I could've said to Marconi. I got out my notepad so I'd remember every second for when I retreated from the world.

Shirley was nothing like my self-effacing mother. At first I couldn't write down enough of the way she fizzed mousse from a can into her hair and then flung her head backwards – suddenly under the light I saw she had good cheekbones after all – while she dragged her hairbrush through the waterfall of her hair. She threw the golden fall from one hand to another and caught it triumphantly, plumped it up, now fluffier because of the mousse, and shimmied it into a clasp with a wiggle of her big round bottom. I wondered why she did her hair in hiding when I would have paid to see such beauty on stage.

The men were turning away when Marconi called them back.

Get a load of this, he said.

He grabbed my sleeve and yanked me down.

Shirley was unbuttoning her blouse so that her white shoulder pads and then her bra showed, and her bra was unexpectedly all black lace and prettiness, not at all similar to the beige bandage-like devices my mother wore. Shirley may have had a plain face but she had beautifully carved breasts. She turned her body from one side to the other looking in the mirror at their pretty mounds, then she reached inside one of the cups of her bra and altered the folds of something tucked inside – a brown woollen sock, we all saw. Everyone whistled and laughed, but she reached inside the other cup and worked that brown sock as well, tucked it in, checked both breasts for symmetry, then buttoned up her shirt, pleased with her secret and beautiful self.

I knew it'd be worth your while, said Marconi, now vindicated, while the other men hooted and catcalled and slapped their thighs. I will admit it now, I failed at this first test to live the life of honour. Would it help to say that no laughter came out of my mouth? It would be a lie. I copied the grey men, and slapped my thighs just like them.

Completely unaware of us, Shirley put on her lab coat, her protective cap and glasses, opened the door and walked back into the stark lab, serenely defying it.

After that, I didn't want to perv. When they huddled around the TV set to have another dekko, as they called it, I did another job. I worried that they'd chiack me, and comforted myself that soon it would be over, soon I'd go back to my aloneness. I'd been tricked by my books that insisted on the allure of the world.

My mother was right, the world was a small and pitiable thing.

But day by day I gave the world another chance, just one more chance. And so it was that on my tenth morning of being a grey man I was standing at the hospital's grand front window, prising the screen wire off and cleaning it and letting the wind in, full of pollution from the traffic, it's true, but also full of the excited shouts of children and the barking of dogs lolloping in the stretch of green verge below and the turning of flowers to the sun and the singing of sap in the trees and the swooping of tiny birds in the blue air. I leaned out the window almost dangerously, hoping someone down below would see me, some mother with a child, perhaps, who'd point and say, There's someone who's part of the hospital.

That's when she came into view. My love.

So at last I can write it down.

CHAPTER 5

An accident affects my destiny

IF MOST PEOPLE HAD BEEN LOOKING out that window that particular morning fifteen years ago, they probably wouldn't have noticed my love. (I can't help calling her that, but will try to restrain myself from here on.) They would've merely registered a girl in a white lab coat that flared in the rays of the early sun and disappeared in the long purple shadows. Or their attention might have been caught by the girl when she lurched to the kerb outside the hospital gates, tipping precariously in the moment before she put out a steadying foot, and trundling her bicycle by its handlebars into the car park. But then they would've looked away. They definitely wouldn't still have been watching as she wheeled her bike past the young sentry with the darkly slicked hair who glanced at her, the way he'd glance at an insect. So they wouldn't have wondered why her lab coat swayed and strained at its buttons as she bent to chain her bike to a post in the shelter. But I watched as she walked across the car park, looking up, fearful that someone might see what she believed she would become. Someone who could guess her secret ambition.

By then anyone else's eye would have moved to more interesting sights, to the fat schoolboy hosing the kiosk footpath for his mother the kiosk woman, flopping the hose so the water snaked, turning the water on harder and holding the hose against his trouser fly, and laughing at the silver arc of water falling like rain on the cars while drivers peered out of their windows, puzzled. Then his mother in a sagging dress lumbered out holding a bucket of red roses against the jutting veranda of her bosom, and yelled at her son and his magnificent waterworks. He turned off the hose and the water looped in disappointment onto his shoes. She banged the bucket down on the wet footpath, stuck a price tag in it, and ushered him inside by his shirt collar. One by one, in a circle around the bucket, the red rose petals fell.

A car wet from the boy's hose slid through the gates, driven by him – oh, how the name still rankles! My rival – the eminent Professor Gunther Mueller.

The sentry guard's hand reached to his forehead in a tentative salute, then drooped, not sure if the scientist was famous enough for a salute, but as a compromise he patted the car as it slid by, wiping a ribbon of dryness along the vehicle's dripping rump.

Mueller noticed nothing, not the hosing, not the guard. He sped into the parking space labelled with his name, then reversed just as rapidly at the very moment when a thin figure walked into his trajectory – the young white-coated girl. I wanted to call to her to watch out, but even if I had been capable of speech, the wind would have whipped away my warning. There was a sound that might've been a bump, she fell, her arm reaching out to break her fall, her arm crumpling, her body suddenly on the ground. Mueller, intent on his parking, straightened his wheels, moved forward just missing her, checked his wheels again, reversed, almost drove over her feet, stopped and went forward. He was a meticulous parker. Meanwhile she lay as still as death, her hair stretched out on either side, feathery like the wings of angels, broken. At last, satisfied, he wrenched on the handbrake, opened his door, reached to the back seat for his briefcase, slammed his door and loped off.

At the sound of the slam, her splayed fingers trembled and became a fist. She punched the air, she lifted her head, put both hands behind her for balance, and she arched a leg to sit up, a bare and poignantly slender leg. And then I saw that her coat had come open and crimson had burst out, not blood but the red silken flames of her dress. They set the wind on fire. That's what took away my breath, right at that moment, her beautiful long leg, the red silk whipping around it, and now as she staggered upright, the curve of her slender waist, and the way she leaped up. That's how I came to see her, always leaping.

She walked a step and felt for the buttons on her lab coat, but they had rolled away. She wrapped the coat around her, clutching it tight – but one of the seams had burst and there were only torn white threads all the way from her armpit to her knee. Then she looked around for her assailant.

Stop! I heard her shout. Stop!

She was utterly without deference.

Mueller was far off, his briefcase bumping impatiently against his legs.

It was like my dream.

Now I've remembered it in every detail, I'll lay the pen down, and rest. And mourn a little.

I don't know why I hadn't seen her before. Somehow I'd missed seeing her for ten whole days. Perhaps she'd been away, on holidays, or off sick. But the thought niggles – if I'd missed seeing her, did I see the world at all?

Now. I must say it. Now.

She was one of my murmurers.

After she'd shouted out, I discovered that she was a murmurer.

'He didn't hurt me,' she'd murmured to me.

'No one can. I'm made to do something extraordinary and until that's done, I'm invincible.'

So that's why I was first drawn to her.

My murmurers. How easily the word sprang from my fingers, when I was putting off admitting it. I was lulled into typing it by the reliving of that life-changing moment. I had sworn to admit to everything but that. I feared how ridiculous the word murmurer would appear, not to readers, for I intend there to be none, but to me on the blank white page. Now that she's gone.

But I see that the word murmurer is just an ordinary word, like a nightmare examined in the sunlight over a cup of tea.

So:

As I became a silent stutterer, I began to hear murmurs. At least, it appears to date from that time. The murmurs seemed to seep out from a place where my thoughts didn't go. On some days the air was shouting with murmurs, sighing and weeping and snivelling and laughter of all sorts, hysterical giggles and deep-throated guffaws and polite chuckles and mean-spirited scoffings. There were the urgent bristling murmurs of men, the grey slurred murmurs of old ladies, the cooing murmurs of young girls, the anxious murmurs of mothers. I heard snatches of things I was too young to comprehend – jealousy and love-making and perfidy and fear, all mixed up with frettings about the price of bread and apples and dresses and houses, and, once, someone's plan to murder a brother.

The murmurs were all unbidden. Sometimes I held my hands over my ears to block out the din of suffering or laughter or stupidity or wisdom or inanity. On a bus, crossing a street, in church with the morning light breaking into rainbows through the stained glass, at the times when I wasn't thinking of anything in particular, just about tying my shoelaces, for instance, or breathing to sing a high note, another murmurer would start up. I'd whirl around, searching for a face with moving lips, but there'd only be an impassive profile, lowered eyelids, stilled muscles or, sometimes, no person there at all, just the empty air.

I couldn't will people to murmur, though I tried many times, sending them questions in my thoughts.

Who are you? I'd ask. Show yourself!

It never worked.

I was so young that I assumed everybody heard murmurs. In fact, on the noisiest days I wondered how the world could bear it.

So when my father banned me not only from school but all excursions into the street, it was, in a way, a relief. Over time, the murmurs faded of their own accord. Only then did I tell my mother.

You weren't just hearing people's thoughts, she said. You become part of people so much, you enter their haunted souls, she said.

She thought for a while.

After what you've told me, it's as well you're hiding away from the world, which doesn't offer much, anyway, being as it is, tiny and pitiable.

I accepted seclusion. Though sometimes, as I leaned out the window, I wished the murmurs would start up again, for company. I never stopped mourning the loss of the choir. I would've put up with a cacophony of murmurers to keep watching the flight of my little boy's voice up into the vast and echoing spaces of the church.

My mother often glanced at me suspiciously.

This murmuring you used to hear, she began one day when she was washing up.

She banged down a saucepan on the kitchen bench.

What do you hear me thinking about? she asked at last.

I shook my head.

Nothing? Not even when I'm thinking about your father?

I shook my head again.

This was when my father was still alive, and my mother would often sit up on the sofa crying long after he'd gone to bed. After one night when I'd heard her cry almost until dawn, she said:

You must've heard me cursing last night.

I heard nothing, I wrote.

She still didn't believe me. So she gave me another lecture about honour, and at the end she asked me all over again what I'd heard her murmur, until I realised that in her mind she must've been cursing my father to hell and begging that he rot there.

———

Until that moment at the hospital window, no one had murmured to me for years. Until the girl.

I realised that she was the sort of woman my mother could've been, the sort of woman my mother knew too late that she should've been.

So now, to keep everything in order, I must remember my mother's last day.

My heart still clenches at the memory and at my ineptitude. Why didn't I run down the stairs into the street that day and hail someone for help?

If I had, might she still be alive?

On the last day of her life, a summer's day like this one but with such humidity that my underarms squelched, my mother had leaned out our window and –

Admit it.

She contradicted everything she'd ever said.

If I'd known what was to come, I would've listened harder. As it was, I was preoccupied because she was in danger of toppling.

I wrote her a note: You'll break your neck!

She took no notice. She was straining to gaze up at the crossroads where a Greyhound bus was picking up passengers bound for far-off cities. She was in profile, and her right side, the side my father had kissed, the side without the strawberry stain, was turned to me. She was silhouetted against the derelict offices opposite, and the brothel. She'd pinned up her russet hair but it was falling down her neck and pasted across her forehead in damp ribbons. I noticed that she was panting, but I didn't think anything of that, given the humidity.

I got it wrong, she was saying.

I thought she was talking about the bus timetable. She always knew when the buses were leaving, in fact she had a timetable stuck to the wall, as if one day she planned to leave too. But she looked up at the sky, which I remember as a deep and mocking blue.

There are only a few years when everything is possible for a woman, she said. Every woman knows that. But some know what I didn't. It doesn't have to be when you're young and as pretty as you're ever going to be.

She laughed then, her choking kookaburra laugh, my father would've called it.

Not that I was ever a beauty, she continued. But I could've come into my own. I didn't have to wait for his death.

I could see she was full of regret, and a parent's regret makes a child squirm, even a grown-up son. I was then eighteen. I squirmed not only from guilt, but confusion. It had been a given between us that the world was not something we wanted anything of, let alone any power over. I reached out to cradle her hand, wanting to write down that we should go for a spin in the country in her Hillman Hunter to clear this nonsense out of her head, but she started at my touch, as if she'd forgotten me and had only been talking to herself. She was trembly and too warm, and her pale skin had a sweet and sickly smell. She shook me off, still talking.

A woman's got to know when it's her time, or she misses out, she said.

As I have, she added.

Only then did she let me lead her to the sofa, where she slumped. I laid damp cloths on her forehead and fanned her and dashed out to call a doctor, and dashed back because I didn't know how to. But within the hour, she'd died. Only then did I run into the street and hail a policeman, gesturing to him to follow me.

But this girl. This murmuring girl. She began following the man who'd knocked her over, limping at first, then gathering her strength, the torn coat flapping. She was holding her arm in an odd position, that was all, but she strode like someone so intent on a purpose that she wouldn't be deflected by anything. She followed Gunther Mueller to the lab's car park door. He opened it and let it slam behind him. She strode to the same door, opened it and shut it. She was as adamant as him, but quiet. Even against the din of the street I heard her quietness.

Most people wouldn't have noticed her entry. They'd have thought her unremarkable. But I did. I noticed her, and I kept on noticing her until –

Order. I must keep to chronological order.

I had to watch her, to be part of her life. I knew I'd never create a book, or music (though some days, foolish with hope and sunshine, I thought I might sing in a choir again). But I had to be part of the creation of her.

CHAPTER 6

So I became a spy

I HURRIED DOWN through the hospital corridor to Shirley's lab,
Shirley of the black lacy bra. Someone was inside, sneezing with a
loud hrrmph – it had to be Shirley. I halted. What crisis could I
invent to justify being here? A crack in the wall caught my eye and
I bent, pretending to examine it. Then there was a flash of red and
the young woman passed right behind me in a rush of air and light.
(She must have gone off somewhere since I saw her – to the Ladies,
perhaps – and then followed me down the corridor.) I tried to
breathe her in. She wasn't the sort to have perfume on, I should've
guessed that. She smelt of sunshine, that's how I remember it.
Maybe a little of the dust and tar of the car park, though I might
be making that up. And peppermints. I later found out that she had
a habit of crunching peppermints as she rode her bike. She didn't
suck them. Sucking peppermints is for patient people. She'd crunch
through an entire packet on her ride home, the way you'd expect
of someone with wild and secret ambitions.

I thought recklessly of opening the door for her. But she might
have said thank you, and expect me to say something in return,
something difficult, like 'No worries'. So I didn't open the door. I

just examined the crack, tapping on the wall with my knife, listening to plaster.

She left the door ajar. I peeped inside. Shirley was lighting a Bunsen burner, but she looked up when the younger woman came in. She blew out the match, her eyes taking in the torn lab coat.

What happened to you? she asked.

Before the girl could answer, Shirley went on:

Don't let Professor Mueller see you like that. You know about him and his rules.

Who cares! said the girl. He's hurt my arm.

She was taking off the coat, and her dress flared out in the ordinary, dull lab. But it was the way she spoke that made me peer. She spoke like Tesla, Rutherford, Volta, Einstein and Marconi, and like the taunting schoolboys of my childhood, in fact like an ordinary Australian, in those days of our dingy city still a matter of shame. The defiant, tumultuous celebration of our country's accent in theatres and public places was hundreds of kilometres away, in other cities. In Sudlow, if you were educated, or at least wanted to make believe you were, you aspired to speak like the Queen of England, as if you were waiting patiently in line for the throne, related to Her, not to our dust. Even my father, in his dingy shop, attempted to sound like one of Her equerries.

If he carries on about my coat, I'll tell him what's what, the girl was saying in an accent so broad that I had to struggle against my prejudices.

Show me your arm! said Shirley.

The girl shrugged and didn't move.

If you're bruised, that'll be a memento, said Shirley. From the winner of the Prize next time.

She was smiling, imagining herself with such a man.

You could be the inspiration behind his fame, she added.

But the girl didn't have such expectations. She stood watching the flame of Shirley's Bunsen burner flicker as it turned from orange to blue. Then she seemed to shake herself into action. I heard her opening cupboards and getting down solutions from the shelves, favouring the hurt arm. I discovered later that her job, like

Shirley's, was to make up solutions and buffers and cultures for the scientists, and to wash up their glass bottles and what I learned to call glassware. She and Shirley weren't university trained, they'd only been to technical college, and so they were the servants of scientists, with little hope of promotion.

I could tell immediately that the girl was unlike any woman I had seen so far, that she was as clear and guileless as a young white sapling in the tangle of green bushland beyond our city's fringes. Perhaps that was why the grey men hadn't bothered with her – she'd have gazed directly at them, with no thought in her blue eyes but that she should see them more clearly, if they were worth seeing, and they'd have paused and swallowed, their hands hanging uselessly by their sides, until they went to hammer a loose board or change a shrivelled washer in a tap.

I set to work before I could go home and reconsider the question of honour and spying. I went to find a drill to make holes for the cameras and monitor they'd been using on Shirley, abandoned now that they'd moved on to poker. I ransacked Stores for sound recording devices. By this time I was inspired, and remembered the little shed out in Samuel Craven Sudlow's courtyard. It was crammed with antique gardening equipment, scythes, a pitsaw and even a plough, which I pulled out when I thought no one was looking and left lying beside the garbage bins, where they might still be today.

Matron was looking.

Well done, Galileo, she said as she passed. You're worth whatever they pay you.

When she'd gone, I put my equipment* inside the shed, and it became my second home.

....

* He attached lots of details of equipment from forty years ago. He obviously relished it. There were pages and pages of diagrams with arrows and details of circuitry. I left them out, I hope you don't mind. – T.

As soon as I dared I returned to Top Lab to drill the holes. I knocked.

Come in, Shirley said in a loud, singsong way, her head bent as she swirled a flask over a flame.

I'd timed it badly. The younger woman was out of the lab.

Yes? Shirley said importantly, not looking up, but suddenly her hair fell out of its protective cap and crunched over her face.

I wanted to tell her that it was imperative I drill holes. But no matter how much I writhed, no sound came out. So I had to write a note:

'I'm to drill. Okay?'

Shirley scarcely looked up at me.

Don't ask me. Ask a scientist, she said sulkily.

Of course I knew I shouldn't spy, but how else was I going to see her often? My heart was cramping to see her often. I had to spy. I decided that there would be rules, strict rules for spying. In fact, I wouldn't spy like the grey men had on Shirley, I wouldn't be a peeping Tom, of course not, because I am a sensitive, truthful, compassionate and honourable man. I would be like someone who happened to be in the lab, except that no one could see me. I wouldn't watch anything intimate, if anything intimate happened, and that wasn't likely in this stark place, because it was only a science lab with no intimacy at all.

But still I dithered. I wished I could talk it over with someone, but there wasn't anyone, and I couldn't talk. I'd read the great philosophers in my library. The problem with philosophers, though, is that while you might agree with all their arguments, their arguments seem to pertain only to other people's lives, not yours. Anyway, a fierce hot wind was pushing me, and all I could do was let the wind have its way.

I found out her name that first morning while I was drilling. Shirley kept checking the clock and at last she let out an excited oh!, jumped up from her work and began cleaning out a coffee percolator.

Since my exile into the world, I'd noticed that it had become fashionable in Sudlow to drink not tea but coffee freshly ground from beans. When I'd fulfilled my daydream and had gone into the

Rive Gauche Cafe with a note requesting a pot of tea, I'd been sat at a table so far back I was almost in their sink. The Rive Gauche placed its fashionable coffee drinkers up the front to suggest that this was an establishment cognisant of the ways of cosmopolitan Europe, as distinct from the Tudor milk bar up the street that served greasy Chiko Rolls and sloshing cups of hot water with a somewhat damp teabag on the saucer.

Shirley's percolator must've been brand-new, because later I found the box in a rubbish bin with its crumpled brown paper wrapping. Suddenly Shirley was eager and interested in what she was doing, double-washing all its parts, running the water clear, drying it. She filled its bowl and spooned in fresh coffee and placed it on a mat over a Bunsen burner, watching it come to the boil, and then she took it off the heat.

She called to the girl.

Come on, I've got it ready. Come and try it, Eva.

So that's when I found out her name.

Eva. Like the first woman in the world.

Eva came back in. Again, she passed so near I could almost feel the heat of her crimson dress against my skin.

Isn't it a great aroma? said Shirley. So . . .

She paused, lost for words. She held up her hands to shoulder-height and let her fingers explore her thoughts, twinkling in the air.

European, she found at last.

My mother has a percolator, said Eva.

She has?

Shirley was disappointed.

She came from Europe, explained Eva. She grew up and worked there.

She worked there! Doing what? asked Shirley, clearly impressed.

Clothes, said the younger girl.

She clearly didn't want to go further with this conversation.

What was she doing with clothes? asked Shirley.

She was just doing clothes, Eva said to Shirley in her broad accent, and sat down, pulling the mug of coffee close, almost protectively.

Shirley saw the evasion but had to persist.

Where in Europe?

Paris, said Eva. She seemed almost ashamed.

You don't look French, said Shirley, now a little jealous.

My dad wasn't, said Eva. He was from here. She came here, to join him.

To Sudlow? Poor woman! said Shirley, hoping for more, but Eva didn't give her more.

I moved quietly around the lab, tapping the wall and pretending to listen to the plaster, my mind in a swirl. She was not only from the rough classes, she was ugly up close, no beauty after all. What had I been thinking? I'd been deceived by distance. Her head was too large for her body, her mouth was big and her nose too long. But she lacked something more – a quality of nonchalance, I decided – the way she held herself so stiffly. She didn't seem shy so much as preoccupied. And her dress sense was alarming, now I could see it in detail – all froth and ribbons, clothes from an earlier era, her mother's perhaps. There was no need to watch her through cameras, there was no need to risk my job, there was no need to be dishonourable. A nerve began to pulse in my temple. I was irrationally angry that, from a distance, she had aroused such a passion in me, this skinny, clumsy, rough young woman. I stopped tapping the wall and turned to go. But then, I glanced at her one last time.

Now that I look back, I know there's a precise moment when you fall in love. If you're watchful and if you happen to be gazing at the person before that moment, during it, and afterwards, you actually see them change before your very eyes. No, I swear it is not you who changes. It is them. Their faces change, their bodies change, their very bones dissolve to align themselves anew. Fat becomes sweetly plump, skinny becomes svelte, old becomes experienced and wise. Even the fabric of their skin softens, tightens, becomes more rounded. You laugh at yourself, but underneath there seems a greater truth, that before you saw them imperfectly, and now you see them as they are. So you become their hostage.

Perhaps it was a trick of the light, perhaps the sun passed under a cloud, but what filled my sight left me almost winded. I saw that she was thin, yes, but as a young plant is slender-stemmed; her face was wide, yes, but full of odd and unexpected architectural proportions, and her eyes were hauntingly blue. They seemed to take in and reflect light, so you looked at her and felt you were looking out a window at an endless sky. She was plain-faced but when she turned, there was a glimpse of beauty that threatened to become astonishing, so that already I was in suspense to glimpse it again. She had an adorable upper lip that lifted like a song.

Fix your lab coat, Shirley said. Or you'll be in trouble. Get your mother to, since she's in clothes.

I could tell from the restless tone in Shirley's voice that she was yearning for excitement and determined to wrest it from this stern, resistant lab. She wanted fear, anxiety, disaster, anything different from what she had. There is so much I can tell from a voice, when I have none.

Eva shrugged and said nothing more. The mere action of her thinking made me into her audience. I wanted to stop pretending to work, to come over and bend to glimpse even the movement of her eyes.

Do you think he'll go a bit crazy with grief? Shirley suddenly asked.

Who? Eva was startled. (I saw now that she had excessively long, dark eyelashes.)

Professor Mueller, said Shirley. Your assailant. About missing out on the Prize.

Eva laughed without humour. The man was impossibly important, a man who'd never notice her, an awkward young girl, whereas Shirley with her sophisticated ways might get to speak to him.

It was only a rumour, she said, shrugging.

He's so odd, he must be a genius, said Shirley. I love the way he doesn't bother with chat.

She checked her reflection in a metallic bit of the equipment.

Though he would, I'm sure, with the right woman.

I kept tapping. The laboratory hummed around us. Despite Eva's flamboyant dress, she seemed as much a part of the lab as the equipment which she jumped up to check from time to time.

Who would you like to walk in that door? Shirley suddenly asked.

Eva seemed shocked by the sound of Shirley's voice, so deep had she been in her own thoughts.

How do you mean? she asked.

What *man*, explained Shirley, a little exasperated that of all the people she could have worked with, all the handsome, charming and eligible young men in the world, she'd been allocated this ungainly adolescent. She inspected her own pink fingernails, as pretty as seashells, ready to drum them on the workbench.

Eva stirred herself.

Someone who talks about interesting organisms, she said at last.

She added a name.

Here's my note:

'McConnell.'

McConnell? Shirley said. There's no McConnell here. Never heard of him.

Eva said no, he didn't work here, in fact he worked in another country, or at least he used to.

Here's another note: 'Planarian worms.'

Then she talked so fast I couldn't keep up, about some scientist who thought that knowledge might be edible and might be transferable from someone to someone else by injection, or even cannibalism.

Cannibalism? interrupted Shirley. You're interested in humans eating humans?

Worms eating other worms, said Eva.

Apparently, for ten years this McConnell had trained Planarian worms to scrunch up their bodies in response to a burst of light as they swam along the bottom of a trough. Then he cut up the trained worms and fed them to untrained worms, and the untrained ones seemed to know automatically to scrunch up their bodies and twist away from light. But the experiments were disbelieved, partly because other scientists couldn't repeat them and get the same results, and partly because it's hard to know when a worm is calm enough to register shock.

Shirley, impatient at the turn the talk had taken in this special coffee break with her new percolator, glanced up the stairs to make sure no one was coming down, shoved pipettes to one side of the bench to make room, and pulled her starry white make-up case out of a drawer. She checked her lipstick, now faded.

Watch out, say if someone's coming, she said. Especially him.

She inclined her head upstairs.

But Eva didn't watch out. She was too busy explaining another experiment where naive worms who'd eaten trained worms seemed to know which route along the trough the trained worms had taken. Other scientists couldn't duplicate this experiment either and claimed that the worms hadn't learned a route, they'd just followed the previous worm's slime. Speculation raged about what the cannibalistic worms had actually eaten – was it a bit of a trained worm's brain or just its body, and where was a worm's brain anyway? McConnell's experiments seemed to lack the gravitas expected by other scientists, and his standing bottomed when he started a newspaper called *The Worm Runner's Digest*, and published not only his work but accounts sent in by high school students of what their worms seemed to remember.

What did they remember? asked Shirley, interested enough to pause, her lipstick in the air like a wand.

To follow each other, said Eva.

Shirley went back to her mirror.

But why I'd like to date him, Eva continued, ignoring a sudden guffaw from Shirley, I'd like to ask him why he thought new knowledge in the brain of a worm could be measured by its behaviour.

Shirley slammed shut the make-up case, stood, grabbed both their cups, washed them under a gush of water so loud nothing else could be heard, and banged them down on the sink.

And McConnell didn't care what anyone thought, said Eva. It's so brave!

I knew then – Is it true, or did I realise it later, after I knew her better? I knew it always, from this moment, that for Eva, the ways of other people were never going to be her ways.

Shirley was watching her, hands on her hips.

Don't you ever think about sex? she demanded.
There was a pause.
Eva looked up.
All the time, she admitted.
And then she became a murmurer again:

'I've been wanting to make love to someone right from my first day at kindergarten, when I looked at a row of little boys with their rounded legs sticking out of their freshly ironed shorts, and I thought, One of them will be mine! Maybe two! Maybe all of them!'

Then her murmur stopped.
I tapped and drilled and pretended interest in the wall as long as I dared, just to be near her, though she was so engrossed in her work she never lifted her eyes to mine. Then I took my time sweeping up, hoping she'd notice what a meticulous worker I was. But finally I was defeated by Shirley's exasperated sighs, and I left.

CHAPTER 7

During which I acquire a rival

I WENT IMMEDIATELY TO MY SHED to try out the equipment, just a mechanical test, I told myself. Only to see if it all worked.* Later, I'd try to reason out the thorny moral problem of spying. (I was finding that morality was more complicated than I'd ever imagined, even when I sat to reason it out in my favourite armchair with wide, comforting arms, a very forgiving cushion tucked at the base of my neck.)

I'd barely gone into my little shed when my microphone picked up footsteps clumping down the stairs from the lab up above the girls, the lab where the scientists worked. Both the technicians looked up, Eva with trepidation, Shirley with hope.

Looking back, I can see that it was one of those moments when events are going along in one direction, and then suddenly everything moves in another direction altogether, perhaps for always.

----

* Another three pages of detail about equipment follows. If you wish, I could send this material to you. – T.)

But I had no premonition of where those footsteps were going. How could I have? (I am becoming defensive.)

Hide, whispered Shirley, and pushed back her protective glasses glamorously.

My coat's his fault, whispered Eva.

Go now! ordered Shirley. Hope was reddening her nose.

I want – began Eva.

Go! ordered Shirley.

Eva went.

Shirley grabbed the pot with its coffee dregs, poured a little water in, shook the pot and began heating it up as Gunther Mueller appeared on the stairs and came down ready to swing out the door to the car park, deep in thought. His hand on the door, he sniffed and glanced over his shoulder, where something was calling to him from a long distance. He struggled to remember where he was. I had an intimation then that, caught unaware by a familiar smell, as he was now, dark shadows rushed at him from his past, and he had to push them back, though they wouldn't stay pushed back.

Percolated, said Shirley, her voice as rich as any brew. Much nicer than the Rive Gauche's. Would you like some?

He was still pausing.

She was finding a clean cup and holding it up. She didn't want to lose him just because the coffee had run out.

It'll be a minute's wait, she said, hovering over the pot.

Seconds now, she added. It'll give you a lift. There now – and she was pouring.

Drink it up, she said.

He came over uncertainly.

Why don't you sit? she said.

He sat obediently, pulling impatiently at his khaki trousers. (He always wore khaki, nothing else.)

Milk? she asked.

Yes, he said.

Shirley smiled, went to the fridge, found the carton of milk and, holding it level with her breasts, offered to pour it for him.

He was still fighting between the dark past and this woman with a crimson smile, whose name he'd never noticed.

Thank you, he said, and blew on the coffee to escape her eyes. It will take time to cool, he said, and smiled his sweet, apologetic smile.

He was one of those people whose silence makes everyone's attempts at light conversation seem addle-headed. Now that she was faced with the object of her desire, Shirley couldn't think of a thing to say. He couldn't either and pretended a sudden interest in the walls and ceiling, even screwing his head around to look in Eva's direction but seeing nothing.

Worms! Shirley blurted suddenly.

Gunther said nothing.

We were just talking about worm experiments, she said, holding up her hands and twinkling them around her shoulders.

Some experiments with worms – not in this lab,

she added, because he wasn't helping her.

The point is, there were trained worms and untrained ones, and they ate each other and some of them remembered something that they'd never known to start with, she said.

She petered out and dropped her hands and threw her head back, to laugh unnecessarily.

There was the slightest pause.

James V. McConnell, the chemical nature of memory transfer substances. Refuted by Bennet and Calvin in sixty-four and later by Byrne and twenty-two others, said Gunther. Taken up by Georges Ungar using mammals. McConnell's a fool. So is Ungar.

Their names were on the tip of my tongue, said Shirley.

They both fell silent again.

Between them was a lab diary, one of those much-thumbed, exhausted-looking exercise books that labs use to record in minute and ponderous detail the experiments that go on. I found out later that theirs was a record of the solutions that had been requested of them: what they'd made up, when, and in what concentrations.

The diary up to date? he thought to ask, to break the silence.

Of course, said Shirley.

He opened it. After a while, he looked up. He was now on much surer ground with a diary in his hand.

You forgot the date here, he pointed out.

Shirley started. Oh, sorry, she said.

Must've been . . . he calculated the date based on the surrounding ones and wrote it in.

Can't be too careful with these diaries, he said. They're evidence. If you make a breakthrough, you can prove to the whole waiting world –

What would we have a breakthrough in? asked Shirley. The washing up?

She laughed.

He copied her and flashed another of his rare smiles. I had the feeling that he hadn't often laughed in his life. But something had caught his eye and he began to read seriously. Shirley sat back, her lab coat falling open as she crossed and recrossed her legs in jeans she'd ripped in lines across her knees. She tweaked the denim so a little more of her knees showed. She could've talked about how long a rip should be if he'd given her half a chance.

He looked over his glasses at her.

I can't read the writing, he said.

It's not mine, she said.

Please read it to me, he said.

Reading aloud was something Shirley would normally have loved to do. She began as excited as a child, she was intoxicating with her clear skin and her rounded cheeks. 'On Monday morning,' she began, 'one of those dull depressing days . . .'

She stumbled. She knew Eva shouldn't have mentioned the mood of the day. The temperature perhaps, if the heat or cold might affect the results, but not the mood it stirred in Eva. She seemed to try to improvise the rest of the entry. But she had no choice, she had to read on:

'. . . one of those dull depressing days that makes the lab feel like home, I came in, set up the experiment and noticed that –'

Her voice thickened, slowed.

Dull? Depressing? The lab *feels* like home? Gunther repeated.

I know, said Shirley. I saw that too. A lab shouldn't *feel* like home, or, at least, you shouldn't say so. It's a workplace, not a home –

And what's this, *noticed*? She noticed? Does a scientist notice? Doesn't a scientist *observe*? asked Gunther.

Observe. Of course observe, said Shirley. We don't *notice* anything.

Why? he quizzed, more confident with her now they were talking about science.

Why should it be *it was observed*, not *I observed*?

If it's I, then she gets the blame, Shirley guessed. But if it's *it was observed*, then it wasn't necessarily her, and no one's to blame.

No! he said. It shows that we aren't subjective. We're reporting, not noticing, nature. We're as rigorous as nature. We reflect it. Nature's facts are observed objectively.

Of course, she said weakly.

He waited, so she had to read on about an observation of a solution that made, according to the report, *the laboratory glow with excitement*.

I can't believe this, he said.

Nor can I, she said. She crossed her legs and laid the diary down. Unfortunately, he could still see the page.

And the rest? he asked. The pencilled part, down the bottom.

So she had no choice but to read on.

'I am so bored, I notice the music of blowflies. My life has never slowed down like this to notice blowflies. Blowflies seem to buzz on three or four notes as they fly towards you or away, but they actually buzz on a monotone.'

She looked up, saw his demanding eyes.

Then it makes –

she took a breath –

another little observation.

She tried a laugh, paused.

'He has defeated buttocks,' she read. Not yours, I'm sure, she added.

She put the book down.

I haven't had a chance to read it over – it's just little details, she said. That she noticed. I mean, observed.

He passed his hand over his face. In his agitation, he said:

But it's the details that count.

Life is lived in the details, agreed a voice from the back of the room, behind a huge microscope. It was her voice, Eva's voice.

She hadn't been able to resist joining in the conversation.

Gunther's head swivelled to gaze in the direction of her voice. He rose to his full height and walked towards her, slowly, belly-first, swaying lightly like a seahorse. I watched him and thought, She can't be hurt by a seahorse.

It was only later that I saw how wrong I'd been.

It was a long, long walk, his walk to the girl who'd commented in a lab diary on his buttocks. He switched on lights as he went, until light stretched all the way to the girl who was standing up slowly, her eyes frightened, defiant. He stopped at the last window, turned sideways, pulled up the blind, turned back to her, and came to the corner of the workbench.

Where are you from? he asked.

Here, she said.

He looked around him at the rows of empty workbenches.

You work in the hospital? he asked.

Here, she said.

Doing what? he asked.

I work with her, she said. With Shirley. I wrote up the lab diary.

That's no lab diary, he said.

She took a breath.

But there's no objectivity, she said. An experimenter disturbs subatomic particles so it's impossible to say exactly where the atoms will be, she went on unblinkingly. Or how fast they'll be. So if I say the observation didn't come from my specific head but from out there in the world, it's a pretence. I'm an experimenter and the experimenter is part of the experiment. The observation isn't a thing disconnected from me, it's not real.

Werner Heisenberg. First year undergraduate physics, he said grimly.

I haven't been an undergraduate, I haven't studied at university, she said. But I read.

We're scientists here, not philosophers, he said calmly, almost smiling.

She swallowed, unable to decide whether to argue back.

Science has to consider *how* we know, as well as what we know, she said. That's why someone like McConnell is interesting.

They glared at each other.

He's not, he said.

Gunther was the one to look down.

Are you going somewhere afterwards? he asked.

They both gazed at her dress. His eyes travelled from her angular face to her long, pale, flawless bared throat ending in the frothy bodice of the crimson dress, then to the curve of her slender waist with a shining purple sash, and a full skirt that had been cut into many sections and joined with either a red satin ribbon to match the silk, or a purple satin ribbon to match the sash.

It's my mother, she told him incoherently.

Your mother? he prompted.

She makes them, she said. My lab coat . . . she started, and petered out.

He bent and examined the microscope.

You're aware this isn't on? he said. You know your Heisenberg, but you can't switch on a microscope? You know that to work a microscope you have to switch it on?

He bent to find the switch to turn it on.

What were you going to look at? he asked.

I wasn't, she said. I was up here hiding from you.

Hiding, he repeated.

My lab coat, she said. That's why I haven't got it on. You ripped it this morning, you knocked me over in your car and it got ripped.

I didn't knock you over in my car, he said.

In the car park, she said, although her voice trembled, as if the accident no longer seemed real.

So my coat is your fault, she said. And I'm a reliable technician.

But her face said more.

What are you going to do about me, her face said, though she was silent now. Where is your dull life going, when I'm not dull at all?

There was something so sure, so vehemently, so poignantly confident about her, despite her shyness, that it seemed almost a promise. I saw then that the ends of her lips twitched up as she spoke, so that you felt she was confiding in you and withholding some secret amusement at the same time. She was adorable!

But he must have seen that too.

Who has the defeated buttocks? he asked, with a hint of a smile in his voice. Not me. I'm far from defeated.

I caught my breath. This wasn't going well. It was going well for her, but not for me. Then it got worse!

Around her neck lay a string of red beads, wooden, heavy beads that contradicted and highlighted the delicacy of her skin. He pressed his finger gently on them, picked them up and held them away from her body, weighing them in his hands, warming himself on their warmth.

I'll always think of you in these beads, he said.

I wanted her to say:

Why would I care?

But she didn't say that. She made a sound, but she was dry-throated and there were no words. The muscles of her face were loose, her lips slack, her eyes mesmerised, wide, too wide for their sockets.

She's thinking of saying something rude, I hoped.

But when he drew his hand away from her beads, she put her hand blindly to them as if to seal in his touch.

More coffee? called Shirley's voice from up the length of the lab. She was now very busy examining a measuring cylinder. They had forgotten her.

She began walking towards them, still holding the cylinder.

I just wanted to ask if you'd like – she began calling.

The man moved away from the bench, looked at his watch, determined not to be overwhelmed again by Shirley.

More coffee? Shirley repeated.

I must go, he said to Eva, as if he was confiding in her about his life.

He turned away, once more withdrawn, shy, studious.

Shirley followed him to the door, but he banged it shut after him.

Eva was sashaying down the lab from one empty workbench to the next. I believe I could hear her humming.

You'll never be a scientist! said Shirley angrily. In future, try to write like one! No more of that rubbish in the diary! You could've got us both sacked! I'm off to the coldroom. We've got work to do, remember?

She wiped her hands on her lab coat and walked out, her blond hair unleashed and swinging.

The young girl, alone now, was still touching her beads.

My heart was turning in its cage, watching her.

Shirley returned with two Eskys, glanced at her, sighed, threw one down in front of her, then plumped down on a stool with the other.

You shouldn't have let him touch you! she shouted. She couldn't let it go, it obsessed her.

He only touched my beads, said Eva, then added:

Besides, I wanted him to.

She paused.

I willed it, she said.

Willed? You don't will something in a science lab, Shirley said.

I willed it because he needs rescuing, Eva cried.

Rescuing? repeated Shirley.

Can't you see – began Eva.

He's an eminent scientist, said Shirley, and you're just a nobody. Like me, she added generously and then generosity got too much for her jealousy.

But you're in an awful dress.

Eva shrugged, and after a while Shirley went back to her work and pretended to concentrate. All the time Eva worked, her hand strayed to her red beads.

Then I knew I had waited too long to exile myself into the world. All that wasted time hiding from the world when I could've roamed it searching for her, finding her, finding a way to speak, to speak to her, to love her, to make her love me. Why, why had I been content with books, with music, with my poor company when a creature like her lived in the world? Why had it taken me so long to come down the few steps of my staircase? It could've been so simple, I could've walked into this hospital and there she'd be. Why hadn't I done it? And now it was too late! Just as I found her, why, the very same day, this awkward scientist had whipped her away from me. She could've rescued me. If I'd appeared before her, she who so wants to rescue someone, she might have said, Oh, there's someone who's in a mess. She might have rescued me!

CHAPTER 8

I resolve to know the meaning of love

I SCARCELY SLEPT, moaning with regret all through the night. At dawn I longed to go right then and there into my little shed to see her again, in the desperate hope that she'd come at dawn too, though why she'd do that I didn't know. I just wanted her to still be there for me.

See him for what he is, I murmured to her face in my head, in the forlorn hope she could hear me the way I heard her.

See him!

But I didn't know what he was that she was supposed to see.

I made myself stay at home for breakfast, but I hurried it so fast I burned my tongue on my tea. Top Lab was deserted but I was at the hospital window early, hoping she hadn't come yet, straining to see her amongst the traffic. Desperation made me cheeky. All the jobs on the blackboard would've taken me to far-flung parts of the hospital, so I picked up the chalk and, mimicking the scrawl of one of the senior nurses, I added on the top of the list, squeezing it in:

'Will someone unstick the front windows before we expire?'

Then I turned screws on the front windows and oiled hinges while I waited for her.

Matron came in for her shift.

Onto your first job already, Galileo? she smiled, while I blushed bright red.

At last Eva rode into view on her bicycle, the lab coat repaired, and it saddened me how quickly the moment that had brought us together had been stitched away. But she was my new life, and that nothing could change. She put out her foot as she always did, to steady herself against the kerb, and trundled the bike in past the guard. As she bent to chain up her bike in the shelter, I glimpsed a flash of green silk under her coat. She straightened and looked around, and then I was crushed. I couldn't deny it. Her long, pale throat was stretched like a swan's in hope as she gazed around for his car. When she saw he hadn't arrived, her shoulders slumped. As she walked across the car park, she stumbled and almost fell.

She hadn't heard my murmur. Murmurers never do.

I did three jobs quickly, and then I hurried out to my shed. Eva was moving like someone possessed. Shirley said little to her, pretending to be absorbed in lining up Petri dishes on the bench, but her eyes darted, taking in every detail of the girl. When Eva went to the toilet, Shirley glanced at her watch. Eva didn't come back for some time. At last she drifted through the door, dreamily trailing her forefinger along the bench. By then Shirley was labelling the Petri dishes with a black felt pen. I wrote down every word they spoke.

You forgot your plates. You've let your plates dry out, said Shirley.

Eva jumped at the sound of Shirley's voice.

You've left them too long. You'll have to start again, Shirley said.

Yes, said Eva quietly. I'm sorry. I'll have to start again.

She was subdued, withdrawn, unhappy. They worked with their backs to each other.

At the morning break, Shirley made the coffee and called Eva.

I don't want coffee, said Eva.

Shirley came to her, hands clenched on her hips.

Why not? she demanded.

I'm sick, said Eva.

Lovesick? mocked Shirley.

Eva nodded.

You've got to get over this, said Shirley.

And then she added something that made my heart jump:

You're nothing to him.

Exactly! I wanted to shout.

Eva was shushing her frantically.

He might hear, she whispered.

He's not even in the building, cried Shirley. He hasn't come in today.

Eva hung her head like a child. There were brown circles under her eyes. She had the sort of skin that shows every mark, every sleepless night.

You shouldn't have let him touch you like that! said Shirley.

You were flirting with him! Eva's voice darted out.

I wasn't flirting. I was being charming, roared Shirley. You weren't. You went completely –

and she did a mock collapse.

Their faces lit up each other's, like fires.

Then Eva looked down, defeated.

I'm clumsy and he's clumsy, she croaked. But you're the one who talked about having sex.

You're thinking about having sex with him? If you do, the Board will sack you, blustered Shirley. (I could tell that she was making this up as she went.)

Eva shrugged.

I could slap you, Shirley said so vehemently that spit jumped out of her mouth, but she didn't care. She walked away.

It went on all day, Eva anxious, silent, touching her beads, watching the door, hoping it would open; Shirley jealous, frowning. Both of them made mistakes in their work, both of them had to throw work away. At five or thereabouts, Shirley stalked home, and Eva followed soon after.

I stayed late, guiltily finishing all the jobs not done, but I initialled them on the chalkboard alternately with an M for Marconi and an R for Rutherford, a lazy man, even fatter than me, who glowered at the lawns I raked and flung his cigarette butts on them. I raked up his butts and went home.

That second terrible night, I tried to reason with myself. I'd lost her just when I'd found her. But who was I? Gunther was clumsy, it was true, but I was worse. By midnight I had admitted that I was too shambling to be anyone's lover. I didn't know the first thing about loving, I was like a prisoner peering out at a silver sheen of ocean from a slit in a door, unable even to walk out onto the sand and crunch its grit under my toes.

By dawn I had a plan.

I would watch her fall in love with him, and learn what love meant to her, and how to do it, how to love her.

Oh, I know I could have learned about sex in other ways, I could've visited the brothel, I wouldn't have needed to speak for the women there to know what I wanted. But fool that I might be, it was not sex that intimidated me, though I'd never lain with a woman.

Once I have Eva in my arms, the rest will take care of itself, I said. The problem is, how to get her there.

So there was only one decision to make: I would stay longer in the world for her, longer than my month. I would wait for her. Even if it took a year. For the next year, I would watch this love affair to know how it is done. Especially how it is done with her.

I was sure that she couldn't love him for long. For a few months, maybe, no more. He was too silent, too inscrutable, and too old. I was the right age. She was only a little younger than me. For her, I could wait a year.

I'll let him teach me, I thought, I will learn from his mistakes. She will tire of him, I thought, when she begins to come into her power.

I glanced out my window, thinking of my mother leaning there, her face damp with regret. Perhaps at that moment my mother was seeing into the future, sensing the woman that one day, despite all her warnings, she knew I'd love.

Perhaps that's why she died then, to give way to Eva.

I wanted him to touch me, Eva had said. I willed it.

If willing something was good enough for her, then I could do it too, this willing. I would will – what? His death? Ah no, not his death. That would not be honourable.

His ill-health? Almost as dishonourable. Worse, it would make Eva pity him.

His misery?

I turned my eyes towards the sky and said:

Burden him.

In that moment, how I secretly longed for his death!

But all I willed was:

Make a terrible burden fall on him.

Was that dishonourable?

At the time it seemed not dishonourable, but inspired. At the time, in the way that sometimes your absurd life slips suddenly into the divine, early morning sunlight burst through the clouds and my dreary street was seared by a shaft of yellow light that reached into my apartment and touched my forehead, like the pictures of prophets ringed in light in the illustrated Bible I had as a child. If the priest had opened the doors of his church at that moment and looked up, he would have thought I was a modern prophet blazing with the light of God.

My mother's words and my cursed frozen tongue were going to make me into a voyeur.

Do I sound full of self-pity? I was stooped with self-pity.

CHAPTER 9
My rival becomes strangely burdened

THAT MORNING, SHIRLEY WAS FIRST IN, and by the time she'd arrived I'd already done two little jobs. So I settled into my shed and watched her make her first pot of coffee, and go to the coldroom where her cultures were stored. The car park door opened to reveal Gunther. He looked just like he usually did, the same khaki clothes, the shy awkwardness. He didn't look burdened, and, I have to admit it, my heart sunk. His eyes jerked immediately to Eva's workbench. He checked his watch. She was late. Surely she'd be pedalling up the road right this minute, weaving her white-coated figure between the cars. I wanted to hurry back to the hospital and look out the window to watch for her, but instead I watched him dither at the mail table.

It was one of Shirley's jobs, I'd already noticed, to sort the mail and deliver it to the scientists. She'd first run to her little powder room to remember who she was under her lab coat and protective cap, then she'd stroll casually up the stairs to Sandy's office, down the corridor and across to Lab Two and out the back to the Animal House where Hugh, the parasitologist, worked. She'd chat at doorways, her hands twinkling in the air, sometimes dropping letters like huge snowflakes as she spoke. But she was under instructions to leave Gunther's letters on a little table in the lab, and every few days he'd riffle through them, often leaving some unopened, piling up. Now the pile gave him something to do while he waited for Eva, so he stood ripping envelopes open with his door key, glancing cursorily at the letters and throwing them back onto the table.

Shirley bustled in from the coldroom. She was surprised to see Gunther, but quickly recovered.

Coffee? she asked.

Burden him!

He sized up the dwindling pile of unopened mail. He had to find another ruse.

What do you think? she persisted.

Yes, please, he said.

He flashed her one of his vulnerable smiles.

She indicated the letters.

You have to expect all this. With your fame, she said.

Shirley's smile seemed lost on him, as usual. I could almost see him blush.

Burden him!

Burden him!

He came to the last envelope, a large yellow packet. He sighed, took his time to slit it in a precise straight line, shook out its contents and threw the envelope down. Soon after, Shirley arrived with a steaming mug.

There you are, she said. I remembered how much milk you like.

He didn't notice.

It's better than the last coffee I gave you, she said. The other day, when I gave you that coffee, I didn't realise that my assistant had left only the dregs.

He wasn't listening, she could see. He was staring at a newspaper cutting that had fallen out of the yellow packet. Later she claimed that his eyes weren't moving over it, just staring into space, paralysed.

She put the coffee down beside him on the table.

Would you like a chair? she asked.

He didn't hear.

She went back to her work, washing up the glassware, glancing at him from time to time, breathing as if she was going to speak but finding nothing to say. Eventually Eva opened the door, in yellow organza under her lab coat. She hesitated when she saw him, but he didn't look up. Shirley made a silent face at her and slid her eyes meaningfully towards Eva's work.

He noticed nothing, not his coffee cup Shirley had set near him, not the chair Shirley had set behind him, and not Eva.

It had succeeded! My willing it had worked! Something in the newspaper cutting had blinded him to everything!

He went on reading. The newspaper cutting fluttered in his hand and I glimpsed a photo, though of what I wasn't sure. He was also holding what seemed to be a scholarly article, with a number of pages clipped together, and his lips were moving over them as if he was learning them by heart. His face had somehow acquired a different shape, it seemed longer, older. His shoulders, his whole torso drooped towards the pages, all of him was in the reading. Even his briefcase, which I hadn't noticed before, seemed to crouch into his legs.

Something's wrong, Shirley whispered to Eva. Terrible news, maybe.

Then the door creaked open again and Dr Charles Sanderson came in, the other scientist from upstairs. He was one of those short, thick-spectacled men who are always taking charge, so for a long time I thought he was more important than Gunther, not the other way around.

By assiduous backstabbing, he eventually became Gunther's boss – but I must remember it all in order.

Charles Sanderson was the opposite of Gunther. He was unfailingly pleasant, standing very close to the dullest people as if he'd never met anyone so interesting, and he'd lean his upper body slightly backwards in delight and surprise as he listened, and open his eyes wide – they were already magnified by his spectacles and seemed like green ponds you could dive into and all your worries would float away. He had a way of opening his mouth a little too wide so you could see the spit surfing around his teeth and gums when he spoke. But it wasn't repulsive, it made him more believable, as if he was even ready to show you how his body worked. I could tell he bewitched people, so they felt he was their best friend and they never noticed he was everyone else's best friend as well. Call me Sandy, he'd say confidingly and open his mouth to show you his surfing spit.

Much later I heard Shirley telling Eva that when the hospital Board had been considering whether to reopen and refit the old labs, Charles Sanderson, a scientist who claimed promising research on a cancer cell (his 'little molecule', he liked to call it), had astonished them with a daring scheme to finance the labs, the staff and his research. It all depended on his luring the eminent Professor Gunther Mueller away from a distant university and back to our city, where Mueller's old and ailing father lived. Once Mueller was safely ensconced, Sandy's scheme went, all sorts of triumphs would flow on – the entire scientific community would be buzzing with interest in the news, and universities all over the country, perhaps even the world, might send postgraduate students here for off-campus training under Mueller and pay the hospital for their training. Last but not least, Mueller's speciality, immunology, was certain to attract funding from Sandy's very good friend, Doris Rockwell, the grieving daughter of the local mining tycoon. The whole of Sudlow knew the story of how Doris's only son, born with a hole in his heart, had died because his immune system rejected the transplanted heart. Doris might even become financially interested in Sandy's little cell and the hospital would benefit from that, of course.

Now is the time to act on Doris, Sandy had urged the hospital Board. Strike while the iron is hot!

The Board, which prided itself on being fresh-thinking, ambitious and enterprising, recognised Sandy as a man after its own heart, and drank a toast to 'our man'.

A Board member in his cups even suggested that a statue of Sandy be made and placed next to the memorial of Samuel Craven Sudlow, but no one was quite sure where that was.

So Gunther Mueller had been brought to Sudlow and, fortuitously, a blaze of glory now surrounded him because he'd almost won the Prize. Sandy's scheme was a great success, so far.

Now Sandy, coming into Top Lab from the sunlight outside, almost walked into Gunther.

Sorry, he said, and pushed his thick spectacles further up his nose.

When Gunther kept reading, absorbed, Sandy put his hand on Gunther's sleeve.

There's another journalist outside, no appointment of course, but this one's flown in from Melbourne.

Gunther ignored him. Sandy wasn't used to being ignored.

I told him to come in – is that all right? He's from *The Age*. I know you're busy, but it'll help marvellously with funding. Just what the lab needs. Doris will be very impressed.

Gunther looked at Sandy's hand as if it was an insect he needed to brush off, and looked from Sandy's arm to Sandy's face.

No journalists, he said shortly.

Nonsense, said Sandy. After such a triumph. Besides, we need to impress Dopey Doris. We need this attention! Come on, he added as if he were speaking to a child, and he did a jokey twist of his body so that he could look at what Gunther was reading.

Get out! Gunther shouted.

Just then the journalist, a shorthand notebook in his hand, put his head around the door.

Oh good, I'm in the right place, he said when he saw Sandy. A bit of a rabbit warren here, and all empty!

Empty, yes, but bursting with important ideas, Sandy began.

Gunther took in the stranger and spoke suddenly:

Professor Mueller is not here.

Sandy started, but recovered.

That's right, he said, I'm afraid Professor Mueller isn't in today, he won't be in, he's got a slight problem, he'll be in tomorrow.

He was steering the journalist back out the door to the car park.

By the time Sandy returned, Gunther had opened the door of the tiny office under the staircase, Shirley's make-up room.

He'll see my mirror! Shirley whispered to Eva.

But Gunther sat down blindly at a desk, pushing an old typewriter out of his way. He was so burdened, he buried his face in his hands.

Sandy stood at the door.

Bad news? he asked sympathetically.

Gunther didn't reply.

Is that a research paper? asked Sandy. He was trying to edge closer to the desk, craning his neck, to find out the author.

Not bad news, I hope, said Sandy.

What? Gunther asked.

Haven't been pipped at the post, have we? Sandy asked.

Pipped? Gunther repeated. He suddenly seemed to have developed a slight accent.

Our rivals? asked Sandy. In immunology?

He wasn't in the least interested in Gunther's immunology, I found out later, but he used words like our and we so that people thought he cared about them. Gunther didn't understand this.

Your rivals? asked Gunther.

Yours, said Sandy. Then he read aloud the title of the paper in Gunther's hand: 'Die Autistischen Psychopathen im Kindesalter'. What's that mean, autistic?

No, Gunther shouted. No, no, no, no, no.

Sorry, said Sandy, backing off. Obviously not rivals.

No, no, no, shouted Gunther.

I thought the paper looked a bit out of date for rivals, said Sandy. Rivals, of course, would be contemporaries.

He was blabbing.

The newspaper clipping was lying on the desk. Gunther clapped his hand over it, to fend off Sandy's prying eyes. His shoulders were shaking oddly, as if he wanted to flap his arms and fly away.

I'll leave you to it then, said Sandy, and went out.

It should be shut, shouted Gunther.

Sorry? asked Sandy, hopefully popping his head back around the door.

The door. Shut the door, said Gunther.

Sorry, said Sandy and shut the door, just as Shirley was miming her relief to Eva that no one had noticed her hanging mirror. She immediately became preoccupied in her work, busily lifting the lid off a Petri dish.

Professor Mueller – he's in a state, Sandy said unnecessarily.

Shirley put the lid back on the Petri dish.

It came in his mail, this thing that's put him in a state, she said.

She was delighted by the unexpected diversion.

Sandy licked his lips. After all, Shirley was of little consequence.

We must leave him to his correspondence, he said.

It wasn't just what you saw, said Shirley. The scientific paper, I mean.

That I didn't see, corrected Sandy.

I saw something else, said Shirley. She seemed a little frenzied herself.

I saw a newspaper clipping with a photo of rows of specimen jars. People's brains, I think. And a headline – something about a Nazi killer.

A Nazi criminal? cried Sandy.

There was handwriting scribbled over it. In purple ink. It's not every day that people scribble in purple ink, she said.

Sandy gazed into her eyes, temporarily distracted by their brown depths.

Vehement writing, in purple ink, added Shirley.

Vehement? repeated Sandy.

Impulsive, said Shirley.

Really, said Sandy.

Eva's voice came so suddenly, they jumped.

The envelope's still here.

Eva pointed to the mail table, where indeed the torn envelope lay abandoned.

Look at all the addresses it's gone to – Sydney and Melbourne and even Tasmania! said Shirley.

There's a sender on the back, said Eva.

She read aloud: 'Helene Haussman, London'.

I thought it might've come from a woman, said Shirley. Being in purple ink.

It's not from a lab, there's no logo, said Sandy. So who is this Helene Haussman?

She's traced him, said Shirley suddenly. Because of his fame.

Oh, I don't think he's that famous, began Sandy.

But Shirley was warming to the subject.

Maybe the TV news we saw here, maybe it was broadcast in England –

Oh, I don't think so, Sandy interrupted.

And someone, Shirley continued, undaunted,

this ordinary person, this Helene Haussman, she'd once known him, maybe back in Austria, and she saw him and remembered him. I mean, you can still see the little boy he once was, don't you think? And she thought, well, there wouldn't be many labs in Australia because there aren't many people in Australia, and they probably all know each other. So she sent off something she knew would mean a lot to him.

Something about autism, said Sandy.

You think I'm right? asked Shirley, pleased.

Absolutely, said Sandy, too quickly. Absolutely.

They gazed silently at each other.

Women are so intuitive, said Sandy.

Do you think she's an ex – she hesitated, and her tone became almost shy –

an ex-lover?

Gunther? Not likely! said Sandy. Do you think? Hardly a Romeo.

He's got a certain fascination, said Shirley. And he's so clever.

Sandy's face stiffened.

Oh, I don't think he's that clever, he said.

Do you think he's an ex-Nazi? asked Shirley.

My heart thumped. If Gunther was an ex-criminal, then my troubles were over. I'd just have to find a way to prove it.

But Sandy was laughing.

He's too young, he said. He's old to you, but he's too young to have been a Nazi. The interesting thing is – why would a paper on autism upset him so much? Then he added, lowering his voice,

Ask Lotti. She'd know.

Was Lotti his childhood sweetheart? asked Shirley.

I have no idea, said Sandy. But they both lived in Sudlow years ago.

He seemed thrilled with Shirley's deductions, though I only knew why much, much later. You're a natural detective! Amazing deductions! he said, over and over again, until even she looked up suspiciously. So he quietened down, put the envelope back on the mail table, on top of the letters Gunther had discarded, and began to straighten up the pile. Shirley helped him, though it was only a small pile and he needed no help. Their fingers brushed each other's. He was floundering in the vivacity of Shirley's face, the pink and whiteness of it, like spring blossoms in the gloom of the lab. He couldn't resist her.

Keep a watch on him, Sandy said, nodding his head towards the room where Gunther still sat.

Tell me if you notice any more clues.

Yes, she said.

Amazing deductions, he said all over again, and she demurred, saying that it was obvious, anyone would've drawn the same conclusions, and he laughed warmly at her modesty.

Back to work then, he said, nodding at her Petri dishes but not moving, so it was unclear whether he was talking about her or himself. He let his hands drop, stood, and straightened his suit coat.

What orders has Lotti's lab sent you? he found to ask.

She told him. He must have known the answer, because all orders were checked by him, I later found out. As she talked she became more excited, and so did he. They both forgot the man bowed with grief in the room behind them.

Then Sandy walked lightly up the stairs, Shirley returned to her work, and Gunther eventually stumbled out into the morning, as if mornings for him would never be the same again.

CHAPTER 10

My rival's troubles are hinted at

I PENITENTLY GOT OUT THE LONG LADDERS and climbed up on the roof and cleaned dead leaves and dirt from around the chimneys for the rest of the morning, even though it wasn't on the job list.

At lunchtime Lotti thrust open the door.

Lotti and another scientist, Narelle, worked in the second lab in the far wing of the hospital, analysing the blood of patients for the doctors, as the scientists in Top Lab didn't. They were both the sort of women my mother would have witheringly called spinsters. As they strode through the hospital talking in ringing tones about chemicals with long names, they didn't seem pitiable at all; in fact, I was a little afraid of them and kept out of their way.

Lotti was middle-aged, with a lively, ruddy face and grey hair pulled back fiercely into a bun, her body shapeless except for thin, sharp shoulders that pushed sternly at the cotton of her blouse, almost piercing it. She flouted the rule of lab coats, and I'd already noticed she treated Shirley and Eva like her equals. I liked her for that.

But she hardly looked like anyone's childhood sweetheart.

Eva half rose from her stool, expecting Gunther. She knocked it over in her excitement, which exasperated Shirley again.

Lunch, announced Lotti in her declamatory way. Coming?

Then she took in Eva, on her feet, with the stool fallen. She seemed fond of Eva. How could she not be? I thought then.

Good heavens, girl. What's wrong now? she asked.

Eva felt behind her for the stool, found it on the floor and scrambled to right it.

Man trouble, said Shirley, with an edgy laugh that wasn't at all infectious.

Men aren't worth troubling yourself over, little one, Lotti told Eva kindly. You're so lovely they'll flock to you but until they do, relish –

Gunther, Shirley added.

Oh, said the older woman. She turned away from Eva and began clenching her fist near her stomach, which protruded a little, distorting the pattern of her checked skirt.

Shirley, oblivious, went to the sink and ran the water fast, although there were only her small, dimpled hands to wash.

Lotti, what do you know about Professor Mueller? asked Shirley. You knew him *before* he came to the lab, didn't you?

Why do you ask? Lotti seemed suddenly cautious.

Would you have guessed he'd become famous? Shirley pursued.

Lotti gave a loud laugh that said nothing.

Shirley came over, drying her hands on her handkerchief, her usual good nature reasserting itself.

He got a strange note this morning, scribbled on a newspaper clipping. It was written in purple ink, she said. Did he leave a sweetheart overseas? A Helene – she paused.

Helene Haussman, said Eva.

How would I know? said Lotti.

But she relented enough to say:

He was just a boy, barely a teenager, when his family came here.

You knew him then, said Shirley. What was he like?

As a boy? Lotti asked and when Shirley nodded, she cried:

You expect me to describe him!

Is it so hard? asked Shirley.

Lotti sighed. She sat down on one of the stools, but her hand was still in a fist, and she addressed only Shirley.

His parents had to get out of Austria – she began.

Because of the Nazis? Shirley interrupted.

Everyone was escaping them in one way or another, said Lotti.

That's exactly what she said. 'In one way or another.' What did she mean? What was she trying not to reveal?

But Shirley and Eva didn't seem to notice.

Anyway, continued Lotti, his parents used to visit us because my mother had come out from Vienna too.

Why did his family land up in this place? Shirley said.

Lotti shrugged.

I never asked. To hide, I suppose. They'd had a terrible time. Gunther's mother never stopped talking – perhaps she was trying to make up for his father. His father! He'd say nothing, he'd just sit and stare at the carpet. He wouldn't make any effort, even when my father brought out the cognac. It was the war, you know. My father hated their visits. You expect me to make conversation with that ghost? he'd say to my mother. But they'd bring home baked strudel, which made my mother cry with homesickness. I'd be hanging around, only understanding bits of the conversation, always in my best dress, because my mother wanted me to entertain Gunther and make a good impression on him. Imagine what that was like, try-ing to entertain Gunther! He was worse than his father!

She gave a high, hard laugh in memory of those times.

He never spoke to me. Not a word, though he spoke English. He'd come straight in out of their car, not even a hello, run out to my father's garden shed, pick out a spade, always the same spade, and spend the visit digging holes – deep holes. He could stand up in them. No one could get him to stop. My father would get mad. Not only did they ruin a good Sunday morning, but the boy's ruined my roses. Why didn't you protect them? he'd say to me afterwards. As if I'd had any chance. After a while, the visits had to stop because my father's rose garden was full of holes.

Lotti gave another of her hard, raucous laughs.

One time, she said, there was an old phone book thrown out on the back porch, and he picked it up and I thought, Aha! A game, at last! But he just read it to himself, in utter silence. And then he spent the rest of the visit making me check the book so I could listen to him reciting a page of phone numbers at a time. He'd say, J. Smith UA 2630, and I'd hurriedly look it up and there it'd be, J. Smith UA 2630. Then it'd be J.E. Smith's turn, LA 7994, and I'd check and, sure enough, there it was. No one could shut him up. The thing is, he was absolutely accurate.

He was trying to impress you. After all, you looked so pretty in your best dress, said Shirley. Have you reminded him of this?

I wouldn't bring it up, it'd embarrass him, said Lotti. He's reinvented himself. I went to Melbourne University and he was there. He'd changed, almost completely. He'd grown up, I suppose. We had conversations. Real conversations. Well, maybe not conversations. He'd talk about his theories. He always had theories. He'd interrupt lectures, just blurting – no, announcing – his theories to the lecturer as if he couldn't stop himself. So in some ways he hadn't changed. But they were interesting theories. Wrong but interesting. I think, in the end, the lecturers rather enjoyed him. They'd ask him out for drinks, to hear his theories.

She stopped abruptly.

I don't know any more, she said.

Did you get sweet on him? Shirley asked.

It was Lotti's turn to blush.

That's my point. We never talked about anything personal. That's what I liked about him when we were students. We talked about work. In science in those days, twenty years ago, a woman had to choose between work and men. Most of the girls would be hanging around after lectures in the courtyard. There was a special low wall where they'd sit, waiting for the men to ask them out. We called it the Matrimony One wall. I never sat on that wall. I'd chosen science.

Her hand, which had been clenched all this time, relaxed.

Besides, I never found a man as interesting as the work.

She glared at Eva, no longer indulging her.

I'd choose men any day, said Shirley, to break the tension. That's why I work in science! To meet men!

And she roared with laughter, so no one knew if she was joking.

Lotti ignored her.

Gunther's not interested in people. Only science. So keep away from him, that's my advice, she said to Eva.

It sounded more like a threat than advice.

Let's go and have lunch, said Shirley, to be a peacemaker.

Coming? she asked Eva.

No, said Eva.

Lotti followed Shirley out the door. Eva stared at the wall, touching her beads.

Later in the day, Eva excused herself to go home early.

Just write up the diary, then go, Shirley said, her voice a little softer now, eased by the rhythm of the work.

I have, Eva said.

Shirley picked up the diary. Her eyes flicked over it.

Fine, fine, she said.

Then she saw scribble in the margins of the page. She had to turn the diary around to read aloud:

'We are made for danger.'

Can't you stop yourself? she shouted.

I don't want to, said the girl.

From then on I saw that Eva was struggling to get absorbed in her work, but every now and then she'd drift off, her eyes glazing over, her hands straying to her red beads. She wore them constantly, and she'd press them gently against her throat. One day I swore I could see on the monitor a discolouration on her flawless skin, as if she was wearing them at night and pressing them against her throat in her dreams. She probably went to sleep saying his name to herself and woke with it drying on her lips.

I'll murder him, I thought dishonourably.

But then she murmured to me, and I'm sure it was only to me:

'When I was about twelve, I was wandering around the shops, and I peeped into the open door of a church. There were curtains somewhere, I don't remember where, but they fell in a great swoop, the light picking out their soft richness. They were grand, a dark, mysterious velvety maroon. There seemed to be nobody about and I couldn't resist creeping in to run my hands over that richness. I wasn't used to churches, only dress fabrics, and velvet was my favourite. Before I could reach out my hand, I heard a noise behind me, a giggle, and I swung around to see a group of children sitting in rows watching me. I turned to run away but a priest who was standing over in a dark corner lecturing them, said: You're late, sit down. He'd mistaken me for another child, I suppose. I had that sort of face.

'I sat down stiffly. They were all girls, except for one boy, and his eyes were on a patch of red hanging over the back of one of the pews, a jumper, an ordinary red jumper, a girl's, with white flowers embroidered on the pocket. A sleeve was dangling towards the floor. The cuff edges were unravelling. The minister said something, maybe he announced a break, and all the children got up and moved off, except the boy. He waited till their clamour died, then he went over to the jumper and picked up the dangling sleeve and propped it against the back of the pew, the way my mother's customers propped up the round bodies of their babies. But he couldn't let it go, he stroked it with his spindly, adolescent fingers. His face softened, and his eyes became like pools at midnight in the bush, as if the whole black swoop of sky had fallen into them.

'Celia must've forgotten it, the priest said, suddenly arriving in our consciousness.

'The boy put the jumper down, and followed Celia.

'My mother had explained that no man would fall in love with me because I wasn't neat and clean enough. But she was wrong. This boy loved Celia, who'd thrown down her jumper untidily. I couldn't wait, from that moment on, to have a lover, a lover like that boy, a man who'd love even the thrown-down clothes I wear.'

Now it came to me, the wild hope that she wouldn't tell him a memory like that. She would only murmur it to me.

CHAPTER 11

My rival reveals a fatal flaw

VERY SOON, the mystery about Gunther Mueller deepened. Matron had told me to go to the children's ward to repair the bathroom window sashes before the doctors made their rounds and blamed her for the children's coughs. I hadn't been to the children's ward. I'd always been frightened of children – oh, the fears I have to admit to if I'm to remember how it all came about!

So I put off going to the children's ward, and because I'd already done all the jobs on the board that morning, I skulked to the nurses' tearoom and had the inspiration of filling up the sink with warm, soapy water, taking down all the clean cups and scrubbing away at their stains as if stains really mattered.

One of the nurses came in, shifted her chewing gum to grunt a greeting, put up her feet on the coffee table and lit a cigarette. Her eyes bored into my back. I didn't like to look around so when I finished scrubbing the cups, I checked them all and rescrubbed some.

Are you a germ freak or something? the nurse asked, puffing on her cigarette.

Sorry, Galileo, I shouldn't have called you a freak, she added. We've been told not to call you a freak.

I made myself wash the whole lot again so she'd think I hadn't heard. But Matron was bearing down the corridor flanked by the doctors so I bolted guiltily into the children's ward. Not a face turned in my direction. They were watching a small boy who was bent over, pretending to plug and unplug imaginary electrical cords into imaginary wall sockets. He stood up and attached their imaginary other ends to his legs, arms and neck. Then he stood stiffly to attention and lifted his right arm, for all the world like a mechanical arm, to his head. His hand, palm down, fingers stretched out, thudded down on his head an imaginary bottle cap. He lowered his arm to his side and stood to attention again. After a second of stillness he slid out his right foot describing part of the arc of a circle, drew the other foot beside it, lifted his right arm again in the same angular way and thudded another lid onto his head, the neck of another bottle on a production line. He stopped, bent over to another imaginary wall switch, unplugged his imaginary wires, replugged the wires and moved again on his production line.

When the performance was over, I burst into applause, then, when all eyes except the boy's turned to me, I realised I was the only clapper.

A stout little nurse about my age, black hair flying importantly from under her white cap, came bustling over.

It's not an act, she hissed in a manner that seemed copied from a much older woman.

I stepped back, ashamed, but she went on in a normal voice:

We've been ringing all morning for someone to fix the bathroom window sashes, and she led me across the ward, past the boy who'd begun to put bottle lids on his head again.

We were passing between him and his imaginary wall switch.

Be careful, she said to me, turning her face, her lips open so I glimpsed a Lavender Lifesaver floating in her mouth.

We wouldn't want to disconnect Billy, would we?

She wasn't joking. None of the children laughed. I didn't either, now. She took a large step over the wire that wasn't there. I did the same.

I got to work. Half an hour later, when I'd finished in the bathroom, the boy was still plugging in his imaginary wiring, clamping bottle caps on his head and unplugging himself, but now he had visitors: a thin, bony man and a stern-looking woman.

Billy, the woman called to him in a cold, fierce voice.

Billy, we're here, echoed the man.

Although he was only a few steps away, Billy gave no sign of hearing. He's having such fun, I thought. Why don't these officials understand?

Some of the younger children took up the call:

Billy, they're here. Billy, your mum and dad are here.

His parents? I was startled. But Billy heard nothing. He kept putting lids on his head and sliding around his production line.

The boy's deaf and his parents don't know, I thought.

As I crossed the ward, I saw another child who wasn't watching Billy. He was banging his head against the wall. I ran over to him but I couldn't hold him still, though I was four times his size. He screamed as I touched him, threw himself out of my clutches and kept banging his head.

The little nurse came up.

Don't handle him, he hates to be handled, she said. It's no use.

Nevertheless I grabbed him, my body bending with his strength as he plummeted towards the wall. His screams were ringing in my ears, but I couldn't bear to let him go.

Give up, she said to me, but she grabbed him too by his other arm, so we both swayed with him, we almost fell with him, losing our balance, righting ourselves and toppling again. More shining strands of black hair flopped out of her cap.

It's no use, she repeated, even while she tried to steady him. He won't stop, he wants to kill himself, don't you see? Give up.

She let go. The boy thudded against the wall. She prised my fingers off the boy's arms.

Can you hear me, even if you can't talk? she asked me.

I nodded yes.

Your mother was probably lovely to you, was she? she continued.

I was so startled, a word dislodged itself.

Yes, my voice squeaked.

Her pretty eyes narrowed.

They said you couldn't talk. But you can when it suits you!

I stepped back. The boy thudded against the wall once more and we both reached out to grab him. She spoke over his screams as we swayed with him:

These kids, they won't talk. Won't even hear, though they're not deaf. They were born in this hospital, they were beautiful babies, I helped to bring them into the world, so I would know. But their mothers have destroyed them. They've taken away the kids' wish to live.

In my astonishment, I let him go and he banged his head. There was a slash of red on his forehead, but she kept speaking:

Their mothers don't hit them or starve them, nothing you can see, they just send out these messages through the air, messages of hate, they really want their kid to die. It's true, she added as she saw uncertainty move across my face. All the doctors say so. And the kid obeys. It dies. Or it does its best to.

As if the boy had heard, his body suddenly became limp. He crumpled onto me, a weight I staggered under.

That's better, darling, she crooned, bending over him. I was so close I could've counted the tiny freckles on her rounded cheeks.

You lie there, she crooned to him. Have a relaxing little faint.

She turned her face.

I'm Deirdre. Who are you? she added with the same rapid change of direction as before, and I realised she was talking to me. But surprise wouldn't dislodge my name out of my throat, and certainly not while I was trying to keep the boy upright. I tried for G, but all that happened was my cheeks filled with air, and the boy slipped further down toward my waist. She watched me with curiosity.

Brain damage, that's what you've got, she said at last with a professional air. Let's get him into the bed.

I half dragged, half carried him.

It took every puff of breath out of my body. Together we laid him down.

He'd be better off dead, she said.

He was like her blood-streaked doll now. She tidied his rumpled pyjamas, watched him for signs of breathing, and turned and checked the ward. The mechanical boy was still putting lids on his head, but the other children were ignoring him.

Then the door swung open and Deirdre groaned. I looked up to see that Gunther was in the ward. I hadn't seen any of the scientists in the wards before, so his appearance took me by surprise. But more surprising was her reaction.

Not him again, she whispered. You know what madness he said the other day? He said that Billy might be incapable of speech. And I said, Professor Mueller, I nursed Billy as a baby, and later on his mother brought him here for weighing, and I'm here to tell you, he was perfectly normal. He could babble like any baby. If he can't speak now, we all know why.

She called out to Gunther:

Have you got permission to be in my ward?

He took no notice of her. He was watching Billy, as mesmerised as the children had been. I thought I'd better go, in case she asked me to remove Gunther. The boy had been heavy enough. But as I passed Gunther, I saw that his eyes were glossed with tears.

CHAPTER 12

I fall into the Slough of Despond, but so does my rival

I DIDN'T GO TO THE HOSPITAL for a few days. The weather was cold and blustery with grey skies and black clouds scudding across it. I went back into the state I'd inhabited much of my life since my mother died. I barely moved around my rooms, and lingered in my pyjamas until late afternoon, my body weighted with a grief I had no name for. Eva's blue eyes kept flickering through my mind, as if I were still watching the cameras and seeing the stain on her neck where she'd pressed the beads too deeply. I longed to sit beside her and take her hand in mine, but if I did, what could I do then?

I was coming into my own too slowly, I would be too late for her, like a man who falls in love with a woman much older than himself.

Wait for me, my love, I murmured (soundlessly of course), just in case it was some use.

Wait for me.

Then rain fell, strong urgent swoops noisy across the windowpanes so that the church and the brothel and the street dissolved into grey fuzzy shapes. So did my self-absorbed plans. Of course, said the rain, of course Eva wouldn't wait for me. She didn't even know of my existence, and if she did, she wouldn't care. Because of my spying lenses, I'd seen her up close, the sort of closeness only a lover would normally have as he lay with his arms around her. Those spying lenses had blurred my judgment and made me feel like her lover. How I groaned with my foolishness! I'd made the greatest mistake, lingering in the world longing for love. I'd give up my pact from this very moment.

If I gave up the world, the rain promised, it wouldn't matter. Nothing would. The mocking of the nurse in the tearoom, the sneering glances from Marconi, none of this would ever matter again. According to the rain's promise I could lie on my sofa with a cup of tea cooling for the rest of my life, listening to music and reading. I plucked a book at random from the nearest shelf. I would have to begin to ration my reading because I was already halfway through my library, too fast if I lived to be a hundred, as I hoped I would. I turned the book around. It was my favourite, *War and Peace*, with my melancholy mascot, Peter – that was his name – walking out unarmed across the battlefields, gaining wisdom.

When the rain cleared, I leaned out the window and watched the traffic up at the corner, every car shining, washed clean. A bus roared by importantly, heading off to a distant city. The sunshine, yellow and fresh as a lemon, enticed me back into the world. That, and the promise I'd see her again.

So I walked to the river to watch the wind whip the waves until they seemed like people rushing head-down to catch a bus. It surged up in me again, the yearning to be part of her life. After all, I'd promised myself I'd wait a year for Eva. And already Gunther had been burdened.

I walked towards the station with its nineteenth-century con-trivances of crenellated turrets, onion dome, and ornate wide vaulted entrance, now plastered with posters for rock bands. Per-haps I'd spent too much time in the proximity of the eyeless Samuel Craven Sudlow, but I wondered if he'd built the hospital and the labs because he'd believed in the future glory of this city of stone, or because his heart was moved at the grief and poverty just beyond his muddy carriage wheels. I hadn't any time to contemplate further because a crowd hurried by me to a little kiosk tucked inside the sweep of one of the station's Italianate arches. Men halted, picked up a copy of the local paper, *The Sudlow Echo*, slammed down a coin and strode off. Up till now I'd never thought of buying a newspaper in case someone spoke to me, but I jangled change in my pocket, found a coin, put it down on the counter, picked up a paper, and it worked! I'd become a man who could buy a newspaper! In the space of almost a fortnight, I'd got a job (though unpaid), been issued with a uniform, fallen in love, burdened my rival and learned to buy a newspaper. In triumph, I sat down in a quiet park and read the headline: 'A Beaten Scientist'.

Here is the clipping, folded carefully, the print faded on the folds:

Professor Mueller, recently rumoured to have been considered for a major Prize for Medicine, has announced that he plans to retire from his groundbreaking work in immunology. 'I've recently been informed of a debt I owe, a moral debt which I must honour. I am in debt for my life,' he said. Professor Mueller declined to say who informed him, or to whom he owed his life, or why, or what his new work would be to honour his moral debt.

CHAPTER 13

During which my rival makes an enemy and I make a plan

I CAME BACK TO A TROUBLING SCENE, though I should've rejoiced, for it meant that my rival was being burdened more and more. At the hospital cafe I saw Gunther leaving with Sandy, Lotti and the old parasitologist, Hugh, from the Animal House. They'd just paid their bill. From the way they were gathered around Gunther, with Sandy patting his shoulder, I could tell that something had been decided, something that Sandy had wanted and Gunther hadn't. I lingered in front of the lolly stand, as if nothing was more important than my decision between Minties or Jaffas, straining to hear.

Hugh, his face dark with anger, had caught up with Gunther. Unfortunately, with the din of the cafe and the whistling of the wind, I couldn't hear everything, only snippets.

But I picked up that Hugh was shouting:

So you're interested in the retards?

He was a man who wore a dark coat however steamy the weather, and his neck was sticking out of his white collar so that he seemed to be pecking at Gunther the way a chook pecks at dirt. I soon found that he was a person who laughed disdainfully at the gaps and foolishnesses in all new theories, impatient with anything that wasn't yet fully known. The wind turned and brought me more snatches of his words:

What are you after, a molecule for the nerves? A gene for neurosis? That's your new secret theory, eh – a gene for neurosis? Let me tell you something. Neurosis is not the province of a biologist. Psychologists worry about emotions, philosophers worry about what that means, but the work of a biologist is biology.

Gunther kept pulling backwards away from Hugh's pecking, and I just caught his reply.

It may be that biology plays a more important part in the emotions than we have so far thought.

His attacker withdrew his neck for a moment, and its bulk slid down into the knot of his tie.

The Russians might think that the emotions are carried on the genes but they're not, he said. The genes carry only physical characteristics.

He lifted his hand to Gunther's chest and knocked on his rib cage as he said:

Like your blond Aryan hair, my boy.

His hand lingered there. Gunther didn't try to resist, and after a while Hugh dropped it.

That's all that's on the genes, Hugh resumed. Physical characteristics. Not the mess of feelings. Why look for a genetic explanation for that mess? Life's the explanation.

So I knew then that Gunther had other enemies besides me.

Sandy came back to rescue Gunther. I was just passing as Sandy said to Hugh:

Gunther's not going to rock the boat. Your work can go on. The funding's safe.

Hugh grunted, but allowed himself to be led away.

Everyone, perhaps the whole cafe, heard him shout to Sandy as they were leaving:

Isn't the point that Mueller *didn't* get the Prize?

———

In the middle of the night I woke to her voice. She was at last murmuring again. I switched on the light as if that could make me hear
better. Her voice hung in the air. But what she'd said, I couldn't
understand. I remembered, as I watched the velvety night, my
mother's words:

You're hearing their feelings. You're entering their haunted souls.

Then, next day, just as I was walking to the hospital and thinking of little more than the thin, bleached weeds breaking through
the hot pavement, her voice came to me:

'Every time I think of him, something flutters deep inside my
stomach, as if that's where my heart is. I am stupid for him, for his
touch. No one has ever touched me before, and no one will again.
All there will ever be for me is him.'

I nearly turned back home, to give up the world. But I didn't,
because she was showing me that the world is not a small, pitiable
thing after all.

The days lengthened into weeks. During her breaks Eva made lists
of things to talk about to Gunther. One evening I worked late and
tiptoed down the corridor when she was gone. (In those days, the
labs were left unlocked. You could trust everyone in Sudlow, it was
said. But as Sandy became more excited about his little molecule,
everyone was issued with a key.) I read her latest list for Gunther.
It was as I suspected. A list of interesting organisms.

I've written them down.

Cilia. The bombardier beetle. Bacterial Flagellum.

A list as childlike and trusting as the stars in the white heaven
of Shirley's make-up case.

Then she seemed to have forgotten him. She no longer started at
every creak on the stairs that might be his feet, she stopped peering
out the window to look for his particular walk across the car park,
she stopped wearing her red beads. Slowly she mended and became
again the intent, engrossed young technician I'd seen that first day.

Sometimes she went out for lunch with Shirley and Lotti's colleague, Narelle, and though in the cafe she always put her book on
the table, she seldom opened it. I'd try to eavesdrop while I scanned
the headlines of *The Sudlow Echo*. She'd watch the others as they
talked, sometimes twitching her lips in anticipation of their jokes,
but she held herself in reserve behind a hand propping up her chin.
She seldom told gossip and never confidences, but the other two
smiled amiably enough at her and mostly she remembered to smile
back. She never joined them for lunch if Lotti was there.

Is Lotti coming? she'd ask.

What have you got against her? Shirley said at last.

She thinks she owns Gunther, Eva said.

Her throat seemed to swell as she said his name.

And you do? laughed Shirley.

Shirley no longer seemed jealous, but she was still irritated by Eva's
dresses. One morning I came in to hear her shouting:

What have you got on now?

Eva looked down at herself glowing in turquoise.

It's smocking, she said, indicating a puckering above her pretty
breasts. A lost art.

Mum likes to show it isn't lost for her.

But those sleeves – no one wears puffed sleeves any more,
sniffed Shirley.

But see how well they sit, said Eva, turning around so Shirley
could appreciate the back view. When Shirley said nothing, Eva said:

I don't suppose it matters how well they sit.

She seemed to be trying to convince herself.

Shirley was checking the solutions they had to make.

She looked up.

Who are your mother's customers?

No one, these days, said Eva.

That proves my point, said Shirley. Come on, let's get started.

———

Shirley had become preoccupied with finding a new apartment. At lunch she opened out the newspaper on the cafe table, poring over the advertisements. She lived with a strict old uncle who was the subject of many domestic conversations that have nothing to do with this memoir – suffice to say that she often complained about being in trouble for chopping vegetables on a cutting board against the grain of the wood, or rushing out a doorway so fast the frame would shake and it'd go out of plumb in ten years.

Something glamorous, that's what I need in a flat, Shirley mused to the other women. So I can enjoy my new satin bedsheets. If I use them at Uncle's, he'll call me brazen.

For the first time I saw lines on her face, little lines like thorns, guarding her mouth.

Shirley, herself in bright pink stretchy tights under her lab coat and leg warmers with fluffy pompoms that wiggled with her every move, turned to Eva and said:

You ought to think of getting your own flat. Might solve the problem of having to wear those dresses.

It would seem like bolting, said Eva quietly.

About the same time, one of my tenants gave notice from the little apartment next door, number five, the one reduced to a studio because of our bookshelves. My lawyer wrote to me saying that the tenant had moved out and the apartment would be re-let. There followed a little interchange between him and me, more than we'd had for years. I wrote instructing him not to do anything. He wrote back saying that if I chose to lower my income, he wasn't going to lower his. I wrote agreeing. I had other plans, I claimed, though that was too strong a word. I had hopes.

CHAPTER 14

My rival makes many enemies

BILLY HAD DIED. Marconi, who claimed to know everything that went on – sometimes rolling his eyes at me so that I trembled for fear he knew what went on in my heart – said that Deirdre had been laughing with a wardsman at the time about the length of his feet, and she had slipped out of her shoes to show him how tiny hers were in comparison. Suddenly there'd been a loud *crack*. She'd wheeled around to find Billy on the floor. Someone had dropped a nail file and he'd stuck it into the electricity socket to wire himself up. Resuscitation didn't work on that little body.

Then the gossip was rife again about Gunther. Deirdre told me that when the parents had come to the hospital after Billy's death to collect his things and talk to the doctors, Gunther had joined the group. No one knew why, no one had invited him.

He's always here, coming into the ward at all hours, she complained, her breath perfumed again with Lavender Lifesavers, but she was too agitated to think of offering one to me.

He probably wants to watch amputees or dwarves, she said, but he has to make do with the autistic kids.

Apparently, when the boy's parents had come to the hospital, the doctors were all assembled in the ward – the registrar, and Dr Graham the chief psychiatrist, and the assistant psychiatrist, and the chief paediatrician, just as it should be, Deirdre said. Then Gunther appeared. The parents came late, the mother immaculately dressed in a canary yellow suit and matching hat with a veil.

Can you imagine dressing up when your son has just died? And in yellow? Canary yellow? Deirdre asked, and didn't stop for my headshake before she continued:

And the father had a briefcase, he was on his way to work. He wasn't taking time off to grieve, not even for a day. And you wouldn't believe it, but when they came in, they were talking about, of all things, how far away they had to park.

She broke down then, and I took her in my arms, sad for her agitation, and sad about Billy. It seemed the most natural thing, to hold her. She snuggled there, but after a minute she pulled away from me, her brown freckles across her nose almost upright in indignation.

You know what the father said then? she asked.

She mimicked the flat tone of the father.

Should we write a letter to someone about the parking system?

Then she leaned on me again, pacified by my renewed headshaking, and went on:

The doctors pretended not to notice, and Dr Graham said how defeated the professionals at the hospital felt, after all our attempts to reclaim Billy with the best psychiatric therapy available in the country. It was distressing to everyone that this terrible accident had happened, not that he blamed anyone, thank goodness, she added. (The instrument of death had been her nail file, after all.)

I'm sure you did your best, the father had said, smiling for all the world as though he had to soothe the doctors.

We were all so confused by the parents' attitude, she said, that no one thought to tell Mueller to leave. The registrar outlined the Freudian methods they'd used with Billy, and how they'd almost begun to work. But out of the corner of my eye, she said, I saw Mueller getting agitated. You know how he does this with his shoulders as if he's planning to fly –

she mimicked Gunther's shoulder-shaking, the way they'd shaken when he read the letter from Helene Haussman.

I feared the worst, she said. I was right.

Almost begun to work? he'd interrupted, so everyone jerked around to look at him. What rubbish! *Almost* begun to work! When does a cure *almost* begin?

Then Dr Graham said to me, as if it was my fault:

Nurse, what's this intruder doing in your ward?

I can't stop him, she'd told him. I don't have the authority, but she couldn't be heard above Gunther. He was saying that psychiatry might work for normal brains that were troubled, but not everyone had a normal brain, and Billy certainly didn't, his brain was abnormal. Not troubled. Billy's brain made different connections. So it was absurd to assume Billy thought like Dr Graham and could be helped by what he dared to call 'wittering on about repression'.

Wittering? Dr Graham had said. You're not just insulting me, you're insulting Freud's work in 1916, Klein's in 1946, de Monchaux's in 1963 and Bion's – none of which you'd know but all of which explain how the logic of the unconscious takes over after unbearable trauma. It's well known that there is the breast that satisfies so the developing child models future experience on his satisfaction, and there is the breast that does not satisfy, resulting in unbearable trauma, sadly.

With this he'd flung a dark glance at Billy's mother, said Deirdre, and, I have to say, her breasts didn't look like the satisfying type.

Billy's problem was not about breasts, Gunther had said. These children connect more with objects than with people. Billy didn't love people, he loved electricity instead.

But Dr Graham wouldn't let him get away with that.

Billy loved electricity because it generated sensations that made him feel 'Aha! At last I exist!' explained Dr Graham, trying not to shout. And don't we all at times get overwhelmed by the vast ocean of not-me around us, and have to find a way to rediscover ourselves in this vast ocean?

We're talking about a differently formed brain, not a poem, Gunther had said.

But Dr Graham had an answer to that.

Tustin taught us that one must enter into poetic experience to understand autism, Dr Graham said. Which I can enter, and obviously you can't.

Can't you see that the child inherited a different sort of brain by a mechanism we don't yet know? said Gunther. Can't you accept that there are children who aren't little copies of you?

Get him out of here, Dr Graham had ordered.

Deirdre had laid her hands on Gunther's chest and tried to push him out, but he wouldn't be shifted. Then pandemonium broke out, and Dr Graham told him to go back to his microscopes because he was upsetting the parents, and when he wouldn't, he shoved Mueller, but only a little, said the nurse, loyally. And then Mueller had grabbed the doctor's stethoscope from around his neck and hit him across the mouth, she said, her voice squeaking with the incredulity of it all.

Mueller is mad, utterly mad, she said. And the poor doctor's lip was split, spurting blood. Then I managed to call for an orderly, but by that time Mueller had gone. Poor Dr Graham couldn't speak, the blood was pouring out, and the registrar had to ask the parents to leave. I treated his lip. The registrar said later that under the circumstances, he'd forget about my nail file. Then would you believe it? Mueller applied to autopsy Billy's brain!

Afterwards, Volta found me in the corridor.

Taken a fancy to her, have you? he demanded, nodding in the direction of the children's ward where Deirdre was still on duty.

All I could do was nod.

Don't you dare do anything I wouldn't do, he added. Then he bent over double in laughter, and out of relief I copied him. We roared together and slapped our thighs with mirth at the notion that I could do anything with a woman. But he stopped laughing before I did, and told me that I must put up some shelves in the geriatric ward quick smart. As I walked off, I saw him slip into the children's ward, hoping that since she'd been friendly to me, she'd have a little bit of friendliness left over for him.

I put up the shelves with care. I didn't know if Volta had the right to tell me what to do, but I didn't want to take any chances. Because if they took my uniform away and told me to go, I'd never see my beautiful one again.

Gunther caught Sandy just as he was leaving, and held out a letter.

For your wealthy friend, he said. I've filled out one of her forms, requesting funds. To do autopsies on the brains of autistic children.

While Sandy stared, he added (I wrote it down exactly):

I want to do measures of the level of various neurotransmitters and their metabolites, as well as receptor populations and activities in various brain areas, to get some sense of the state of regional neurotransmission.

That's not what we were hoping for from you, said Sandy. The Board would be deeply disappointed, after bringing you back to Sudlow at great expense.

Gunther said nothing. The letter flopped in his extended hand.

You should run it by the psychiatrists, said Sandy. Nice bunch of fellows. I assume you know them.

His voice was without irony. His mouth fell open to show the innocent gushing of his spit.

To put it mildly, said Gunther, this is another approach altogether.

He shook the letter so that Sandy had to take it.

Autism, said Sandy. Not very common. Only four kids in every 10,000, they say. Whereas immunology problems, I don't need to tell you, that's where the need is. And cancer, of course. But Doris doesn't seem interested in my little cancer molecule despite its promise and our many talks – so why would she buy autism? She wouldn't. She wants your immunology work. That's what she'll fund.

Gunther stared at his letter in Sandy's hand.

It's higher than four in 10,000, he said at last. Much higher. It often goes – he stared so piercingly at the letter that Sandy felt obliged to tuck it into his pocket – unrecognised.

Gunther turned on his heel and went out to his car.

Sandy watched him through the open door. Eva had gone and Shirley was putting on her coat.

I'll pass it on all right – to the garbage bin, he joked to Shirley. She didn't smile. He looked down again at Gunther's form, and I hoped, despite my jealousy, that he was having a change of heart. But he wasn't.

Have you seen these forms Dopey Doris gets us to fill in? was all he said. The woman knows nothing. I don't suppose you have to know anything when you're a tycoon's daughter.

He showed Shirley a form, which seemed to be largely blank spaces. Shirley was relieved to be talking about forms rather than about Gunther.

That's certainly not a proper form, said Shirley. It's not nearly bewildering enough.

She even gets in a handwriting expert, said Sandy. To assess whether we're sincere!

Does she ever promise money for your research? asked Shirley sympathetically.

That's my point, said Sandy. Never!

He winked at Shirley, and dropped Gunther's form into the bin. After he left, Shirley pulled it out again, considered it, changed her mind, and threw it back.

I almost intervened too, thinking I could retrieve it and post it to Doris. That would be the honourable thing to do. I knew where she lived, everyone in our city knew that grand mansion on the right side of the river, on the right bend, with the security guard and an angry Alsatian. Deirdre had told me she'd nursed at least half a dozen children who'd tried to pat that dog. But I didn't retrieve the form because my jealousy right there and then inspired a new and terrible theory about Gunther: what if his interest in doing autopsies of brains was because of his father? What if it was really a collection of brains that Shirley glimpsed in the newspaper cutting, and what if they'd belonged to Gunther's strange, silent father? What if Gunther was planning to complete his father's work?

CHAPTER 15

I begin to understand his fatal flaw

THE RAINS CAME AGAIN, huge, hungry, drenching rains with reports of floods in the backblocks. I didn't want to walk to the hospital in all that rain. It would be streaming down the hill, over-flowing the gutters, sheeting across the footpaths. I'd get my shoes wet. But I didn't want to miss seeing her.

The Hillman Hunter! I thought. A good man for climbing hills!

I still checked the Hillman Hunter once a month, so I knew it would start. I found the keys, grabbed Taruffi for luck, ran down-stairs, unlocked the garage, turned on the ignition, pulled out the choke knob, and the Hillman shuddered into life. I backed it out into the street, only banging into a no parking sign – which straightened up pretty well with a bit of pushing and shoving. It was early and there was no traffic, but nevertheless I drove fearfully and very slowly to the garage where my mother used to go. The same man was there at the garage, standing in his doorway gazing at the rain. He still had a young boy's face but now it seemed to have been cut and pasted into the middle of a receding hairline and a double chin. I didn't mind him chortling at the way I jolted to a stop in front of his bowsers, because it allowed me to chortle at the change in him.

Often wondered what became of you, he said. Still a man of few words? I nodded and held up my money, and he filled the tank amiably enough. He even patted the car fondly as I drove away. There was a funny noise and when I glanced in the rear-view mirror, I saw that he was frantically signalling me. I found I'd been dragging along his sandwich board saying Cheap Car Washes Today. I ran back to reinstate it, and we both gave each other the thumbs-up, which made me feel I knew the ways of the world. He watched me drive up the street and I was glad I didn't bump into anything else.

I bent low over the steering wheel so I wouldn't attract any attention, and at the hospital I slid into a space so easily I wondered why people found parking hard. Only when I was locking up did I see that the space was reserved for Professor Mueller. But the other spaces were at right angles, and I didn't know how to turn the car around. So he lost his spot, which seemed a good omen. It must've been my lucky day because I found out later that his car had broken down in the rain, and had been towed off for repairs.

The next day, after studying Taruffi over dinner and practising on my sofa as if I was making a pitstop at Le Mans to hand over to my co-driver at four am, I managed to do an almost perfect right-angled turn, not even grazing the bumper of the car beside me.

The rains kept up. On the third day I drove past Eva on her bicycle, splashing rainwater with every push of her feet. She was hunched over her pedals, a green plastic raincoat funnelling with wind and barely covering a blue party dress. I had been thinking about her so constantly – she was my companion when I was mending gutters or cleaning my teeth – that I somehow forgot she didn't know me at all. I pulled over, proudly parallel to the kerb, opened the back door on her side, and honked. She frowned, looked behind to see if another car was approaching, swerved and pedalled around me.

As I watched her huddled figure, I felt infinitely sad. I had to become more than a watcher.

Murmur to me, I said.

But she pedalled on until she was just a distant shape.

That afternoon the sun broke through so late that the shadows of the hospital buildings formed long, macabre shapes.

I'm off to hang up our wet washing, said Shirley to Eva. I left it in the bottom of the machine and if my uncle finds it there, he'll make me do it all over again. Why don't you go before there's another downpour?

Eva looked up, nodded and went on with her work. But after a while she packed up and clattered down to the parking lot and unlocked her bicycle. I heard Sandy coming down, calling up to Gunther:

They still haven't fixed it? No worries. I'll give you a lift.

He put his head around the door.

Everyone all right here for going home?

Finding the lab deserted, he checked the coldroom – so he'd been hoping that Shirley might like a lift as well. Gunther caught up with him. The rain had begun again, and the ground was already slicked.

Sandy was unlocking his station wagon when he noticed Eva with her bicycle.

Would you like a lift? His fatherly concern carried up to me.

No thanks, she said. She was already threading her way through the puddles.

Are you sure? he called again, then, to persuade her, he appealed to Gunther.

She's riding home, in this.

She's probably used to it, said Gunther, his voice impersonal, as if he wasn't thinking of her day and night, as I was.

Then he opened the passenger door and sat down.

I think you should accept my offer, Sandy called to her.

I'm used to it, Eva called back, perhaps a sardonic repetition of Gunther, and she waved.

I'd noticed that Sandy sometimes glanced at my Eva. He wanted Shirley, I was sure, but sometimes he seemed to wonder whether Eva might be more useful. Now his car caught up to her at the hospital gate. Her sodden dress dragged down, catching in the bike chain. She was bent over releasing it, the rain in her face, her hands already black with grease.

He insisted on giving her a lift and she capitulated. As he pulled open his car boot for her bicycle, I thought:

Gunther will see where she lives, and I won't!

Jealousy took over, more determined and capable than me. I became purposeful, dashing down the stairs, my fingers plunging in one jacket pocket then the other for my car key. As I ran to the Hillman Hunter I saw that Sandy was bent over his boot, settling her bike amongst a tea urn and a pile of folding chairs. A box of gilt-edged Bibles toppled out. He probably even told people what to do at church.

I switched on my ignition as his station wagon edged out of the gate. The Hillman Hunter sputtered and died a couple of times until I remembered to use the choke, but I had a few moments because Sandy had stopped to exchange a greeting with the sentry in his usual familiar way. By the time he'd got to the traffic lights, which were red, I was right behind them, feeling so elated by my quick actions that if there'd been no windscreen in front of me, I could almost have reached in and rung the bell on her bicycle.

We drove through the suburbs. Looking back, I admit I used to drive the way a cockroach would, bent white-knuckled and low over the steering wheel, watchful, expecting capture at any moment. But Sandy sat back, chatting to Gunther, one hand on the steering wheel, the other emphasising his opinions. Sometimes he waved to other drivers. To follow him, I had to drive like him, which meant barely slowing down for corners and running every orange traffic light. It was a frightening but wonderful freedom. It made me feel that I could be like him, organising everyone, waving my hands around like him, speaking effusively, being the world's friend. I was so elated to be visiting Eva at home – that's how I thought of it – I found myself humming. I scarcely noticed when we left the shops behind.

We crossed the bridge over the river that flowed almost like gravy, so thick and brown it was with rain, past the refineries with their long, grinding conveyor belts, then the miners' cottages, all identical and jammed against each other to stay upright, their back yards ending in glum rows of outside toilets next to back fences of rusty corrugated iron. Occasionally old people stood with folded arms desolately watching the rain from damp front porches, and a clump of children in a graffiti-scrawled bus shelter smoked cigarettes, the sort of children who chiack passers-by, so I was glad I was safe inside the Hillman Hunter. It all had a subdued look, saved only by the occasional angophora which had somehow escaped the axe – grand salmon-coloured trees that grew straight and tall like a tree should, then, when they thought your neck was too strained to keep looking, their boughs suddenly broke free of all expectations and leapt and twisted and turned and bulged and danced and laughed themselves into the sky. But nothing else in this landscape laughed. We passed the Aboriginal Reserve, the finest in the whole country, Deirdre had told me when she was nursing a dark-eyed child from there who filled the ward with her giggles. Maybe it was the finest, but it looked very desolate now with the paint peeling on its wooden fences and, inside, a children's playground with broken swings and a collapsed roundabout. Wisps of blue chimney smoke uncoiled hopefully into the rain from a huddle of cottages.

Soon we were driving beside a strip of brown marshy weeds, wild and high as a human, and beyond I glimpsed a new curve of the river. Up ahead on the road was a huge old powerhouse, disused now, with high rusty pulleys and smokestacks and shattered windows. Grey–green scrub choked a driveway. Sandy turned into a laneway I hadn't noticed before. I didn't dare follow him but drove to a road on the other side of the powerhouse, and swung to the right. I came to a dead end in a bank of high reeds. I got out, fearing I'd lost her, and clambered on my bonnet. Sandy, beyond the reeds, was pulling her bicycle out of the boot, and his box of Bibles toppled again into the mud. Between us, in a tiny lane at the back of the powerhouse, was a rubbish dump – old cars without their wheels, mattresses exploding puffs of white filling, and piles of rusty tins and cans and broken beer bottles. I wondered why he'd let her out there.

She took her bike, thanked Sandy and began to wheel it away. Sandy went to Gunther's side of the car and spoke to him. Then he called out to Eva.

She turned, her face almost lost to me in the rain.

May I, I heard, then the wind took his voice away.

She stood smiling, acquiescing while the rain poured on her.

The two men, their coats held above their heads, slammed their doors and followed her. I pulled my coat over my head too, and ran past the marsh reeds. There lay an old wooden house that had once been pretty, with wide verandas on all sides, and turned wooden posts topped with filigreed brackets, and generous stone entrance steps flanked with decorative urns leading to a wide front door with stained glass inserts. But it seemed as if a giant's fist had punched the house and made its boards swing loose and shattered its window glass, which was patched on the inside with cardboard and newspapers, and gored part of its roof. There was new silver roofing piled on the ground, and one section of the roof had recently been repaired, so someone had started to care for it.

Everything spoke of poverty, but the intense young girl in her wet raincoat swung open the front gate for them and ushered them up a path of broken, uneven stones to the porch. She dragged her bicycle up the steps and propped it against the front wall. The house was angled towards me, by some chance twist of the lane, and I made out, as she put her key into the lock, a sign in faded letters:

Parisian Couture.

It swung lopsidedly.

Something about the pathos of that sign made me ashamed. Ashamed of knowing about the tiny hairs that grew above her lip, about the particles of sleep that sometimes dusted her eyelashes, ashamed to see the misery that was her home, ashamed of how comfortable my parents had made my life. No wonder she'd left school early! And now she must be the only person her mother made dresses for.

All the secret, embarrassing things I've hidden about myself came flooding over me – why I haven't even admitted to this memoir how large I was then. Not large, not heavy. How fat I was.

Quite agile, but fat. I knew that if I had any honour at all, I must stop spying, in fact I must turn on my heel, return to my car, drive back into town, go straight to the hospital and the lab, close up all the spyholes and take away the camera.

I stood trembling because I was torn by honour and by a fever that must have been love. It was love that had entered my veins, invaded me and held sway. I had to be near her. To miss seeing her for a day, that seemed worse than death itself. Loss opened up in me a chasm I would never clamber out of.

So I crept closer, heading into the paddock of rubbish.

She opened the front door.

Mama, she called into a dark passage.

I crept closer still, with the smell of the sluggish river in my nostrils and the creaking of the reeds around me. A wind taunted me, banging doors inside the house. The sky grew darker, with ominous black clouds rolling across, blown by a gale way above us.

Leave, I told myself, but still I paused. It seemed to be another of those moments when you wait for a sign, any sign, to tell you how to live honourably. And because you're waiting, it comes, as if we're linked to the world in subtler and stranger ways than we know. From deep inside the house, the opening bars of Handel's 'Lascia ch'io pianga' from *Rinaldo* came floating out above the reeds – my song, my special solo in the church choir. Surely this was a sign, that she was playing for me, she was playing Handel's grand clumps of chords, the way they gather for strength, tremble there, then settle into peace. I could've sung the song to her, I could've showed her how the mute's voice could unexpectedly leap beyond the piano and soar across cadences like a bird soaring over this stagnant river, and then, satisfied, settle back into the nest of her piano. One day she would play for me, and I would sing to her.

Permit me to weep over
My hard fate
And sigh for freedom.
How I sigh for freedom.

Then her hands moved into the minor part of the song, and suddenly the piano was wispy with hesitation, right on the leap that insists that the intolerable fetters can't be tolerated, that they must be broken – there was a wrong note. A pause. Silence. Only the crackling of brown weeds weighted with rain. Then she began again, switching back to the chorus, searching inside the music for its former grandeur, but she couldn't find it and the spell was broken.

I knew then that, however dishonourable it was, I must be near her, for my life's sake. One day, I'll sing that music for her, the way she should hear it.

The paddock was slimy and treacherous with puddles, so I had to watch my footing. It was unlikely that anyone inside the house would be peering out at the dark. They'd be watching her play, they'd be talking small talk. Sandy would be saying something ingratiating like, What an interesting spot, you must almost have a view, so close to the river, indeed a little outpost of Paris.

I almost tripped over a broken kitchen stool someone had thrown away, its white paint peeling in long strips. I picked it up so I'd look like an ordinary scavenger if anyone should look out at the rain. By this time she'd resumed playing, this time a preoccupied ripple of chords moving into a dirge I didn't know. I was just drawing near the side window of the house when the back door swung open and Sandy came out, one hand hoisting his coat over his head, his other hand holding a saucer with a candle.

I'll be fine like this, he was assuring someone in the house as the candle flickered. He went down a path heading to an outside toilet.

So that was the excuse he'd found to look inside her home – no doubt to use the knowledge if it became useful to him.

The path wound in my direction, and I had to duck low. Then Eva came out – so she wasn't the pianist! Could it be her mother? She teetered on the top step, still under cover, uncertain if she wanted to be with the turmoil of the music or out in the rain. On impulse she came down the steps and veered off into the oozing, dripping garden which had once been ornate with stone edgings and a bird-bath. She wandered, rain streaming down her body, to a wooden swing hanging from a bough of a grand jacaranda. Suddenly she tugged at its seat. One of the old ropes broke and the seat dragged lopsidedly on the ground. Then she couldn't stop herself, she began angrily ripping at plants in a little kitchen garden plot, tugging at them so they lifted out of the wet ground by their roots. She threw a handful into a sodden heap, turned to a new patch and tugged them out as well.

Looking back, I'm sure that the music and the presence of Gunther in her home had stirred some secret turmoil in her.

She only stopped when Sandy emerged from the toilet, his candle still flickering, and asked her what she was up to. She started as if she'd forgotten him. He offered her a place under his hoisted coat, and they went back into the house side by side. There was a crescendo on the piano and I could resist no longer. I crept up to the side fence.

Sandy stood loose-armed, still at the back door, still with the candle flickering. Gunther was sitting on a piano stool, which creaked under his weight, his face dark. So he was the pianist, and the music had stirred him as well, because Sandy and Eva had barely come inside before he was saying:

The problem with this country is that you've all been cowed by Freud. He's my countryman but we got over him! The Austrians got over him. The Austrians accept that the brain can be organically misformed. But in this country, and in America, and in England, it's Freud and his half-baked followers and their poetry about the unconscious and full breasts. Without graphs, without measurements, without controls. Never, ever does someone say: Could there be a structural, inherited alteration in this brain?

I could hardly credit that anyone would play Handel and think, not of love, but of the brain. But then my sympathies switched sides and I was wishing that Gunther wouldn't confide in Sandy like this. Sandy would find a way to use it – but I'm racing ahead of myself.

Order. Order must teach me.

At least Freud offers hope, Sandy said evenly. If we thought a brain was organically deformed, if it's inheritance that deforms it, then there's no hope.

Freud offers hope to the unhappy, said Gunther. But unhappy people are not what I'm interested in.

Anyway, said Sandy, look what biologists have offered people with mental problems – lobotomies! Pioneered by Moniz, who, I'm sorry to mention it, won a Nobel Prize. Though, of course, most prize-winners are very worthy. And the also-rans, let's say, the contenders, also worthy.

Sandy was smiling genially.

As we know, he added, bowing his head to Gunther.

I'm advocating science, not butchery, said Gunther quietly.

Not to mention, said Sandy – and now I saw that his friendliness had slipped off like water, and underneath showed reefs of brutality –

not to mention eugenics. Biology offered eugenics!

Sandy spat the word.

Eugenics? How did that come into the argument? Eugenics is bad science. A misunderstanding of Mendel's scheme of inheritance, said Gunther.

Eugenics, repeated Sandy, but Gunther didn't seem to be getting the point, so he added:

As practised by your countrymen!

By the Nazis. *On* my countrymen, Gunther said sadly.

Practised so well, lashed Sandy, that no scientist in this country would dare to consider that biology makes us who we are, and won't dare to for many lifetimes. And no funding body will. And certainly my friend Doris won't with her bequests. Imagine us asking Doris for money to fund Nazi-type eugenics! So don't you, with your Germanic name, consider working in that direction in my lab. Or they'll think we're harbouring Nazi ideas. And we'll never get Doris. Then where will our lab be?

Gunther slammed down the piano lid.

Is that what you're all thinking? he said. That because I escaped the Nazis, I must be like them? That because I once stood on the same patch of earth as them, I am – how to say it? Tarred with the same brush?

No, of course not, said Sandy, suddenly friendly again, coming over and patting Gunther on the shoulder, so Gunther could see the innocent spit sloshing in his mouth.

That would be foolish. It's just what other people might think. Doris, for example. She's a rich woman grieving for her son. How would we explain these subtleties to her?

But I was the Nazis' victim! said Gunther. I was a kid when I left – a victim! How can I be a Nazi victim and a Nazi at the same time?

A victim? How were you a victim? Sandy's voice rang in surprise. You're not Jewish, are you?

I imagined he'd shaken his head because Sandy persisted:

Explain how you were a victim. Then maybe we'd all understand.

I saw then that it was unbearable to Sandy not to have solved the mystery surrounding Gunther, the strange letter from Helene Haussman that had come to the lab, the newspaper cutting she'd sent about a Nazi killer, and the way they had pivoted Gunther into his obsession.

It was becoming unbearable to me, as well.

There was a pause, during which Sandy pretended he was preoccupied with blowing out his candle, as if there was nothing more important than saving some of the wick. And Gunther opened the piano again and played chords, dissonant, despairing chords. He wasn't going to tell Sandy anything more – I suspect not because he feared Sandy's machinations, he was too innocent for that, but because his heart was too full to speak. Compelled by his anguish, I found myself crouching on the ground, my bones creaking, my feet crunching twigs.

I can't see how you could've been a Nazi victim, persisted Sandy who, like Gunther, simply couldn't help himself. He was as driven as any of us.

Gunther spoke at last.

The piano's out of tune, he said.

No one plays it now, came Eva's voice suddenly, rescuing him.

I heard him ask who used to play it, and her reply was soft, and I didn't catch it. But then she said:

My mother used to tell me how she'd been a top mannequin in the great fashion houses of Paris, and it was expected in those days that a mannequin should be accomplished.

And now? I heard Sandy ask.

She's asleep, said Eva.

I mean, does she still model? he asked, aware, like I was, that here in this battered house lurked another secret it might be useful to discover.

My mother? Model? repeated the girl in surprise, and laughed sadly.

You wear her clothes? guessed Sandy, and Eva was quiet, so she must have been nodding.

And then she murmured to me, as if she'd been reading my mind:

'So many people ache with secrets we'd love to tell. Gunther, my mother, all her customers in my childhood. Everyone pretending that nothing is wrong, that they can go about their ordinary lives, when something extraordinary is destroying them.'

Then she broke off, because Gunther was speaking to her.

What have you got in your hands? he was asking. He had to ask it again because she was absorbed in her murmuring to me.

Herbs, she answered at last. I used to plant them. To make concoctions. I was just a child – I was always in my way a scientist . . . she wound down.

May I smell them? he asked.

They're nothing special, she began.

But she went over to him, as if he had her on a rope, and opened her hands. In their heat, the torn plants from her childhood lay forlornly. Gunther bent his head and sniffed, then smiled slowly at her. She was enclosed by him again, we could all see that, utterly enclosed as if she were alone with him. Only now and again did she escape, and then to me. I was her escape, even then.

The herbs smell of you, he said.

He reached out and pushed her wet hair off her face.

You should take off that wet dress before you catch cold, he said.

For a minute I thought he was going to unbutton it, like a

mother would, but all he did was cup her hands, still holding the limp green herbs, in his own. When he takes his hands away, I thought, her skin will be warm with him, as mine was when Deirdre touched me. But the little nurse meant nothing to me, compared with Eva. Gunther didn't take his hands away, he sat on the spindly piano chair cupping her hands, breathing on her breasts, not looking at anything but her eyes.

Sandy's feet creaked on the bare floorboards. It took a long time for her to turn around and remember him.

She struggled out of the moment and found something else to say.

Would you like something? Something hot to warm you? Tea?

We'll have to go, Sandy said. Thank you, but we don't need tea.

Eva moved, her whole body swayed with her effort to speak.

Your fingers, she said to Gunther, speaking slowly, like someone mesmerised,

they suit . . . what was it you were playing at first?

Handel, he said.

Then he added:

Why are you working with us in that snake-pit?

It was as if he was asking a child.

Because of science. Science should give meaning to everything, she said.

He smiled.

I was like you, he said. Once. A long time ago, it seems, though it's only a few months.

And now? she asked, lifting her chin and daring to gaze at him as she had before.

But all he said was:

You're not wearing your beads.

We'd better let her get warm and dry, Sandy said in his fatherly way. Off we go, then.

Gunther stood, the stool creaking, released from his weight.

Sandy disappeared down the hall.

Eva glanced after him, and said so softly to Gunther that I had to strain to hear:

Do you know something that – she inclined her head in Sandy's direction – they don't?

I mean, about autism?

It seemed preposterous, her question, but even more surprising was his answer:

Yes.

They stared at each other, now equals.

There's evidence? she said.

Observations. No measurements. But observations that suggest inherited structural differences. I was sent a paper, he said. From overseas. It took me by surprise – in fact, it took my breath away.

Why don't you show them this paper? she asked. Sandy, the hospital Board – everyone.

Coming? shouted Sandy from outside.

I mustn't, he said.

Why not? she asked.

Are you coming? shouted Sandy.

It would be misinterpreted. They'd have too much on me, he told her.

He turned on his heel and left.

Eva stared after him. I ducked around to the front of the house, to see the farewell. It was lucky I did. The rain was sheeting off the gutterless part of the roof. Sandy and Gunther were on the wide veranda bracing themselves to run through the front garden.

I'm going now! cried Gunther, and loped into the downpour.

Eva came out and stood watching. Sandy was about to follow him, but she blurted:

Why won't you back him?

She was standing on one leg, like a bird.

Sandy, always eager to be friendly, couldn't help himself looking around at her.

You know he wants to study autism. Why won't you back him? she repeated.

She seemed cramped with urgency, as if she was about to burst like the clouds.

Sandy laughed at this blurting child who seemed to have forgotten that farewells had been made.

Because autism is part of human behaviour and that's what psychologists study, not biologists, he said.

She stared at him, fierce, unflinching, much stronger than him.

But the brain is a chemical and mechanical system, so it's also what a biologist could study, she said.

Not if the study of the brain is for the study of human behaviour, Sandy retorted.

He glanced at the downpour, back at her, took in her trembling intellect for the first time, lowered his voice and said:

He's too old for you.

Then he ran.

A minute later, his car roared in angry triumph against the rain and thunder, and drove away. Eva shivered on her doorstep, unwilling to give them up, watching until their tail-lights faded.

She went back inside and sank on a chair at the table, looking at her hands, turning them over and over as if she'd been the one to play Handel. Now she had a cause to love in him, and my heart sank.

The floorboards creaked again and an old woman in a black nightgown shuffled out. Eva looked up, her face suddenly bright. The mother barely greeted her – I could tell it was her mother, because though her face was ruined, she still had Eva's strange beauty. The nightgown was almost an evening dress, with an elegant flared skirt and a deeply cut neckline that revealed her withered chest. I could easily believe that she'd once been on a catwalk.

Who was here? she asked, in a heavy French accent. All the shouting on the porch! Like cats!

People I work with. Scientists. They drove me home, answered Eva.

Scientists! hooted the mother.

I gathered she didn't have much time for scientists.

Was that the sort of party scientists have? she said.

One played the piano, said Eva, her voice thick. Anyway, it's not late.

There was a little pause, and then she added:

You never used to mind visitors. Before him.

He likes his peace, said the old woman.

They both sighed.

After a while, the old woman noticed a plant lying on the floor, one of the herbs that Eva had brought in, curled up and drying now. She shuffled over to it and picked it up.

Something ripped it out, she said. By the roots. Perhaps a wild animal.

Eva did not respond.

But as I drove home, she began murmuring again:

'When I was a child, my mother loved her customers, she'd welcome them with cups of tea that I had to run and make. She was happy then, happy to hear endlessly their talk of love. That's why they came to her, they came for dresses that were remedies for lost love. I'd stand in the corner, holding pins, because my mother wanted me to learn the trade, to take over. That was her plan for my life.

'I remember that the grocer's wife would tell my mother about her husband's mistress, and my mother would hold her and they'd weep together over the way he'd buy roses for the mistress, never for her.

'My mother always had a remedy for lost love in those days.

'You wear this and he'll shower you with rose petals, my mother would say, raising a hemline so we suddenly saw that the legs of the grocer's wife were beautifully shaped, so beautiful you'd forget how lumpy the rest of her was.

'Or the mayor's wife would arrive, haughty but with a twitch in her left eye, and sooner or later during one of the fittings, she'd clutch my mother's hands, and say urgently:

'He watches shop girls at lunchtime. What will I do if he strays? The shame – it will be so public – what will I do?

'Without another word my mother would cut the neckline of the new dress to reveal the woman's pure white bosom, as white as whipped cream.

'He won't watch anyone now, my mother would say.

'I remember a washerwoman, she'd have been about thirty years old, a thin, gangling woman with red and wrinkled hands. She told my mother that she was in love with a married man. My mother nodded, that's all. She never judged, she just made the woman a sheath dress that showed how marvellously slender she was, with pointed lacy cuffs that hid her shrivelled hands.

'When the man's wife came in, confiding that her husband had a mistress, and a wizened frump at that, my mother said nothing, but made her a nightgown as embroidered and magnificent as any wedding dress.

'My mother never offered advice, she never criticised. She just designed, cut and sewed to solve the problems of love. Her customers always obeyed her as they swayed and pouted in front of the mirror, stretching the fabric across their breasts and turning to see its effect on their buttocks. My mother had a knack with cutting. She could turn bulk into voluptuousness, bonyness into a tapering figure; she could make the wizened have a strange, wise beauty.

'Or that's how I saw it then.

'Sometimes women would burst through our front door – in those days it was always on the latch – radiant, hugging my mother and holding her hands, and crying in gratitude.

'I don't know how to thank you, they'd always say. He's back. We're in love again.

'My mother, never one for hugging and kissing, would wipe away the women's tears from her own shoulders, and say:

'Who can explain the promises that dresses make?

'She said she'd learned the secrets of the queens of Europe from her time as a model in Paris, and, until I was a teenager, I believed her with all my heart. I wanted to be a model in her place, and then a dressmaker. I wanted her life. But when I found out it was all a lie, I wanted to study truth instead. I couldn't tell him that, when he asked. He'll probably never ask again. He's in so much pain, he doesn't want mine. He couldn't bear it.

'My mother never solved her own problems of love.'

The murmurs paused. Then after a while, she told me:

'Of course I couldn't be like her. Why did I ever think I could be? When everything went wrong, I yearned for something pure, something that had nothing to do with the lies of love.'

CHAPTER 16
I make my love a home

SHE MIGHT BE VERY BAD at choosing men, Shirley was saying to Eva one day when I turned on the cameras. They were both mixing chemicals at the sink, side by side.

Lotti? I wondered. Were they discussing Lotti? Narelle? Eva was saying nothing, though Shirley kept glancing at her, watching her face as they worked.

A terrible judge, added Shirley. Then, to prompt her, she added: Don't you think?

Choose? Eva echoed in confusion. Do people choose people? I thought love just happened. It just fell on us.

Shirley tucked an errant strand of hair into her protective cap.

It's good I'm here to guide you, she said.

Dad seemed kind, Eva said, her eyes on her work. If she chose Dad, she chose well.

So they were talking about Eva's mother!

Why did he leave then? Shirley asked.

Eva paused. She bent over the solutions, pretending she was absorbed in checking the quantities, that the levels of chemicals were all that mattered. She didn't want to answer, but Shirley was persistent.

Don't you remember? she asked.

There were lots of arguments, Eva said at last. About . . .

About? prompted Shirley.

I was much younger. I don't know. Well, he said their marriage was built on a lie, said Eva. If you really want to know. A lie.

Shirley, I could see, was longing to ask more, but she gave up and tried another tack.

Where did your mother meet this new man? she asked.

Oh, he's nothing. At the shops, said Eva. At least, he's a handyman.

Aha! Maybe he's the roof repairer, I thought.

At the shops? quizzed Shirley. What, at a fashion parade or something?

No, just at the butcher's, said Eva mournfully. He helped her carry home the meat and came in for a cuppa and never left.

You might be getting in their way, said Shirley. Imagine what it's like for them – and she carried off to the coldroom a full, sloshing bottle.

That's when I decided that I should waste no more time. What Eva needed was a home of her own. Once I'd settled that in my mind, the other decisions were easy: that I was the one to make it for her, and that it should be in the little vacant apartment next to mine.

Looking back, I blush at my arrogance. But I must remind myself: I had only recently come into the ways of the world. Events were happening in a tangle. Rushing between leaky tap washers and my cameras, I scarcely had time to contemplate the modest life, let alone the life of honour. Both require contemplation. Time to sift thoughts, to question possibilities, to consider if there is any true decency or honour at all. I never knew this before, having had all the time there is.

I refurbished the apartment the way I imagined a young girl would like, with roses on the cornices, and taps wrought into the shape of swans and a claw-footed bath with heated towel rails and a stained-glass window, and a kitchen gleaming with all the latest conveniences even though she was a lab technician who had no time to cook, and a little balcony for her to sit out on and watch the goings-on in the street outside the brothel and the church. I spent hours with colour charts, imagining her face and hair against a gold background, then a lilac, then a watermelon pink. I painted the ceiling blue, the same blue as her eyes, and, in the end, I painted her walls cream. I put in adjustable lighting and I built in a wardrobe, and I made a bed copied from a thirteenth-century Italian drawing in one of my mother's books on the Renaissance, a plain high box surrounded by wooden blanket boxes which could double up as seats. Perhaps the bed was designed for a woman with many children who'd play while she read, but I imagined myself lounging on the boxes, sipping tea and gazing at Eva. We'd talk science, or at least she'd talk science and I'd listen, she in her bed, and me lounging on the boxes. I went into the apartment every day to watch the sun swing across her room with the turning of the planets, so that when she'd moved in, I'd be able to imagine her watching it too. I ran my fingers over everything as if I was caressing her.

I haven't yet admitted that I took out all the insulation between her wall and mine. It meant I'd have to creep around my apartment when she moved in, but that wouldn't be a problem. And I put in a peephole, high up, so I would always be able to see her.

When she moved in.

Of course, I was naive to think she'd move in. But I had all the naivety of hope.

And of course I was dishonourable to spy. But the peephole gave me a view only of part of her room, the balcony and the window with its chair. I couldn't see her bed.

I must remember that when I upbraid myself. I never saw her bed.

CHAPTER 17

A painful lesson

I DIDN'T GET A CHANCE to go to my shed in the courtyard for
days. Marconi and I were replacing all the rotting windowsills. I
tried to sneak away several times, but Marconi would follow me,
asking me where I was going and could he come.

You're a dark horse, he said. You might be up to something.

I shook my head sadly. I was up to nothing.

I've got to keep an eye on you, he said, and the purple scar on
his neck glittered.

While I hammered and sawed, my mind bulged fatly on what I'd
done for her. But I hadn't any idea how to entice her to her new
home. There is no mercy for a spy, no comfort. Especially if the spy
has no choice but to spy, because what he sees has become essential.

I came back to find Sandy telling Shirley and Eva about the previous night's formal dinner, a glittering evening when Doris
awarded money to science projects all over the country that tugged
at the strings of her heart.

They're her words, said Sandy. We're not to do projects that
deepen the knowledge of science. We're to do projects that tug at
Doris's heart.

Did we tug at her heart? asked Shirley, pleased to put a delicate emphasis on 'we'.

Absolutely, said Sandy, beaming. We got the biggest cheque. Gunther's reputation with immunology tugged at her heart more than anything else. We're guaranteed funds for five years, just as I'd hoped. So I'll be able to look further into my little cancer molecule.

She should be pleased about that, said Shirley. Such useful work.

She doesn't know, said Sandy. She'll be pleased when it succeeds. A budget can be pushed around a little. Oh, the string-pulling I've had to do. I deserve a bit of a reward.

Of course, she would've been impressed seeing Gunther on TV talking about the Prize, said Shirley. I was.

Sandy's face twitched.

That Prize was never more than a rumour, he said.

Does Doris know that? asked Eva.

Sandy didn't reply.

Did you take your wife? Shirley asked him, tactfully conscious that she should change the subject.

Of course, he said. But she was bored. All the shop talk.

He smiled at Shirley.

Next year I might invite someone who understands me more.

He'd been leaning on her workbench. Now he pushed himself off, straight-backed, fancying himself as a boat pushing off down our murky little river and out on to the wide ocean.

The point is, he said, we'll be able to do research on whatever we like – particularly what I like – and put our city on the map. That's the bottom line. Sudlow. That's what I told the hospital Board. I said, You know those globes that people have on their desks? Soon people will be able to spin them around and say, There's Sudlow, the city where they make the big breakthroughs in science.

Soon after, several new researchers were employed to assist Gunther with his immunology work – at least at first – and they were all to work in the barn-like, empty lab that had belonged solely to Shirley and Eva. There were five men – boyish, friendly Tony, handsome Mark who whistled tunelessly as he worked (irritating the others) and hung on Sandy's every word, Jim with a receding chin and an alarming Mohawk hairdo gelled into spikes (I heard Sandy advising him on his first day that no Nobel Laureate had ever sported a Mohawk, and next day and from then on poor Jim looked flat-headed, dowdy and a little disappointed), bespectacled, pony-tailed Chris who kept a copy of Proust in his jacket pocket and planned to become a poet when he'd made his fortune in science, and Robert, who always wore the same thin knitted tie and spent his lunchtimes puffing Gauloise cigarettes in the car park while he frowned over the trotting guide. Shirley was delighted, and whisked off several times a day to renew her crimson lipstick. For her, it was almost like a party. When she came back from lunch to find half a dozen small lab fridges had been delivered, I heard her crying out: What are they for? Drinks?

But for Eva, the lab prickled with their inquisitive male eyes. Sometimes it was hard for me to hear her amongst the male voices, and sometimes chattering scientists got in the way of my camera. I had to sneak into the lab one night when no one was there and make a new peephole and find another camera in Stores. I feared that, sooner or later, one of the men would look up from his work and say:

What's that lens doing there?

Though the men were mainly working with Gunther, it was Sandy who seemed to organise most of the work. He had become, as he put it, the head of the lab by default – this last jibe was aimed at Gunther, who never noticed it. Nevertheless, he often found time to stride around the lab. What's new? he'd say, over someone's shoulder. Good, good, he'd say, even before their explanation was finished, and he'd push his hands into his pockets proudly.

Despite her shyness, Eva was always watching the scientists and asking questions. Why are you doing it like that? she'd ask, her eyes on the dish or the beaker. There was no hint of flirting. She was driven by curiosity. One particular man, the charming Tony, began to seek her out. Every time I got to my shed, he seemed to be talking over his work with her.

Come and see this! he'd be saying to her.

It seemed very fiddly, unimportant work, to cause such excitement.

There's a note somewhere of what Tony said one day – aha! Here it is.

I'm trying to make the cell walls leaky, he told Eva, so the plasmid can go through. Then I'll screen the colonies to see which ones have the insert.

So they must've been trying to put bits of one cell into another cell, though why they'd want to do that, I didn't know. But she did, and she'd nod, eyes wide.

He had copper hair and a splatter of boyish freckles across his nose, and a warm grin. His bench was near her sink and as she washed up she'd lean over and peer at his work.

I began to hate his boyish grin.

Eva knew far more than anyone would expect. One day she said to Shirley:

I'll collect Mark's glassware. His incubation should be through by now.

How do you know? asked Shirley.

Mark's bench was at the far end of the lab.

Eva ignored her and hurried off. She came back triumphantly a few minutes later with the glassware to wash.

Perfect timing, she said to Shirley.

Are you sweet on Mark? Shirley burst out. To know when his incubation would be finished?

My heart lurched. Despite his dreadful whistling, Mark had long, wavy fair hair which fell beguilingly over one eye, and a strong, tanned face. Could Shirley be right?

Eva laughed.

I just know what people are doing. Don't you?

Shirley shook her head.

Why not? asked Eva.

It's not my job, said Shirley loftily.

It's like taking part in a revolution! Eva said at another time to Shirley, whose face that morning had been stretching and collapsing with smothered yawns. Now Shirley allowed herself to yawn openly and say that if all revolutions were as boring as this, they'd never catch on.

The man that Eva had no respect for was Hugh, the loud man from the cafe conversation. She'd laugh at anything about him – his jutting neck, his choking tie – and one day I heard her tell Tony that farmers would send in the droppings from their sick cattle and Hugh would work out what was wrong, but using ancient methods from last century, so often – here she clutched Tony's arm and doubled over with giggles, and plopped on her stool weak with laughter – he'd only figure out what was wrong after the cattle had died.

Was she cruel? Would she be cruel to me?

Hugh thinks he sees the big picture and we don't, I heard her whisper to Shirley one day. But the big picture he sees, nobody's looking at any more.

Shirley made noises in her throat to show her sympathy.

Despite the revolution! she said.

Eva nodded vigorously and went off to collect glassware, and didn't notice that Shirley was grinning at her.

Then one morning when I was at my shed early, Gunther was hailed by Tony, who held a Petri dish containing the usual puddle of slime.

I'm getting different results from the ones they got in America, Tony said. Could it be significant? Could we be onto something their lab doesn't know?

He explained his results, with Eva straining to listen in, her hands moving absent-mindedly in the sink full of water.

Gunther told him to repeat the experiment in case there'd been contamination. But he was obviously pleased.

In the next few years, we'll be opening the book of life, he said in his shy, smiling way.

Then I felt almost sorry for my rival, to utter such foolishness in front of his junior scientist and his technician. He'd feel very silly afterwards. He wouldn't be able to hold his head up in the lab for a while, till they'd all forgotten it. Opening the book of life indeed! Why, even a little child would mock him. A bricklayer might as well call a lump of concrete 'life'. I'd only just arrived in the world and already I knew far, far more about it than him. I'd always known that life was a tiny and pitiable thing, but even that is more complicated and interesting than a bit of slime in a glass dish. And life might stop being tiny and pitiable, it might become falling in love, and longing for love, and losing love, and leaving your apartment to walk out into the world.

I laughed aloud at him, then I had to clap my hand over my mouth in case someone heard me, someone expecting me to be hard at work fixing toilet cisterns instead of sitting in my shed.

I waited for the faces of Tony and Eva to break up into mirth, or at least to see that their face muscles were suppressing it. But Tony nodded, as if something very true had been said. I'd been misled by his boyish face and the way he spoke without conde-scension to Eva, disregarding the difference in rank between them. Now I saw that he too was an arrogant fool.

But my biggest surprise was to come.

The book of life! Eva exclaimed. That's it, exactly. What a per-fect way to describe it.

She had entirely forgotten the washcloth in her hand, which was dripping on the floor.

I'll be here. I'll be here at the right time in history. I'll be around when the book of life is first read.

Shirley couldn't resist calling out:

No you won't – not if you don't finish the washing up.

Tony smiled and agreed with Eva that, yes, she had indeed timed it well.

I left my shed, banged the door shut and stalked out into the hospital grounds. I found a bucket and picked up stray autumn leaves and crushed them to smithereens. I could never belong to her world, nor did I want to if she thought life was a puddle of slime. I lit the incinerator and watched the flames roar, and hurled more and more leaves in, so burnt leaves spiralled darkly into the air. By the time I got home, I'd talked myself into such a fury that I swore I'd abandon my mission. The world was full of beautiful girls who weren't already in love, and who didn't believe that life was just a puddle of slime. I didn't need this particular, gawky, obsessed girl. I didn't need love at all, or the hospital. I could stay in my apartment, just like my mother had said I should, I could go back to my books and my music and my isolation. I put on my dinner and banged saucepans on the stove and smashed a cup against the kitchen tap and spilled an entire can of tomato soup all over the floor.

As I crankily stooped over the dustpan to sweep it up, a perverse daydream flickered through my ungovernable mind.

One day she'd be lying in my arms after we'd made love. But she'd turn her face away and say sadly:

Our paths are so different. You weren't there when we opened the book of life.

And I'd be able to say:

I was!

You! she'd say. You're not a scientist. You wouldn't understand.

And I'd say:

I learned it with you. I was there, every moment, with you.

After all, I said to myself in the morning, I'm a good watcher. I can watch her watching them. I can write down everything they say, and learn it. It will be the schooling I missed out on. When I read what I wrote down, it'll be my own book of life.

From then on I tried to pay attention to the talk for her sake, and though there were days when I entirely sympathised with Shirley's yawns, sometimes it started to interest me.

The word DNA kept coming up. Here's where I should start, I thought. My library's old encyclopaedia – it took an evening to find the volume – just gave it a longer name, as if it was determined to thwart my love – deoxyribonucleic acid. So I decided to wait till their obsession with DNA was over. Soon, science would move on to something more comprehensible – like mice, perhaps. I could tell her a thing or two about mice, since I now had a whole family of them behind the fridge. They scampered around the apartment when they thought I was asleep.

At last Shirley rescued me by swallowing her pride and saying in a low voice to Eva while they were pouring out solution:

Why do they keep talking about DNA?

Eva looked startled.

The whole world is, she said.

I must've been out of the room when they explained it to you, Shirley said defensively.

So Eva told her that DNA is an acid that contains all the information that makes us who were are, and we inherit it in different patterns, called G, A, T and C.

Which is why you've got such beautiful blond hair and I haven't, she ended up, touching the blond tendrils always swooshing down from Shirley's cap.

One of your parents probably had blond hair and the other didn't. So why did you get it? That's the question.

There's nothing new in that, said Shirley crankily. People have always known their children might inherit the colour of their hair.

But how? said Eva. We've only connected one hundred and fifty genes to specific chromosomes, but soon we'll know them all. And we'll know how the huge set of genes – and it does seem as if it's going to be huge – you inherited from your mother mixes with the huge set of genes from your father. Which ones get switched on? Which ones get switched off? And how? What are the simultaneous steps, the alternative steps, the sequential steps? That's why everyone's trying to learn the new techniques of experimental embryology and cell biology.

Oh, they're trying to see inside people! said Shirley.

After a while she sidled back and said in the same low voice:

Why hasn't anyone figured all this out before?

Eva explained that for a long time people thought the answer was to do with the structure of DNA, but no one figured it out until 1953.

Watson and Crick discovered it, she said. However, an essential clue for them was secretly seeing an x-ray photo (taken with a special camera and an exposure of over a hundred hours) by their colleague, Rosalind Franklin. Every other photo before hers had been blurred because no one had realised that there's a dry and wet form of DNA and they'd been getting images of both, combined. Her photo made the structure clear. She was writing up her discovery in an unhurried way, but Watson and Crick published first, received the Nobel and didn't credit her.

It's a cut-throat world, this science, said Shirley thoughtfully, and I wondered if she was having suspicions about Sandy, as I was.

The problem is, every time there's an answer, it only creates more questions, Eva said, ignoring her.

(Why didn't she pause and think about what Shirley was saying? Because, in her adorable way, she was right then too immersed in her own thoughts – even at that moment her beautiful upper lip was lifting.)

Like, she continued, could we control the switching on and off of genes so that we could change what you inherit? Not us –

she added because Shirley was pouring water into Eva's sink to remind her of her job.

Okay, okay. I'm just employed to wash up. But Watson and Crick realised that DNA carries information on the rungs of a spiralling ladder, and now people are beginning to discover what that means. We can watch them discover it, we're at a turning point in history. By the time you're middle-aged, you'll know why you are blond.

I know now, giggled Shirley. It's from a bottle.

I began to see that, despite her lowly job, Eva felt utterly a scientist, dedicated and relentlessly searching. I knew then that she would one day come into her own, and she knew it. Though how she did it would be in her particular way.

Even then I didn't realise that there were many disagreements among the scientists until one day Hugh, the parasitologist, came into the lab from his Animal House.

Sandy, I think we're overlooking something, he said loudly.

Sandy, who'd been enjoying the hubbub, turned around impatiently. Gunther continued talking to Tony about his work.

Hugh's about to give us the big picture, the one that no one wants to look at any more, I heard Shirley say and giggle. She was standing near Sandy, who shot an appreciative look at her. All talk gradually came to a standstill.

I have a proposal, Hugh said. I suggest that we defer all work until we have a proper, complete set of information about one living thing. Just one living animal. Look at it, Sandy – he turned around to Sandy, who was clearly irritated –

it'd clear up all this confusion. Everyone here is confused. My way, we might end up knowing what we're doing. If it takes five years let's give it five years. If it takes ten, so be it. If we have to work with other nations, we should.

He threw his head back.

Imagine what he could do to Sudlow's standing in the international community! said Sandy to Shirley.

Shirley whispered to Eva:

Do we have any?

Gunther's here, she said.

But Hugh heard none of this.

In fact, that's the way to go, he said. An international collaboration on one tiny animal. I offer myself as coordinator!

What tiny animal, Hugh? the irrepressible Shirley called out. What about my uncle's budgerigar?

Sandy stopped him and explained that his parasites, being simple organisms, were not what the world was currently investigating.

It's the gene where we'll get our breakthroughs, he finished.

Hugh opened his mouth and shut it again with a loud smacking noise. His poking neck slid into his collar.

Isn't that so, Gunther? said Sandy.

There was a silence, and then Gunther, battling his shyness, explained that they were now interested in complex, not simple animals – animals whose immune systems operate in startling ways we don't yet understand.

Hugh stalked off to the hospital cafe, where he'd discovered, he told everybody later, an excellent local red, Sudlow's finest, kept behind the counter and only served to special people.

———

I began to make notes on all their talk, so one day it could be mine with her.

Here's a note: apparently Sandy was telling Shirley that the cells of higher organisms can change their biochemical make-up during their development, and Shirley cried out laughingly:

Really? Even their make-up?

Shirley was always joking, wanting to make the lab less stern.

Whereas Eva was always showing off how much she knew.

Bacteria cells have no nuclei, she told Shirley one day, when Sandy was nearby. (I'm sure she'd noticed Sandy's presence.) They make far fewer substances, they have far less genetic material. Whereas in an elephant, the ovum becomes an adult with cells that somehow become tissues and organs and a trunk and a tail. But how? And there are interruptions within the genes. No one knows why, though maybe it's to make room for evolution.

Looking back, I suspect that Eva was hoping she'd get promoted to doing science work without having to leave Sudlow and go to a university a long way from her mother, and from Gunther.

Sandy, in his turn, was often a little nonplussed by her. It made me proud, the way he'd gaze at her unblinkingly, and walk away. I suspect that sometimes he went upstairs to look up what she'd said. Later, he'd use it as a way to compliment Shirley.

It's very good the way you're keeping yourself and your junior up to date, he'd say.

Thank you, Shirley would say. Since I have so many responsibilities, I get her to report all the latest research to me.

Very good, very good, he'd repeat.

I heard Eva say, in answer to a question from Shirley about the difference between bacteria and elephants:

It's a long road from bacteria to elephants.

I don't know if she invented this saying, but she said it so often that to me it became hers.

When it was discovered overseas that the amount of DNA in the nuclei of mice was a thousand times more than in bacteria, Eva was exultant. She'd brought in a paper she'd found it in.

Wait till Hugh hears this, she said.

I could tell Shirley was still confused about why some animals were considered higher than others, but she just asked for a copy of the paper, and then, when Eva was out of the lab, she passed it on to Sandy so fast I was sure she hadn't read it.

My assistant and I thought you might be interested, she said to him.

He beamed at her.

As a leader I've always been a good delegator. As long as my helpers are up to scratch.

Within days he'd announced that, given all the new research coming in on mice, the lab was to have its own Mouse Institute – in Hugh's Animal House, to Hugh's fury. Sandy was particularly interested in breeding a type of mouse for experiments that, incidentally, turned out to be the perfect mice for his experiments on cancer cells. I was pleased about the mice, thinking I'd be able to befriend them. I remember thinking that I might write a note asking if I could clean out their cages, so I'd be in the same room as Eva. But I didn't dare.

Once, when he turned to go, he made a careful joke, which I suspected he'd rehearsed:

It's a shame we can't study elephants instead. But how would we fit them in the lab? And what would we do with the carcasses?

Shirley giggled as he disappeared up the stairs.

How would we fit them in, she kept repeating to Eva. He's so funny!

It's exciting, cried Eva, when she and Shirley were alone. One day, just by examining people's genes, we might be able to see what they're really like. Don't you see – you won't need to go on a date to find out.

I considered slipping a note to Eva with the poet's lines inspired by the beginning of the French Revolution:

Bliss it was in that dawn to be alive,
But to be young was very heaven.

(Read after my mother's death, so check between her bedroom and mine.)

But I knew I had to bide my time.

Hundreds of mice arrived and soon many of the researchers seemed to be trying to purify a mouse protein, and complaining because the techniques were awkward. It seemed that they had to suck solutions into their pipettes. Constantly I heard them quoting Eva:

It's a long road from bacteria to elephants! they'd say.

It became a shared joke, like the jokes between the grey men, and considered funny even though everyone had heard it before.

I was very proud of her.

(Later on I read that it was a common saying among scientists far away from Sudlow, so she didn't invent it.)

I wish I could've listened more, but of late I'd been followed by Marconi several times, and I was beginning to think twice about anything untoward that I did – not that I was going to give up my shed. I became very cautious, circling around the grounds with a rake or clambering over the roof pretending to look for leaks, but really checking whether he was lurking in my courtyard. My times there became less frequent and even more precious.

One day I was watching when Tony told Gunther and Sandy he'd read that it might be possible to introduce entirely new genes into an animal using a virus to help. The new word was recombinant DNA.

Sandy nodded as if he already knew all about this.

Of course, of course, he said. And who knows, we might be able to cure any illness soon.

He glanced at Gunther and added:

Except mental illness.

Sandy wanted to copy the experiments because, he said, if they had an unusual development, it would put this lab at the forefront.

And then we wouldn't be so dependent on Dopey Doris! he finished.

Isn't Doris his friend? Eva said when Sandy was out of earshot. Why's he always calling her dopey?

He's just cranky because she doesn't value his cancer work, said Shirley.

But Eva wouldn't let it go.

His lab, he means, said Eva. He wants to put his lab on the map. And it's not even his lab! If anything, it's Gunther's lab. Gunther's success has brought in all these scientists.

But Sandy's molecule is looking very promising, said Shirley. And he's not only a great scientist, he's the one who knows how to build on success.

So he should be trying to keep Gunther happy, said Eva.

That's true, said Shirley.

They worked quietly for a while.

I was about to go back to reattaching a stair runner when they began talking again.

If this place is going to use bacteria to put new genes into the mice, I'm going to resign, said Shirley. Who knows what might happen to us? Maybe we'd have giant mice running around. Or mice with an infectious sort of cancer. It might even stop us having babies.

You still want babies? asked Eva softly.

You think I'm too old? asked Shirley.

Of course not! But we're at such a big moment in science. We're making history, cried Eva. Imagine having to give all this up for a baby.

CHAPTER 18

My rival begins to decline

GUNTHER WAS NOW COORDINATING the work on immunology but, it was said, in rather a distracted way. He took to lingering in Top Lab like Sandy did, but I could see that he wanted to be with Eva. The new scientists jostled for his attention, asking him details, and he'd talk problems over with them, but he'd arc towards Eva, though constantly interrupted. He clearly thought no one would notice it, but everyone did. Then, when he stood at her sink, as if by accident, pretending he urgently wanted to speak to her neighbour, Tony, he'd fall silent. He wouldn't even watch her. His eyes would flicker on her, then away, to the floor, to the glassware drying on the bench, anything. She'd keep working in her engrossed way, but glance at him from time to time. It was meant to look as if he was musing over some deep problem, and perhaps he was, but it wasn't immunology. Other men who came up to talk to him because he was silent would stop, their eyes darting between him and her, and they'd tactfully turn and walk away.

After a while, Eva would find a way to break the silence, to mention something to him about the work she saw going on around her. But all these attempts met with wordless nods, as if nothing that she said could interest him. Perhaps it couldn't. Perhaps that was the problem between them, that he wasn't interested in what she had to say, only in her youth and beauty and enthusiasm for him. Whereas I was fascinated with every movement of her mind.

Then something would shift in him and he'd fumble for words and talk about his work, trying to address Tony as well. When Eva spoke again, the scientists would strain to listen, to weigh up her sentences, to hear what intellectual interest an eminent though eccentric scientist could find in a girl employed to wash up.

Eva would especially admire him when he said something authoritative about science that seemed to dismiss all their work. Or so I thought at first, and then I realised, because she did, that he was talking about the bewilderment of a search for truth.

One day he said:

Are we finding our way in the dark? Or are we just going around in circles?

Sandy, who was passing at that moment, gave a guffaw of disapproval. But her whole face glowed until she was entirely beautiful. He saw it too, the charm of her beauty. I watched him gaze at her. I raked the lawns angrily all afternoon.

Another time, when Mark had said that the problem was finding the right questions to ask, which I thought was very true, everyone nodded. I nodded too. But Gunther didn't. He seemed to be taking the idea deep inside his body, to see what his body made of it.

Have you ever thought that questions simplify things out of all recognition? he said after a while. Maybe even destroy things? That they might need to stay complex, that complexity might be what's needed? That nature's complex and we have to live with it? That this endless search for the right question, for the right way of measuring, for the right ruler, might be leading us astray, might in fact be simplifying and ruining what we set out to achieve?

Sometimes I felt I could respect him as a rival. If I had to have a rival, he was a worthy one. I was impressed by his knowledge. You'd have to have a lot of knowledge and be at ease with it to discount it like he did. But then jealousy would take over my finer feelings, if I can call them that, and I'd brood, and believe more and more that he had other knowledge, a dark secret, perhaps a terrible heritage.

I began to think I wasn't the only one to be suspicious of him. One afternoon I had to burn old bandages at the incinerator, a long, hot and filthy job. Before I went to the ablutions block to clean up, I popped into my shed just in time to hear Hugh telling Gunther he was a heretic.

I grabbed my pen and paper. I knew that Hugh had been simmering since he'd lost his Animal House to the Mice Institute. He'd been relegated to a walled-in corner in Top Lab, and blamed this humiliation on Gunther, who stood for the waywardness of the new DNA science. He'd been waiting for his moment, I could tell, and his speech was slurred, so he'd probably had another bottle of Sudlow's finest red from behind the counter of the cafe, and could wait no longer.

Looking back, I have to admit I was hoping that Hugh was about to say something that would destroy Gunther in Eva's eyes. Eva quietly left the sink where she'd been washing up. Her adorable upper lip was lifted, taking in Hugh's fury. It was such an enchanting upper lip that I missed a lot of what Hugh said. I've had to reconstruct it from the odd words scribbled across the page, often crisscrossing each other. What they said probably didn't happen quite the way I wrote it, but it's close.

Gunther's heresy, according to Hugh, was his belief that the message in the DNA could be changed by a protein.

That's the same as saying that the environment can change DNA. That we are who we are because of something in our environment, and that contradicts what Darwin said. That's the same as being a Lamarckian, he accused.

Tony and Mike argued with him while Shirley, near my camera, asked Eva quietly what the fuss was about. Eva, her sky-blue eyes wide with wonder at Hugh's rudeness, explained that a Frenchman, Jean Baptiste Lamarck, a professor of insects, worms and microscopic animals in 1802 when Darwin was only a child, had reasoned that we can change what we inherit in our cells by our 'felt needs', as he put it, so we are who we are not by chance, like Darwin said, but because of our needs and desires. So his water birds knew they needed webbed feet and grew them, his rams grew horns because of their bad tempers, and his giraffes grew long necks because they wanted to reach the tastiest leaves. Then they gave birth to baby giraffes with the same long necks. A Lamarckian today would say that the cells can tell the DNA what to do, as well as obey it, she finished.

It's a lovely idea, cooed Shirley, and it was Eva's turn to roll her eyes heavenwards.

It's against Crick's central dogma, she whispered.

Crick who? asked Shirley.

Crick and Watson – I told you just the other day, said Eva. The ones who stole Rosalind Franklin's photo and worked out the structure of DNA.

It's hard to take in these abstract things when you're sitting on a chair with a rip in its vinyl, Shirley began.

Mike heard this, nudged his friend Jim, and turned around.

A woman scientist is a contradiction in terms, he said.

Watch out or we'll contaminate your dishes, Shirley slung back at him.

If you're a Lamarckian, Eva whispered, ignoring them both, you say that the animal's changes happened because of some problem the animal came across in the environment. If you're a Darwinian, you think that the changes were internal and accidental and nothing to do with the world. The animals whose changes happened to suit the world prospered by having more offspring.

Though I wrote this down I agreed with Shirley, and doodled on my page, imagining the satisfaction of giraffes that all the pain they'd gone through to stretch their necks had been worth it, because the neck length they'd achieved lived on after them.

It was clear even to me, his rival, that Gunther understood the new science and Hugh didn't, but Hugh had a score to settle. He'd lost his Animal House because of Gunther's success. Suddenly he accused Gunther of being in sympathy with the Stalinists.

Why the Stalinists? cried Tony, looking around at the others and pulling a face in Hugh's direction.

In Russia, Hugh explained, scientists had to sign up as Lamarckians, so the peasants could think that what they'd learned in such pain wouldn't be lost on their offspring. Their children would inherit what they'd learned. Even the winter wheat was supposed to be able to teach the spring wheat how to survive a cold snap. And if scientists dared to disagree, he finished up, they were disappeared. Sent off to a Gulag, or worse. None of this reactionary, decadent Darwinism that what you inherit is fixed.

He poked his head towards Gunther.

The trouble in all this European research we're competing with is that Europe regards the rest of us as barbarians. Especially us, here.

Everyone was too surprised to speak. Into the silence, suddenly Eva's voice rang out, a little shrill, a little nervous, but determined.

Hugh, you can't lump all of Europe together.

Her face was tense, but her voice was sure.

Hugh faced Gunther.

He's one of them. He thinks he has some private knowledge of science.

There was an uproar, but Hugh turned to Eva.

And who are you, to speak out of turn? he said. Only a bottle-washer, I'm told. Yes?

This last word was thrown to Shirley, who flinched to be called a bottle-washer by implication.

If we can't contradict, Eva said quietly now, this would really be like Russia. We're not priests bowing to some dogma, we're observers!

Shirley, awed by Eva's response and suddenly motherly, came over and put her hands on Eva's shoulders, which were still shaking from her outburst.

Leave her alone, said Shirley stoutly. She's very . . .

Shirley paused, searching for a word, and they both looked instinctively to Gunther.

She is, said Gunther, speaking into the silence, and now Eva was trembling to hear at last what he thought of her . . .

Reliable, said Gunther.

I could almost hear the disappointment in Eva's breathing.

See him! I murmured to her. See who he is!

But still she didn't.

Matron decided that several of the doors needed rehanging, and when I'd done that – it was decided that with my bulky strength, I was the man for the job – all sorts of work on door frames followed. It took weeks, with Matron constantly checking on me. When I returned to my cameras, I found to my despair that relations between Gunther and Eva had deepened. Sandy's plan for graduate students to come to Sudlow for a term to study under Gunther had succeeded, and three had arrived. Gunther asked Eva to explain lab techniques to them.

They'll like you, he said, in answer to some cautious comment from her I'd come in too late to hear.

I wonder what you've done to deserve this, Shirley said after he'd gone. She spoke with narrowed eyes.

By the way, you've never explained, what are you trying to say by wearing those dresses? Obviously there's a message.

Eva sighed.

I can't refuse my mother. She has lots of problems, Eva said. Besides, I grew up with these silks, but she couldn't make them up for me when I was little because I'd tear them. She had to wait till now.

Sandy doesn't approve, said Shirley.

Afterwards, when Shirley had gone out, her heels clicking self-righteously on the lino, Eva stopped work and went over to the window and stood gazing out. Her voice came to me, and I wrote it down:

'I could forget him and turn my back on Gunther if I had a girl-friend to confide in, to weigh it all up. It's loneliness and ineptitude that's pivoting me into this. All I want is someone to see in the evenings, in the lab or in a cafe, someone to have cups of tea with,

someone with time for me. It seems easier finding a lover than finding a friend.'

But from then on she dressed more circumspectly, more in the
current fashion, and in dull, lifeless materials, fawns and greys.
Her mother and she had compromised, I think.

Two nights before Eva taught his students, she abandoned
sleep, she told Shirley, to study.

He just wants you to explain what we do, said Shirley impatiently. Anyone could do it. I could, if required.

When the students quizzed Eva, she became incoherent, examining their questions for hidden meanings. Their questions seemed
to stick to her skin like a lie detector, to see what she was made of.
She'd give meticulous answers, convoluted and lengthy because of
her timidity.

My students say you're very well read, Gunther told her one
day. But almost incomprehensible.

Sometimes I found her incomprehensible, though it never
stopped me loving her. She was as clumsy and innocent as Gunther
and, looking back, I see how needy she was.

Tony, her neighbour in the lab, must've seen that as well. He
had such a natural, good-looking ease about him that anyone
would wonder how it was that there was any ugliness or meanness
in the world, when he made it so simple to be friendly.

One unseasonably warm day in late autumn, Gunther hadn't
come back after lunch. Throughout the afternoon Eva waited for
him, glancing at the door occasionally in her absorbed way, checking that it still stood open. He'd become such a part of her
thoughts that this was no interruption, and her hands worked
rhythmically.

Tony interrupted her. She was concentrating so hard, she didn't
notice him for some seconds.

Like an ice-cream? he said.

She looked around.

Everyone's gone, she said in surprise.

A vanilla ice-cream? he repeated. Or something more fancy?

I could see, in the round curves of his freckled face, in the way he held his small nuggety body erect, there had been in his life only peace and an absence of humiliation. She might see that too, and long for that in him, to make it hers, I realised. While he would see in her the shadows of a childhood suffering, and consider it mysterious, even romantic. I cursed myself. He'd glanced at her hundreds of times over the equipment, the taps and the bottles and the Bunsen burners, and yet I'd never prepared myself for this attack. He posed a greater threat to me than Gunther because this could be a true love match.

Anything you choose, she said.

He left, and the room seemed restored to her and to me, but he popped his head back to ask:

Strawberry?

Yes, yes, she said.

When she could no longer hear his footsteps, she bent her head to her work, but her fingers had become as clumsy as her discomforted mind. Something was demanded of her, something she didn't quite have the sophistication to handle, that's how I see it now, though at the time it puzzled me.

She jumped up, ran to Shirley's drawer, and pulled out Shirley's make-up case and wound up Shirley's crimson lipstick. It was the first time I'd noticed that Eva didn't wear make-up, her colouring was so lively. She ran towards Shirley's little powder room then halted, looked around and saw a machine with a strip of metal on its edge, and used it as a makeshift mirror, just like Shirley sometimes did, rounding her mouth into an o as she'd seen Shirley do, circling her lips with crimson, rubbing them together, peering, repainting, re-rubbing. She glanced around, fearful that she'd heard his returning footsteps, and as her face whirled past me I saw that she'd painted on herself a clown's mouth, grotesque and unnuanced, that mocked her intelligent, finely carved face. She grabbed a piece of paper to wipe it off but the mouth refused to leave, and now he was genuinely returning, his footsteps in the corridor, all she had time to do was scamper back to her workplace and hide Shirley's lipstick under a rubber glove.

He came in panting.

They're half-melted. We'll have to lick urgently.

He handed her an ice-cream and went to grab his stool, bringing it one-handed over to her workplace. It was only when he sat down that he saw her clown mouth. He lowered his eyes and addressed himself to the ice-cream, licking assiduously, but his face was working in a way that was not just about eating ice-cream. Slowly she forgot what she'd done to her face, or perhaps she convinced herself that it wasn't as visible as she'd feared, and so they sat side by side like children, dangling their legs from the high stools, pushing their hot tongues into the ice-cream's coolness, absorbed in the task of licking.

Suddenly his ice-cream collapsed onto her knee, bared by the skirt of her dress.

They both laughed.

I'm sorry, he said.

I haven't got a handkerchief, she said.

I could lick it up, he suggested.

No, she cried, but when she saw he'd taken this as a rebuff, she nodded, too shy to speak. She had no words. Nothing like this had ever happened before.

He bent to her smooth knee. He swirled his tongue around its curves while she kept licking her ice-cream. I could scarcely bear to watch. She even allowed herself to giggle, as she probably thought Shirley would have done, to prove that she was not a deeply serious person. Though this was too terrifying to be fun.

Delicious, he said, straightening up again.

So that she felt safe at last, and so did I – though only for a second.

There's ice-cream on your fingers, he said. He laughed to show that the game had begun again, a new development. He leaned over and licked her fingers.

No, she said at first, but he didn't stop, and she gave herself to the pleasure, her eyes half closing.

He had moved closer, licking her ice-cream.

Their faces were very close.

I didn't think, she began, confused, uncertain what she thought.

It was the lipstick, he said, licking her lips now. He pulled away long enough to ask:

Do you always put on lipstick to eat ice-cream?

At this precise moment, Sandy appeared. Perhaps he'd walked down the steps quietly, or come in from the car park. I hadn't noticed, I'd been too jealous. He craned in, looking for Shirley, his early evening shadow menacing. I was longing to signal to them to break apart, but they didn't. The kiss seemed to go on and on. Then at last Tony withdrew a little and whispered something, his lips moving but his voice too low for me to hear.

I can't. I've got my bike, she answered.

Please, he said urgently.

No, she said.

All this time Sandy had been watching, like me, but I knew that he would never be a helpless bystander. His breath was coming in jabs. His eyes glinted. Silently, he withdrew. Eva, her head still bowed, wiped the kiss off her mouth.

Yes, urged Tony, easing his face close to hers again. He was dragging at her hand, to take her home to his place, I suppose.

No, flashed Eva.

Tony sighed, straightened and carried his stool back to his bench, pretending a carefree shuffle that contradicted the serious-ness of his face. Out the window, the sky mocked the orderliness of the laboratory, a wild sunset clamouring against the glass.

Both of them tried to go on with their work. Then the phone rang. Tony answered it and spoke to one of his friends. He cut the conversation short and began packing up.

Are you sure? he called to Eva's back.

Yes, she nodded more than spoke. He slouched out. She looked after him, uncertain. She crossed her arms and put her head in them and rocked herself. Her hands moved on her arms, to chafe them or comfort them, I wasn't sure.

I watched her wheel her bicycle out of the hospital grounds, until she was just a white fleck amongst the traffic.

But she didn't murmur to me.

I didn't go back to my little shed for a few days, maybe a fort-night. I was sick at heart, to think that I could lose her to anyone who kissed her. Up till that moment, only Gunther had seemed a threat. But when I looked at Top Lab again, there seemed to be a gap where Tony had worked. Then I picked up a snatch of gossip that Tony had received a letter from the hospital Board saying that his project was no longer to be funded by the Board and his serv-ices were to be terminated immediately. From then on, I never saw Tony again.

The sooner Eva had a home, I decided, the better. The home that I had made.

Then Shirley came in with news that she'd just moved into her new apartment, all alone, away from the apartment she'd shared with her difficult uncle. Excitement made her break into a jokey dance step, just at the moment when Gunther opened the door to go upstairs. He stood and watched.

The work going well? he asked Shirley, who stopped her dance, embarrassed.

I've got a flat, she stumbled.

He looked bewildered.

A flat what? he asked.

Shirley sighed imperceptibly. She and Gunther never quite understood each other.

Just then Sandy came in.

She blushed bright red, but kept on.

I'm just explaining that I've changed my life, she told Sandy, trying to include Gunther in her glance. I've left my cranky uncle to scold himself, and I've rented an apartment to live in. Would you like to drop by and see it? Oh, I'm asking everyone, not just you, everyone, but one by one, because I haven't got many chairs, only two . . . She petered out.

I'm very busy right now, Sandy said rapidly. Family commit-ments, you know.

He bounded up the stairs and Gunther followed.

Shirley made a face at Eva.

Does his heart beat for me? Does he want to lay his lips on mine? Is he a goer? she asked. Or not?

I always believed that when the time was right, a path would open up for me with Eva, all of its own accord, the way a path had opened when I rode on the hospital mower. I couldn't imagine myself accosting her and asking her out as Sandy accosted Shirley about a fortnight later.

Every time I'd watched them through that day, Shirley had been worrying about the wrinkles that, she said, had appeared overnight under her eyes.

When Eva had gone and Shirley was wiping down all the work-benches, there were heavy footsteps on the stairs. Sandy came in.

Working late? he said unnecessarily.

He held his head oddly, angled, ingratiating. I was about to switch off the camera, but I hesitated.

Like a lift home? To the new flat? he said. Not that it's still new, I suppose – that was a while ago, now. I suppose everyone's tramped through.

He laughed, realising he hadn't been his usual urbane self. He seemed slightly flustered.

My friends drop in, Shirley said defensively.

Of course, he said easily. You're a very independent young woman. As it should be.

He lingered, watching her work.

After a while, when the silence grew oppressive, she thought of something to say, something that they had privately shared.

Do you think Professor Mueller has recovered?

(Shirley was always deferential. She tried never to say 'Gunther'.)

Sandy started.

Recovered from what? he asked.

His correspondent, she said.

When Sandy didn't react, she prompted:

The woman who sent the newspaper clipping and wrote on it

in purple ink. Remember? About the Nazi killer. She sent a mysterious research paper as well.

Sandy laughed.

Gunther is a danger to himself, he said. We all love him, but he gets himself into these states. A good scientist but a loose cannon.

His face muscles worked. I was beginning to suspect he resented all talk of Gunther's success. He leaned forward conspiratorially.

He's made it very difficult for our lab, he added. We need to be on good terms with the hospital. Doris insists on it because she got attached to the doctors here when her son was dying, the way women do. Especially Dr Graham, the psychiatrist. That's why – he looped his fingers into his belt –

it's a good thing I'm around.

Sandy checked to see if the lab was indeed empty and leaned further forward so his face almost touched her hair.

There is even a rumour that Gunther put himself up for the Prize, he said.

Shirley gasped.

Is it possible? she asked.

Sandy shrugged.

If you know what you're doing. A letter on someone else's letterhead, which you could steal, you know.

That's being rumoured? cried Shirley loyally. Isn't a man innocent until he's proven guilty? Who's passing on that gossip? I won't wash up for them.

Sandy shushed her again.

I can't tell you. But I agree it's unlikely – he's too naive. He wouldn't even be cunning enough to steal the letterhead. Anyway, we've all benefited – it impressed Doris greatly, our little blaze of media attention, so don't pass the rumour on.

Shirley agreed, but he made her promise, a touch more anxiety in his voice than seemed necessary. Then she smiled at him and kept wiping the workbenches. He watched her, suddenly doubting.

What do you think of Gunther? he asked.

He's not my type, she lied.

What's your type? he asked.

Her cleaning cloth had just reached the equipment that Eva had used as a mirror. I could see her pausing, worrying again about her wrinkles. She looked up and noticed his eyes on her, soft and shining with hope. Something shifted for her at that moment, a resignation, an acceptance of what was possible, after all. Or perhaps I'm reading that into the moment, which was just her reflection in a piece of equipment.

My type is a man with experience, she said softly.

Really, he said.

They gazed at each other in some sort of understanding, or misunderstanding.

Sandy twitched slightly. He had to return to Gunther, as if Gunther was a thorn in his side.

He seems to find the young girl who works with you – what's her name? – attractive.

Oh, Eva, cried Shirley in exasperation. I try to help her, I'm always trying to help her! Do you find her attractive? Her . . . youthfulness?

Me? he asked. His own lips were wet with saliva.

He considered the question, as if for the first time.

I wouldn't want to upset the apple-cart, you know, with Gunther. It's important that he stay with us. He'll be happy while she's around. A leader has to think of these things. Anyway, she's a bit angular – all pointy nose and elbows. I wouldn't want to meet those elbows in bed. Nice legs, though, and eyes. A man could lose himself forever in those blue eyes. But she's so unformed. Get a dog young, you have to teach it tricks.

He paused; they both did.

I like a woman who already knows tricks.

He tucked his thumbs into his belt.

Her face darkened a little, working out if this was a compliment she wanted. She glanced at the confident way he was fanning out his fingers. She smiled to herself and looked down. For the first time, her hands no longer moved on her work.

He swallowed, unsure.

Look, he said, I'm sorry I didn't come around when you asked last time, but do you need any help now with your flat? Hanging pictures or something?

Have you had a fight with your wife? she flashed at him.

He laughed in disbelief at such a question, and then his lips seemed unable to go back to their usual place. They trembled, because perhaps it hadn't been funny after all.

I do need some help, she said. She looked at him levelly.

Anything, he said, spreading his hands and almost knocking over a Bunsen burner.

I've got satin sheets that haven't been used, she said. They need to be tried out.

He swallowed, his Adam's apple pumping.

Can I get your coat? he asked.

Shortly afterwards, they clattered out together.

I'll follow your car, I heard him call to her, his voice warm with sexual excitement.

I went home cowed, and I relived that scene all night. If that was what I'd have to do some day with Eva, I should give up the world right now.

CHAPTER 19
During which, despite it all, my plan begins to work

WHEN GUNTHER DIDN'T APPEAR in the lab for several weeks, I allowed myself the hope that he never would again. As day after day went by and he still didn't show up, I began to believe it. So I acted. Looking back, my timing was wrong, but who can know these things? I was so full of yearning.

I pinned up an advertisement in the bike shelter to the effect that a benefactor to science possessed a small but attractive and newly refurbished apartment, and wanted it to be the home of a young woman scientist for a negligible rent. Anyone interested was to apply to my lawyer.

Then I wrote to my lawyer telling him that the only acceptable applicant would be called Eva.

I waited.

Sudlow is cruellest in winter, and especially cruel that year in the old, damp, high-ceilinged hospital. Mould crept like a sinister black insect up the walls and had to be scrubbed off every second day. Many of the wards and even the beds smelled of damp. Howling gusts of wind spun around the grounds and whistled down the chimneys and poked chilly fingers up under the windows no matter how often we tried to make them snug, and banged doors shut or strained to blow them open. Every time it rained, drips clanged into tin buckets, no matter how much tar we painted on the complicated roof. The ancient boiler that heated the entire hospital kept breaking down. All in all, I was too busy to sit in my shed and watch my love and try to guess if she'd noticed my advertisement.

One day, on the tail end of some exchange between Shirley and Eva, I came in as Eva said:

Sometimes nothing works out. And then, when you're least expecting it, an answer comes.

She may have been talking about her work, but since that was largely just making up solutions, I allowed myself to think she was talking about the apartment.

Though my lawyer received several letters, none of them was from a young woman named Eva.

Someone pinned up on the noticeboard a newspaper photograph of Gunther accepting an award in Denmark for his immunology research – so he was travelling, and would one day return, as of course I should have guessed. There was a mention of invitations from various universities. I watched Eva go over to the noticeboard and count up the universities: five. He'd be gone a long time, I could see from her face as she turned back to her work.

Funny how the world encourages you when you don't want it to, she said to Shirley.

As Sandy says, none of us can do anything we like, said Shirley.

Then one afternoon, all my hopes were dashed. Eva was working later than anyone else, and I had crept out to watch her, marvelling once again at her slender hands and intelligent face, when suddenly the door swung open. She didn't look up, she wasn't expecting him. I wasn't either. But there he was, watching her, in his travelling clothes, a khaki coat, the usual khaki suit, a khaki tie partly unknotted.

I came straight from the airport, he began.

He couldn't go on. He seemed choked.

She continued what she was doing, as if she didn't need him, as though the longing for his touch had left her and she was free. I exulted in that.

Hello, she said, smiling wanly, absorbed in her work.

I caught the first plane back that I could, he said.

She laughed dismissively, and my heart sang.

Really, she said.

He sighed imperceptibly and leaned against the bench. He seemed to be trying to say something more. It came out with a slight accent from his childhood.

Because of you.

She smiled as if she thought he was joking.

Come and have a drink, he said.

But that would make me late for dinner and my mother's expecting me, she said.

I wish, he said and paused, we could go somewhere to talk. I've been longing for that.

She kept her head bent to her work.

You could come and visit me at home, she said. After dinner, of course.

It's a bit hard to talk there, he said.

Yes, I know, she said.

Do you ever think of getting a little place on your own, like Shirley? he asked.

Her face fell. She didn't like being compared to Shirley.

Then we could really talk, he finished.

With that, he almost bolted out the door.

Just a few days later, Eva wrote to my lawyer asking if she could see the apartment. So she'd known about it for a while. I feared the worst, that Gunther would pursue her there. When the lawyer told me about her letter, I dashed off a reply:

No! My plans have changed! Under no circumstances show it to her!

But I didn't go down to the mailbox to send it. The night was too dark and I was too tired. So her appointment with my lawyer was made.

I tried to leave work in time to see her reaction to the apartment, but that day every single heater in the hospital broke down, and I worked well into the evening. The next day, Eva apparently rang the lawyer saying she'd like to take it. She even named a day when she'd move in. Could the key be left in a letterbox? Then she added:

Who is my benefactor?

My lawyer told her that it was one of the conditions of the offer that the benefactor remain unnamed. However, he added, it might interest her to know that the benefactor's kindness was in memory of his mother. Why did I want her to know that? Because I longed for her to know something about me, anything at all.

The adventure of my life was about to begin. We'd live side by side, only a wall between us, looking out at the church and the brothel, clattering down the same staircase, perhaps even passing each other on it. She'd almost be like the sister I never had. Do you condemn me, a condemned man? I thought then, This might be the only way I'd ever be able to love her.

How my heart lurches still.

Before she moved in, I heard the end of another conversation between Eva and Shirley while they dried the glassware.

So you see, Eva was saying, I'm turning out to be a bolter.

You're also reliable, Shirley said. Remember – even Professor Mueller thinks that. You're reliable!

She laughed as she spoke, a short, rasping laugh.

I asked her to come with me but she won't, said Eva. There wouldn't be much room, but at least she'd get away from Cuthbert.

Cuthbert! The man from the butcher's, that's his name? What sort of a man is called Cuthbert? cried Shirley. It must be true love, for her to put up with a name like Cuthbert.

She might bolt from her mother. But she'd never bolt from me.

They worked away in silence for a while, and then Shirley looked across at Eva.

Just don't get too carried away, she said. With all this freedom. Don't let it affect your work.

She moved in during the day while I was at work. When I came home I found the little I could see of her apartment littered with cardboard boxes. She seemed to be one of those people who are meticulous about some things and disregard others, which I'd never known before. Her mother's dresses lay in a heap under the window on the floor, a tumble of red and turquoise and black and pink, while a box crammed with a jumble of spoons, knives, forks, plates, a battered saucepan, a kettle with a rusting handle, an egg whisk, a worn bread knife, a stained egg lifter and an unopened packet of Billy Tea balanced near the edge of the chair. I could just see that her books stood upright on the shelves and I suspect that they'd been transported in alphabetical order and meticulously placed like that, unlike my library.

She did not tidy up for days, which I found endearing, that she cared so little about domesticity. I felt it made her a true scientist.

It seemed a great accomplishment to have her there beside me. The greatest accomplishment of my life.

CHAPTER 20

During which my plan founders

I DIDN'T FEEL EXULTANT for very long. The next afternoon, Gunther came down to Top Lab and headed straight for her bench – no arc, no manoeuvring, no seeking out her neighbours to chat with. He headed straight for her. Mark was around though not within earshot. Gunther planned something, I could see.

And she could see it too. The stern, uncompromising lab was instantly brighter, more colourful, even festive because of his presence. For her, it was as if the walls had been hung with bright streamers. I could see her almost hug herself with the pleasure of him. So she had reverted to her old fascination, she must've really longed for him to be there while she worked, how plaintively she must've longed for that, despite herself. And how seldom I could admit it.

This time he was calmer and even rehearsed, the way he threw back his head as if he was about to make a speech.

Come for a drink, he said.

But I've got to check the cells at seven, she said.

He didn't know what to say to this, I could see, so he picked up her lab diary, leafed his way through it and checked on her graphs.

He looked up shyly.

This is how we met, you remember?

No, she said. You ran into me in your car.

He smiled his rare, sweet smile that lit up his eyes, he was so amused. He still didn't believe her, he was so unaware of other people, he didn't even notice when he ran them down!

He seemed less intense now when they talked.

You probably want more important work than mixing solutions, washing up, being everyone's servant, he said. Why didn't you go to university?

I left school early, she said. My mother . . .

She gave up, stopped any pretence of working.

Oh, I want to do something important, of course –

Important to whom? he interrupted, his voice thick.

Why, to me, of course, she said.

She must've hoped he'd ask her this. She almost seemed to be making a speech.

If I ever had my way, and I was a scientist, I'd choose problems that are on the edge of knowing, she said, almost pompously because it was so important to her. Problems you know only approximately where you stand, and from this point you have to go further.

I blushed for her – she was over-earnest and gauche. But he didn't notice this.

We're two of a kind, he said.

They both breathed with relief.

Suddenly they were back to being intimates, as they'd been at her mother's house that rainy day.

I'll come back with you, he said. To check your cells.

His voice, attempting to sound casual, squeaked instead, so he had to clear his throat before he said:

So will you come for that drink?

Where? she asked, I think for something to say, because I believe at that moment she would've followed him to the desert beyond Sudlow, though she wouldn't always.

The Roo Bar, he said. It's quiet. We can talk.

She nodded, too excited for speech.

I quickly packed my own bag and headed for the Roo Bar, which I'd seen but never dared go in. I'd never dared enter any pub, and I feared that a bar with a name like the Roo Bar would only let in Ernest Hemingway sort of men. But I had to be with her. So I slipped out of my uniform in the Gents and back into a pair of trousers, shirt and tie, straightened my back, puffed out my chest and did my best to swagger into the Roo Bar. It was part of Sudlow's most popular pub, the Duke of Wellington, and I could hear noisy drinkers in the brightly lit main bar, but few seemed to want the moody silence of the Roo Bar.

Trying to be manly, I leaned near the cash register and pointed to one of the two beers on tap. I went for the Old over the New because it sounded more genteel. I imagined Hemingway would approve. I held up a note and gestured for the barman to pour himself a drink as well. (I learned that trick out of a movie on TV. I think it had Humphrey Bogart in it.) He pulled my beer and, after checking that the coast was clear, poured himself a nip of Glenfiddich, raising an eyebrow as if he couldn't speak either. We clinked glasses.

The room was shadowy with wooden veneer panelling, a navy nylon carpet and a stuffed Big Grey kangaroo mounted on a mahogany shield, with a brass plate saying Mulga Creek 1935. The roo was rather moth-eaten when I looked at it more closely, and one of its glass eyes had fallen out. Over near the window were two old men holding on to their empty glasses and staring out at the refinery, where they'd probably worked all their lives.

The barman scoffed down his drink just as the door opened again. It was Gunther and Eva.

There was a Johnnie Walker mirror near the till and I moved so I could watch its reflection of the room. For months I'd mainly looked at her through a camera so that for me she'd become like an actress on a stage, or like a figure through a doorway in an old painting – distant, remote, poised to walk off away into another life. Now we shared the same air, the same light, and if I dared, I could turn and walk right past her and sigh just at the right moment to ripple the shining threads of her hair. But I stayed where I was, concealed in a shadow, watching the mirror. I didn't look around, even when the old men called out:

Professor Mueller! Honoured with your company, Professor Mueller. Congratulations on your research. We saw you on TV.

Then chairs clattered. He and she had taken up a table annoyingly out of earshot, and he bent over her solicitously. Then he came up to the bar and ordered a beer (New) for himself and a lemonade.

The barman put the drinks down on the rippling bar towel, Eva's with a straw about to topple.

I dared a look along the bar at Gunther, his now familiar profile with his shock of blond, almost upright hair, his deeply set, dark eyes, his thick sensuous lips and double chin. As he waited for his order, he fiddled with the bar runner. He was too absorbed with his thoughts to notice me. I decided it would be safe to move closer to where they were sitting. There was an empty table with a newspaper folded on its shining laminex surface. I scuttled over to it – completely forgetting to do a manly stride – and sat down with a worried frown as if all that mattered was the last-minute scratchings from Sudlow's races. He didn't turn around and she didn't look in my direction, but then, why should they take any interest in me?

As Gunther came from the bar towards us both, the straw fell on the floor. He didn't notice. He was walking toward the beautiful curve of her legs under her dress.

His chair clattered again. I heard it take his weight. I didn't look up from Daylight's odds against Sudden Strike.

Shouldn't we have a toast? I heard her ask.

Toast? he asked.

To the work you want to do, she said.

He clinked her glass with his. They drank. I looked up, repeating numbers as if I was calculating how much I could lose on Sudden Strike at six to one on, and I found her gazing around, and he was following her gaze. It went everywhere, from the sepia photos on the walls of Sudlow's main thoroughfare in the old days, with gentlemen in top hats and long-skirted ladies holding parasols, to memories of our hospital grounds, where a row of graduating nurses sat, their stockinged legs crossed tensely, their faces unsmiling, full of apprehension about their futures, or perhaps just about the apparatus that would fix their youth forever, to the recent action shots of the publican crashing through dense bush after a dark shape that was probably a kangaroo, and driving across the rippling red ocean of the desert, in a muddy Land Rover with a hefty roo bar on the front.

Eva and Gunther sat in silence. Every time I peeked, the level of their drinks was lower, but they weren't meeting each other's gaze.

Will you tell me more about autism? What you know? she asked at last.

No, he said.

Why don't people here know about it? she asked.

Fashion, he said.

He sank into gloom, but remembered himself enough to add:

As Sandy would say, it's the wrong time in history. So the observations – the paper I have – haven't been translated into English.

Couldn't you translate it? she asked.

I don't want it translated, he said.

Why not? she asked.

I told you. They have enough against me already, he said.

There was another long pause.

At last he stirred himself and made an effort.

Did your mother want you to leave home? he asked.

No, she said.

Did she want you to be a scientist? he asked.

No, she said.

He didn't press her further and she didn't offer more. How could he be interested in her if he didn't pursue this? I'd have held her hand and demanded to know more and more until I'd explored her very soul. I'd have watched her eyes flinch and widen, I'd have watched the way her lips trembled with the thoughts she almost dared not say, I'd have comforted her.

She finally said:

I didn't get good marks at school. Perhaps I didn't try. But I want to be a scientist one day, in my own way, she said.

That's not possible, he said sternly. You have to follow convention and jump through hoops like everyone else.

Ask her why she doesn't want to follow convention! Try to find out about her childhood and her mother!

But he didn't. He talked, not even about himself, but about some new DNA finding that he thought unlikely to be true.

Now that you've got that off your chest, ask her more! I wanted to shout.

But he didn't. He wasn't interested. Had she noticed that he wasn't interested? He merely finished his drink. She finished hers.

Would you like another or do you want to go home? he asked. I peeked, and he'd asked this vital question – where they were going next, or at least where she was going – not to her beautiful face, but to her hands, which crouched on the table. He was still unwilling or unable to meet her gaze.

Another drink, please, she said, to my bafflement.

He went to the bar and then she gazed after him, examining the sweep of his back, his shoulders under his suit coat, his rather flat buttocks. But she timed her gaze so that when he returned, she was merely studying the roof of the refinery out the window.

Thank you, she said.

She still kept her eyes slightly averted.

There followed another silence so long I began to doubt my concentration. Had I got lost in my thoughts about Golden Purse's lengthening odds on a wet track? Surely some curiosity about her would've niggled at him. He had all the time I longed to have to know her as I longed to know her. But he said nothing to her – nothing, nothing! Time seemed to curve in on itself through the long dusk. White cockatoos screeched past the windows, cars honked in the six o'clock rush hour. But these two people were still gazing at the publican's muddy Land Rover, the rows of coloured liqueurs, the glasses held stem up, the barman with his back to the room gazing at himself now in the Johnnie Walker mirror by the till and squeezing a pimple on his otherwise handsome face, and the moth-eaten Big Grey from 1935 – they examined everything except each other. This can't be how to flirt, I thought.

Then she murmured to me, almost in answer:

'He's not perfect. He's not what I really want, but I don't know how to bind men to me. I don't know how to charm, like Shirley does. I've always resisted those charming ways my mother wanted to teach me, to smile readily, to remember to nod when men talked, to look admiringly, to say, ah yes, to ricochet between trivia and importance, but to stay on trivia, to mention important things only apologetically.'

At least, even at this moment, she'd murmured to me.

She finished her glass.

Another? he asked.

I'm awash with lemonade, she said. I should go home.

She began to make those shuffling, rustling sounds that people make when they depart, unsatisfied, hoping for something that hasn't quite transpired. It was that tension about them that gave me hope, that they tantalised each other but, ultimately, she knew and I knew that he'd disappoint her. Then there would be room for me.

At that moment he stood up with such suddenness he bumped the table they'd been leaning their elbows on, and tipped his glass so beer spilled and frothed onto his pants. Then there was a flurry about finding something to mop it up with, first a stiff coaster, then a little handkerchief she found in her bag (grey, to match her dress), then he used his big, rather grubby man's handkerchief, and she insisted on helping him, and he found a beer stain darkening her dress, and after all this they were red faced and laughing and tousled, and she was tossing hair out of her bewitching blue eyes with their dark lashes like stars.

He cleared his throat.

Thank you, he said. That was one of the most interesting talks I've ever had with anyone.

It was for me too, she said politely, but I know she lied.

May we do it again? he asked.

Yes, she said.

Of course she had to say yes. She could hardly say no.

She picked up her bag and coat.

Are you going home now? she asked.

Yes, he said.

Who's at home? she asked.

Aha! Was she suspicious of his father as well?

An aged parent, he said. Then he added:

I'm not good with people. I never have been. But –

He was looking straight into her eyes at last.

I want to sleep with you, he said quickly. Now that he'd raised his eyes, anyone could see why he'd not done it before. They were shouting with desire.

She gazed back at him, at his desire.

You do? she asked and laughed at him, her eyes flashing, so that blue fire leapt at him.

Stop! I wanted to shout. Don't! You know he's not interested in who you are!

But he pushed his chair back under the table because he was even at this moment a methodical, tidy man, and she copied him.

Now? he said breathlessly.

She paused.

I've got to go back for my cells, she said uncertainly.

Of course you're not sure! I longed to shout. Take notice of your uncertainty. He's not unkind, he's just wrong for you. Can't you see how wrong he is?

But they walked side by side across the floor and he changed his step to fit with hers. At the door, he stopped.

What do you like talking about? he asked her, suddenly animated and smiling.

Interesting organisms, she was able to say at last, also suddenly animated. Now her words were tumbling over each other.

Here's my note – I wrote them down:

Cilia. How they don't fit with evolution. How evolution doesn't work on the molecular level. The parts of cilia can't have evolved bit by bit, each new mutation would've contradicted what had gone before, the only sort of mutations that made cilia fit for survival were the ones that happened when cilia had already evolved. It's the same for –

She paused for breath because he wasn't opening the door, he was just looking at her.

Even then he couldn't keep quiet, and let her speak as I would've.

For the human eye! he said.

And for poison fangs of snakes! she said.

And for haemoglobin! he said. Some traits may have got fixed in place because there was no competition, or the useful gene might've dragged some useless genes along the chromosome.

She was nodding.

Natural selection isn't everything, she said, and added, giggling:

We should mention that to Hugh.

She opened the door for herself. He forgot to let her go first, he was walking through, turning, grabbing it before it shut, remembering too late to hold it open as she passed, so it almost grazed her arm.

You're a heretic too, he said into her eyes.

Worse than you, she said into his.

They went down the stairs in unison. I crossed the bar floor and stood at the window, watching them loiter on the street, giggling now like children released from school, too deep in the moment to think of going anywhere. I swivelled a little catch in the window and it flew open so a breath of wind whisked into the stale, flat, silent room, and their voices came to me on the wind, both talking at once, her voice trilling a little in her excitement, his voice running under hers, like a soprano and an alto in a choir.

There's some new work being done on bacteria, she was saying, that could explain how evolution seemed to take a huge leap.

Lynn Margulis's work? he asked. You've read about Margulis's work?

I read everything, she said.

You're on the ball. It isn't published in full yet, he said.

It was then that tears came into my eyes, for I longed more than my life was worth to be in his shoes.

Then they walked off towards the lab.

CHAPTER 21

I briefly contemplate poison

I WENT TO THE GENTS and smashed my fist against the walls.
Poison. There must be many types of poison in Stores, to which
Volta has a key. There must be slow cumulative chemical concoctions to slip into his percolated coffee, secrete in his cafe lunches,
shove up his snoring nostrils, poisons to deflesh his bones, to stop
his odd brain. Poisons to finish him.

But I had to find another way to destroy him, an honourable way.

I knew that in her apartment she'd be making love with him, and
I couldn't bear it, I couldn't bear this terrible knowledge. In every way
I'd brought this pain upon myself. There was no one to blame but
me. So I stayed at the bar, drinking with the barman until closing time
when he asked me and the two old men to leave. They clung on to
me for support with their frail hands as we stumbled down the steps
and I clung onto them for company. I walked them home to their sad
little rooms in a boarding house near the station. They didn't mind
the screech of the coal trains, the older one said gummily:

Makes us feel we could hop up on them one day, and leave it
all behind.

Even if I found a poison in Stores, I couldn't murder Gunther or he'd have a martyr's death, and she'd mourn him forever. I must wait, must wait, must wait. That's what my steps ringing out on the pavement told me. I walked till one in the morning, because if I heard him making love to her, I'd rip down the walls and kill him.

When I eventually went home, there was no sound from next door. I made myself shower and clean my teeth. I put on my most comfortable pyjamas. I even made a cup of hot milk and honey, stirring it slowly, and pretended to myself I was interested in the radio for five minutes, turned down low.

Then I could take the suspense no longer.

I pulled a stool over to the peephole. At first I saw nothing but the moonlight on the tumble of their clothes over the chair.

I imagined them in the bed, uncovered, him gnarled, big-bellied, thick-thighed, hairy. She would be beautiful, smooth, deep-breasted, beyond comparison. Her hair would festoon the pillow, her legs would be underneath his, not daring to move. He would be sleeping, she wouldn't be. Her eyelids would be fluttering. Her arm would be underneath her head. She would be breathing in time with him, breathing in the smell of him, her outbreath moving the hair on his chest. And she'd be foolish enough, my adorable one, to relish this, that the man with his heavy, important body was hers at least for a few hours. He'd resist her intensity even in his sleep, he'd turn away from her, his knee pushing against her soft tummy. She wouldn't move away from him. She would want him, however he lay, she would long for him to fill her bedroom.

Talk to me, I pleaded. But there were no murmurings. Perhaps his presence was drowning her.

I must've stayed there for ten minutes, staring at the moonlight on their clothes. I began to notice that they hadn't fallen randomly. I saw that even in their impatience, his impatience at least, she'd given thought to the arrangement of her underwear on the chair. After all, it was decorated with what I could tell was Brussels lace (and as my mother would have said, Brussels lace isn't worth wasting). She would have liked him to notice. She would have wanted him to see the twining lace on the bra cups, she would have wanted him to imagine his hands holding the sweet burden of her breasts not only for an evening, but a lifetime. He wouldn't have noticed her Brussels lace, I was sure. He scarcely noticed who she was.

Just then, as if she'd sensed my thoughts, there was a creaking of the bed. She must have withdrawn her feet so that they tipped over the cold edge of the mattress, and she slung her long legs down to the floor.

What's going on, Eva? he asked in his sleep. His mouth would've smelt of sleep, but he'd called her name.

Sleep on, she said, her voice deep with delight. Because he'd murmured her name, she probably believed that her delicate hands held his heart.

When the room was filled again with his snores – his snores were unfurling through both our apartments and perhaps down the entire sleeping street – she padded across the room and I glimpsed her beautiful naked shape near their clothes, considering them. I had to look away. I couldn't bear it. It was like looking into the face of God.

But then I allowed myself to look again – how could I not? His clothes were flung into shapes like strange khaki birds that could not take flight. I imagined she was thinking that it was something they could talk about if he woke, those shapes, like children lying on a hill of grass might talk about the shapes of clouds. If they could laugh about whether his singlet looked like a dog or a bent old man or a bird, it might give them both the feeling that they'd touched each other's souls. But his underpants on the floor were slumped, huddled, disappointed. She wouldn't have expected his underpants to crouch. So she scooped up his clothes and laid them on top of hers, and on top of them all she laid her bra, her Brussels lace.

I am a honourable man, though in love, so I got down from my stool. My foot slipped in protest as I landed on the floor.

Who's that? I heard her call.

I stayed stock still, and only five minutes later did I creep into my own cold bed, and lying there was like taming a wild animal that was scarcely me. I reasoned it out like an equation in mathematics: the peephole was not to see her naked body, but to understand how to love her.

I lay tossing and turning, unable to stop the image in my mind of her padding back to bed through the white streetlight, startlingly naked. Some people, unclothed, are more naked than others, as if nakedness is a comparative state. My mother getting out of a bath never seemed particularly naked, her good-natured, amiable breasts wriggling as she clutched at doorways and rummaged in drawers, her thighs dimpling, her skin like a sausage casing stretched around her vital organs. The only other naked women I'd seen were the reclining nudes that the great masters painted, and they weren't startling like Eva – they were clothed by the artists' explorations of beauty. Whereas Eva's intense nakedness made me long for her with every cell of my body.

I kept thinking of how in that fleeting glance I'd allowed myself she seemed sad.

Tell me what's wrong, I whispered to her.

Then I heard her murmur, one of the few times ever a murmur has come when bidden:

'You could never become a model. In the great fashion houses of Paree, they'd never stop laughing at you.'

There was a pause, and then her murmur added:

'I have one daughter only, and she looks like a fish.'

If I'd been Gunther, her thoughts would have woken me. But they didn't wake him. And she didn't know me, I was nothing to her, though she was everything to me. And it was too late.

To stop thought, there was only one thing to do – read. I happened upon *The Complete World Angler* and read for three hours. It was the only book my father ever bought, and it bored me to sleep.

I woke to a fierce elation, the way that sometimes, in the darkest moments, the mind finds its own aberrant path into joy.

I could think of nothing but her that day. Rutherford was waiting for me and demanded that I help him hose out every garbage bin. Then he insisted we check on a new sort of gasket that had been installed in all the troublesome cisterns.

You're not with us today, said Rutherford. Some sheila on your mind?

He thought he'd made a very funny joke.

It was dark by the time I got home. I unlocked my door quietly and peered into her room. Their clothes were again flung down in disarray, his shoes pigeon-toed, one of hers on its side. I imagined them covered by a light sheet, Gunther asleep, Eva facing him, her left shoulder a golden oval, her face close to his, examining every pore and wrinkle and sag. He'd sag a lot, especially his face crushed against a pillow. He was far, far too old for her.

The room was still untidy but during the day she'd bought and hung new yellow linen curtains, with clumps of threads that mottled the white streetlight. She hadn't ironed the curtains but pulled them straight out of the box, so they fell unevenly, stiff and furrowed with creases.

Darling, she suddenly said. It was her speaking voice, not her murmuring one.

I imagined Gunther jerking his head backwards with a noisy snore that became a whimper.

Jesus Christ, he yelled. He leaped out of bed and passed right under my spy-hole, pale, thin-legged and large-stomached. (I made a mental note to exercise mine into flatness.) And she'd been right, his buttocks were definitely defeated.

Where's the bathroom? he shouted sleepily, opening a wardrobe door, then another, then the bathroom door slammed shut behind him.

He turned the water on with a cry of the taps. (I made a mental note to change her washers.) He'd come out any moment wrapped in a towel. She must have gone to the stove and lit the gas, and got cups out of the box she'd brought from her mother's, and the unopened packet of Billy Tea I'd glimpsed on her chair. There are always kettles to be filled, tea to be made, to weld one moment onto another. I remembered I'd learned that with my mother. We drank many cups of pale tea after difficult conversations, sometimes instead of them. We drank a lot of tea over the Facts of Life. I felt a little puff of pride that I already knew how to do this, how to smooth over the jagged edges. Surely I was well on my way to being Eva's ideal lover.

He was still showering, the kettle was whistling. There was a crash outside. She moved under my peephole to the window. She was dressed in a mauve petticoat slightly uneven at its hem, caught up on one hip. I looked out the window too. A neighbour in a crumpled dressing gown was dragging out her garbage, heaving it across the cement yard. Eva's body was bowed in sympathy.

Gunther must have come out of the bathroom at that moment.

I won't have time for tea, he said. I imagined him framed by the bathroom doorway, totally naked, pink and moist and large. Somewhere, from one of the apartments, a child screamed, like my heart.

Why? she asked. Your father can manage.

He said nothing.

I don't know how you feel about me, she said.

Against the streetlight, she was only a spindly girl after all. Even her voice didn't seem to belong to her, it seemed to bounce off the shine of the floor.

Isn't it clear? he asked. After what we did?

There was no intimacy, she said.

Intimacy? None?

He must have been towelling himself dry.

I would have liked to talk, she said.

About interesting organisms? he asked. Or is that stage over now? You probably want to compare –

he paused

– our childhoods.

He spat it out with unexpected vehemence.

Childhoods? she asked, puzzled.

Women usually do, he said.

No, she said.

Aren't you going to ask me about mine?

There was a strange, high note in his voice.

No, she said.

He came over to his clothes on the window chair. He walked so confidently to find his shirt, his trousers.

We are equals in this – I could see him gesturing towards the space in the room, and then the bed.

She moved, unaware that the petticoat was almost transparent and made her look vulnerable, of no consequence.

He shot one of his quick looks at her.

Aren't we? Equals?

Do you know how I feel about you? she asked sadly.

He waited until he'd buttoned up his shirt, all the buttons.

That you like me enough to do it with me again? he asked.

Then we're not equals, she said.

He pulled his trousers up over his belly. It was as good as a shrug.

But as he was about to leave, he relented. By now she must have been sitting on the large bed, marooned, but her body enigmatic.

We haven't even kissed properly yet, she said. We're doing it all in the wrong order.

There was silence, then, amongst the tumbled bedclothes.

Does that fit with your dream of romance? he said, afterwards. It'll be easier when we know each other. You find it difficult too.

What? she asked.

Being with someone, he said. I'm not good at finding my feelings. It doesn't mean I have none. It's just where they are, that's the problem. And I'm scared of you.

Scared? Why? she asked.

You might winkle out my secrets, he said.

Secrets? What secrets? I thought.

We'll talk more, he said awkwardly, and the night swallowed him.

Her room was silent. I imagined her in bed in the mauve petticoat, her arms lying bare on the sheet, the way a child sleeps, but she wouldn't be sleeping, she would be staring wide-eyed out the window at the planet's slow turning. Suddenly I heard her sit up. Then she began to laugh, ripples of giggles, a child again, rolling around the bed in a tumble of mirth until her room and mine were full of giggles. Then she subsided and fell into a troubled sleep.

I listened to her for a long time. Even to listen to her sleep, to imagine the tiny puff of air out her nostrils, her arm thrown back on the pillow like a ballet dancer, the curve of her hip under the sheets, it was enchanting. I was so in love with her, then. When I went to my own narrow bed, I found her murmur on my pillow.

'We do this act of taking off our clothes, which from babyhood we were instructed to do only with familiars, we press ourselves hard against each other as if we wanted to pass through each other, and yet with him there seems no intimacy at all.'

In the morning, I was in that mist of waking when I remember with a bright glow that something good has happened, but it's lost in dreams, and I'm fearful to go searching in case the reality is only a memory of a ray of sunshine, or someone's sudden smile, or light glancing off a murky river. Then I heard the clink of hangers in her wardrobe, and she came over in her mauve petticoat and picked up one of her mother's dresses slumped in a pile near the window. In the filtered yellow light through her new curtains, her mother's dresses shone like foil.

I wanted her to murmur to me then, but there was no sound, only more clanking of hangers against the inside of the wardrobe.

So I had to learn patience, to wait on the movements of some-one else's mind.

When she went to the lab I let myself into her apartment, to change the washer, I said to myself. When I entered the room, I almost ran away. She was one of those people who fill the rooms they live in, so that when they leave, the spaces seem brooding, waiting for their return. Everywhere was her smell of flowers and sunshine and peppermints, even on the chilly air that blew through the open window billowing the new yellow curtains. I found on the floor their little price tag. It must've been what she'd found and giggled at, relieved that it hadn't stuck to him.

I come from Paradise, the tag said. It was meant to say Paradise Furnishings but someone had obliterated Furnishings by stamping over the price, twenty-five dollars. I carried the little tag into my apartment, where it still is. Here. Straight out of Paradise.

———

Sick at heart with jealousy, I stayed home. She had gone early to the lab, running up the street to the bus. I don't know why she'd abandoned her bicycle. She'd made her bed neatly, so I suspected he would come home with her that night.

I was angry all morning. I hated being her benefactor if she was going to keep bringing him home. But then I remembered: if I wasn't her benefactor, I had no place in her life.

Then suddenly, at lunchtime, just when I was about to go to work, they burst in and made love feverishly against my wall, for there was much bumping, and something crashed, perhaps a little table I'd placed there, and he was whimpering to her:

I can't bear needing you, you know I can't bear it.

She was whimpering back. They were like two feverish, sad animals. It was me who couldn't bear it, this life I had created for myself. I ran a bath to hide the sounds in the gush of water and the scream of my taps. (My washers needed changing too.) By the time I'd towelled myself dry, he was telling her to go back to the lab by bus, he didn't want her to arrive on her bike because that was more noticeable. She was to enter the building via the hospital and come down the corridor. He was such a particular person, he'd read the timetable. You'll have to catch the one-ten bus. But be quick about it, because there isn't another until one fifty. Then it's two thirty-five, but don't get the two thirty-five because it's an express. It doesn't stop until it gets past the mountains. Have you got small change?

Did you memorise those times just for me? she asked.

He didn't answer her. I could've. He'd have glanced at the timetable somewhere and it had stayed in his memory, the way he'd read a phone book at Lotti's and recited it. I would've liked to remind her – but of course I couldn't.

He was at her chair near the window, opening her wallet to check for change. He was extraordinarily gentle with her about details, like a mother. She submitted to all this as she'd done to his love-making.

Just as he was going to the door, she burst out:

I'm as discreet as anyone would be. That Shirley –

So she'd been confiding in Shirley and Shirley had gossiped!

He shouted back at her:

They're finding every reason they can to thwart me. If you let something slip again, I'll lose all hope!

Then he ran down the stairs and strode across the car park while she watched from the window. I knew she was willing him to turn and wave, but he didn't wave. He was one of those people with a stiff, accusatory back.

She threw open the windows and made a pot of tea and sat down on her chair with a little square white cardboard box. Inside were two jam pastries she'd carried home from the cake shop especially for this moment, except that she'd probably hoped they'd eat them together. She poured the tea and her hand hovered over the pastries, choosing. I watched her say eeny-meeny-miney-mo, just like a child. She chose one carefully. Then she changed her mind and devoured them both. Afterwards, she picked up every crumb on a moistened finger. And then she buried her head in her hands and sobbed.

She missed the one-fifty bus because she was murmuring to me.

'What I want to know is what he sees in me, the story of the life a renowned scientist like him would imagine for me. There must be a story for me and I don't know it, but he might. A story that my mother never knew.'

He doesn't imagine your life at all, I murmured back.

But I don't think she heard.

I made myself go to work every day, so I couldn't listen to the sadness of her love. It seemed that she'd learned sadness from her childhood, and she'd always be sad until something shifted, I didn't know what. At that moment, she'd find me.

Every night I stayed at the hospital as long as I could until Matron sent me home. Then I'd go to the Roo Bar and drink with the barman and the old men. By the time I'd come home, Gunther would've left.

One evening they came back just after I had arrived. They'd

been to see an old musical, *Guys and Dolls*. He hated serious films. They blundered into her apartment, a little drunk, already talking.

I was lonely in my childhood, she was telling him.

She must've been easing herself out of her shoes because I heard them fall as she flopped on the bed.

Sorry, I mentioned a bad word, I heard her say.

Leave your beads on, he said.

She must've been wearing the red beads.

Childhood, I mean. I mentioned childhood, she said.

So I knew she was already exasperated with him and trying to pique him. He ignored this.

Did you notice the nightclub singer's song? he asked.

What song? she asked lazily.

The blonde who wanted to be married? he asked.

What nightclub singer? she repeated.

You know, in the beginning, the one who wanted to get married, he said. The words of her song came right out of Franz Alexander's book, *Psychosomatic Medicine*. Franz Alexander, he repeated, as if the name should mean something to her.

My countryman, but not my soul mate, he continued. Alexander listed personality problems and the diseases you'll get from them. So if you have infantile dependency, you'll get gastric hypersecretion. Problems with your father give you gallstones.

She laughed, to agree with him.

You must've noticed the words.

And he sang, in a strange, tuneless drawl, a lament that just waiting for a marriage proposal could give a woman a cold.

His singing was appalling! He couldn't keep a tune, and he had no singing voice at all!

I was sure I could hear Eva giggling at his tunelessness.

She got a cold from waiting for him? Was she waiting in a draught? asked Eva.

The point is, said Gunther, slightly testy – the song says she'll get a cold from being unhappy.

And she wouldn't? asked Eva, missing the point, to my delight.

He groaned.

Once it's in musicals, everyone thinks it's true. It's popular culture! What chance has a biologist?

It's just a song, she said mildly.

It's what everyone thinks in this country, he cried. That everything, a cold included, is in the mind! A cold is caused by what goes on in the mind. We don't have bodies any more. We only have minds. Every problem can be explained, and with enough talk it can be solved. This person is manic? He was taken off his potty too young. This man's bronchioles are going into spasm? It's his repressed desire for his mother. Popular culture says that we're not prisoners in genetic handcuffs after all.

But that's positive – it means we can all be saved, she said reasonably.

Saved? he shouted. We're stuck. I'm stuck. That's the whole problem.

There was a pause, and a creaking.

Go on, I murmured to her. Say, What do you mean by stuck? How are you stuck?

But she didn't hear my murmur.

He told her then that Freud's theories gained hold when organic cures were terrible. Insane people used to be whirled till their ears bled, or they were castrated, or given high doses of oxygen or carbon dioxide, horse injections, icepicks through the eye socket to the brain in order to destroy the brain's pre-frontal lobes, or electricity to shock the brain into submission – that's still going on, he said. Not to mention lobotomies. Moniz got a Nobel for that one, as Sandy reminded me, he added.

There was a pause.

The brain is proving to be so complex, he said, that it's easier to say the way people behave is their choice. Or it's caused by their life problems.

I didn't think she'd been listening.

But McConnell showed different behaviours are inheritable, she said suddenly. You know, the worm man.

A fool, murmured Gunther absently. It's hard enough without fools.

Gunther always became impatient when she talked. It meant that he had to listen to her, rather than to himself. So she fell silent.

Why don't you want to talk about childhood? was all she said.

I knew she'd been trying to pique him. She was already tiring of him. I heard the bed squeak more, so he would be lying beside her, stroking her, because how could he not?

Take off your shoes, she said.

I'll be leaving soon, he said. I'll keep them away from the cover.

I could see his feet jutting off the bed.

They lay in silence. She was tense, I guessed, at the thought of him going.

I love your beads, he said. You wear jewellery like my mother's.

Your mother! she exclaimed. What was your mother like?

He sighed.

Beautiful. Clever. But she's dead now, he said.

And what was your father like when he was young? she asked.

Aha! The vital question! Did she suspect his father like I did?

I can't remember, was all Gunther said.

There was an edge to his voice, so she didn't question him further. But he wanted to talk, and perhaps she sensed this.

The mother –

he said, suddenly sounding as if he was quoting, his voice oddly singsong

– was a very bright and extremely nice woman whose life was not easy. She complained of nervousness and headaches. She was also very sensitive. She found it hard to cope with the fact that her son, who was obviously her one and only interest in life, was such an odd child and did so badly at school.

Why are you speaking like that? asked Eva, sounding a little frightened. Are you repeating something well known? Who's the boy?

But he ignored her.

She constantly took his side against the school and fought desperately against transfer into a special school for retarded children, he went on.

The bed creaked as Eva sat up.

What's that from? she demanded again.

Something a doctor wrote about odd people, he said.

Clever people are often a little odd, she said, struggling to be gentle and reassuring, trying to hold on to the softness they'd been in.

He sighed again, and lay back, creaking the bed again.

I don't like to be touched, he said, a little crankily. It's making me edgy.

So I touch you the wrong way? Do other women do it the right way? she asked, petulant now, unsure of him, unsure of herself.

I hate it, he said.

You don't like making love? she asked.

That's different from being touched, he said.

There was a terrible silence between them.

What women? What other women? he demanded bitterly.

Lotti! she cried. Does Lotti touch you the right way?

Who's Lotti? he asked.

She was drawing into herself, away from him.

I'm trapped, he suddenly cried out. They keep saying, After you win the Prize next time, after you win, you can do what you like then, but how can I keep going when I'm not doing what I have to do?

There was a terrible anguish in his voice.

Then, unexpectedly, he wrenched my heart.

Sometimes I think that I'll die trying to repay this debt, he said.

Will you tell me what the debt is? she asked.

He said nothing.

Soon afterwards I heard his snores. I think she would have sat up in bed. She would have been tousled, deep in thought, gazing out her window into the white fluorescing fire of the streetlights.

She woke him, and he left.

CHAPTER 22
An awful silence prevails

ONE LUNCHTIME when I saw her slip out of the lab, I couldn't help but follow her home, even though I had twenty more sacks of used bandages to burn. It was becoming a madness, my need.

I took my time. When I crept into my apartment, I knew that their love-making had finished, because he was reminding her about bus timetables again. He was a little irritated. Apparently after each of their shared lunchtimes, she'd been late back to work.

What were you doing on Friday, all that time after I'd left? he asked.

She wouldn't answer him. She'd be sitting up in bed, watching him, the sheet wrapped around her as if she felt it was impolite to be naked once he'd showered and dressed.

Then suddenly, perhaps in anger, she asked:

What went wrong in Vienna?

As soon as the words were out, she knew she shouldn't have asked it. I could see him knotting his tie near the window. He was a man who always wore a tie without any thought that it could be decorative. He wouldn't have noticed if his tie was made of fish skins. Now his head whirled around to her, his eyes bulging:

Why? What are they saying?

He plumped suddenly on the bed, a man waiting to hear terrible news.

I've heard nothing, Eva said miserably.

Who talked? he asked. Who knows?

No one talked, she said.

Did you gossip? he asked.

I don't know your secret, she said. I just meant . . .

Eva started then stopped, but made herself speak:

I just meant, you seem so troubled about those poor little children. Those autistic children.

They banned me from going into any hospital ward, he cried. The Board, the hospital Board. I'm a danger, am I? They're right, are they, to ban me?

No, no, she said.

But perhaps they were right, I wanted to call through the wall. Perhaps you are up to something!

It was my jealousy, of course.

He came back to the window, fixing his tie although it was already knotted, pulling with hard jabs at the cloth, his chin stuck out like a fighter. He got a brush out of his briefcase and pulled it through his hair reprimandingly, and straightened his jacket with silent deliberation. Then he grabbed his briefcase and banged open the door.

You're like everyone else, he said, his voice echoing up and down the stairwell.

We both listened to him striding down the stairs. As he walked across the car park, he poked his briefcase ahead of him with his thighs, a man intent only on his work.

That afternoon, she got the one-ten bus.

You must be very happy, Shirley said to her that afternoon as Eva soaped her hands at the sink.

Why? Eva asked.

Haven't you got everything you ever wanted? Shirley asked.

No, she said. Have you?

Shirley giggled.

These days, after an assignation with Sandy, she was glowing in the early morning, though it wore off, I noticed, as the day went on.

For several wretched days Gunther punished Eva by walking through the lab without glancing in her direction. She'd gasp in hope and jump up when he came in the door, and fall onto her stool as he'd turn and stamp up the stairs, head down. Every cell in her body longed to climb up the stairs with him.

'Our time together was perfect,' she murmured to me.

But she experienced it differently, I know she did. I knew it wasn't perfect, if only I could have reminded her. She might've recognised this occasionally, but I'm sure she thought this imperfection was essential to living. I could see she was sick with fear that she'd never be touched by him again. She was sure that without him there was nothing. There at her workbench, she couldn't concentrate. She turned again, impatient with her work, gazing at the big clock on the wall. She wore a watch but she needed the big official face of the clock to say, Yes, since you last looked, only eight minutes have gone by. She dragged herself through the hours, only allowing herself to look at the clock every now and then, astonished that the hands had moved on a mere eight minutes. Eight and a quarter, now, and she was turning again.

That's what was wrong with her. In those endless, terrible days she'd learned, and I learned with her, the truth that one of our great writers taught us, that there is the loved and the lover, and that she was the lover. She'd learned that it's the lover who lies to herself, the lover who has to believe that their time together was perfect, even though she'd experienced it otherwise. (I think Puig, which I read before Charlene left the brothel, so try shelves between bathroom and kitchen.)

At night I heard her moaning and crawling on her knees with the weight of the loss of him. It was appalling to hear her moans.

In the morning, I found her at the workbench with her head in her hands. Shirley came in.

Now what's wrong? asked Shirley.

Nothing, said the girl, bowing her head.

Shirley walked out of the lab, her skirt swishing behind her like a reprimand. When she returned, Eva said:

I've done it wrong. Here.

She showed Shirley her calculations. Shirley scarcely glanced across at them.

I'm not surprised, said Shirley coldly. At least you won't get sacked for it.

Eva put her head on the workbench and sobbed.

Men depend on us to do the thinking about love, she said after a while.

So you've become a know-all about men too, Shirley began, but Eva interrupted her.

If I could turn back the clock, I wouldn't bother about love, she said. I'd just think.

Lotti came in to take Shirley to lunch. Eva bent her head over her work. As they were leaving, she looked up.

Lotti, she called, in a voice that was almost a groan. Lotti pretended not to hear, but Shirley looked back.

Eva wants you, she said to Lotti.

The older woman stopped at the doorway, Shirley behind her.

What? she asked brusquely. There seemed a vast distance of floorboards between them.

Eva's face was ugly with pain, all her youth fled. She came towards Lotti, crumpled.

You know him. Tell me about him.

Lotti didn't ask who, she didn't need to.

Tell you what? Her voice was cold, harsh, unyielding.

Please, said Eva, all dignity gone. He's making enemies, he's lost heart in his work, he's going up this blind alley. Do you know why?

Give him up if it's so bad! Shirley said. Love is meant to be happy.

You ask him what's wrong! cried Lotti to Eva.

Please tell me, gasped the girl.

Lotti turned to Shirley. Let's go, she said.

Eva went closer to Lotti, almost crouching.

Lotti, please, she whispered, white-faced in her suffering. Is there a child? Does he have a child?

A child? cried Lotti. What's a child got to do with it?

Maybe there's a child of his, in a home somewhere. An autistic child . . .

A terrible thought came to her. Her mouth moved, she couldn't help herself, so deep was her anguish.

Have you ever –

Both the women were silent, watching her for what she might say next.

It came.

Does he have a child with you?

You stupid, stupid girl! cried Lotti. For a moment I thought she was going to strike Eva. Then she strode out of the lab.

Give him up, said Shirley to Eva, a little more sympathetically now. She followed Lotti.

For the next week Eva didn't come home to her apartment until late at night. One afternoon I noticed she was heading for the Sudlow library. Then, early on a quiet Monday morning when only she and Shirley were in the lab, busily preparing solutions for the day's work, Gunther came in so quietly that Shirley didn't seem to notice. But Eva began gabbling loudly.

I've been finding out about autism, she said to Shirley.

I'm concentrating, Shirley said absent-mindedly.

Eva must have been waiting for her moment to speak. Just as she would have wanted, Gunther stopped at the side table for his mail, and pretended to riffle through it. But Eva looked steadily at Shirley, as if she was only talking to her.

She told Shirley that wolf children might've been autistic children, abandoned and left to the wolves.

188 THE SECRET CURE

Autistic children? echoed Shirley, glancing up at her. What's that to do with you? If you start going on about it like he does, you'll drive us all mad!

She turned on the tap with a flourish.

But Eva took no notice and began to talk about Victor, the wolf boy of Aveyron, who was captured and considered a test of Rousseau's belief that, innately, we're noble. There was a famous dinner party, Eva was saying, with playwrights and generals in attendance, and a beautiful wealthy socialite who sat Victor beside her, thinking he'd be astonished at her beauty, as all of France was. But Victor ignored them all, gulping down his food and racing out the door to leap through the trees as if innate nobility meant nothing.

Eva didn't look up but she would've sensed that Gunther was lingering, still pretending to be absorbed in his mail. She told poor, bored Shirley that autistic children have been considered seers and prophets or the children of fairies or changelings secretly exchanged for human babies, or even aliens left in carelessly watched cribs. She began talking more loudly as Gunther gave up the mail and resumed climbing the stairs away from her. She mentioned that someone called William Bailey came up with a plan to make over what he called morons by a method of gland control. Then in 1943 a doctor, Leo Kanner – in 1943,

she repeated, because the date had made Gunther turn around on the stairs – Leo Kanner was at the height of his profession when he began to study autistic children. He noticed that their parents were aloof and excessively rational, and popularised the idea that parents caused autism, especially mothers – refrigerator mothers, he called them.

I'm going to pull rank, I'm afraid, said Shirley hotly, still unaware of Gunther.

Eva, get on with your work or they'll give you the flick!

But Eva kept talking as if she couldn't stop, about the few animal studies that had been done, but then again, she said, perhaps animal studies were useless because true autism might only affect humans. She began listing scientists who'd identified neurological lesions or abnormalities in children, but these studies had been ignored.

If he – Shirley threw her head in the direction of upstairs – catches you chattering like this, believe me, it won't matter what goes on in bed –

Gunther spoke suddenly.

You left out the Austrian, he said curtly. He began climbing the stairs.

Shirley wheeled on her heel and screamed.

Oh – sorry, Professor Mueller! You're there, you gave me such a fright. It's like seeing a ghost.

The Austrian? Eva said to Gunther, ignoring Shirley. What Austrian? I've read nothing about an Austrian.

No one has, said Gunther. That's the problem.

Eva reached into her handbag and picked something out. It was the strand of red beads.

Gunther, on the top step, turned around just as she was reaching behind her hair to put them on. She looked up at him, utterly still, her hands behind her head, her hair raised. There was so much yearning between them that Shirley said:

I might go and clean out the coffee pot.

She left.

Gunther came down the stairs.

Allow me, he said, and put the beads on her. Afterwards he stroked her over and over, her beautiful, young white throat.

Don't ever ask about my past again, he said. Because what breaks my heart is that I remember nothing.

Later, when Lotti arrived to take Shirley to lunch, Shirley said:

Who's the important Austrian in Gunther's past?

How would I know? said Lotti, in that way she had of being so fierce you suspected she was hiding something.

You don't know? persisted Shirley.

Lotti patted Shirley's elegant wrist and hushed her. Eva was just coming in carrying Petri dishes.

Later, said Lotti. That girl pushes me too far.

They slammed the door behind them.

I followed them to the cafe, though I didn't dare go near them. I walked around listening to the hubbub, the ringing of the cash register and the clatter of trays, as if what Lotti had to say had permeated the air, like the smell of bacon and fried onions. But at least I saw what Lotti regularly ordered for lunch – potato salad, coleslaw and pickles. It became very useful knowledge later, much later.

CHAPTER 23

I find a way to bear this torment

I TOOK TO GOING FOR WALKS whenever they came into her apartment. I tried to concentrate on my stride, my breath in the cold night air, the swing of my arms, the power in my legs. It was another little triumph in my exile into the world, that I became a walker. I worked out a particular circuit, as far as the bus terminus with its cigarette butts thrown on the tarmac by chattering bus drivers, out to the shadowy cemetery with its sad grey headstones under a black sky almost ringing with stars, along to the Duke of Wellington hotel with its crowd of drinkers spilling out onto the street, then I'd about turn and walk back the same way. I counted the steps. Five thousand six hundred and seventy-seven steps. Those were the steps I had to take so I wouldn't think about murdering him. Five thousand six hundred and seventy-seven steps while they made love. But afterwards their love-making would be over. If it takes only five thousand six hundred and seventy-seven steps for them to make love, then their love is only a tiny, tiny thing.

I wore stout shoes and I carried books for weights. I chose Russian novelists because they were very weighty. I got a lot of exercise. My body had been almost like a sofa, I'd lain on them so long. Now it was still fat, but it was beginning to show the odd muscle. Twice Deirdre snuggled up to me, on some pretence or other.

You're looking strong, she cooed.

Though she ran her hand across my chest, I was only aware of it afterwards. I didn't care for anyone but Eva. I never would. I was pacing for my love.

One night when I came in from my pacing, I heard him in the kitchen, his appalling, tuneless singing. The bed creaked, she must've pulled herself up to rest against the wall, momentarily at peace. I could hear the water gushing from the kitchen tap, and the clink of crockery. It came to me that he was making a pot of tea for them both. I'm sure she would have wanted to run out to the kitchen, to laugh with him as the kettle boiled, to rattle cups together, to lean over the steam, but that was what a friend would do. She was his mistress, not his friend. He didn't have friends.

He came in. I could hear cups rattling.

They have saucers, she said a little querulously. You should use their saucers. On the shelf, at the back.

Aren't they all right like this? he asked.

Of course, she said. It's audacious of you.

Audacious? he repeated.

To use beautiful cups without their saucers, she said.

He must have been cradling his cup in his hand.

It's like holding the weight of a breast, he said.

My breast? she asked.

Of course your breast, he said. Then I imagined him burying his face in the breast of the cup.

I'm too young, she said, to have these fears.

He didn't speak.

About betrayal, she added. Treachery. Anguish close to death.

Drink that tea before it gets cold, he said after a while. That was all. Drink your tea.

She obeyed him.

———

Sometimes it seemed that for Gunther she was only a piece of her mother's fabric. Its breadth and length were unsatisfactory, though the texture was passable. He wanted to cut her to shape, a little wider here, a little narrower there, longer, shorter, and nipped in. I wanted to turn and hiss to her:

Can't you see he has nothing to say about love?

But of course, I could say nothing.

Now she became convinced that if he'd stay the night with her, she'd get from him the love she wanted. She mentioned it every time they were together, although she tried not to nag, finding cunning ways to ask instead.

When do you have to be gone by? she'd say. He brought over his alarm clock, and I'd hear him set it in case they fell asleep. Yet he hated the noise of the alarm, he hated all loud noises, and to him, many noises were loud. He'd shout for her to turn it off, blaming her, it seemed, for the din.

Sometimes she'd say:

Will we forget the alarm, just this once? You hate it so much.

But he'd set it.

That's how I knew to begin on my five thousand, six hundred and seventy-seven paces. The sound of the alarm clock being set. The warning that soon after love, he'd abandon her.

She'd say:

Tomorrow night we could make love here and then go to your place. I could even cook you and your father a meal.

He never answered her.

In her distress she developed an eerie habit of sleepwalking, when she'd stumble out of bed and stand at the window, holding on to the window frame and staring into the car park until the cold night air propelled her back to fling herself on the mattress. She seemed much more lovable to me then, because she was fraily human, a little scruffy, a little untidy, a little mad. I'm not sure he would have loved her when she was like that. Not the way I did.

When people in the hospital avoided my eyes, in case they'd have to speak to me, I reminded myself that I was closer to Eva than anyone, and much closer than him. He had her body, but I possessed her soul.

CHAPTER 24

Sandy uses my love as a bait for my rival

FOR SIX MONTHS I WAITED AND WALKED, and tried to keep hoping. Then life changed its course, as life sometimes does of its own accord, without any pushing and pulling from me.

Sandy was officially promoted above Gunther. When Mark was alone with the other men, he said that by rights the honour should have gone to Gunther but Gunther had become an embarrassment, the way he was always talking about subjects better left to the doctors. Sandy, on the other hand, was the natural team leader. He *intuitively* – Mark's face seemed more chiselled and handsome as he stressed the word – made decisions that pleased his powerful friend Doris as well as the hospital Board, and stepped on no important toes.

No one mentioned that Sandy sometimes stepped on Gunther's toes, so perhaps Gunther's toes didn't matter.

Mark added that Sandy's little molecule might turn out to be just what the lab needed – though, Mark said, it was a shame he kept it so hush-hush. He wished Sandy was more open about his research.

The others nodded but said nothing, because Sandy for all his friendliness became grim-faced and monosyllabic when anyone questioned him about the cancer research.

In all my eavesdropping, Gunther never spoke to Eva about Sandy's promotion above him. I don't think he even noticed it.

Not long after, Shirley gave Eva a letter.

It looks official, Shirley said. Eva turned it over and over.

Should I open it now? she asked, holding it excitedly. She was still a little girl in many ways.

Of course, said Shirley, and waited, peering over Eva's shoulder.

It turned out to be an offer of a job in another city.

But I didn't apply, said Eva, bewildered.

Shirley took the letter and examined the address.

It's from the lab where Tony went, Shirley said. Don't you remember?

Tony! cried Eva, and looked embarrassed.

He liked you, didn't he? said Shirley. I heard that you and he kissed one afternoon –

Who told you? demanded Eva.

Around here, the walls have eyes, said Shirley evasively, so my heart hammered for fear the eyes might notice me.

But if she'd noticed one of my eyes, surely she'd have looked straight into the lens.

The muscles on Eva's face were moving.

I didn't mean to kiss Tony, she said. It was an accident.

The letter was an invitation to be a lab manager.

Shirley was disconcerted at this compliment to her junior, but she was generous enough to enthuse.

It'd be so good for your career, said Shirley. She came over to hug Eva.

I'm really thrilled for you.

Eva looked up from the letter.

It would be, wouldn't it? I'd get away from everything, she said. I'd get away from him, she added.

Shirley put down her work and solicitously began cleaning out her percolator, to make them an unscheduled cup of coffee.

This love affair is just making you unhappy, she said as they sipped. It's no criticism of Gunther. Who could criticise him? He needs a different sort of woman, someone . . . she paused . . .

Someone more mature.

I'm growing up as fast as I can, said Eva.

But when they were draining their cups, she had another doubt.

Would I do much science, as a lab manager?

It would be hard to do less than you do now, said Shirley.

Eva went back to her work, then returned to Shirley.

You won't tell Sandy I'm considering this?

Of course not, said Shirley.

Eva was very quiet in her apartment that evening, so I stayed in mine, silently reading next to her, not even interrupting her with the TV news, so she'd think how pleasant her life was, living next door to me. I wanted her just where she was, but without him.

The next day, Shirley was very subdued.

Eva came in, her face flushed, too excited to notice the way Shirley stared fixedly at her work.

I thought about it all evening and I've made up my mind. I'm going to get back my freedom, Eva said exultantly. They gave me ten days to consider it, but I'm going to write back today. Yes, I'm going to say. Yes.

I wouldn't if I was you, said Shirley.

You think I should play hard to get? Eva asked. Make them wait out the ten days?

I thought about it all evening too, said Shirley in a quieter voice than I'd ever heard her use. And I think you shouldn't take it.

But yesterday you said – began Eva.

Your chances here are very good, said Shirley dully.

Chances of what? cried Eva.

You're considered very reliable, said Shirley in the same funereal tone. People respect you. And do you want to break the heart of a great man who needs you?

But what about my needs? cried Eva.
You're honour bound, said Shirley.
Honour? cried Eva.
They've trained you, they've overlooked your mistakes –
What mistakes? demanded Eva.
Little errors, but nevertheless . . . Shirley wound down.
You must stay here, she hissed.

Within a fortnight the hospital Board had offered Eva a new job, the job of lab manager, despite her lack of formal qualifications. She would be given a higher salary, an office and, it was promised, great responsibility.

Two job offers in a fortnight, breathed Shirley. And for the same position. What a coincidence!

Did you tell Sandy about the job offer from Tony's lab? Eva asked Shirley. Is that the reason behind this?

Of course not, said Shirley, reddening slightly but hiding it with a toss of her golden hair.

Then she almost covered her face in her protective cap, and she was unusually busy all day. Too busy to talk.

I kept hearing about Eva's promotion as I eavesdropped. She's an intelligent girl, the men scientists would say when Eva was in the coldroom. But don't qualifications matter anymore?

In her apartment that night I heard her say to Gunther as he dressed (I'd just come in from my walk and I was trying to hear them above my panting):

Why did Sandy offer it to me?

I don't know the way these things work, said Gunther. Aren't you delighted?

Yes, she said dutifully.

Sandy mentioned it to me, said Gunther. He thought it would help you to settle down. We'd all like you to settle down.

She didn't hang out the window to watch him walk across the car park. She stayed in bed, leaning back against the wall as if she was in a prison.

The next night she told Gunther she'd been to see her mother to report her success.

They've made you the real scientist then, her mother had said. Not that you could be a model like me. At least you are important now. It is what you really wanted all along, no? To be important?

Perhaps, she told Gunther, it was what my mother had always wanted. That's why she was always saying that she'd been a model in Paris. To make herself important.

And you don't want to be important? Gunther asked.

I just want to talk about interesting organisms, she said.

Wait a minute, I longed to shout at him. Did you notice what she said about her mother? Did that mean her mother hadn't been a model?

But he hadn't noticed. Hadn't observed. Though he was a scientist, he didn't observe nearly as much as me.

Eva's new job was exacting and tiring but at least she didn't change labs, so I could still see her. A little cubicle was built for her, sadly not by me. No one thought to ask me.

In her new job no detail was allowed to escape her attention. She learned about all the equipment, every screw, every flask, every batch of cells, every order, every issue, and there were issues no one had ever considered before, such as where the new photocopier should be (in Gunther's office, Sandy insisted) and where the tea urn should be (where Gunther's table for his letters used to be).

She organised stores and transport and she made starter cultures and plated *E. coli* for Gunther's students from distant universities, and she kept track of the petty cash.

She became, as her mother had said, very important.

After a month, Sandy brought in champagne.

The best lab manager we could've had, he told the scientists. Even better than me.

Everyone said that was impossible, but that she was doing very well.

Mark added quietly:

Considering where she came from.

(How I hated his handsome face.)

They will break her, Sandy with his schemes and Gunther with his obsession. And how am I to rescue her?

CHAPTER 25

During which my rival becomes an object of general suspicion

THEIR BRAINS ARE UNDERDEVELOPED in some way, Gunther was saying one night as I came back from my walk.

I was startled and climbed to my peephole. He came into view, his towel just falling off him, telling Eva that somebody had done autopsies overseas, just like he'd wanted to do, on four people who'd been killed simultaneously in an accident. Apparently they all had autistic-like symptoms. But Gunther had no faith in the autopsy reports. The researcher didn't get the full picture of their lives from the relatives, he didn't question how the abnormalities developed, when the autism had been first observed by the families, or how autistic they really were. For all the researcher knew, they might have had some illness that just looked like autism.

What stupidity! What a waste! he finished. Why couldn't I have had a chance at it?

Were they related, these people? Eva asked.

There was a mother and son, and her brother and his child, her nephew, he said.

What abnormalities did the autopsies show? she asked.

There was a long pause.

None, he said. But that proves nothing.

Perhaps in autism the brain mechanism that links memory and sensation are impaired, he said.

She was struggling to follow his thinking.

Would you be able to see an impairment in an autopsy? Surely if it was obvious, it would have been noticed, she said.

He was drying his legs after his shower.

Not if he wasn't looking out for it, he said. You of all people should remember your Heisenberg. You quoted him once. 'We have to remember that what we observe is not nature itself, but nature exposed to our method of questioning.'

It would be an inherited brain underdevelopment, he went on. That's why Billy's parents seemed almost as aloof as Billy. Hugh talked about a gene for neurosis, and of course that's absurd.

He laughed to himself.

But a brain *structure* – an odd neuronal inherited structure.

He was dressing, not looking at what he was doing. Then he stood up straight.

Now if I could find that, it would be worthy of his death.

Whose death? she asked.

He was putting his wallet in his pocket. His eyes came back to her from a long way off.

Billy's death? she asked.

What are you talking about? he asked.

She changed tack.

We always think, Well, if someone's brain isn't like ours, they must be retarded, she said.

I'm not saying that! he cried. I'd be the last to say that. Can't you understand who I am?

Has anyone suggested that autistic children mightn't have undeveloped brains, but ones that have developed too fast? she asked.

I heard him open the door.

Whose death were you talking about? she asked again.

He slammed it and ran down the stairs.

She was going to overtake him, I thought, at least in this matter of hunches, which scientists seem to respect in an apologetic, covert sort of way. As they should. Hunches belonged to my sort of world – and Eva's.

The pupil is going to overtake the teacher.

As if to prove me right, one night when I came in late on their conversation, she was saying:

At least McConnell realised that the brain extracts he fed to untrained worms must've had a particular amino acid sequence.

McConnell? I remembered that name – Planarian worms! – the Planarian worm man she'd told Shirley she wanted to date.

McConnell realised that it would have been the molecular code to do with their memory that was transferred, she was saying. Ungar believed that they'd found a peptide, an inheritable peptide, passed on from the trained worms to the untrained worms. He thought it was responsible for them knowing to react to light.

There was silence.

I know Sandy would laugh, and as for Hugh . . . she petered out.

I'd better go home, was his reply at last.

She was too excited to stop talking.

McConnell believed that phobias might be molecularly encoded, she said.

There was a longer silence.

Do you think – she began.

We don't want to cling on to the work of a fool just because it's convenient, said Gunther.

I heard the springs in the mattress squeak.

If there was some way . . . she hesitated. It might be that DNA is not only inherited but can pop in from outside –

Pop in? he repeated.

Introduced, she corrected. Sorry, introduced. And make the gene mutate.

Pop in? Where did you get the idea that DNA can pop in? he said.

Barbara McClintock thought that genes can jump, she said.

But *pop in*? Darwin never hinted at that. That's Lamarckian, he argued.

She ignored him, as if he was just a mosquito buzzing, as he'd often ignored her.

– and when they jump into different places, they have different effects, she said.

That's not *popping in*, he said.

It might be, she said. So it might be possible to look at the DNA of a person with autism and compare it to the DNA of a person without autism, as a control, then . . .

She trailed off.

No, no, he said, bothering to follow her train of thought at last. For a start, if you did that, how would you know that the DNA of the control person is normal, standard DNA? That's the problem that's always dogged zoology – surely you know that? You should do some proper study. All this wild, random reading you do!

But we accept a standard skeleton, she said. Somehow, despite everybody's structure being different, we've got a standard skeleton.

He laughed mockingly.

Whose DNA will be the standard? Yours?

If the brain is as complicated as you say, there might be no standard way that people organise their memories, she said. Maybe we can't even talk about an odd brain. Maybe my memory, for instance, stores differently from Shirley's, and Shirley's stores differently from Sandy's and – what if it's worse? What if Sandy's memory stores things differently in the morning than in the afternoon and differently on Sundays than it does on Mondays? Maybe there's no ideal brain.

I heard him groan.

Is this why you sleep with me? he asked. To have someone to talk this rubbish to?

Because I love you, she said, almost absent-mindedly.

A lot of science is foolish, she began again. Until someone shows it isn't. If autism is a genetic disease in which someone is missing a gene or has a defective gene, you might be able to isolate a normal gene and grow lots of it, then work out the tissue where it's needed, work out what mechanisms go into the making of the gene, and maybe you could supply those too and then figure out how to deliver the gene to the defective cell – are you listening to me? Or maybe you could chemically change the environment so . . . What's wrong?

He was dressing now, in protest. He was right under my peephole. His body was getting bulkier while mine was getting more muscular with all my walking. I had been trying not to notice his penis, but now I couldn't help noticing that it was, shall I say, less than I expected, and much less prepossessing than the penis in *Broome's Anatomy*, even allowing for scale.

I have a note here:

'florid, crisscrossed with lots of raised, purply veins'.

Now he was pulling clothes over his flabby middle-aged belly. All he said was:

Sandy's coming around to my point of view. He knows I'm in the grip of a hunch.

Did you hear anything I said? she asked.

He's always nice to me, said Gunther.

He's nice to everyone, said Eva.

This is what being a scientist is, to be in the grip of a hunch, Gunther said.

So he was allowed to have hunches, and she wasn't – because she wasn't a scientist. I was beginning to understand his way of thinking.

Not a word went in, she was saying resentfully. All my thinking aloud, and not a word went in.

If a scientist has a hunch and he's right, he's a visionary, a brilliant loner. If he's wrong, he's just a maverick, a shabby loser, Gunther said.

There was a long pause and, though I strained and peered this way and that, I couldn't see what they were doing. Then he stood up to go, still displeased with her, I could tell, by the angry way he jangled the change in his pocket. I watched him stalk underneath my peephole with his briefcase.

Anything wrong? she asked, temporarily defeated.

No, he said.

He was going out the door when I heard him say:

I don't know why I come here. You don't listen to me, and you talk pure science fiction!

It's going to be possible, one day, she was shouting after him even when he'd slammed her door. She sat on the chair where I could see her in her mauve petticoat, staring not out the window but at the blank oblong of door he'd just walked out.

When she heard him reach the car park, she jumped up and yanked at her heavy window. She leaned out and yelled into the sleeping night:

One day I'll move DNA from one species to another, I'll make some amazing organisms and one day I'll be able –

he was now pulling open his car door –

to swap . . . she paused, corrected herself,

to exchange, that's it, not swap, to exchange DNA between flowers and animals, so animals grow petals and flowers grow ears, and . . .

But her words were drowned under the revving of his engine, while all around apartment lights flashed on and heads appeared.

She ignored them.

One day I'll put a firefly gene into a wattle flower so the wattle lights up! she shouted. Then you'll see I'm right, and you're wrong!*

Without a wave, he drove off.

I was learning that when he shouted at her, it didn't stop her loving him. In fact she became almost proud that she could absorb his anger into herself, as if his anger was a confiding. She became more fleshy, like a lily.

A year passed. Eva busily managed the lab, and she still wasn't allowed to do any science. Gunther still visited her, though not

---

* Shirley tells me that shortly after this, in 1986, a firefly gene was inserted in a tobacco leaf. Eva's actual prediction came true in 2002 in a London flower exhibition, well after this memoir was written. But of course you'd know that. – T.

every night. He seemed more and more depressed. Often I didn't have to go out walking because I could tell from the snores that he'd just fallen asleep on the bed, fully clothed. Sometimes she'd drive him home in his car. I imagined him grunting goodbye, kissing her hair or eyebrows or anything that collided with a brush of his lips. She'd sneak her bike out of the back of the car without his neighbours hearing, put his car keys in his pocket, and as he stumbled down his path, she'd pedal home. She still loved him. She wasn't ready to give up on him. She was trying to believe that what she had of him was enough.

Now that Sandy was the lab head, he was diverting the scientists from Gunther's immunology work to learn and practise new techniques of genetic engineering. He talked about isolating particular genes and trying to understand them. For a scientist, understanding genes wasn't like understanding love. With all the talk of switches and pulleys on the gene, it seemed more like understanding a Ford assembly plant. I learned that gene molecules are arranged in sequences which the scientists hoped to decode. Looking back, I wonder now how much of the lab's research was really aimed at helping Sandy work on his cancer molecule. But no one seemed suspicious and the Board trusted Sandy entirely. Everyone was swept up in the excitement that this lab in unknown Sudlow was part of a surge of international discovery.

Eva suggested weekly meetings to Sandy.

News is coming in so fast that we should keep everyone up to date, she said.

Sandy rubbed his chin.

There's enough slacking around. We wouldn't want time wasted.

He alone resented the world for its annoying habit of making new discoveries when Sudlow still hadn't. He must've felt that if he didn't acknowledge them, they wouldn't be so important. But he called the lab to attention a few days later.

I've just decided we need weekly meetings, he said. News is coming in so fast. We must all keep up.

They had the meetings just near my spy-hole. Everyone was

required to come, even Hugh, who sat up the back half asleep. Sometimes he snored loudly, or at least pretended to, and he never stayed for long, but Sandy saw it as a triumph of his leadership to have Hugh there, though snoring.

No one asked me to attend, of course, but I tried to juggle my jobs so I could write everything down, to talk it over with her one day.

Soon the news came that an overseas lab had discovered that some DNA sequences had nothing useful on them at all. They were just junk, it was said. Hugh made a show of waking himself up, to protest that the economy of Darwin's evolution wouldn't allow junk DNA of no use to the organism. So quite clearly all of the new science was a vast and expensive mistake. Then he stalked out while everyone acted as if they hadn't heard him.

At another meeting Gunther told them that foreign DNA had been integrated into plant cells. This seemed to mean that cells weren't just reliant on what they'd inherited.

Who'd believe that? Sandy asked. He didn't like Gunther to know something first, and so he was quick to scoff. Everyone agreed that perhaps a mistake had been made, except Eva.

Get yourself more in the picture and do some proper study, said Sandy to Eva.

I never stop, she said.

Proper study, repeated Sandy.

He always had to have the last word.

But the meeting I remember most was when Gunther told them that mouse embryos injected with foreign DNA had integrated it into their cells. Gunther was almost chatty in his excitement. Apparently the embryos had been implanted into surrogates who'd given birth to mice with the foreign DNA.

Just like I predicted, cried Eva.

Gunther paused, mid-sentence.

You did?

Why, she said, aware of everyone's eyes on her, I predicted that soon we'd be able to move DNA across from one species to another.

That's no prediction really, said Sandy easily. Hybridisation has been going on for millennia.

I mean across mating boundaries, said Eva.

You couldn't have predicted that, Sandy said, laughing.

She bravely turned to Gunther and continued:

You remember – you said that what I'd said was science fiction. I'd said that one day I'd be able to put fireflies in wattle, and you took no notice of me and drove off.

The shape of their bed was suddenly huge in the lab, like a noisy, clanking ghost. It took up as much room in the lab as it did in her apartment, as much room as it did in their minds. Mark and Jim giggled. Eva knew she'd gone too far to stop.

It shows that the idea of unique organisms will become old-fashioned, she said.

Hugh stalked out of the meeting again muttering, but Gunther spoke as if he'd noticed nothing personal in what she'd said.

This method, injecting embryos with DNA and then implanting them in surrogates, is very interesting, especially if it could be applied to diagnose genetic disorders, he said. Especially genetic disorders of the brain.

Shirley came into Eva's office later.

Don't worry, she said to Eva.

My big mouth! moaned Eva.

It's all right, said Shirley. Everyone knows you do it with him.

Gunther must've been embarrassed because he didn't visit her for a week. I had a rest from my long walks. Soon their affair would be over, I was sure. Every night we spent the peaceful evenings together, more or less, Eva and I, listening to each other's cooking or TV, or sleep. But eventually Gunther came back, and I resumed my lonely walking.

Hugh wasn't the only one who lost interest in the discussions. Surprisingly, though Gunther kept up with all molecular research, even when it wasn't in immunology, he'd lose interest as soon as the discussions began. To Sandy's irritation, he'd just wander absent-mindedly out of the meetings like Hugh did, and though Sandy would call after him, asking him a question, Gunther wouldn't turn around. It was as if he was deaf. Sometimes he'd leave the lab and drive away. Often he didn't come in for days.

When Eva turned up for work alone, it was assumed that Gunther was mooching at home with his aged father, watching TV. Ostensibly he was still working at immunology, but everyone agreed that his heart wasn't in it.

One night in late 1982 I came in after dark, flushed with triumph because I'd been to a supermarket for the first time ever. *The Sudlow Echo* complained that our city was the last in the country to get one, but for me it was a celebration because I could at last change my diet from my standing order of chocolate biscuits, tomato soup, ham off the bone, blackcurrant jam and Vegemite – without needing to say a word. I walked into the shop head held high, striding not scuttling, and I tried to deliberate like any other shopper on the merits of the lamb cutlets over the lamb chops, the fresh ricotta cheese over the Philadelphia Cream, the sweet gherkins over the spiced gherkins – not to mention the sweet spiced gherkins. I felt extra brave because of my uniform. No one would laugh at a useful citizen in a grey uniform. So I made myself stroll with the respectable matrons amongst the fruit and vegetables as if I was meditating in a fragrant garden. There weren't many other men there, to be sure, but the women who caught my eye smiled at me encouragingly, wishing they had shopping husbands like me. Oh, the sweet and perfect roundness of the red tomatoes when you haven't been near a display of tomatoes since you were a child, and the green crunchy lettuces with their curving leaves, and the broccoli and the lustrous purple eggplants that were causing a stir in Sudlow in those days. So continental, said the ladies to each other, giggling with daring.

I held bunches of translucent red grapes up to the light. I weighed cut slices of golden pumpkin in my hands, and considered taking home the leaflet that showed how to roast them with thyme. Amongst the large purring fridges there was a hush as soothing as I remembered in church. Even when I walked up a ramp to the checkout, the cashier, a young girl as smooth and fresh as a peach, needed just one glance at my uniform and she attended to my purchases as if I had every right to be there.

But anyway, I digress into my commonplace life.

I came home to hear, even as I mounted the stairs, a terrible commotion in Eva's apartment – a demented, high-pitched screaming, a rhythmic banging on the wall, and, under it, a man's voice singing, of all things, what seemed to be a nursery rhyme in German. I threw the shopping on the table and crept to my peephole, though the noise was so great that if I'd marched around with an entire brass band, no one would have heard.

He'll kill himself if he doesn't stop, Eva was calling out.

There, to my horror, I saw a child, an autistic boy from the hospital. I knew him by his height, his skinniness, the poignant tangle of his curls that I'd watched Deirdre struggling to trim. He was banging his head on the wall near the window in an unchanging rhythm – so that was the thumping I'd heard. Eva stood nearby, distraught, her arms reaching out to stop him with every thump, but she'd obviously been warned against that, as I had, so all she could do was watch.

We must get help, she said, whenever she could be heard.

Gunther kneeled nearby in an attitude of desperate prayer, I thought at first, but, no, he wasn't praying, he was singing the nursery rhyme, the same German phrase over and over, while on his bare wrist he tapped out its rhythm.

Listen! he'd say to the boy. Listen.

And he'd tap again.

But the boy heard nothing. Blood was pouring out of a gash on his forehead and splattering the wall, so that there was a horrible dark stream coursing down it.

Your jewellery, said Gunther suddenly to Eva, interrupting his song. Shiny jewellery.

His face was drawn, and his own pale hair striped his damp forehead.

Why jewellery? asked Eva in bewilderment, but she went away and returned half a minute later with a tangled handful of diamantes and pearls. Gunther dangled them in front of the boy's bloodshot, unseeing eyes, sang the phrase in German again and twirled the jewels to catch the light. For a few seconds even the boy was dazzled and his head-banging ceased. In the sudden calm, I heard Eva gasp with relief. But then the boy tired, or perhaps his vision blurred, and he turned away and thumped the wall again.

I promised that I would write this down the way it happened, so I have to confess it: I fled. I grabbed my coat and fled into the dark streets to find a policeman, or even to go back to the hospital and find a doctor, though how I would communicate, I couldn't imagine. A note! I could write a note! But then I thought that perhaps the hospital shouldn't be told. So all I could do was run. I blundered along, stumbling over kerbs and irregularities in the pavement, strange cries falling out of my mouth in a way I seemed unable to prevent. My footsteps rang out like shrieks. Luckily the streets were deserted and I lost myself in unlit alleys, and halted panting against back fences. Finally I came to the Duke of Wellington and, almost sobbing with relief, I pushed open the door of the Roo Bar and ran in. Only the barman was there, quietly wiping glasses. The almost domestic orderliness of it, the bright light and the man's careful hands moving on the glasses as they sparkled, slowed my steps. I sat down on one of the stools. To my astonishment, a word popped out of my mouth, a long and complicated word.

Glenfiddich.

Even in my distress, my own voice startled me, as if it had come from another place, out of my pocket, for example, or the ends of my hair.

You look like you've seen a ghost, the barman said wryly, but he poured the whisky and put it down in front of me. Of course I wished I'd used my moment of speech to ask for help, not for a whisky, but how to begin to explain what was happening in that terrible room? I tossed the nip down almost in one gulp and, by then, my tongue seemed to have locked itself back into its usual unreachable place. The barman saved me.

Another? he asked, and all I could do was nod and indicate that I'd buy him one too – like Humphrey Bogart would do.

At some stage, after my third whisky perhaps, police sirens raced down the street, making my heart lurch and the barman look up from his work.

A lot of craziness in this town, he said, and I made a mouth of disapproval like I'd seen the nurses make, and nodded knowingly, as if I too was daily oppressed by the madness of human nature.

I left shortly after, stumbling through the night back to her.

In the car park a lone white police car was flashing its blue sign on and off, so the row of letterboxes with their numbers – mine was number six – and the row of steel garbage bins (from which I'd hammered out a few little dings made by the continuing wayward-ness of the Hillman Hunter) were illuminated theatrically for a moment, then forgotten, then lit up, as if garbage bins were impor-tant in the world's schemes. The apartments were all in darkness, except for mine and hers, and there was an air of exhaustion about the place. Two policemen were just then emerging from the building, striding with the resignation of men who have peered into the writhings of other human souls and decided that if that's all there is, they might as well go and eat hamburgers with cheese and pickles.

They threw open the doors of their car, slid into their seats, switched off the flashing lights, started the engine and eased into the night.

I ran up the stairs and checked my apartment, which was just as I'd left it, with the shopping strewn on the table, and the bag of tomatoes, so triumphantly purchased, now split and fallen to the floor. I peeped into her room. The boy had gone. It seemed that Gun-ther had gone as well. The wall was scrubbed clean, but her books and dresses were thrown on the floor under the window. She'd turned the lights down low. All I could hear was her breathing, and my heart clenched for her, the way she'd suddenly catch her breath and sob a little, then sniff and breathe normally, until she discovered an unexplored well of anguish and sobbed again. From the occa-sional creak I guessed she was lying on the bed, trying to sleep.

Next day the hospital was bubbling with gossip. The nurses said that last night Gunther had crept into the children's ward and kid-napped the boy. Deirdre said to anyone who'd listen that she'd just popped outside to turn off a dripping garden tap – her only crime was that she'd wanted to fix it – just at the moment when the madman had snatched the boy away. Everyone said that the police had failed in their duty because they'd let Gunther off with a caution. Hanging's not good enough for him! all the grey men said, especially after Marconi claimed that the madman had planned to murder the boy and cut him open to show the psychiatrists that his brain had been missing all the time.

Sandy told Shirley that Gunther was becoming a liability. If he couldn't be kept on the rails, what was the Board to do?

He flung an accusing look at Eva, who said nothing.

It often happens with minds like his, he said. It's better to have a good, solid working intelligence. Then everyone knows where they are.

That night Eva came into her apartment alone, and I heard her moving about, clanking the hangers in the wardrobe, opening and shutting cupboard doors and drawers until the room was unusually neat. She was probably trying to find comfort in order, like I do.

When she had been in bed an hour or more, but with the lights dimmed, not off, so I guessed she was hoping for him, there was a soft knocking. He usually let himself in with his own key – something had altered between them. She passed directly beneath my peephole as she walked around the bed to the door, almost shapeless in a white cotton nightgown. She let Gunther in silently, then went back to bed. He trailed behind her. He sat on the end of the bed and all I could see was the occasional movement of his foot to some rhythm inside his head.

They were going to send him away to die, said Gunther, after a protracted silence.

She said nothing, so he continued:

There's a home at the edge of the desert. It's for incurable children. Families pay for a widow to look after them, an ex-matron. She feeds them and cleans them but there's no treatment for them, no stimulation. They're kept sedated but they often mutilate themselves, as you've seen, and die young.

There was a long pause.

What if the diagnosis is wrong? cried Gunther. What if he needs help for a little more time, a few months, a year maybe, until something has altered for him? For instance, until people stop expecting him to be like them?

Eva still kept silent. I imagined her lying there, her feet moving on the sheets.

One day, Gunther said after a while, I'd gone into the hospital with my car keys in my hand – that little nurse, the one who hates me, she'd stepped outside again, this time to flirt with one of those men in grey uniforms – and without thinking, while I watched little Allan, I'd been tapping a rhythm on my own wrist with the keys, some silly tune from my childhood. And suddenly, without looking at me, without even glancing my way, Allan began tapping on his own arm. The same rhythm. The very same rhythm.

Eva stirred.

The same rhythm? she repeated dully.

Yes! I stopped, and then, to be sure, I tapped again, the same silly song, and the boy listened. I thought he hadn't heard, but he tapped it again. I still couldn't believe it, so I stopped and started again, and he stopped and started too. He was reacting, Eva, he was acknowledging me, he has intelligence, he has a sense of timing, maybe he even wanted contact but in his own way. I gave him that. No one else has.

There was a long pause.

Why didn't you tell the nurse? asked Eva. There are people whose job it is, proper people to tell these things to.

Gunther groaned.

I've been banned, remember? But I wrote to the hospital Board, and to the Sudlow Board who decides which of these children's cases is hopeless and which isn't. That's why Allan has been in the ward so long. They had to think about my letter. They took their time to deliberate, but eventually a group of their psychiatrists and social workers came to try to talk to him. To talk to him! Of course it failed. Talk means nothing to him. Yet all the time they insisted on making eye contact with him, turning his face around to them, and eyes terrify Allan, eyes say too much.

How do you know? asked Eva dully, but he didn't answer her.

Then they tried their ultimate test. They said if he could tie his shoelace, they'd rethink. They think that's a test. Some of these children don't understand what a shoe is for. Allan doesn't. Why would he want to tie a shoelace? Of course, when they held it out to him, he couldn't do it. So they demonstrated in front of him how they tied their shoelaces, and one of them pulled off his own shoe, the laces undone, and told Allan to tie it. So Allan put it in his mouth. That showed they were right, that Allan is incapable of contact.

He put his head in his hands.

It's the same everywhere, he said, for people who are odd. If they're out of line, punish them.

Unreachable, she corrected. Not out of line.

He's not unreachable, can't you see that? he said.

Did you tell the parents? asked Eva.

The parents! groaned Gunther. The parents want to put Allan out of their lives for the sake of their other children. The parents don't know how to stop expecting him to be normal.

And now? asked Eva.

He's going to the widow's.

Tears streamed down Gunther's face.

Another long silence followed.

I'll let myself out, he said, and soon the door clicked behind him.

I am still unsure why you have sent this to me. I have refrained
from correcting this garble of science reported by a nincompoop,
but I would suggest you refer to appropriate texts on the subject,
even mine:
A Short History of Molecular Biology, published by Rumsby Press,
England, 1988.

Nevertheless, I will bear with it.

Professor Gunther Mueller

CHAPTER 26

I am plunged into an unbearable history

LOOKING BACK, I'm ashamed of what happened next. Of course that night I was troubled for him, as she was – who could not be? I was troubled when I woke and over my breakfast. But at smoko in the hospital, Volta was talking to the grey men when I came into the tearoom.

This place is stacked with retards, he was saying. He interrupted himself.

Oh, hello, Galileo.

They all fell silent. At that moment a little voice started up in my mind, saying the words my mother used to shout:

I'll show you!

I nodded to everyone in a friendly way, as if there was no little voice, and I busied myself making a cup of tea while they all watched to see whether a retard should be let loose with an urn of hot water and a teabag. I must use Gunther's setback to do something that would make them respect me, the little voice said. I must become a hero. I must prevail. Anything to help me with Eva, I thought greedily – and dishonourably.

Ironically, Gunther's respect for his hunches inspired me to respect my own. I'd long had a hunch that whatever he was hiding was shocking. I knew that it was connected with the newspaper clipping about the Nazi killer, and that grisly photo of specimen jars, and with a strangely silent, perhaps guiltily silent father, and a burden – the burden I'd willed on him.

Sandy, Shirley, Lotti and Eva knew all of this – except my part in it – but each had their reasons not to denounce him. Denounce him. Surely that would be honourable. The very word thrilled me. I had to be the one to find out the mystery behind him, so I could denounce him for Eva's sake.

The next time he visited her, I didn't walk the five thousand, six hundred and seventy-seven steps. I eased the Hillman Hunter into the street instead, and waited. He wasn't there long. He came out of the building and headed off in his car.

I followed him, a steady half-block behind, and I allowed myself a little pride that I could drive quite unobtrusively by now. There weren't many cars on the road at that hour and the traffic lights were all green, so I didn't have to bang on the brake pedal. The dark streets were dreamy, still wet after another drizzle of rain.

Without warning he turned into a quiet back street. My tyres screeched as I spun around the corner after him. The screech frightened me, and after that things went awry. The street was lit only at the far end, and my end was shrouded in shadows. I meant to stop the Hillman Hunter, fiddle with the glove box and pretend to look up a street directory. If he noticed me, he'd think I was just someone's lost visitor. There was a distance between us of about twenty houses, all silently sleeping, with that cowed look houses take on late at night, as if protesting that the lives in them are entirely unremarkable. But somehow I lost my presence of mind and instead of jamming on the brake, I hit the accelerator, so all my sleuthing was in vain. As he swung into his driveway, I came careering up to him.

Watch what you're doing! his startled face yelled out of his window as I managed to swerve into the bushes opposite, not into him.

I straightened up and drove on, seeing in the rear-view mirror that his house was white with a little porch out in the front and a tall pine tree near the side fence. I whizzed into another road and kept driving in case he was listening out for me. Then I drove around the block, parked in a side street and wondered what to do next. I didn't have a plan, I've never had a plan, only my hope for Eva. He'd be cleaning his teeth now, I thought, and changing into his pyjamas. I took off my shoes and padded up his chilly street in my socks and passed his house. That didn't inspire me with a plan either. A light in one of his rooms went out. I padded back to the Hillman Hunter like a child sent to bed.

By then it was two o'clock and I was exhausted with excitement. I thought about the next morning. Despite his constant late nights, he'd probably be in the lab by eight forty-five. I moved my car to the corner, settled down underneath the level of the windows and dozed. The sun would be high above the rooftops by seven. I'd think of what to do then. Perhaps, I said in that reckless state that sleepiness brings on, when everything seems easy, perhaps I'll storm into his house and find documents that will put both Gunther and his father in jail.

It didn't go quite as I'd hoped. For a start, I slept till nine-thirty, waking dry-mouthed. Rain was thundering on my car roof and the street was awash. There is something very foreboding about a winter rainstorm in Sudlow, as if it's warning of a huge event to follow, the world's end, perhaps, so you are subdued, compelled, waiting. I sat in the car watching the rain on my windscreen turn the street into crazy patterns. I must have dozed again. When I woke again, the rain had eased and it was mid-morning. I opened my door and stood up. I needed a cup of tea but there was no cafe in sight, not even a shop. If I turned on the ignition, I knew that I'd give in to temptation, drive home and get into my soft bed with its gentle, silky sheets and turn on my old electric blanket.

I'd noticed a back lane behind Gunther's house. I felt more comfortable about storming Gunther's back door rather than the front – not that I wanted to storm anything, but a back door seemed less a place for chatting and more suitable for the avenger warrior I now had to become. I tidied myself as best I could, running my fingers through my hair and tucking in my shirt. Then I couldn't prevaricate any longer. I locked up the car and strolled towards the back lane, my hands casually in my pockets.

It took a few minutes to figure out which back yard belonged to the white house with a little porch and a pine tree, because several houses were white with pine trees at the side. All of them had high grey wooden fences. I found an abandoned garbage bin and hoisted myself up on what seemed to be the right fence. The house was very quiet. Perhaps there was no one at home. Between me and a perfectly ordinary white back door was a patch of green-painted cement. Clothes dumb with wetness hung on a line – shirts and trousers, grey, blue – and khaki! – and khaki underpants, the sort I knew Gunther wore, and white boxer underpants, the sort I knew he didn't.

Still without a plan, I hoisted myself up on the fence. It just seemed the next logical action to take. But then a schoolboy turned into the lane bouncing a football, so I had to move quickly, either entirely up and over, or down and run – and then I'd have to meet the boy's inquiring eyes, or perhaps worse. I went up and over but I lost my footing and landed sprawling on the green cement.

I'd made too much noise. The back door opened and a white-haired man peered out. I was face to face with the war criminal.

At last! he said, in heavily accented English, speaking in the quavering voice of the very old.

I've said to Gunther every day that you'll come.

His old head, cocked to one side so he seemed held up by a star, beamed in triumph.

This very morning, I said: This is the day!

I scrambled to my feet. In his hands were plastic bags straining with objects. In fact, at this moment a spoon toppled out and clanged on the cement yard. He didn't bend to pick it up and I was too astonished to move.

He peered at me.

You don't speak German, do you?

My ankle hurt and my wits seemed to have deserted me. But he was nodding enough for both of us.

We heard they send all types, he said. That's all right. We're very grateful. I know many English words. Most of them.

It was as if in speaking English he was showing me a line of shining medals on his shrivelled, white-haired chest, which I could just glimpse under the opening of his shirt. He indicated, with a courteous gesture, that I should enter the house.

The trouble is, we're still not packed, he added. She says – he inclined his head towards the house, perhaps towards a bedroom – she says I'm procrastinating. She says I don't want to leave my job. She says I love my job more than saving my son.

I stood wavering, unsure whether to try to jump back over the fence or not. But he misunderstood my hesitation.

If you will allow me to lead you, he said. It must be confusing. You must go to so many houses.

He began walking inside.

Perhaps you can help me with the finishing touches, he said over his stooped, cardigan-covered shoulder. I stumbled towards the door, kicked the spoon along the green cement, and stooped to pick it up. I wondered if I should put it in one of his plastic bags. By the look of them, he was packing to go to a place where dozens of spoons were needed, their gleaming silver turned into spotted brass. A place where many empty metal tubes were needed, their labels worn off long ago, all meticulously squeezed flat.

He turned around.

Come in quickly, he said, before anyone sees. You never know.

I had no choice but to follow, holding his spoon.

The corridor leading from the back door opened out into a large, airy living room. The walls were bare, the armchairs were stuffed and bulbous, and the slatted blinds at the windows allowed light through but concealed us from the street. It was an unremarkable suburban living room, except that on the floor were hundreds of plastic shopping bags, all lolling and overflowing with a medley of objects, shining coffee-pots with their bottoms blackened, used saucepans, odd pieces of crockery, picture frames, books, mirrors, hats, folded newspapers, and clothes, great musty mounds of clothes.

It's difficult to sort out one's life, he said apologetically. That's the problem with everything, don't you think – the ordering? In my job, order is never an issue. It's all about order. But life outside is so disorderly! Here, please be seated.

He indicated that I should sit on the sofa, and checked if I needed cushions behind my head.

Let me get you a cup of coffee while you think how you can help, he said.

Soon I heard him moving about in the kitchen, water gushing from the tap, then the tinkle of china. I sat because I couldn't think of anything else to do. I tried to assess the house. Along the corridor I'd passed two rooms that could have been bedrooms or something far, far worse. Torture chambers, perhaps, with a rack – not that I was sure I'd recognise a rack if I saw one – thumbscrews (I wouldn't recognise them either), a hand-operated generator with electrodes (that one I could work out), not to mention an SS uniform wrapped around a skeleton.

He interrupted my thoughts by popping his head back to ask if I took milk – perhaps I called it cream, as the Americans do? – and there were some pastries, quite fresh.

I don't know where young Gunther finds them, pastries in these terrible times, he said. He has a good nose for these things.

He touched his own nose, chuckling fondly, and left me on his sofa. The front door was just down that corridor. I could've crept out, and if he'd called the police, perhaps they'd take no notice of a feeble-minded old man. I stood up, and sat down. I was on a mission for my beloved.

So I stared at the bags rustling in a draught, telling myself to leave, telling myself to stay.

If you'd asked me before that moment, I'd have said that a plastic bag is silent. But I'd never sat in a living room with hundreds of plastic bags crammed between a sofa up one end and a sideboard down the other, with only narrow paths to walk between. Hundreds of plastic bags crammed full of objects whisper and chatter and crinkle and flutter in any draught, and even my breath created a draught. As the old man made coffee in his kitchen, the plastic bags around me seemed like a crowd of ghostly humans.

He brought in a rattling tray and put it down on a little doiley-covered table, poured coffee – percolated – into a tiny white cup and offered me milk and sugar. There were no pastries on the tray and I wondered what I should make of that.

You must get it all the time, he said. People in chaos.

His face formed into a charming, unexpected smile that crinkled and lit up his deeply hooded but faded blue eyes. I could imagine him charming his victims with that smile, promising them pastries he never produced, then gassing them.

I sipped my coffee and then, to cover my confusion, I wandered up the avenues of plastic bags as if I was inspecting them.

Chronological order of course was my first thought, the old man said companionably. Though I should throw some things out – but what? Everything seems essential.

He got up, carrying his cup clattering in its saucer, and wandered with me. And so he began to show me how essential all his possessions were, picking them randomly from the tops of the bags, just as they were about to slither out. He picked up a wedding photo which made me gasp, for in Gunther's mother's face I saw Gunther, and a dozen copies of a slim novel.

It's written by Gunther's grandfather, said the old man, and he flipped one open and read me a paragraph, entirely ignoring my lack of German, but there was such drama in his old voice as it gained strength and passion that I listened to every strange syllable. And afterwards, when he fixed me with his glittering eyes, I felt I'd understood.

I remember my father writing it, he said. He took a long time. I remember his closed door.

Something more was expected of me. I thought of bending over and picking at some tissue paper loosely wrapped around a pile of old exercise books, the sort that children use at school.

Stop – don't touch them! the old man suddenly cried.

He'd come so near, his breath was hot on my face. Then he smiled beguilingly, the white-whiskered flesh on his old goose neck trembling.

It's evidence of my boy's sanity, he said. You'll appreciate that.

I smiled a wavering smile, put them back, and instead poked at something shiny and white.

I can't throw that away either, he said, still smiling. Look.

He pulled it out. It was a satin christening dress.

My wife was so excited when Gunther was born, our first, and, as it turned out, our only child. We don't dare have any more, of course.

Gunther had told Eva that his mother was dead, but I nodded again.

I was excited as well, said the old man, but I was busy with my work. A baby is a woman's job. I told myself I'd allow myself feelings when he became a proper person, that's how I saw it, someone you could reason with.

He laughed, a little sourly.

I'm still waiting.

I nodded again, unsure, because after all he was talking about an eminent scientist.

He looked towards the bedroom door, then whispered to me:

I'm the strength for us all. It isn't often asked of a man with an important job.

I randomly picked up a pink silk dress, my mind full of what he was saying.

You'll see my problem right there in your hands, said the old man.

So I tried to concentrate on the dress. Its bodice was gathered into a large rose that would've bared the wearer's shoulder. Out of the plastic bag tumbled white naphthalene balls and a number of identical pink dresses, all gleaming poignantly in the morning light through the slats of the blinds, like disappointed people who've turned up for a party at the wrong house. I stuffed them back into the bag and rounded up the rolling balls. The old man's sad laughter made me look up.

He screams if any woman comes into the house wearing a different dress. He doesn't mind different maids or nurses, but the dresses aren't allowed to change. See for yourself.

I obediently checked the dresses and discovered that they were of different sizes and shapes. One would've fitted the body of a tall, stout woman, another a very thin woman, another a tiny woman.

Gunther can't tolerate change, said the old man.

Even then I merely thought that Gunther must've been a very spoiled child. I packed the pink dresses back into the bag while the old man kept talking. I wasn't really listening to him because I was trying to find a way to leave. After all my deductions and suspicions and hunches, there was just an eccentric old man and hundreds of plastic bags.

So my visit would have ended there, and this memoir would have had an entirely different ending, except that I idly picked up a piece of paper that had dropped on the floor. He took it from me, unfolded it and passed his hand before his eyes. Then he almost staggered back to the sofa and sat so heavily the milk jug on the tray fell over. He ignored it, suddenly a mere stick of a man. It was then that I most deeply regretted my impulsive visit. What would I do if he fainted, if he died? But he rallied himself to mutter:

Life unworthy of life. That's what Hitler called the mental patients who lie on sand or sawdust because they perpetually dirty themselves, and put their own excrement into their mouths. He said these people should be eradicated. He's worked out how many should go – he assumed that out of one thousand people, ten will require psychiatric treatment, five in residential form. That means about seventy thousand people –

He paused.

You were sent, weren't you, by the – he said a foreign word, then corrected himself – the underground sent you, didn't they?

But he didn't wait for an answer.

No one dares speak up. People get prosecuted, or worse, if they're known to . . .

His sad old eyes roved over the ordinary furniture.

Don't they?

I nodded again, uncomprehending.

They say it's treason to speak up, that's the accusation. So no one speaks. Friends go silent when you mention it.

Words were tumbling out of him now.

You don't know who's your friend, who'll inform on you. A friend of mine, an acquaintance really, a judge, protested that his wards of state who'd been sick had suddenly been taken away and gassed. His protest went all the way up to the Minister of Justice – Justice, hah! My friend threatened to instigate charges, he didn't care what happened to his career, he told me, but it wasn't his career that suffered. He and his wife have suddenly disappeared. Just like that – they've disappeared. Their home is as empty as a tomb. You walk by there – I'll tell you the address – you'll see. Cobwebs have fanned over the windows, the mail is piling up outside their door, no one dares collect it, no one dares show that they were friends, no one dares show that they were involved. Including me. Only Galen, the pastor, he's now talking about it out in the open from the pulpit. You must know about Galen's sermons? He said that: 'We are not dealing with machines, horses and cows whose only function is to serve mankind, to produce goods for man. We are dealing with our fellow human beings, our brothers and sisters. With poor people, sick people, if you like, unproductive people. But have they forfeited the right to life? Have you, have I the right to live only so long as we are productive, so long as we are recognised by others as productive?'

At least he's started people whispering. Did you hear what Galen said? people now ask, and then, if they trust you, they say: Is it true? Is it true? It can't be! But it is, it is. There's an awful tearing at your gut, because the unthinkable is suddenly happening.

At first we heard life unworthy of life was just for permanent inmates of asylums who were taking up the beds that sick soldiers needed, and we all said of course we wanted our country's good, if the lifelong inmates had to go, they had to go. Of course we wanted Austria's health. When you slide into evil, you wonder where the slow slide started – don't you? Where exactly things went wrong? And I think it was that, that we turned our backs on those lifelong patients. We agreed to it. We never thought it would touch us. We all said that our families have problems, but they're worthy of life, they're not like those patients.

Now they're gassing our children and our parents – you know that, don't you? But is a child unworthy of life because he wears spectacles? Because he has a harelip? Because he needs an x-ray? Because he has asthma? Because he wets the bed? Is an old person unworthy of life because she has to be looked after? Because she has an artificial limb? And the mental patients on sawdust – were we satanic to dismiss them? Who can decide who's worthy of life? Only God can, not politicians, not us, and God isn't saying a thing.

I must've been making noises.

He peered at me over his own spectacles.

You're in danger too. Being a mute. They exterminate stutterers, of course they'd exterminate a mute.

I nodded, not knowing what else to do.

He was still holding the letter that had prompted this. He looked down at it and read it. He forgot me for a moment while he read. The page seemed heavy in his hand.

Of course, it will mean nothing to you unless I translate it, he said. This is from my goddaughter, her last words –

his voice broke –

I'd watched her grow up. She was so vivacious, we often said she'd be a great actress in the cinema. Then she began to have fits. She had epilepsy. She went to hospital, and of course the convoys came. Her doctor, I've since found out, sends the convoys for most of his patients because it's good for his career. Her father, who'd often argued that the long-term mental patients should be eradicated, gave this to me for safekeeping the night before he shot himself.

The old man read in a shaking voice:

'Dearest beloved Father,

Unfortunately it cannot be otherwise. I must die as a martyr for everyone's sake. Today I must write these words of farewell as I leave this earthly life for an eternal one. I embrace you with undying love.

Your only daughter.'

The old man wiped his eyes.

This beautiful girl had to be a martyr? How dare these politicians make judgments on the worth of anyone's life!

I took the letter out of his trembling hands and tucked it away in a plastic bag, as if that could comfort him.

Of course they claim she died of breathing problems, he said. They're good at faking death certificates. I've seen many in my job.

He looked up, suddenly startled at his own words, and all my suspicions came tumbling back. I thought: Aha, a slip. He's not only seen death certificates, he's probably ordered them.

So of course, Gunther is in danger as well, he added.

I wheeled around. One of my rare words came out.

Gunther?

He passed his hand over his eyes again.

That's the dilemma. She – again he inclined his head towards the bedroom, which he must have shared with his wife – is always saying that we must leave now. She says I'm risking my own son. But I tell her that I've got to stay here, to save other people. I'm allowing the murder of many but saving some.

I stared at him. How could he be risking his son?

Go now, he said in a choked voice. I'm too tired to work any more.

As I was leaving, he muttered:

Come back tomorrow.

His voice stayed in my mind:

Allowing the murder of many but saving some.

CHAPTER 27

I become a welcome visitor

I DIDN'T GO BACK TO HIM IMMEDIATELY, I let weeks accumulate. I couldn't make sense of what I'd seen and heard. Was the old man making it all up? Was I finding out the truth about Gunther? Was there any essential truth about Gunther to be found out? For a week I told myself I was too busy with my tap washers and my doomed love, too busy for the sorrow of an old man with a wandering mind, especially an old man reliving a catastrophe that belonged to another time and another country. As if it had nothing to do with my country, with me, with Sudlow. As if pain lessens with time or distance. I know now that it doesn't.

While I dithered, Gunther burst into Eva's office with news.
    Allan's back! he shouted. Little Allan. The little boy who was sent away to die, surely you remember?
    Her voice was heavy.
    How could I forget? she said.
    But he didn't die! Gunther said. They were wrong. The assessment was wrong. He recovered.

Where is he? asked Eva. Dread was thickening her voice, that Gunther might do something that would get him into trouble all over again.

In this hospital, said Gunther. I just saw him at the admissions desk with his arm in a sling. He fell off a swing, just like any child. His parents brought him in. Of course no one told me. But the main thing is –

He sat down heavily.

Apparently the widow sent him back. She kept him for three months, then she sent him back. She said that they'd been wrong, that he'd be able to survive. Just like I thought. He can't speak but he's intelligent, anyone can see it. Isn't that wonderful?

How did you find all this out? asked Eva warily.

The parents told me everything. Of course, they didn't know –

He stopped.

They didn't know who I am. I just said I remembered him.

He was so excited he rose and paced around the room.

It proves that I've got to leave the lab, said Gunther. I'll study medicine and then everything will be different.

After that he began travelling to a distant city to study medicine part-time, often staying overnight, but he kept up his work in immunology. At the university he was given credit for his work and permitted to miss lectures but he still seemed impatient as a student, and often he didn't even bother to go there. When he went, he constantly criticised the lecturers and argued with them as he'd done when he was young, except that while to Lotti he'd been an angry young man full of promise, now he was just an angry man.

They're fools, I'd constantly hear him say.

One day he'd called out Idiot! to the lecturer, and he'd been escorted from the lecture theatre.

I don't know how I'm going to last this out, he said to Eva. I don't need to study. I just want to do autopsies!

I still had to find out who he really was, so I visited his father again. Since I was now an invited visitor – though it was some time since I'd been invited – I knocked boldly on the front door. It was a terrible mistake. My knocking seemed to echo through a silent house. I banged more loudly, and at last I heard feet shuffling along the corridor. The door opened only gradually, as if it too was stricken by age. The old man peeked out. He seemed much older than the last time I'd seen him, in the way that the very old, like the very young, seem to age before your eyes.

I smiled a warm, friendly smile and stuck out my hand to shake his, but he only glanced at me, growled in German – it certainly didn't sound like a greeting – and shut the door in my face. I stayed where I was, waiting to see what would happen next. Nothing did, except that his old man's fingers poked at the slats of the blinds, his ancient blue eyes peered at me, and then the slats closed. After a few more minutes of staring at the paintwork on the door, I gave up and walked back to the Hillman Hunter.

But my mind didn't give up. Allowing the murder of many but saving some, it chanted. Allowing the murder of many but saving some.

Had Gunther found out about my visit? Had the old man realised I wasn't from the underground? Had I dreamed it all?

Then one day when my life had shrunk to little more than throwing leaves into the incinerator, a new thought crossed my mind.

The front door! That's what went wrong with my visit. He wouldn't expect the underground to knock on the front door! The underground would come surreptitiously over the back fence, as I had before.

By dawn I'd concocted a plan. If the old man let me into the house again, I'd ransack those plastic bags for the newspaper clipping and the photo from Helene Haussman. If I could find that, perhaps then I'd have enough to condemn Gunther.

The next morning, as soon as Gunther was safely at the lab, I climbed over Gunther's back fence and this time landed neatly on the green concrete. Again he heard my thump, almost as though he'd been waiting for it. The back door opened.

Where have you been? the old man said, smiling. We'd almost given you up.

There was no mention of my visit to his front door, so perhaps my hunch had been right.

He led me into his living room just as before.

Ready to work? he said.

As we walked between the plastic bags, it seemed to satisfy him if I moved objects fussily from one bag to another. I'd move an old toaster from a bag with saucepan lids to a bag with jugs.

Very good, very good, he'd say.

Sometimes I'd make an entirely absurd move, for example reclassifying hammers and chisels not with tools but with cutlery.

Just right, he'd say, as if we were getting somewhere at last, though I suspected that when I was gone, he'd put the tools right back where they'd come from.

He made me coffee again, though his old hands trembled so much the saucers were awash. When I went back to organising, he said:

Forgive me, but it makes me marvel. I've been waiting all this time for help – and who should they send but a mute!

He paused for thought.

Mind you, it makes sense. If you're tortured, they won't get much out of you.

I worked on while he sat and watched. Once he led me to bags full of newspaper clippings and my heart leaped. I pretended great interest in classifying them by date, so I knew that they were all in German, all from Austria and from the year of 1943. None was the clipping from Helene Haussman.

I should get back to the hospital, I thought, and just then I saw that our organising had led us towards the tissue-wrapped school-books, the ones he'd prevented me from touching on my first visit. Luck seemed to be playing into my hands, for at this point the old man excused himself and I heard the clank of a toilet seat. I crept over to the books, ripped off the tissue paper and flicked one of them open. There was nothing of interest – just a muddle of wavering horizontal lines. I opened the next exercise book and the next, and learned nothing. Then, in the next book, I paused. The lines of scribble were becoming more deliberate, growing to be

234 THE SECRET CURE

jagged, reluctant loops. Sometimes the pen jabbed the paper so angrily, it dug into it like a knife into flesh.

Suddenly the old man was running across the room to me, his eyes narrow with fury, his old mouth an open gash. He grabbed the books out of my hand.

You're trying to steal the evidence! he shouted.

Before I could move, he'd shoved me against the wall and pinned me with his unexpected, bony strength. He punched me in the stomach, and I collapsed on the floor. After a while I got up.

You shouldn't have touched the books, he said.

I staggered to the front door, intent on leaving. But as I reached the doorstep, he began to talk, weaving the past into the present again.

He told me that his wife had found a doctor for Gunther, one with his own small hospital.

He's a fine man who defies the Nazis and doesn't register his patients. That's brave, as you'd know, added the old man.

The doctor says they're all in danger, he went on, his staff and the children, and he is too. But the children in the most danger, the doctor warns me, are the children who can't write their own names. Like my Gunther. It's taken the doctor twelve months to get Gunther to accept a pen in his hand, and the boy has only recently agreed to let his pen touch the paper. The noise! he shouts.

The old man said it in German, remembered me and translated. Stop the noise!

My boy can't stand the mere scratching of a pen on paper. He doesn't understand why we're trying to make him write. My wife says it's as if the boy is willing his own death. I have to find strength for all of us. But you see – he waved the book – this is proof that he's not feeble-minded. The good doctor says that my son is a model of his type of problem. He's going to write about him in a paper.

I walked slowly back down the corridor as he opened the school-book, now as friendly as before he punched me. He held the book up for me, like a teacher does for his pupils. I came closer. I saw that one of the lines wasn't meaningless after all. It had resolved into a huge, clumsy

G.

There was a pause in the room. Even the plastic bags seemed to have stopped their whispering.

I was totally unprepared for what happened next. My father, though often angry, had never cried, and in nearly all the books I'd read, the heroes didn't cry. Almost the only man I'd ever known cry was me. But now the old man seemed to crumple, as if I'd hit him in the stomach. Bent low, he was making strange mewling noises. His breath was coming in quick gasps, and he was clutching at his heart. At first I didn't know how to comfort him, I was too shy to comfort this man who'd been important – for what, I didn't know, but now it didn't seem to matter. A man shouldn't touch another man, I thought. But then I reasoned that he was just like my mother, only a man – perhaps all people are like my mother. So I led him back to the sofa, and sat beside him and put my hand on his shoulder.

I stayed with him most of the day, kneeling with him to sort out shoes, all of which I suspected had been sorted again and again. As I moved between the bags, I sometimes noticed things that wouldn't have belonged to Gunther's family, such as a little girl's lacy dress, or a doll's tea set. I wondered if they'd belonged to his goddaughter, but I tried not to think of the child who might once have worn that dress, or played gravely with those little cups.

Looking back, the old man taught me something about love I'd never known. When I was with him, following his words, his breathing, his sad life, he seemed as poignantly human as anyone. Only when I left him did I remember that he might be a criminal and essential to my mission to disgrace Gunther. So I have come to believe that if soldiers were to sit in the homes of their enemies for a while, they'd forget their missions too.

I went back again and again to Gunther's house, each time moved by the old man, each time wondering why I came. But when I drove away, my doubts would plague me all over again.

Then one day, when I was ready to give up my mission to disgrace Gunther, the old man led me into the room which, on my first visit, I'd thought might hide a photograph of Hitler, at the very least. I was almost embarrassed to see an ordinary room, a single man's bedroom.

Gunther doesn't have much to do with his father these days, the old man said, switching from the past to the present with bewildering ease.

He used to collect phonograph records. But now he lets me use some floor space.

It was a very neat, almost boyish room, with bare pale green walls, a narrow bed made up with a green chenille coverlet (I could just see a grey and yellow striped pyjama leg poking out from under the green-slipped pillow), a neat row of shoes and a pair of slippers all in a line in front of the lowboy, and a few oddments – a hairbrush, comb, nail clippers and a toy microscope – placed with even spaces between on top of a dresser. A khaki dressing gown hung on a hook on the back of the door, and the lowboy stood shut. It didn't look like a room that could hide anything, except that over in one corner, near a fireplace that had been boarded up with a piece of green-painted masonite, more plastic bags whispered at our approach.

I remembered the old man's sudden violence and knew I wouldn't be permitted to snoop, so I did as he asked and carried some bags out to the living room. But when I went back in again for more bags, I pulled at the piece of masonite in front of the fire. It was firmly nailed on. On my next visit, I opened the top drawer of the dresser, only to discover Gunther's familiar khaki socks. Each visit, I opened another drawer but I made no discoveries. The lowboy had a set of drawers, and I inched them open as well. I even checked under the bed but all I discovered were balls of fluff. When I was taking out my last lot of plastic bags, I tried the hanging section of the lowboy. There was a folded blanket on the base, and under it, a shoebox.

I threw the plastic bags down on the floor, and in the din from the clattering of many old phonograph records, I riffled through the box. There were bills and receipts and scribbled telephone numbers, but right at the bottom was the research paper, 'Die Autistischen Psychopathen im Kindesalter', and underneath it was an envelope addressed to Gunther in purple ink. And inside, there it was at last – the newspaper clipping with the photo!

I tucked it all inside my shirt, meaning to return it later (I never did). Then I collected the phonograph records, put them back into their plastic bag and took them out to the living room where the old man was immersed in sorting through saucepans. I tapped my watch, looked worried and gestured towards the door.

Come back tomorrow, the old man said, as he had before. We're running out of time.

I was just driving off when I glimpsed Gunther arriving in his car. For once he was early. I slipped down as low as I could, and kept going.

My mind should've teemed with ideas on what to do, but it didn't. It seemed to be mired in sadness as I read the clipping. The clipping was headed:

'Unquiet Grave for Nazi Victims'.

It reported that memorials had recently been held for the remains of children and babies killed in Vienna under the Nazi euthanasia program for medical research, and in the program for killing incurables.

In the middle of the article was the photo that Shirley glimpsed in Gunther's hands, the photo of rows of specimen jars. The camera had been angled so that three of the jars were in close-up, and in them were, the caption explained, human brains – the brains, according to the article, of children admitted to hospital with harelips, stutters and learning difficulties. Once there, the children had been injected with lung infections by a Nazi doctor, Heinrich Gross, and then left outside in the winter snow to die. Dr Gross, the newspaper cutting said, had recently been tried by the court in Austria and forgiven. He still practised as a doctor and boasted, the article said, that his collection of children's brains was 'unique in the world'.

Below the photo of the specimen jars was a picture of a little boy, perhaps five years of age, dressed in a short-sleeved white shirt, a tie and braces. He had hair precisely parted over the temple in the fashion of the '40s, sweetly wide-apart eyes and the anxious smile of a child who often displeases adults and can't understand why. The caption said he had been declared an idiot, possibly autistic, though he was very musical. He'd been sent to hospital and put in a caged bed after he'd broken a window. His family received news of his death in 1945, along with an invoice for the costs of his care. His name was Fritz Haussman.

Across the newspaper cutting was scrawled, in purple ink just as Shirley had reported, the words:

Since he lost his life, what have you done with yours? Helene Haussman.

The scientific paper was written by a Dr Hans Asperger in 1944. It was entirely in German, so I flicked through the pages, trying to guess what it was about. It seemed to describe four boys, perhaps four patients. Each of the boys was called only by his Christian name. None was called Fritz. But one was called Gunther.

I decided to have the paper translated. But I didn't, not then, not for a while. Because I still wanted to condemn my rival, and I feared that if I read it and understood him, I wouldn't condemn him at all.

CHAPTER 28

I hold new hope that my love will come to her senses

I WAS BEGINNING TO FEEL that now I'd lived in the world, I knew less about it than when I'd first walked into it. I seemed to know less and less how to live, how to think. I seemed unable to make any moral judgments at all. I no longer understood what honour meant, or if it had any meaning at all. I kept on working in the hospital, and spying on the lab when I could, and listening to their conversations in the apartment when he was there, and living silently beside her when he wasn't. I felt that I should make a decision to stop, but decisiveness seemed to exist in a place where I wasn't, beyond our city, out in the desert perhaps. The old man's plight had taken all my certainties away.

Besides, I was in a habit of loving her, and love had given my life its reason and its structure. I never thought of giving up the world now, and going back to my isolation. She was still the reason I left home every day. I'd check on her early every morning, her room still dim with sleep, her breathing just audible, and I'd go to the hospital and when I didn't have a job to do, I'd check on her in the lab at morning tea, and again at lunch and afternoon tea, and during the evenings. It's strange, the way feelings are different from what you'd expect. I had been so immersed in learning about love that I'd felt like a student of love as I peeped into her apartment, the way students feel that their responsibility is only to learn, that one day they will have the life they were learning for, but until then, learning itself is enough. I had no idea what to do once I knew how to love. I had no plan.

As she came into the lab one day, she suddenly murmured to me, in a way that she hadn't for ages:

'I wanted to love properly, and it seemed the only way to do that was to search out the most demanding passion, the man who needed me the most. It wouldn't be heroism, but a relief to know I'd gone for the hardest love my mind could bear. If only for that reason, to love despite the odds, and not fail.'

Early in 1983, Gunther received news that he didn't take into the lab, only to Eva in her apartment. I came home to hear Gunther sadly explaining the details to her. I wondered if I should be honourable and go out walking, but since there was no sound of the alarm clock being wound, I stayed.

It seems that an American scientist who regularly did autopsies of the brain, a Margaret Bauman, had reported the autopsy findings of a young man with autism who'd drowned. She'd found many brain abnormalities in (here he repeated them several times and I wrote them down) the hippocampus, subiculum, entorhinal cortex, septal nuclei, mamillary body, selected nuclei of the amygdala, neocerebellar cortex, roof nuclei of the cerebellum, and inferior olivary nucleus.

Eva tried to comfort him.

At least they can't say autism is the fault of poor parenting anymore, she said.

He wasn't comforted.

Apparently Bauman had done other foetal studies and knew that the abnormalities must've begun before birth, even before the first thirty weeks of gestation.

So they'll know you were right and they were wrong, said Eva. Sandy will say that. Everyone will. You'll be away at university, but I'll take it into the weekly meeting.

That was no comfort for him either.

Every scientist gets pipped at the post, she said. Every now and then.

That wasn't the cause of his grief. I knew it, but she didn't.

I could've paid my debt by doing that autopsy! he kept saying. I could've paid my debt.

I had troubles of my own. I suspected more and more that Marconi was spying on me. Every time I walked into my courtyard to go to my shed, I saw him lurking on the veranda and I'd have to pretend I'd only popped out to disinfect the garbage bins. Now and again, to vary this, I fiddled with the fountain as if I'd been told to get it going again, as if it was important that water should play once more on the eyeless head of Samuel Craven Sudlow.

Marconi was around so often that I took to carrying a broom out to my shed so I could look busy just for him.

One day I heard a low whistle just as I was about to put a key into the padlock on my shed. When I turned around I saw Marconi, and he laughed at the look on my face. I was so frightened that I signalled towards the administration area and made little running movements with my fingers, and then I dashed back into the hospital. Luckily the chef was hunting for me. The fridges had iced up again along with nine dozen cutlets, and I was just the person to dig them out for lunch.

About the same time, I overheard a conversation between Shirley and Sandy that changed everything for me – and, as it turned out, for Shirley.

They were in the lab having a drink after work. There was some difficulty about going to Shirley's apartment, I can't remember what, so Sandy had brought in a couple of bottles of Sudlow's best red. Drinking in that stern lab was against the rules, but Sandy was head and so it didn't matter, he said.

I came into my shed when Sandy had drunk so much, he was keeping himself upright only by gripping the workbench.

He's no genius, he was saying. He's just a fanatic.

So they must've been talking about Gunther.

His immunology work when he was younger must've been impressive, said Shirley, who'd always been loyal to Gunther.

Sandy threw his head back laughing so loudly and crudely that Shirley got up and shut the lab door in case he was heard all the way down the corridor. As she came back, he said:

The world knows nothing about him. Never heard of him.

Shirley was looking at her dishevelled lover with some distaste.

I think I'd better drive you home, she said. Your wife won't know – I'll drop you at the corner. You're going to have a terrible headache tomorrow.

She was a little dishevelled herself, her blond hair hanging in tendrils down her face.

It should've ended there, but Sandy wasn't able to go anywhere. He tried to sit down on a stool and it skidded away across the floor.

Gunther was never considered for the Prize, said Sandy.

Your wife will put you into bed, Shirley said, taking his drink away and pouring it down the sink.

It was only ever a rumour, Sandy went on, and then he began chortling again so raucously that I could barely make out his next words.

It grew and grew – with a little help from me. And you, he said.

She gazed at him, still holding the glass upside down in the sink.

From me?

He was too drunk to answer her directly.

I started the rumour, he said, and got the Board all fired up. But I didn't have to do much. Sudlow was waiting for a genius. Suddenly he was it!

But he was a genius, said Shirley, eyes wide open.

I'm the genius, shouted Sandy. To my eternal damnation! He's no better than anyone. No better than me. Think about it – don't any of you ever think? Am I the only one around here who ever thinks? Think about it. Dopey Doris, awash with money, loses her son because his immune system rejects a new heart. Hmm, I think. I entice from Melbourne an immunologist of a little, only a little eminence who hails from an exotic and mysterious European background, and I begin a rumour that he's being considered for the Prize. And everyone makes it easy for me and cheers me on – the hospital Board, Dopey Doris, Gunther, you – everyone. Everything falls into place, at least it did until he started this autism caper.

Shirley was now holding on to the bench too, her knuckles white.

His near-win was a lie? You tricked us into believing a lie?

You're all such fools! Sandy yelled. Such stupid, trusting idiots! Never asking the important questions. Never in science, I'm sure, because you don't ask them in life! No one questioned it. Not Eva, who thinks she asks all the right questions. And not him, who asks all the wrong questions. I run rings around the lot of you in smartness, and I got away with it.

Shirley had plumped down on a stool.

Wait a minute, she said. The letter from that woman in London, the one with the German name who saw him on TV – what about that? cried Shirley.

It was a blessing, a coincidence, that she happened to track him down just at the right time for me, said Sandy. Of course she hadn't seen him on TV. Why would Europe be interested in a little news item on a slow day in Sudlow? You – it was you who came up with that fairy story. I've always wanted to tell you that.

Sandy slumped off the bench and slid onto the lab floor while Shirley watched, unmoving.

I'm like God, he said. He made a drunken attempt to click his fingers. There was no sound.

But is this how God feels? he continued. Disappointed that no one can see how simple his artifice is?

His fingers scrabbled on the floor for his drink, as if he thought he was still standing up. Then his head tipped over on one side and he began to snore.

Shirley pulled on her coat, collected the empty bottles, opened the windows to air the lab, and walked down the stairs. I heard her pause and come back up. She was about to kick him in the ribs with her elegantly shod toe. But she relented, took off her shoe, and kicked him instead with her stockinged foot. So I saw that Shirley, in her own way, also thought about the life of honour.

Next day Sandy phoned in to say he'd been in a fist fight in the Duke of Wellington, defending Darwin, he claimed. When Shirley heard that, she threw a stack of newly washed Petri dishes at the wall while Eva watched open-mouthed.

I hope you're going to clean that up, Eva said sternly.

I'm going to clean up my entire life, said Shirley.

Later she bustled into Eva's little cubicle and asked:

What are you going to do about Gunther? Isn't it about time you got on with your career? Do some study? You're such a know-all. Get a qualification! Stop fussing about love! Start being a scientist!

CHAPTER 29
Marconi changes my destiny

IT HAD TO HAPPEN. Marconi caught me when I had just opened my shed door.

I've been wanting to get you when the other blokes weren't around, he said. But you're always such a tricky bugger, always rushing off somewhere.

I surreptitiously pressed the door shut again with my elbow and leaned my bulk against it. He'd have to prise me away before he could look inside. In the bright sunlight, his purple scar gleamed cruelly, like a snake. I was breathing heavily.

But so was he. He was looking around to make sure the coast was clear, and I suddenly realised that he was nervous too.

I didn't trust you when you first came here, he said. I thought you were tricking us. But you've been fair. You've pulled your weight. And I've figured out you've got a stutter.

I nodded wildly. I couldn't work out where this conversation was leading, but it seemed all right to agree I had a stutter.

You want to know how I know? he went on. Because –

here he unexpectedly skittered away from me and peered down the path at the veranda, and checked behind the lantana that I'd clipped back to the far side of the courtyard, and then he came back and spoke rapidly:

I had a stutter too. Not like yours. More a stammer. But I got it fixed. Then I came here to Sudlow, to get away from all the rubbish that stammering brings. I wanted a clean start. So now I'm helping you, but if you tell anyone –

he held his huge fist in front of my face.

I shook my head.

Okay then, he said.

With that he pulled out of his pocket a crushed, stained pamphlet.

I've been carrying it on me for ages, he said, but somehow you were never around to take it.

It was about a new treatment at a clinic in another city to cure people with stutters.

He stood near me, breathing noisily, making sure I got to the end of the pamphlet and all the time keeping watch on the path and ducking his head to see behind the lantana.

What do you think? he kept asking, and I'd nod, to show I could think.

It's a long way from this place, he said, too impatient to wait for me to read right to the end. You'd have to leave here. But that will do you good. Getting away from –

his huge hands indicated not only the hospital, not only the lab, but, I feared, my little shed whose very door was threatening to swing open if I moved –

away from the stupid stuff you do, eh?

I was so terrified at what he might know about my spying that a word popped out of my mouth.

Yes, I said. It was almost a yelp.

He took the pamphlet out of my hands and tucked it into my pocket.

Don't let the others see. But tell you what – I'll ring up for you. Book you into the clinic. I know all the people there. I'll tell them I'm sending my mate. What do you think?

The shed door seemed to be opening wider of its own accord behind my back.

I nodded, to finish the discussion.

Tomorrow? Want me to do it tomorrow? Come in early, before the others. I'll set you up.

He was just about to clap me on the back when Volta's head appeared at an upstairs window.

Damn, said Marconi, and left before he got caught helping me.

I let Marconi set me up, as he called it, because I didn't like to refuse him. But I couldn't bear to leave Eva. At last I went back to Gunther's father one more time, in the hope that something about the old man's meandering mind would show me what to do. I waited as usual until Gunther was safely at the lab. Again, it had been weeks since I'd been there, but when I climbed over his back fence he came out of his house beaming.

We're all ready to go, he said. There's nothing left but to decide when and where.

But after he'd made the coffee, he faltered a little as he set down the tray on the sofa.

You'd better tell me straight why they're delaying getting us out, he said. Are they criticising me? What have you heard?

He busied himself with the doiley on the tray, setting it straight, smoothing out its ripples.

Tell me, boy! Speak honestly. I'm a straight talker. I can take it. Tell me why you didn't come back earlier.

He forgot to hand me my cup. His old hooded eyes fastened on me. He must've mistaken my confusion for doubt.

It's because of my job, isn't it? She – he indicated his bedroom, which I knew by now was empty – said you wouldn't come back if they found out about my job, and I feared she was right. But here you are, back again, and I've made up my mind to come clean. So you can pass it on to whoever's in charge. I wasn't telling the truth entirely before. I had to pretend not to know exactly what's happening in our country. In case you were a spy, after all. But I know what's happening, I know it very well. Too well. And if I tell you how I'm helping our countrymen, you can tell them. What they don't know is that in my job I'm saving many.

Allowing the murder of many but saving some, my brain recited.

What he told me was that when the Nazis had begun to implement their plan to exterminate seventy thousand incurables, he'd been in the army, in active service. Unexpectedly, he'd been offered a desk job, supposedly in accounting.

It turned out, he said, that I'd been recruited to account, all right – but for death. My job was to keep a tally of the incurables going off in the convoys to Hartheim to be gassed. The system was very complicated, since there were participating nurses, doctors and hospitals all over Austria who had to notify the officials when they had patients who were deemed unworthy of life – sometimes just one or two, sometimes a small group. Then the convoys would arrive and take them away. The problem was that with growing public unease, particularly around Hartheim where the stench of burning flesh was becoming unmistakable and clutches of human hair were said to swirl in the breeze, the officials were anxious to know at any one moment how close they were to fulfilling the target figure of seventy thousand, or how much further they had to go. I was attached to the Community Patients Transport System, as it was called – the convoys – and once a week I had to report on progress.

When I found out what my job really was, he went on, I didn't know what to do. I couldn't refuse – I couldn't back out and say, This is evil! They'd have shot me right there and then. But I couldn't go along with it. How could I, when my own son might at any moment be considered unworthy of life if some neighbour complained about the noise at home?

So I've come up with a solution (here he eerily switched to the present) and here's what I want you to tell the network, however you go about telling them – you write notes, don't you? I finally thought, I'll use the job as a way to save some of my countrymen. Not all of them, but some. It's easy enough, when I'm there at my desk with all the paperwork here (he was gesturing as he spoke), and the stamps at my elbow here, and important signatures I can copy, and everyone's assumptions that I'll do what I'm supposed to do.

But I don't. Well, I do and I don't. If a convoy driver tells me he's transported five people from such and such a hospital to Hartheim, I don't write down five, I change it to six, sometimes even seven. Never double – that might get me shot! If a driver tells me twelve, I change it to fifteen. I've got to be careful, you know, I can't get carried away. I can't make it, say, one hundred and twenty. Someone might notice. But I'm doing my best. If I can trick them into thinking they've got their seventy thousand when they've only got sixty-five thousand, that'll be some old people and children they don't kill.

I was too agitated to stay still while I listened. I got up and walked around the room, the plastic bags swishing in my wake.

The old man's voice followed me:

That's why it took me a long while to ask the network to help. I knew we should escape for Gunther's sake, and I also knew that the longer I held off, the more people I could save. Now, this terrible tension is ruining my wife's health. He's more biddable than he used to be, but often he yells uncontrollably, and people talk. What if the convoys come?

I left that unbearable room and went down the corridor and opened his back door. I hadn't noticed before, but the house was on a slight rise, looking over a valley that backed on to bushland. The ordinary morning rushed up to me, smelling of flowers, and the roofs in the valley below gleamed like placid water, and up in the bush, a sandstone cliff reared up gold. Between the slats of the side fence I glimpsed a bare-chested man in shorts starting up a motor mower. A woman, her head in pink curlers, her ample body covered in a loose white dress, was hanging a bathroom mat on her Hills Hoist. They were chatting about dinner. She saw me and nodded in a neighbourly way. We stood, the sad old man and I, on his back step and we breathed in the air, and found that Sudlow felt like peace.

Then he started talking again.

Sometimes I think I could've stretched it all just a bit further, he said, prompted by the peace to remember where he was.

Sometimes I think, when the driver told me twelve and I wrote down fifteen, why didn't I write down sixteen? Who was that sixteenth person I could've saved? Was it a little girl who'd now be a mother with her own grandchildren? A bed-wetting boy who might just have been timid? An old grandmother who needed a few last years with the family she'd brought up? But if I had written down sixteen, I'd be asking the same questions about the seventeenth. Or if I'd written down seventeen, is that the one more lie that would've got me shot, and my wife and child as well? And should I have stayed on and risked my son's life? What did the man do who took my job? Was I a murderer or a saviour?

That day I stayed with him for much later than I intended, just moving objects between bags. He didn't ask me why. He knew I wanted to be there with him. After a while he heard my growling stomach and brought in a tray of food – a loaf of brown bread, butter and grapes, and more coffee. We cut the loaf into thick slices and buttered them, and we drank our coffee in unison, two lonely souls puzzled about the life of honour, whatever honour is when the world becomes bewildering.

At last I got up to go and he walked to the door with me.

Thank you, he said in his courteous way. His old face seemed clearer.

You know what I'm going to do for the rest of the day? I'm just going to sit down on that sofa and do nothing.

At least, I think that's what he said, because he lapsed into German.

Further to my previous comments, my father and I endured many years in each other's company in total silence after my mother's death. I had no idea of his job in Austria. He never told me. This comes as a great shock. All I ever knew about my family's history was that I had to be smuggled out of Austria, and my mother once mentioned that I hadn't been developing at the normal rate. It is true that the paper by Hans Asperger changed everything for me, as well as the newspaper clipping sent by Helene Haussman. I'm afraid I couldn't remember her brother. Now I wish I'd shown the paper and the clipping to Papa. It might've started us talking.

Professor Gunther Mueller

CHAPTER 30

I give up my love but begin to speak

THAT NIGHT GUNTHER TOLD EVA he was going to give up medicine. When she tried to change his mind, he admitted he'd missed most of his lectures in the last three months.

What were you doing? she asked. While I thought you were driving there?

Watching daytime TV, he said. *General Hospital.* I'm not learning much from it.

As he lay on Eva's bed, I could just see his feet in socks, the big toe turned up to the ceiling. She sat at the little chair near the window, checking invoices, a little relieved at the peace when he slept. They seemed like an old married couple.

There was no place for me.

The next two years have very little to do with this memoir. I don't remember much about them. It's enough to write down that I advised my lawyer I'd be away for some time, I packed a few belongings in one of my mother's old suitcases, I sought out and farewelled only the woman who'd given me my uniform (who turned out to be on the hospital Board), and I travelled across this huge continent to its very edge to learn to speak. I had to stay in the clinic Marconi had recommended for a month at a time while my reluctant mouth learned to produce the noises my brain asked of it, to slow them down and draw them out and then to speed them up. I was a difficult patient, they said, the very worst ever. Far worse than my friend had been. Perhaps I had no motivation, they said. Was there no one at home I wanted to speak to?

I tried a second treatment course, and a third.

After a year I could produce stammering sounds with much wrenching and writhing. Everyone said this was a great improvement because at least they knew I was trying to speak, though they didn't know what I was saying. A friendly doctor told me not to go back home.

You failed there, he said. Try new horizons.

He helped me book a trip around the world that became three trips around the world, and when I returned to Australia I went straight back to the stuttering course again, mute.

If it doesn't take this time, we'll have to give up on you, the same doctor said.

It didn't quite take. My stammer was audible but still incoherent. In despair, I went for another trip, this time to Paris, in memory of Eva's mother. By day I wandered conscientiously but dismally past its fine architecture and magnificent statues, keeping my thumb at the right page in a guidebook and trying to admire the things I should. At night I slept long hours in my hotel bed and I was pleased if half the next day was lost in sleep. I tried to forget all my dreams, because dreams can hold you hostage almost as much as love. One day I was passing the book's favourite cathedral in Paris when I heard, through the open doors, my music, the music of my childhood, the music Gunther played on her piano: Handel's 'Lascia ch'io pianga' from *Rinaldo*.

I burst inside, out of the blinding sunshine, into a gaggle of people, desultory tourists dressed like me in jovial floral shirts. They had books like mine in their hands and they were gaping at the vaulting ceilings and the pillars. All round us the long, majestic chords of Handel were striding apart and closing again, like stylised stuttering, I realised for the first time. Memories of the past buckled my legs so I had to lean against the cathedral's cold stone walls. I wanted to sag into the ancient flagstones at my feet. How could I have left her? How could I have abandoned her when if I'd held out a little longer, she might've been mine? I didn't want to wander the wide world. All I wanted was to crouch once again in a rain-swept paddock, holding on to an abandoned little stool with its paint peeling off, with her near me, only a thin wall between us, and my heart surging with the belief that one day I'd court her, hold her, sing to her.

Then I couldn't help myself. Though I couldn't speak, I could sing. What did it matter now if my father forbade it? Who was he but just an angry man? Suddenly it was as if he'd never belted me for my stutter, only for his own. So I sang. I allowed my throat to open. Is that right? No – I sang at first in a whisper:

> *Permit me to weep over*
> *My hard fate.*
> *And sigh for freedom*
> *How I sigh for freedom.*
> *May sorrow break the chains*
> *Of my sufferings.*
> *I pray for mercy.*

Then my voice began to swell of its own accord, not in defiance, but in the love I'd had for him before everything went wrong, in my love for my mother, in my love for Eva, for Gunther's father, even, in the end, for Gunther and his sad childhood. I tried to send my voice out over the ocean to them all, but especially to her. Old women in black swung around with frowns to hush me, and a fat priest ran over waving his brown cassocked arms. But I couldn't stop singing, I'd been silent too long, and no one could stop me now. My voice rode out as it had when I was a child, out into the immense spaces above our heads.

I only hushed when the organ subsided. And then I began again, this time without the organ, because Handel's 'Lascia ch'io pianga' has no end.

The organist, a swarthy man with a brooding face, came up to me when I'd finally fallen silent. In a heavy French accent, he explained that in the evenings he played piano in a smoky little bar, just for tips, he said, but sometimes drinkers late at night left good tips. The customers always wanted him to sing, but he couldn't.

Would I sing while he accompanied me, just for tips?

My stammer was bad but at least he knew I was trying to answer him. It took a while to force out:

Why me?

You sing with such feeling, as if you've seen a lot of life, he said.

So I sang in his bar in Paris while around us late at night, people made deals and bargains and love. Sometimes they'd approach the piano and rattle some coins into our jar, but mostly they'd simply slip out into the dark. Between us we earned only small tips, and I was never sure anyone ever listened, but I didn't care. I was prac- tising for her. I'd become a counter-tenor. And afterwards, when I sat having a drink with my new friend, I began to talk. One night I told him about my love for Eva.

Why don't you go back to her? he asked.

So I came back to my country, to Sudlow, to my apartment, to my job at the hospital – the authoritative woman gave it back to me, with a salary this time, and many congratulations on my audible though still fragile speech – and to my spy-holes, which no one had covered up or, it seemed, even noticed, and to my peephole into her apartment. I couldn't give them up, even though I had no excuse now, if I ever had.

She was still able to make my heart skitter. She was as strangely beautiful as ever, though her figure was fuller. She was still man- aging the lab, which seemed more relaxed and less stark. Now there were postcards from people's holidays tacked up on the wall, and take-away menus fluttering on the shelves for people working late. The women no longer had to wear protective caps or glasses. I wondered if Eva had brought in these changes. But sadly, she was still with Gunther, just as in the old days. Or so it seemed.

Soon after my return, Clara came.

CHAPTER 31
Sandy strikes again

CLARA WAS A POSTGRADUATE STUDENT, doing her doctorate. They had three postgraduate students that year, down from the usual six because Doris had begun to flirt with another lab in another city, one that seemed more committed to immunology.

The lab needs a new stroke of luck, or genius, Eva said.

I noticed that Shirley pursed her lips at the mention of genius, but kept her silence.

Clara was an extra, a fourth, and Sandy's choice. I heard Eva telling Gunther that she'd been surprised by the addition – the girl's application didn't seem particularly to recommend her.

Perhaps she's for Sandy, said Gunther.

He was leaving for home, pulling on his coat. Everyone else had left.

Sandy's still in love with Shirley, cried Eva. He never got over her.

Gunther shrugged. He wasn't interested in love.

Then Eva found Sandy's note.

This applicant has a special interest in immunology, it said.

Funny that, Eva said to him as he went out the door. There's little in her work record to suggest it.

I knew, the moment I saw her, that my mother would've called her one of the rare ones, a woman who'd come into her power early. What I didn't know about was her luck.

I remember Eva as I saw her then, in her late twenties but looking middle-aged, pushing her glasses up her nose as she hurried through a door, frostbitten from riding her bicycle – she still did that, the same bicycle, though showing signs of rust – her jacket half off, half on in the sudden swamp of heat from the out of control lab air-conditioners that we were never called upon to fix, a pile of accounts threatening to topple out of her arms, pausing as she saw, bent over one of the microscopes, a tall, slender stranger, blond hair falling across her face in a careless veil.

I was just on my way outside to remove autumn leaves from the gutters, but I stopped.

Who are you? Eva was demanding suspiciously.

The girl righted herself.

I hope you don't mind, she said, indicating the microscope. Someone left a slide in and I was just . . .

Conscious of the fierceness in Eva's eyes, the girl trailed off. She said her name, but clearly Eva could scarcely take it in because of the shining pinkness of the girl's face, and the colour and light of her eyes, and her blond hair billowing and effervescing and spiralling.

You said to come at nine, but I couldn't wait, I was so excited to be suddenly accepted by this lab, she said. I didn't think I'd have a job, and then Dr Sanderson contacted me.

I could see already Eva knew, as you sometimes know ahead of time, that this girl would change everything for her.

One of Eva's papers fluttered onto the floor. The girl bent to pick it up, a dancer's bend.

What's your name? Eva asked again, and the girl had to repeat it.

A lab coat, you'll need a lab coat, Eva said fussily, and told the girl where to find one. As she walked out of the office to get the coat Eva watched her long legs, slender in black stockings and incongruously big shoes that made her seem more delicate.

Tie that hair back, she added.

When the girl returned, I saw that she even made a lab coat look glamorous.

My love – as I still called her because I hadn't given up hope, not for a minute – showed Clara around the lab and talked about the work she was to do for Gunther.

It's not groundbreaking work, she warned. You mightn't want to stay.

Eva assigned her an obscure corner, behind a door, near a sink that nobody used any more. It was Eva's old sink (and near my camera). After all, the girl wasn't going to do anything important.

Then Shirley came in. Shirley's face had thinned, and her mouth turned down in a disappointed way, though when I looked carefully I could see that it wasn't disappointment at all, just her cheek pouches slipping towards the corners of her lips. She'd become an unremarkable dresser. While I'd been away she'd begun a university correspondence course and would soon get her degree. She'd become a proper scientist, immersed in her work.

I caught a look of concern for her on Eva's face, and several times Eva glanced upstairs, waiting for Sandy to appear. When he finally came in from the car park, however, he ignored Clara, and I wondered if the girl wasn't for him at all, but for some other purpose.

On the other hand, Shirley was sharp with Clara, and told her to go to the kiosk for Eva's favourite biscuits for her morning coffee.

Shouldn't I be setting up my work? Clara asked.

Don't have tickets on yourself, my girl, said Shirley.

Eva was busy for the next two months, especially fending off criticisms of Gunther, who seldom turned up for work. I could tell, from Eva's glances, that Clara was always hovering on the edge of her mind. But I also saw that Clara was watching Eva.

One morning Clara left her corner behind the door and was talking to the men scientists, her voice carefully casual. I heard her ask:

What do you make of them?

I guessed I'd stumbled upon a conversation about Eva and Gunther. Just then, Eva came in quietly and heard the same question.

She hesitated just outside the door, so I knew that her old bright carelessness of other people's opinions was falling off her. I was startled by an aching sense of loss for the girl she used to be.

I think she was a real scientist once, said Clara. Endlessly attracted to working out something. She was probably an idealist, she would have imagined science as putting a bit of the creation in place, that's how she would have seen it.

You're the idealist, cried Ben, one of the new boys, gazing at her beautiful face.

She laughed, but continued:

What do you think is going on with her and Mueller? Are they destroying each other?

There was only the tap-tapping of Ben's fingers on his plates, and the fluttering of the take-away menus hanging from the shelves.

There are worse ways to go, said Ben. At least she's feeling something. More than you can say for him.

Then the phone rang in Eva's office, and she coughed and walked in, and took the call, and afterwards sat with her head in her hands.

Clara came to Eva's office the day she was to post off a large order for chemicals, a task that irritated her because it used up so much of her time. She'd taken to eating biscuits to nurse herself through the day, and in between them she'd crunch celery or carrots, as if she was trying to make up for the biscuits, that's how I saw it. Gunther was supposed to be upstairs in his office but he'd gone home to have a sleep.

Sleep at my place, I'd heard her urge, looking at her papers so he wouldn't see her yearning, which hadn't left her, despite the years. But he shrugged, said goodbye, and she had to make do with that. She watched him leave and reached for another biscuit. Just then she became aware that Clara was standing at her door.

Can I have a word? she asked.

Can it wait till tomorrow? Eva asked.

I've got an odd result, Clara said in an urgent voice, and came in. Eva didn't invite her to sit down. Clara began to talk about her odd result.

I have an undated note here:

'C doing recombinant DNA experiments introducing an antibiotic gene into *E. coli* cells, so that *E. coli* cells would begin producing antibiotics.'

So my results don't make sense, Clara finished.

There was a pause. Now that Clara had stopped speaking, the tick of the clock on the wall became insistent.

What do you think? prompted Clara, but I could tell Eva was thinking of nothing, the way you do when misery seems to swell in you and take all the room there is.

It's just the usual problem, Eva improvised, not sure of her ground because she hadn't been listening.

No doubt you've made some mistake in the experiment.

But what if I haven't? What if they're wrong, not me? asked the girl.

Who's wrong? Eva asked.

Everyone but me, Clara said.

Eva sighed. It was a cloudy afternoon, that dismal grey of cities, with a sky the colour of cement. She probably felt very old next to Clara's freshness.

I know you're impatient, she said. But to be a scientist, you have to love it all. The rote work. The drudgery. The irritations that the Petri dishes aren't clean, the water's contaminated, the equipment's failed, the company you keep in the lab. You even have to love it that you're probably never going to make a breakthrough. Don't feel obliged to astonish us by overturning an old, established result. It's been known for twenty years, proven in labs all over the world. Gunther himself published a paper on it when he was young.

I know, Clara said. I've read everything. She was talking fast, to cover her embarrassment.

The point is, the contamination is proving it. I had one dish here, that I was trying to put foreign DNA into and the other dish had the antibiotic-resistant cells. I must've contaminated one with the other when I used the swab. The antibiotic-resistant cells now contain the foreign DNA when they reproduce. Maybe we should always use the antibiotic-resistant cells when we want to work with foreign DNA.

That's a big leap to make, said Eva.

I thought I'd tell you, said the girl. Maybe you could tell him. Because I shouldn't be contradicting my supervisor.

Then the girl said something that overturned everything.

Should I pretend it never happened? she asked. Should I forget it, and, one day, when I've got another job, another boss, should I think about it then, not now?

Eva suddenly became her old self.

Tell it to me all over again, she said. I'll listen properly this time.

And she did. Afterwards, she took a breath. She said the fateful words:

This may be important.

Clara reached across the desk and grasped Eva's hand, which was still holding a biscuit.

Sorry, she said, because she'd knocked it onto the desk, where it crumbled. Thank you, thank you, she said.

As she went out the door, she added:

I thought you'd give me a good hearing. I've been lucky with this result and –

her intelligence seemed connected with the speed of her smile – I'm lucky that you're here.

Thank you, Eva said, surprised.

But when she'd gone, Eva drew angry doodles on her writing pad. I could see she didn't want Clara to be lucky. Clara was already lucky, being beautiful and clever. Eva wanted Clara's science to be good, but not lucky. Luck should come to ordinary people. Luck should come to Shirley.

She wrote a note to Gunther, went up to his office and put it on his desk. Then she worked till dawn, so I did too, to Matron's delight, keeping vigil to find how the possums were getting into the roof. Before Eva left for home, she went up to his office, came back with the note and tore it up. I guessed that she wanted to tell him about Clara's luck, in case there was a way it could be her luck too.

When I checked in the next day, Eva was trying to avoid Clara's eyes. She kept shuffling papers importantly. It made her feel powerful, I think, after all her powerlessness, to have Clara's hope to herself for a while.

About your result, I'm biding my time with Gunther, she said at last. Waiting for the right moment.

I'll repeat the experiment as long as it's saying something to me, Clara said.

For a few days Eva glanced at Clara's elegant back as she repeated the experiment. I could imagine she thought that in Clara's company, anyone would be suddenly alive, anyone would float on her quick mind. With her, the air seemed charged, so that nothing was grim, dour, unbearable. It was charged with Clara's luck.

Gunther was in a bad mood. He and Eva had to go to lunch with a few representatives from a large multinational company that might sponsor them, now that Doris was turning her back.

I don't see why you can't go without me, he said as they came into the lab from the car park. They'd arrived together by chance, he in his car, she on her bike.

That's what a good lab manager does, he added. She lets the scientists get on with their work.

These days he'd long stopped arguing for the work he really wanted to do. In fact he'd almost forgotten, anyone would have thought, until they saw the way his eyes turned down habitually now, glazed with something that may have been guilt. He obviously felt, as the saying went, like yesterday's man.

I could tell Eva had dressed for the occasion, choosing a blue suit with shoulder pads. Till this moment she'd been stepping briskly, pleased because at a lunch with sponsors she'd sit near Gunther, they'd be successful together. But clearly it was nothing to him to be across a table from her.

That's probably why she decided to tell him then about Clara's luck.

I've got a surprise for you, she said. An odd result from your student.

He grunted and followed her into the lab, to Clara's corner. She was bent over the bench. A bare stretch of glossy back showed between the end of her jumper and the start of her trousers. A silver bracelet glinted on the shelf above her.

Gunther leaned on one of the fridges and asked Clara for details, which she gave him.

I just happened to contaminate the control, she ended.

Gunther levered his bulky body off the fridge.

Very interesting, he said.

It doesn't mean anyone's been doing it wrong when they didn't get this same result, she said.

It was as if she had to repeat the whole mantra to prove that she wasn't proud of her luck.

You must take results like this with a grain of salt, in case they're not true. There's always a way to confirm things, Gunther said.

Think of experiments that will give a clearer picture of what's going on, Eva put in.

I don't know how it will all turn out, Clara said breathlessly, her eyes alight. She gazed only at Gunther.

Eva cleared her throat.

It's such a chance, she said to make the girl break her gaze and look at her, whether you happen to do something useful and observe it. It's the dark side of molecular biology, where things might happen and you mightn't ever observe them.

The girl still looked at Gunther.

This could be important enough to help us at the lunch, Eva said to him.

You're right, Gunther said, remembering her briefly, but impatiently turning back to Clara and her experiment.

It'll give us all a spurt on, he said to her, smiling at her so that she beamed and light bounced between them.

What's more, it will give me something to think about while I sit through this dreadful lunch.

———

That afternoon, just after everyone had left, I watched Eva look around, go to Clara's workbench, take Ben's folder and place it over Clara's gel.

That evening, Eva was dry retching. Gunther didn't visit her, and she seemed to go to bed early and sleep deeply. The next morning, I heard Clara wail about her gel.

You put your folder on it, she said to Ben.

I'm sure I didn't, he said.

You should be more careful, Eva said to Clara.

For the first time I noticed that one of Clara's top teeth was broken.

Yes, she said, abashed.

She was so achingly young.

Like Eva once was.

Slowly I put it together: Sandy had employed the beautiful Clara to work as Gunther's assistant, in the hope that Gunther would fall in love with her and through her get back to immunology. But I wanted Gunther to fall in love with her too, and that made me an unlikely ally of a man I was sure was corrupt. So how corrupt was I?

Eva still held her weekly meetings to keep everyone up to date. Hugh had resigned while I was away, and Sandy never deigned to come to the meetings these days, but somehow she'd persuaded Gunther to attend, and the students were there. Eva had taken to bringing in a large cake to make up for the breakfast the students would miss by coming. It encouraged attendance. This particular morning, they were passing around the cake when I came into my shed.

Would you like a piece? someone said to her.

Eva patted her bulky hips, her bulky stomach.

Maybe just a tiny one. And I'll take a large one for Gunther.

Gunther was missing, and so was Clara.

Eva put her folder down on the seat she was keeping for him, next to her, with his cake on top. They always sat together, a united front, I'd heard Eva tell him.

At this particular meeting, Ben was scheduled to explain his research. He waited at the little whiteboard she'd carried in, leaning on the pointer as if it was a golf club.

Will I wait for Gunther? he asked.

And Clara? said somebody else, but Eva merely checked her watch.

Perhaps you'd better start.

Ben began. Suddenly the car park was echoing with footsteps. The door burst open. It was Gunther, his coat swinging from his shoulder.

Ben stopped talking.

We started without you, he said to Gunther.

That's okay, Gunther said. Right behind him walked Clara, as elegant as ever, her cheeks bright, her coat also swinging from her shoulder.

We started without you too, Ben said to Clara. Nobody laughed. She took no notice of him. There was a self-consciousness about her. Gunther sat in one of the two seats near the door. Clara paused, then sat down beside him. Knowing all eyes were on her, she tossed her hair behind her. A few shining tendrils fell on Gunther's shoulder, then slid off. Everyone's eyes were on that slow slide.

Eva murmured to me as if she'd noticed my return:

'He doesn't catch my eye and acknowledge me, acknowledge our life together, when he's with her.'

One of the girl students looked over at Eva, to check how she felt. Eva closed her eyes against the pale and curious face. I'm sure her heart hammered. After all, she didn't know whether they'd spent the night together or just met in the car park. Neither did anyone else, including me.

Ben hadn't begun again. He lined up his golf club pointer as if there really was a ball on the floor, uncertain how to get past this moment. Then, mercifully, one of the students said that on his graph, the growth of his cells was erratic. It seemed as if the boy hadn't noticed the tension in the room.

Ben stopped lining up his golf club.

The problem is, the cells I'm studying are real buggers, he said.
The little group exploded into laughter as if he'd made a joke.

The cells went out of control and that graph, okay, it wasn't my
average result, just my best one. The little things went wild, I couldn't
grow them evenly, I had plates scattered all over the bench –

Everyone was laughing as if they'd never stop. Except Clara,
Gunther and Eva.

Ben switched off the overhead and looked at Gunther.

I'm still recovering, Gunther said.

No one moved. Not a chair creaked.

From the traffic, Gunther explained. I'm still recovering from
the traffic.

Eva stumbled to her feet and talked to distract everyone. She
talked about loving even exasperating organisms. She said that
molecular biology was on a hunt through an architecture that science was only beginning to glimpse.

Our minds resist this intricate view of the world, she said. (By
now I was taking notes again.) That's why we need so much
research into things that no one can see the point of right now.

The group filed out, Clara with them. When they'd gone, Gunther came over to her.

He jingled change in his pockets.

I slept in, he said at last.

She breathed.

Then you won't have had breakfast, she said. And I've saved
you a piece of cake.

When no one was in the lab, I saw her go to the emergency stores
cupboard, get down some sodium hydroxide and sprinkle it on the
sink near Clara's workbench. Most of the others would be out over
the next few hours. Clara would probably be the only one to use
the bench. Her elegant hands would burn.

When Clara came in, she went straight to Eva's office and
knocked.

This morning, she began, and stopped.

Yes? Eva asked coldly. What about this morning?

I'm sorry I was late, Clara said.

There was a gap so jagged it could have cut my darling.

Don't be late again, was all Eva said.

I wouldn't have wanted to miss your talk, Clara said.

Why? Eva asked, daring the girl.

When you talk, it makes us remember why we wanted to be scientists, said Clara. All this, it's so tedious. You make us remember why we're here.

Eva went into her office in such agitation of spirit that when she heard a sound beside her, she looked out of the window, puzzled.

Clara ran in.

Do you want me to answer the phone for you? she asked.

Oh, that's what it is, Eva said and picked up the handpiece, but it had already stopped ringing.

What's wrong? Clara asked. Are you sick?

Eva put her throbbing head in her hands.

Yes, she said. Go away.

Then she asked Clara to go to the hospital kiosk and buy some medicine for nausea.

Of course, Clara said, and left almost running, with a troubled backward glance. Eva listened to her steps hurrying away, put on gloves, found a thick rag, went to Clara's sink, mopped up the sodium hydroxide, and threw the rag in the bin.

She murmured to me:

'I'm tired at the very thought of love, yet it clings so closely, and you can't wash it off, not because it's natural, or right, but because it always stays sticky with promise.'

As she went back to her office, Eva accidentally knocked Clara's handbag onto the floor. She picked it up, but she lingered for a moment looking at it. Clara always left it handy. She often had to move it somewhere else because it was in the way, but she kept it nearby, as if she was always ready to depart when she knew enough, when she was ready to go on.

Eva didn't open it. She went into her office, but she looked behind her again at Clara's handbag. I should've remembered then that Eva had called herself a bolter. I'd taken it for granted that she'd always stay where she was.

Eva's jealousy seemed to be making her sick. She lay in bed for days, moaning and vomiting. Gunther didn't visit her. I heard him tell her he feared it was catching.

One afternoon I was in my apartment when she came back from work early, still weak, and Gunther followed her. She suggested that they have a cup of tea on the balcony in the last of the afternoon light. I think she suggested it because that's what proper couples did, they sat together, easy in each other's company, and had cups of tea, and every now and then they'd share a thought. Gunther spoilt it a little by pulling out an afternoon paper and an apple from his briefcase but I could see that she tried not to mind.

May I have a bite? she asked.

He lifted his head, sniffing. She was baking a chicken although the aroma seemed to be making her sick again. She must've been hoping he'd stay to dinner.

Will we eat it in bed? she asked.

He didn't answer her and didn't hand her a share of the apple, as I would have. He was gazing at her withered pot plants on the balcony. It was a dry, cold winter.

Not more chicken. I've already had chicken sandwiches today, he said.

The cafe's chicken isn't like my chicken, she said easily.

It wasn't the cafe's chicken I ate, he said, and stopped so she had to ask.

Whose?

Clara's, he said. Clara's chicken sandwiches. One. Only one. Just a bite, he said.

She stood and walked away.

Were they good? she called, her voice casual.

So so, he answered, his head in the paper.

Do you think she's beautiful? Eva called to him. Her voice was thin, as if she was struggling up a hill.

Who? he asked, not looking up.

Clara, said Eva.

I haven't noticed, he said. Is she?

So so, Eva said.

She came back and sat down, examining the pots.

You don't have golden hands, Gunther said, with a garden.

No, she said.

Gunther returned to the subject that was preoccupying them both.

It's her luck I've noticed, said Gunther. Her blessed luck. I haven't had a breakthrough for a long time. How many scientists ever have a breakthrough? But her! She comes along and – bang!

He clapped his hands together.

Eva sighed, and said:

I want to go and study science. At last. So I can be a proper scientist, like Shirley, like – everyone. I'm – she said it loudly, deliberately –

I'm resigning. As from this moment.

You can't, he said. You're too good at your job. I need you there, organising it all, making it all happen. Anyway, Sandy would never employ you as a scientist.

Why not? she asked.

Because I'm there, he said.

You have only ever seen me as reliable! she burst out. You've never said I was clever or inspired or able to put disparate ideas together. All you can see is that I'm reliable! You know I'm smart and you loved me for that at first, I could tell, but then the more they thwarted you, the less notice you took of my ideas. But I'll go somewhere else, she said, her chin defiant. I'll study and become a scientist somewhere else.

You made too much of your hunches, he said.

You had radical ideas, she cried. Once!

You'll never leave me, he said.

Do you love me? she asked.

You're part of everything I do, he said.

That's not love, she shouted. That's just habit.

I want things to stay the way they are, he said. Isn't that love?

She went back to the kitchen and brought the chicken out on a platter, with potatoes and a salad. They ate in a terrible silence.

She vomited the next morning and when she went into the lab later she was still bilious. Gunther was already there, early for him. He was with Clara.

I remember the way she came upon them. He was fiddling with a microscope that had been left on overnight.

He was saying:

I think there's where it happened.

This is my memory: he's bending over her, his fingers lingering on the plates as he explains. They mirror each other's bent arms. A noise at another workbench drowns out their conversation, so that I strain to hear.

Perhaps the mixture slid into the buffer, he's saying.

He's holding her cells, the plates in a row all along the length of his hand.

When you're faced with something like this, all you can do is go back and try it again, he says.

She laughs, self-deprecating, tossing her blondness away from her beautiful face.

It'll have to be a late night tonight. I want to get it right, she says.

He's walking away from her, but he's still carrying her cells, unable to put down something that she's touched.

Put them into the incubator and they'll be through by – he checks his watch – six tonight. You won't be home too late.

She's standing, reaching out her arms for the cells.

I'm going that way. I'll do it, he says, the eminent professor, carrying her cells.

But they can't tear themselves apart, they're like people on a liner and a wharf, holding on to a billowing streamer.

If I – she laughs, she's uncertain whether he should do this for her. If I'm making a mistake – she began.

We all make mistakes, we're human, he says, walking backwards. You're human, very human.

It's so human, science, she calls to him.

He pauses, breathes in her words as if they're a revelation.

Anyway, you're lucky, he says. It's made this lab exciting, at last.

He walks backwards until he reaches the swing door.

Eva left early, still sick. Gunther was staying late. He'd found new interest in immunology, just as Sandy had hoped. He was coming to the laboratory regularly, and working long hours while Clara worked with her cells. I went home, but I could tell Eva hadn't come in yet, though she'd left work two hours ago. Then I heard her open her door and lie on her bed, groaning softly, and weeping.

Gunther knocked on the door about midnight and came in.

I watched you with that girl, I heard her say without any preliminaries.

That girl – Clara?

His voice was confused.

You're in love with her, she said. I watched you. You can barely leave her alone. She will leave you when she's ready! Eva cried. And I'm finishing it with you.

If you finish it with me, I'll make sure you never become a scientist, he said. Nothing must change! Nothing.

They were like children raging.

At last he lay back with her on the bed, and they were more or less at peace.

Reluctantly, I put on my shoes, ready to go out into the frosty night. But before I left, I heard him say:

You were right.

About what? she asked.

Clara. That girl, he added, as if it needed clarification. She's only so-so to look at.

You've started noticing her looks, said Eva.

You told me to, he said. I wouldn't have noticed. I don't notice people. I only noticed her because you told me to. And because of her luck.

I believed him. But, looking back, I know that Eva didn't.

CHAPTER 32

I am not invited to a party, but I am fatefully inspired

IN THE MIDST OF THIS TENSION, Lotti resigned. Shirley had
come in and told Eva, playing with a paperweight on Eva's desk, a
rounded dome with blue whorls that seemed to vanish into a centre. She tipped it this way and that like a child. Then she put it
down and fiddled with one of Eva's pens. She looked up.

The lab's been Lotti's life. Should we have a party? To say goodbye to an era? she asked.

You think I should organise something? asked Eva doubtfully.

Organise it for her last night, said Shirley. Then we might see
the real Lotti. I'll know what's ahead for a spinster like me.

I didn't go to Lotti's party. I wasn't invited, of course, I was just
a grey man whom no one noticed. Sometimes I forgot this.

The morning after her farewell, everyone came in late, exhausted
and yawning. The students joked a little among themselves, but
when Eva pushed open the door, all joking stopped, and as she
walked through the lab, everyone bent their heads, suddenly preoccupied. She sat at her desk, quietly eating biscuits.

Suddenly Lotti and Gunther strode in together, Lotti proud but frowning a little. Neither of them looked to left or right as they headed for Eva's office. Behind them, the students looked at each other and rolled their eyes. Someone theatrically put his hands over his ears as if he was expecting thunder.

I've come to apologise, said Lotti loudly to Eva. I'm sorry for saying that you're only a fat technician –

and then Gunther shut the door. Whatever happened after, I couldn't hear.

Lotti left, striding down the workbenches of very busy scientists. The door to Eva's office was still open. Gunther didn't think to shut it after Lotti had gone.

He bent forward and I just caught him saying to an increasingly astonished Eva:

You know, I don't remember this long friendship I'm supposed to have had with Lotti. I might have known her at university because she was there three years ahead of me, but I don't remember her before, I don't remember my family visiting her family. I do remember digging wonderful holes. We only had a cemented back yard but sometimes we'd go to someone's house with a garden –

he stopped, looked shocked, and grabbed the desk.

Was that *her* house? Were they *her* father's roses?

I couldn't put it off any longer, after that. I had the research paper translated.

As I read it, I began to realise that Gunther had been doing his best to hide a sort of autism. As an ungovernable child, he'd been in danger of being condemned as an incurable and gassed in Nazi-dominated Austria. That was why his parents had escaped Austria – despite his father wanting to stay to save other incurables – and why, after Helene Haussman's letter, Gunther felt so passionately for the plight of autistic children, to the extent of kidnapping Allan and abandoning immunology. Asperger's paper hadn't been translated into English, and seemed unknown in our country. I could now see Gunther's dilemma: if he'd translated the paper and been

recognised as an ex-patient, it would've given Sandy all the ammunition he needed; on the other hand, if the paper was translated
and circulated, Gunther would have been more able to justify
studying the biology of autism.

I couldn't solve Gunther's problem. But I could solve Eva's, or so
I thought. I became convinced that if Eva was to fulfil her destiny,
if she was to become a scientist, even if she was to settle down to
have a baby, she must leave him. How self-interested that sounds!
But through all those years, I'd always thought of my own interests.
Now I was thinking of hers. And that gave me new clarity.

Looking back – after all the grief, the self-recrimination, the
unendurable sleepless nights, not to mention the years of putting
together these painful memories – I think I knew intuitively that in
helping her to leave him, I might never see her again – never hear
her lively voice, never watch her fine-boned, beautiful face, never
see the colour rising in it as she considered and exulted over new
ideas – that was what I most loved in her, her excitement about living. I might lose all hope that I'd hold her in my arms, that I'd be
able to tell her one day what I'd learned, and how I'd learned it,
and tell her how I loved her. The hope of that had become my life,
and losing it was like losing my life. But for her sake, I had to take
the risk. So I've come to believe that what I did next was, in its
own way, perhaps my only honourable act.

It was a long search to find an example of Lotti's handwriting.
She'd been a tidy, well-organised researcher, and her lab diaries, all
handwritten, seemed to have gone into storage. I could have used
a typewriter, but Lotti seemed an old-world person who in a letter
written from her heart would use a fountain pen. As Eva would've
said, life is lived in the details. So after searching through Lotti's
lab on many evenings, pretending to Matron that I was checking
for possums in the roof cavity again, I at last came upon a current
lab diary of Narelle's. Lotti had made a few entries in it. I Xeroxed
the entries, all of them, so that I could learn to copy her handwriting perfectly. I spent many days copying how she rounded her c and

looped her l, and made a little triangle with her g. Then I lingered in stationery shops, deciding on the sort of paper a woman like Lotti would use. I finally settled on cream paper with a linen finish and I used black ink, like Lotti did.

I was so absorbed in these details that I worked till all hours, and I was regularly woken by Eva vomiting early in the mornings. I am ashamed to say that though I loved her, I was cranky to be woken. Now, of course, I would willingly be woken every moment if she were by my side.

I didn't know Lotti's address but I decided that it shouldn't appear. Eva could, of course, find Lotti's home address within seconds, but that wasn't the point. It had to seem as if Lotti didn't want a reply.

The first drafts, I decided, were not the way Lotti would say things. They were either too gentle, or too vacillating, or too polite, or too stern. Then a story came to my rescue, in the way that stories have always taught me. It was a story in my library about a colonel who, required to challenge a poor journalist to a duel, spent the day of the duel imagining himself as his enemy, eating the same lowly food at the same lowly hotel as the journalist would – pork rinds and the last dregs of stew burned at the bottom of the cooking pot – and drinking the same coarse wine. (Aha! 'The Last Cigar at the Grey Arab' by the Hungarian author Gyula Krudy.)

So I went to the hospital cafe and ate Lotti's favourite food for lunch and again for dinner – potato salad, coleslaw and pickles. Gyula Krudy was right. When I began writing the letter that night, I felt as if I was Lotti.

Dear Eva,

Though I understand you will not wish to hear from me after my rudeness at the party you so generously gave me, I would like to make amends by answering a question you put to me a long time ago.

You will be aware of the political situation in Austria during the Second World War when the Nazis decided to exterminate seventy thousand 'incurables' – children, old people and sick people, those who were taking up medical attention and beds needed for soldiers, or so it was claimed.

There was, in the midst of all this horror, a doctor who saw his way to saving some of the children who'd been brought to him, boys commonly regarded as cretins, the very children who were likely to be killed in the Nazi exterminations. Many doctors had complied with the extermination program but Hans Asperger, for that was his name, put not only his career but his life in jeopardy by publishing a paper defending them. As he said:

'The children I will present all have in common a fundamental disturbance which manifests itself in their physical appearance, expressive functions and, indeed, their whole behaviour. This disturbance results in severe and characteristic difficulty of social integration. In many cases the social problems are so profound that they overshadow everything else. In some cases, however, the problems are compensated by a high level of original thought and experience. This can often lead to exceptional achievements in later life.'

For example, one of the doctor's patients had been thrown out of kindergarten on his third day there, and out of school on the first day after attacking other children and even the coat-racks! This particular boy seemed unable to learn the simplest lessons, his handwriting was atrocious and he stumbled through ordinary sums with great difficulty, but if a problem interested him, he showed an astonishing mathematical ability that seemed innate. He refused to do most of the doctor's intelligence tests, but the doctor realised that the boy could think way ahead of his age about ideas, and he was very good at logical thinking. He'd taught himself to understand negative numbers and when he was only a toddler he'd set himself the problem of deciding which was bigger, one-sixteenth or one-eighteenth, and he'd worked it out. After a year in the doctor's special school, he passed a state school examination and astounded the examiners in mathematics.

Hans Asperger saw that the condition could be inherited. He explained that over his ten years of practice he'd glimpsed odd traits in the relatives of every child with this problem, such as an uncle who seldom spoke about anything but train time-tables, or one who lived in a room alone, whittling. Often the children were descendants of scientific, artistic and scholarly families. He suspected a sex-linked mode of inheritance because all the autistic children he'd seen were boys, and he believed that the autistic personality is an extreme variant of male intel-ligence, gifted in logical ability, abstraction, precise thinking and scientific investigation. 'It is possible,' he said, 'to consider such individuals both as child prodigies and as imbeciles with ample justification.' However, several of his patients had gone on to lead exceptional lives, and one had, at a very young age, proved a mathematical error in Newton's work.

'We are convinced,' Asperger's paper ended, 'that autistic people have their place in the organism of the social community. They fulfil their roles well, perhaps better than anyone else could, and we are talking of people who as children had the greatest dif-ficulties and caused untold worries to their care-givers.'

He was doing his best to save all his children, as he called them, though in the paper he could name and describe only four. Those four in particular would've had a better chance of being released to their parents and afterwards smuggled out of the country before anyone could make further trouble for them.

Gunther Mueller was one of the chosen.

Do you remember that letter Gunther received, the one Shirley claimed was written in purple ink, that set his work on a new course? I have reason to suspect that it was written by the sister of one of the boys who was not saved, reminding Gunther of the debt of honour he owed not only to Hans Asperger, but to her brother. This was the debt he spoke of.

I enclose a translated copy of Hans Asperger's paper of 1944. It's a great loss that it took so long to be translated into English. The good doctor seems to have been a visionary who saw into the workings of the odd mind way ahead of his time and of his colleagues in English-speaking countries, realising that autism is a continuum, as Freud defined all madness, which is of course ironic given Gunther's fury against all the poor followers of Freud.

I've tried to understand why Gunther didn't tell us about Asperger's insights. Perhaps he could not face our reaction. His scars, as you would know, are deep.

Several times I was tempted to tell you, to alert you to who he is, but it was his secret. A refugee has the right to a new life.

Allow me to give you one word of advice. Do not get pregnant to Gunther, for if this oddity of mind is in his DNA, and if you carry some similar abnormality in your genes, it could be disastrous for your offspring.

Yours faithfully,
Lotti

PS: Don't try to contact me. I have nothing more to say on this or any other matter.

I glowed with pride when I'd finished writing this. For a day or so I almost believed I'd somehow received through the ether a genuine letter dictated by Lotti's mind, such is my ability to deceive myself. As if Lotti had murmured to me.

Nothing, however, prepared me for the catastrophe that happened next. Looking back after all these years, I see how impulsive I was to send that letter, but at the time, I believed I had no choice. I broke my own heart.

It has taken me this long to write down my sad story, and many times in the telling I have had to put down my pen because my eyes were misted with tears.

It happened this way: I slipped the letter and the paper by Hans Asperger under the door of her apartment, after I'd seen her stout white figure pedalling down the street to the lab. That day she came home early, sick again. She opened the door but didn't shut it immediately so I knew she'd picked up my letter. I heard her absent-mindedly prising open a take-away food carton as she read. (It astonished me that though she was so sick, she had an insatiable hunger, and for unexpected food: right now the smell of stuffed cabbage permeated my room.) She didn't turn her lights off, so she must have read all night.

At dawn I heard her moving around the room. I didn't look through my peephole. Every waking morning for years, how I have regretted not looking through my peephole. How simply everything might have changed. If I had looked, I might have been able to intervene. But I didn't intervene. I thought that she was just tidying up her room, which I'd always found charmingly messy.

She didn't go into the lab that day, which disappointed me greatly because I wanted to examine her face, to watch the play of muscles over her jaw, to see her eyes that still were the colour of an endless sky. I recklessly supposed she was too ill.

I tried to come home early, but loose bathroom tiles with mould conspired to prevent me. In the evening, when I finally parked the Hillman Hunter, the apartments seemed held in a hush of silence. As I walked up the stairs, some intuition made my heart thump, and I ran up the last two or three. There was no chink of light under her door. When I looked through the peephole, the room was in darkness, but there was a peculiar emptiness about it, an unfamiliar stillness. She had been a woman who could fill a room, but now it seemed more than empty, it seemed hollow.

With a leap in my heart, I grabbed the spare key and ran through my apartment, out to the corridor and, without knocking, I let myself in. The shine of the floorboards, bereft of everything except the furniture I'd built for her, mocked my soul. There were no traces of her, except a broken glass on the kitchen counter. I took that broken glass away, and have it still. I left the door ajar, so that when he came, he too would know that we'd lost her.

March 7, 1997

My life returned to me on this day. I found her at her mother's house. Miraculously, her child led me there. Her child – that's why she left! I thought I'd become a man of the world, but I was too naive to guess she was pregnant.

How long has she been at her mother's house? I gave up watching it!

The child is like her, not him.

Now to find a way. But timing. I must not time it wrongly again.

---

* I found this note, handwritten and tucked in between the memoir and the diary letter. It was in Owen's handwriting. He must've scribbled it after he first came to the house. After all, the dates tally. – T.

Part Two
THE LETTER

15 February 1997

My darling,

I will try to leave before they find me out. I will stay as long as I dare, and, while I do, I've decided to write this. Then I'll find some place to put it and leave instructions with someone – who, I don't know, but I'll find someone – instructions that you are to be given it after your first love affair.

That's if you ever have a love affair. If you can ever read. If you remember who I am, and if you care.

My darling, I've always lived with such hope.

They will tell you I have done illegal and criminal acts. If you can comprehend what they say you'll be hoping that they are making a terrible mistake. But they're not.

I am a criminal. For you, my darling, for you.

So instead of tossing on these damp sheets though the rest of this terrible summer, I will use the night hours between when I put you to bed and when I drift off to sleep to write to you. It will be my comfort, my nightly ritual. I'll prop up the pillows, pour a cup of tea from the Thermos on the old bedside table – your grand-mother's and probably yours now, a dark brown stained oak set of drawers she bought at Walton's in Sudlow just before her wedding day, the handles worked into the shapes of lions – I'll pick up this notepad and a Biro, and tell you why I had to leave.

But where to begin? There are so many subterfuges in my life, I lose track. What's real? What isn't? Perhaps all criminals feel like this. I read in the newspapers about a bitter old woman who murdered her neighbours one by one over the years, terrible murders that required the strength of an athlete and no one suspected her because they'd never seen her out of her wheelchair. She was relieved to be discovered so she could at last confide in the police. The newspaper said she helped the police most graciously, as if they were her friends. They probably were her first friends! I wanted to ask her how she'd got through the years of nights, how she swallowed the yearning to talk to somebody, to ask, 'Was this really me who committed this murder?' Did she long for a lover she could hold through the dark nights and say, 'Tell me who I am!'? Did she long for a daughter she could write a letter to?

I have you to talk to. Only you.

And the acts I did were not to murder, but to give you what you'll need in order to read this letter.

And now that's off my chest, I can sleep.

16 February

I will begin at the hardest part and tell you about your parents. You probably still don't know your father. He is a scientist, Professor Gunther Mueller. He was always eminent, and once almost famous. But he had a rival, Dr Sanderson, who thwarted him. As I write, your father is temporarily overseas visiting another university to teach about his early research, his immunology work. He lost his old fire, but that's another story. He doesn't know what's going on back here, and probably he doesn't care. He doesn't know about me.

And me?

I was only ever a technician, though I had big dreams. I never did well at school because –

maybe one night I'll tell you that.

I began my working life as a scientist in the lab. I was just a girl who made up solutions and washed the glassware. I fell in love with him when I saw him interviewed on TV – as the interviewee, he didn't bother to talk! He was endearingly awkward in an ill-fitting suit. (Your grandmother, my mother, was a dressmaker, so my eye for clothes was trained from babyhood. When my mother walked on the streets with me, she wouldn't see people, all she'd see was the fit of their clothes. 'Look at that puckering in the shoulder seams,' she'd say in disgust. Or, 'The creases in those trousers – who's his tailor? He's got an odd-shaped hip and he just needed the crotch to be widened, that's all.') Your father cared only about grand purposes, so to me he seemed almost like a god, an awkward, tongue-tied god. I thought I could rescue him because I knew about surfaces. I suddenly became studious and read through the nights, even making lists of interesting organisms so we could have a conversation.

For a while he loved me. But he was thwarted and defeated in his work, and then a woman came to the lab who was a proper scientist, unlike me. She was shimmering with ambition, like sun on water. We were dazed with the sunshine of her, Gunther and me, and I think we both fell a little in love with her, with her shimmering. She wasn't ruthless, in fact she was kind to me. She often complimented me – she could afford to. But she shimmered at Gunther. I couldn't do that, not any more. I was also thwarted. The thwarted can't shimmer. And luck came to her. 'I've got an odd result,' she said one day. She wasn't crowing, but she had that assurance beautiful people have, that she would be lucky, she was too beautiful not to be blessed.

I realised how dazed Gunther was with her self-assurance and especially with her luck just at the moment I found I was pregnant with you. He would've stayed with me, I'm sure, he was very faithful, but someone wrote me a letter – Lotti, a scientist who'd loved him since they were teenagers. 'To alert you to who he is,' she said.

I left him because of it. Except that, over time, the letter's changed, the way a person seems to. I read it again just after you were born and it seemed such a spiteful letter, but when we moved here and I unpacked, I found it amongst my soft blouses, and then it seemed a letter of revenge, probably because he'd always ignored her. And now when I look at it here in my top drawer – Lotti is probably in her dotage now – I hold her letter in my hand and it seems like a letter of love.

So as my letter will change for you, every time you read it.

When I first read Lotti's letter, I had a choice: to tell him I was expecting you, or to set him free. Once I'd made that choice and left him, it was too late to go back.

Forgive me for my choice. I've never forgiven myself.

So he's never known about you.

No one in the lab knows about you, except Shirley. My old friend Shirley, who once worked as a bottle-washer with me. She may betray me yet. All the rest, the new scientists there – Abdul, Frank and Jan, the fool of a lab manager Dick E. McLaughlin, the nurses at the hospital, and your father's rival, Dr Sanderson – Sandy, we used to call him – they all only think of me as a cleaning lady. If they think about me at all.

No one knows who I am, or that right under their noses I run the lab. No one knows that for two hours every morning when my cleaning jobs are done, I begin my real work. I research your cure.

I'll keep researching until they find me out. Or Shirley tells. Or he returns.

Goodnight, my love.

17 February

It's such a comfort to talk to you at last.

I think of your twenty-year-old self reading these words, my darling, the muscles around your pretty mouth moving with my thoughts, your eyes gripping them. Perhaps you'll be eighteen. Perhaps you'll let love wait, perhaps you'll be thirty. Your hair will have lightened to blond, I'm guessing, as blond as your elegant grandmother once was. Your cheeks will still be like fresh downy peaches. Your upper lip always lifted with such sweetness – your lips are like mine were. You were a skinny child, but when you were in the bath yesterday and turned to stop the tap dripping, I saw with a pang that at twelve you suddenly have a woman's body, your waist dipping in as if you were willing its tinyness, your hips long and swelling like a bell. I could have shaken you, and you would peal like a church bell across a sleepy blue harbour, waking everyone to wonder. I'm not sure at what precise moment your little girl's body ebbed into a woman's. I was here to notice and didn't see. I have taken for granted so much, as if you would always be near me, unchanging.

In my mind's eye, I see you reading this letter in the room above me, the best room, the dog room you called it, where we spent most of every day through the endless years of your terrible childhood until you began to go in the mornings to the Centre. It was our favourite room in this large, empty house.

Perhaps you don't know that this is my mother's house, your grandmother's. We came here after her death, when you were three. When I was growing up it was a lonely place next to a rubbish dump, but by the time you and I came back, the streets had come down to meet it. Sudlow was admired at last, like the nineteenth-century founders had hoped. 'Where have they been hiding this place?' the newcomers ask each other. Even the old powerhouse near us has become a shopping mall. There's a roundabout at the end of our street. Everywhere are cement footpaths, front gates, trim gardens. I was frightened to come back to the house, and put it off as long as I could – it was dark, cobwebbed, brooding, every room echoing sadly with our footsteps. I almost couldn't bear to enter my mother's room, and only your little face at the door propelled me on. I ran across to the windows and flung them wide.

'No ghosts, see?' I said to you, as if you'd been worrying about ghosts too.

Cuthbert, the lonely man my mother married, had renovated and extended the house as if suddenly they'd become sociable and expected a stream of house guests, but he had an accident. He fell

off the roof and broke his neck. My mother died shortly afterwards, out of pity, they said. A broken heart, they said. I'd never
known she loved him so much. There was a great deal I didn't
know about my mother.

Shirley helped us move in, clattering around the forlorn rooms
in her high heels as she carried our boxes overflowing with your
toys, your clothes.

Though she was my only friend I was jealous of her. After I
became lab manager, she'd studied and become a proper scientist.
Being a lab manager, I thought, was useless, a job that was only on
the fringes of science. But now I'm putting it to use.

The grey in Shirley's hair was like ghostly cobwebs.

'You'll liven this place up,' she said cheerfully.

Soon we filled this silent house with our noise, our screams and
wrestles with food, clothes, toys, our fights hung like rattling skele-
tons everywhere. But strangely we never fought upstairs in the dog
room. Outside there was a tree – it's probably still there as you read
this. When I was a child there was a swing hanging from it. In winter it was just craggy grey twigs and a sombre trunk. We scarcely
noticed it against the old wooden fence. But in spring, almost without warning, it was always weighted with purple bells, like your
bell-shaped hips, masses of tiny purple bells that puffed perfume
into our room. It became a huge friendly dog tethered to our back
yard, nudging the window glass to be let in.

I think that's why you called it the dog room.

Do I bore you with these details, my darling? But they have
been our life together, though we didn't share them the way other
people share things. They say: 'Look at that tree', and point. You
and I can't do that. You can't even look where I point.

You'd tear the wallpaper of the dog room as you followed the
movement of the sunlight, from one end of the room to the other,
and in its wake you peeled the shapes of dogs. You'd say the names
of the dog body parts you peeled, as you got older and learned them.
'Ears', you learned to say in your monotone as you tore an ear, then
'nose', 'tail'. Where the paper became whiskery with tearing, you'd
touch it and say 'fur'. I'd sit near you, with the latest computer

Sandy had thrown out and Shirley had brought around. 'Keep up to date,' she'd say. 'You never know – one day you might come back as our lab manager.' Sandy wouldn't want me there because of Gunther, and Gunther wouldn't want me there because of Clara. I'd point this out to her but she'd always say, 'Things change.' And recently she said, 'We've got such a fool of a manager now – there's all sorts of rackets going on and he's too stupid to notice.' How right she was.

Shirley thought that I'd use the computer just to keep up with science, but I did far more – I stumbled across a chat room where two people I didn't know talked about hacking into systems and cracking security codes and passwords. I didn't tell them I was there. Every day I kept eavesdropping, and they kept chatting – explaining codes, telling jokes, teaching each other, playing games on each other, always a little edgy, boastful, competitive. I felt so guilty I even checked to see if you were sensing what I was doing. You never seemed to – how could you? You still have no idea why I'm making these marks on a page. But something about their innocence and excitement made hacking into an adventure, not a crime. I guess they were half my age at least. One day I could bear the guilt no more, and I interrupted them to tell them I was there, and would you believe it – they'd known all along!

Learning to hack was the beginning of my crime.

What I couldn't do then was something that your father had talked about all the time we were together. He wanted to study the brain. The letter from Lotti at last told me why. But because of him, I wanted to examine DNA sequences to research a particular disorder. A disorder that affects the brain. Your disorder, as things turned out. And his. An inherited disorder. That's what else Lotti's letter explained – that you might inherit it from him.

18 February

Last night I didn't even try to sleep, I was so excited to talk to you.

In those days when Shirley visited, her arms would be brimful of bright flowers, and she'd laugh and say, 'See, I told you you'd liven up this place.' She'd stay for coffee and gossip about the lab, though I scarcely knew anyone there any more. She'd tell me about your father and pretend not to know how my heart thumped. She'd lend me money when my pension was running out, and when I'd try to return it she'd laugh and say, 'One day, when you come back to us . . .' (She said that so often, it was like nagging.) She loved you. When you pretended to be a dog and buried some chocolate she'd given you in the garden, she pretended to be a dog and helped you dig it up.

'What a character,' she'd say.

She was always saying that about you:

'What a character.'

As if there is a choice for you.

She's had no children and sometimes I've thought that she might keep silent because of her love for you. Maybe.

Oh, the guilt I have about Shirley.

19 February

So now I must admit how I'm betraying Shirley.

All those years while we were imprisoned in this house with each other, you and me, for whole days, day after day, week after week, I survived by remembering my favourite daydream. One day I'd walk into my own lab every morning, I'd have my qualifications and I'd be a proper scientist. I'd be a little later than the others and the door would be on the latch, there'd already be a quiet hum of busyness, and as I entered, preoccupied faces would lift, they'd clear, and all around there'd be smiles, acknowledging me. I'd be working in the grip of a hunch, working patiently, stubbornly, intently. The hunch I'd had when I was young. The hunch that could cure you.

But it was impossible for me to work on my hunch. Even if I was a scientist, even if I was in a lab, I would have had to copy your DNA – and his and mine – by a cumbersome method of putting your DNA sequences into a bacterium, so it would reproduce them. It would have had to be done by hand, staying up all night with a stopwatch and three baths of different temperatures, always the same different temperatures right through the night, and moving a test tube by hand from one bath to the next every three minutes, making batch after perfect batch. But I was here, with you, no lab, and not a scientist at all.

Then I read on the Internet that someone had invented machines to do it!

It made tears come into my eyes, that my timing was wrong, that my background was wrong, my life was wrong. I'd left the only man I'll ever love because of a spiteful letter. That was when it seemed spiteful.

When I read about the machine, you looked up from the wallpaper. You sensed my sadness. You've been doing that lately, more and more as if you can read my mind. Are you getting better? You came over and pulled out a tissue from the box and dabbed my face, breathing your child's breath on my skin.

'That's better,' you said to yourself when my face was dry.

My face was just a surface you were wiping dry.

You are always forgetting that I am human. And never knowing just how human I am.

So I took you downstairs to the piano and you talked to it till dinnertime, strange dissonances of squeakings and mutterings and grumblings and, sometimes, something that soared like a prayer, but faded.

After you've gone to sleep and the house is still full of you, even the air, I long to wake you up again, to have you near. I go instead to the piano and try to finger the keys the way you did, to bring you back to me.

One day you'll talk to me as much as you talk to it. This I must believe.

When Shirley next visited, she knew all about the machine.

Sandy had talked to his new sponsors. Sudlow would be the first lab in the country with both a PCR machine and an automated DNR sequencer. The very machines I needed!

She started to tell me how preoccupied Sandy is with his little cancer molecule. It's the reason that the new international sponsors have come. He's in and out of the country so much, he asked Gunther to take over the lab. Shirley thinks Sandy's skipping the protocol in his research so he can get it published sooner, to impress the sponsors.

'I record what he's done and I know he used five mice, not fifty,' she said. She told him and he retorted he'd get the same result if he used fifty mice.

'Then he told a lab overseas,' she went on, unable to stop now, 'that he had a special antibody that was responsible for his marvellous results, and when they couldn't reproduce them, one of them came to Sudlow to watch him work. After letting him come all this way, Sandy said there was nothing to show because I'd been careless and spilled the antibody in the fridge! Imagine how stupid I felt! Will anyone ever employ me again? What's more, I think he's more interested in founding little companies than in doing science.'

She asked me what I thought she should do.

'Bide your time,' I said, because a plan had started in my head.

I wasn't interested in Sandy. I was only interested in the machines.

Now I daydreamed that I'd break into the lab to work. Gunther has always been very vague, except about his science, and even then he was a sleepwalking sort of scientist. That and his fights with the hospital were why Sandy had become head of the lab when I was there. Gunther would still be vague, I thought. Besides, I knew this lab like the back of my hand, I knew everything about its spaces, its walls, its smells, its sounds. I even knew the way the planets creep around it through the day and night. But I'd have to break in every night. Thieves return to the scene of their crimes – but every night?

Sometimes we daydream so much, we lose our moorings. Perhaps that's what love is – daydreaming too much about someone, and losing your moorings. So that you think they are god.

But my daydream had some reality. I knew that with the new machines, I could test your DNA, just the way I'd envisaged long ago, long before your birth. I could test it against normal DNA, and see what was the same and what was mutated, for cells can make mistakes in copying their DNA during cell division, inserting the wrong base, or putting in extra bases or leaving some out. About one in every billion mistakes becomes a mutation. I assumed that my mother, my grandmother, your father and you all had two copies of the mutated genes, and I was the survivor, escaping with only one copy. But I may be wrong – I may have the mutations but somehow they're not showing up in my life. I can only test – and testing requires copies of all our family's genes.

One afternoon when I was gazing at the slow slipping-by of our river and thinking about breaking into the lab, I remembered as a child finding my mother's christening gown, bundled up with a nightgown and gleaming dully at the back of her wardrobe – it's now my wardrobe, probably yours by the time you read this. The nightgown was made of pale green satin, the colour of the sea in sunshine, with a diamond of sand-coloured lace over the bust – my mother's word, 'bust'. Over the breasts, my darling. I was about the age you are as I write, a lonely child who rummaged in shadowy places. What I rummaged for, I couldn't have said.

When I'd first come across them, these belongings of my mother, the best model in Paris, I examined them closely. The christening dress was white, of course, made from some heavy old-fashioned cloth hand-sewn with uneven stitches that zigzagged, the sort a child might do. There was a worked button hook at its little neck and the hook was bloodstained. Blood, I thought, so what had happened to the baby?

But the nightgown – ah – its smooth green coolness. It even had a label, it was shop-bought when everything else we wore was home-made. But even better, it was made in Paris.

I stood up and held it against my skinny body and in the pale light of the dressing table mirror, I shimmered, as slippery and mysterious as any mermaid.

My mother was suddenly in the room, telling me to put it down. She grabbed it and I didn't dare resist. But the nightgown did, it ballooned out to me pleadingly, and turned its back to show me that, like the christening dress, it was also stained, a long brown stain.

Only later, when I brushed her hair – I had good training in hairbrushing from your grandmother; it had to be done with the same pressure all the way down the scalp – I asked about the christening dress. Was it mine?

'Mine,' she said to my surprise. It was one of the few keepsakes she had, so she'd brought it with her from home.

I asked her why it was bloodstained.

'Mum wouldn't use a thimble, ever,' said my mother, who always wore a thimble on her slender white finger. She explained that my grandmother had sewn the dress just before the christening, and she didn't have time to wash it and dry it in that harsh winter.

I knew that this French grandmother of mine had eventually been put in an asylum, like her own mother had. Whenever I thought of her, I thought of those wild, zigzagging stitches.

'All the women in our family end up in asylums,' my mother taught me. 'So watch out.'

She wouldn't tell me any more, what they'd done, or if they'd done anything. All she'd say was 'Watch out!'

I bided my time about the nightgown.

Then, when I was brushing her hair again, I said:

'You'd have been more beautiful in that nightie than anyone in the world.'

My mother loved compliments about her beauty.

'I only wore it once,' she'd said. 'It wasn't a nightgown to sleep in.'

I knew I hadn't thrown them out, I wouldn't have dared. Will you be like that with things of mine? But there's nothing here I value, only you and my red beads, because he loved them.

Where had I put these clothes? When you slept that night, I searched through drawers, wardrobes, boxes. The next morning, I'd think of a box in the attic and go up to look while you were banging on the piano, or I'd remember a drawer in a cupboard unopened for years. Maybe that box! Maybe that one! I found them at last in your room, in the drawers under your bed, your great-grandmother's blood on the christening dress, your grandmother's blood on the green nightgown. I unfolded them with a clenched heart, half expecting my mother to shriek from her grave:

'Leave them alone!'

There was only silence.

So if I could break into the lab, I thought, I'd be able to study my genes, your grandmother's genes, your great-grandmother's genes. I could see if they were mutated, and how.

As for your father's DNA, I had an old clock of his that he'd bring when he visited me – how I used to hate his clock, the way it timed our love – and a tie that he wore when he was on TV, and those red beads.

There'd be hundreds of skin cells on them, I was sure.

Your DNA I could take from your hair, of course. I'm always brushing your hair. It soothes you, like it did my mother.

But breaking into a lab every night? – that seemed impossible.

It's cooler now. Seagulls have flown all the way up the river and they're screaming outside at the glow of my lamp. They know how foolish I am.

I'll sleep now. Goodnight, my daughter.

21 February

I couldn't write last night. I'd worn myself out with remembering.

But tonight, my daughter, I'd rather talk to you than sleep.

I was still daydreaming about breaking in every night when Shirley visited again.

She brought news as well as flowers.

Gunther was going away for an extended trip. He and Clara had broken up, and he'd accepted an invitation to visit an overseas lab that had been inviting him for a couple of years. The people there wanted him to teach them his work practices. Now Clara had left him, he'd accepted.

We were sitting at the kitchen table. She put her hand over mine and said:

'I'm sure you've only been coping because he's in Sudlow. Not that I've ever told him you were here – honestly.'

All I could think of was that with Gunther overseas my day-dream would come true. It was as if it had all been planned. Except for how to actually do it.

I didn't think how I'd feel about him when I went to the lab. If I went to the lab. If I could find a way.

When Shirley was in our bathroom redoing her make-up, she left her keys on the table, a big ring of keys – her car keys, the front and back doors of her flat, and the key to the lab. It was the same distinctive key it had always been. I took it off the ring. When she came back she refused another cup of coffee, and rushed off without any keys at all. I had to run after her.

She rang me the next day and came over to pick it up. I'm afraid that I blamed you – I said you must've taken it off the ring.

But by that time, I had my own lab key.

For a fortnight I broke into the lab, not working on your DNA at all. I was getting rid of the cleaning lady.

I rang Shirley ten days later. She told me what I wanted to hear – that the lab was in an uproar.

Another wait, but only twenty-four hours. I had a thousand terrors. What, for instance, if Sandy interviewed me for the job? Or saw me? Or Shirley realised what I'd done and told them?

I dyed my hair red. I practised my mother's accent. I wore a cotton jumper under my clothes to fatten up, a plain dress on top and a pink cotton cardigan over it all. I hoped the air-conditioning worked better than it used to for this bulky pink cardigan of a woman. I knew if I was lucky, Sandy wouldn't see me. I'd be interviewed by the lab manager, a stranger whose name Shirley had mentioned but I'd forgotten. While you were at the Centre I caught the bus to the lab. I trembled my way past the same cracks in the wall that were there so long ago, the same smells, the same clutter. Students flirted with each other in front of a drink machine, looking younger than they used to, almost as young as you. The place seemed very quiet. The sign on the lab manager's office, my old office, reminded me that his name was Dick E. McLaughlin.

'Who are you?' asked Dick. He was just off for his weekly assignation with Jan. On Thursdays they always rented an upper-floor room with a balcony at the Duke of Wellington hotel, I found out later from his emails. She'd already be on the balcony, with a bottle of wine open, the glasses sparkling.

I gave my mother's name. I was so frightened, I had to say it twice. Then I took a deep breath and asked if they needed a cleaner. I told him that I'd worked in a lab in Sydney, and dropped the name of a scientist I'd read about. He'd heard of him too. He nodded.

'Lucky you,' he said. 'But you came back to Sudlow. They all do.'

He sighed.

I remembered cleaning protocols that I'd overseen in my old lab management days and talked easily about them. Dick didn't seem very interested, except in my accent. He asked where it was from.

'Paris,' I said. He nodded.

'I'm still planning my trip there,' he said. He added:

'You're on.'

He left immediately, roaring down to the Duke of Wellington in his silver Volvo. I was almost disappointed, it had been so easy.

Now your mother is Francoise, the new cleaner from Paris.

I knew from Shirley's gossip that almost all the people I'd known had left. The students, of course, sent by the universities from other cities, were always changing. The lab's old benefactor, Doris, had funded the lab because of your father's early work, but when she discovered that his interest had gone in another direction, she took her money instead to a laboratory in Perth, and many of the staff went with it. Only Sandy stayed, and your father, and Shirley.

Sandy, I soon found out, hardly ever comes in. I read all his emails to Dick, and when he's due I leave early, though I'm fairly sure he wouldn't notice me. My youth was a long time ago. He's pursuing more financial deals for his cancer drug and he's now been appointed to the hospital Board, so he's too busy to think about the new cleaning lady. I agree with Shirley – I suspect his claims and his research figures, but who am I?

Shirley's jaw dropped when she saw me.

'I am the new cleaner,' I said in my Parisian accent, just like my mother's.

Shirley is very honest, but she's loyal. Her face tightened. She figured out what I'd done immediately.

'Come outside,' she demanded. Her tied-back hair flopped down in her fury and she didn't notice. She led me out to the car park, near where the air-conditioning units roar, and she roared, drowning them. She said that I'd betrayed her, that I'd made her an accessory to my crime, that she'd never be my friend again. All this was what I deserve. She said she'd have to tell.

And finally she said:

'I can't believe you've done this just to be a cleaning lady! You could've at least tried to take Dick's job. He's driving us all crazy.'

I didn't explain. I didn't want to implicate her.

But I don't have a friend any more.

Shirley hasn't spoken to me again. When she sees me, she looks straight through me.

She hasn't spoken to anyone else – not yet. I've been here since the beginning of the year and still she's silent.

If I hadn't betrayed her, I'd just have stayed in daydreams.

On my first shift at the lab, a mop in one hand and a bucket of dirty water slopping in the other, I examined the PCR machine, there before me, eerily solid, taking up space on the floor the way it had taken up space in my mind. I even wondered if I was sleepwalking. If all that I'd done was untrue. But it was firm, cold and utterly substantial, utterly irrefutable. There was no one around. Just the machine, and me. New light was slanting through the window, dust motes were dancing on top of it in spirals, right up to the ceiling. Even the dust motes seemed to be shouting, 'See what you can do for your child!'

I've already grown so many generations of your DNA that if they'd been you, you'd have stretched from the time of the Crusades until now. Your father's DNA speaks to me every morning. In its own way, it tells me about him, so that at last I understand him.

I don't think I understood him back then. If only he'd talked about himself, about his childhood, about his feelings, about his debt. But I suppose his disorder made that sort of talk impossible. He was doing the best he could.

Sometimes, waiting for the experiment to develop, it seems like waiting for a person. Like waiting for you to come into the world. As you will, with my help.

I grow large cultures of cells, I add to them a compound that produces hundreds of random mutations, I observe endlessly the results to make sense of them. What's alike here? What's different? I sift. I contemplate. I am always with our cells, these ghosts of our family, the ghosts of his.

I remember your father's words:

'On good days I say that if I'm right, perhaps people will condemn me less. He was a brilliant visionary, they'll say.

'On bad days, I know I'm a traitor to all who trust me, a forger, a thief.'

But at least I feel important now, even jostling on the bus home. This afternoon, a large man sat beside me, legs splayed, one of them into my space.

I glared at it.

'Excuse me,' I said.

After all, the fate of five thousand dividing cells depends on me.

Please understand me, my daughter.

I've written all night! It's time to get ready for work!

22 February

This evening you babbled to the clock, the fork in your hand, the kitchen tap, and they all babbled back to you in the little high voices you gave them. You went to that old friend the fridge, you hummed with it and opened and shut the door, opened and shut it again and again so it lit up like a theatre and then the lights went out. You took out the frozen food so it began to defrost on the table, and you screamed when I put it all back in.

'No, no,' you yelled, blank behind your eyes, your only concern your friend the fridge.

On my fourth attempt to reload it I grabbed you, and how you hated my touch on your skin. You bit me, screamed, punched. But when I'm angry I'm stronger than you, I have such strength. I ripped off your clothes and though you wanted your pyjamas on, I pushed you still screaming into bed and switched out the light.

'Sleep it off!' I shouted from behind the closed door. Then I crouched in my bedroom over this letter. I willed for someone to come, anyone, a late-night charity collector, a neighbour who'd lost a key, anyone. No one came. You screamed yourself to sleep.

It's absurd that at home I act as if you're just wilful, that you could snap out of it. But in the lab I search for your biological cure, because I know that you can't snap out of it at all.

23 February

This morning before Laura came, you called me sweetly, as if you'd entirely forgotten:

'Mum!'

I ran in, switching on the light, full of hope of forgiveness. But I forgot how much you hate sudden light. It's as if, after all these years, I can't remember who you are. Who I must be.

'Switch it off!' you screamed, high-pitched, frantic.

You'd just said a whole sentence! A whole, proper sentence! I switched it off, astounded. Are you getting better?

We breathed in the warm, urgent darkness.

'Can I switch it on now?' I asked.

You had the bedcover over your head. I switched on the light. Only slowly did you slide the cover down. I sat and, careful to make sure you could see my hands approaching, I held you.

My temper, my terrible temper. I'll ruin everything with you, I'll drive you further into darkness if I can't curb my terrible temper. Had I ruined everything already? But you'd just said a whole, entire sentence – so maybe I hadn't.

'I'm sorry, I'm sorry,' I said over and over again. You said nothing, you just picked at bits of fluff on your nightie. I never know if you remember my cruelty.

'I came to kiss you goodbye,' I said, my voice even despite the sad, slow movement of my heart. 'No goodbye,' you said.

You seldom speak, and now you'd spoken twice. I was so surprised, I took off my shoes and lay down beside you, stroking your slender neck, almost too slender to support your rounded head. I love you with jolts of terror, love almost beyond bearing.

'Do you forgive me?' I asked softly.

You opened your mouth and trilled a strange sound.

'What?' I asked, putting my ear close to your lips.

You trilled again.

'Yes?' I said, hoping.

Then I heard it, a bird outside the house, up in our purple tree that nudges the windowpane in the dog room. You were imitating the trilling of the bird – perhaps you were the bird. So we lay together, you and I, listening to a bird in a purple tree, and you followed the sound, again and again. I didn't think about missing the bus. The trill in your mouth turned to laughter, you were laughing breathlessly. You paused. The bird had flown away. There was silence.

Then you began again, the same trilling over and over. I didn't notice the time passing. All I noticed was the miraculous sweetness of your red and arching lips while the bird sat singing on a bough inside your head.

Remember this moment, I told myself. Remember this.

Report of ongoing investigation commissioned by the
Sudlow Hospital Board, 17 August 1998

Ref: ghp: 261

This is one of the most unusual cases I have been called
upon to investigate.

Firstly, Francoise Arnoux's entry into the laboratory was
due to a remarkable coincidence. The circumstances are
that the previous cleaner, Hermione Lu, who had held the
job for six months, was dismissed because the glassware
she was responsible for had a contaminant on it which
affected the work of the scientists. Some thousands of
dollars worth of work was lost because of this
contaminant, according to McLaughlin. She was
questioned and cautioned but the problem continued until
her dismissal. It is rare but not unheard of for glassware to
be contaminated, and of course there is the famous
precedent for a successful contamination in the case of the
development of penicillin. However, no such happy
accident occurred. Within a day of Lu's departure, and
before the vacancy could be publicly known, Arnoux
successfully applied for it.

Dick McLaughlin says that he was pleased to accept her
application because he was frantically struggling with
problems caused by the contaminant. Arnoux was readily
available and gave evidence that she was competent, having
worked as a cleaner in a lab in Sydney. He does not
remember sighting any papers proving this, but she
mentioned a scientist he knew and, in his words, 'seemed
to know her stuff'.

Dick McLaughlin, who has been most cooperative in my
investigations, provided the address she had given him, but
the residents of that address said that they had never heard
of Francoise Arnoux. However, older townsfolk of Sudlow
remember a Francoise Arnoux who had been a somewhat
eccentric dressmaker operating from that address many

years earlier. She died in 1988, after two marriages, the first to a Dennis Chatworth, deceased, and the second to a Cuthbert Portman, also deceased. Her nearest of kin, a daughter, Eva Chatworth, was living in the house until recently, but, again, residents of the house (a motley crew, if I may say so) have no knowledge of her present whereabouts. They informed me, as did a neighbour living opposite, that she used to leave early on a bus every morning to work as a cleaner, but they did not know exactly where. (The woman opposite even doubted Chatworth was a cleaner.) Since Francoise Arnoux has disappeared and Eva Chatworth (an airline tells me) has gone overseas, and they were both using this address, even contemporaneously, it would be easy for a careless investigator to assume that Arnoux and Chatworth were one and the same. But I have no hard evidence of this. Further investigations will continue.

I have checked staff records for the last ten years and found nobody who I could connect with Francoise Arnoux. (If you wish, I will go back for another few years, but this will take time.) There have been many comings and goings from the lab, largely due to a fluctuation in funding, of which you would be well aware. Dick McLaughlin has only held the position for two years. The staff members who have been there longest are Dr Sanderson, Professor Gunther Mueller and Shirley Thompson. The first two can shed no light on the mystery of why someone would take the pseudonym of a dead dressmaker. Shirley Thompson has been absent and unavailable for questioning.

I only mention the coincidence of Lu's dismissal and Arnoux's arrival because it was one of several coincidences that may add up to nothing at all. Coincidences, as my mathematics training has taught me, are the commonest things.

I believe that McLaughlin was negligent, even reckless, in not demanding a written reference or in not phoning the

Sydney scientist cited by Arnoux, as I am sure you will
agree. He has apologised, and has drawn up a set of
protocols on all facets of lab management which he will
keep to in future. I fear that this is a case of locking the
stable door after the horse has bolted.*

* Shirley sent me this report which you will know well – but you've never
known what was really going on, I'm sure. – T.

24 February

Today there was danger. In the lull time, six-thirty to eight, the time when I assume I'm safe, I heard the alarm too late. I'd been using the PCR machine. Perhaps I concentrate too deeply. I turned off the machine, pulled out my tubes, and was just rushing out of the cubicle when the lab door opened. It was Frank.

'What are you up to?' he called across the lab, his briefcase swinging at his side.

I had the presence of mind to turn away from him so I could put the tubes into my uniform pocket and pull my red flannel duster from my belt, the better to look like an all-purpose cleaning lady.

'I was wondering how to dust it,' I said.

'Of course,' he said. 'To you, everything is just something to clean.'

He told me that I was not to clean it at all, and I stood between him and it, so that he'd have to reach around me to touch it, because he mustn't discover it was still warm. I was concocting a story about how I'd accidentally switched it on, but luckily he wanted to boast about how he'd helped Sandy persuade the sponsors, and I made such sympathetic noises and nodded so encouragingly that by the time he petered out, the machine had cooled. Then he showed me how to use it, and got one of his facts wrong, but of course I didn't tell him that.

'Don't ever switch it on accidentally,' he ended. 'Someone unauthorised is stealing nucleotide bases and copying DNA. It started just after you came. So be careful – we wouldn't want you blamed.'

Then he said that he wished I was a student. Gunther and Sandy have students and he often has to supervise them.

'You listened so closely when I was explaining just then,' he said. 'As if you were really interested. You listened better than them.'

25 February

Just as I arrived at the lab, the phone rang. It was one of the nurses from down in the hospital, the bright-faced one with a black ponytail that swings as she walks.

'Got a new patient for you, very agitated, he can't sleep,' the nurse said. 'Would you have a moment to come down, do your calming trick with the hairbrush this morning?'

Early in my time here, I'd heard that an autistic girl was in the children's ward. I took in one of your hairbrushes that I've sprinkled with sparkles, and visited her. I said that I'd finished my cleaning jobs early, and I had some experience with autism, and could I help out? The nurse was only too happy to agree. The child was quiet, rocking herself. I approached her slowly and hummed a nursery rhyme so she'd know I was there, and I showed her the brush. I knew about using the sparkles because your father once kidnapped an autistic child and mesmerised him with my jewellery. (Someone had probably done that to him when he was a child.) I brushed her hair the way I'd brushed my mother's, the way I now brush yours.

The nurse told the others that I'm a genius with a hairbrush. I often am. You and my mother trained me well. But even if it didn't work, I only needed a few sweeps with the brush to collect many fresh follicles, so fresh their cells would still be working, each with its full set of DNA instructions.

Once I put the cells through the DNA machine, they reproduced and I had as much of her DNA as I needed – to find out whether or not she has genes mutated the way yours are. To see if the DNA of all the autistic children I test has the same mutations in the same genes.

As I left the ward this morning, the nurse was cooing to the little boy as he rocked himself, but more slowly now. 'Isn't that better?' she was saying to him. 'What a sweet, kind-hearted cleaning lady!'

The DNA machine trundled through its paces just before Abdul came in.

For you, my darling, for you.

26 February

There is no time to lose. This morning there was an email from Gunther telling Dick to find out immediately who was stealing the nucleotide bases. Could it be the same person who'd spread the contaminant? Was the lab in jeopardy? And he was too busy for these management details – couldn't Dick ask Sandy to get on to the case?

But I intercept all emails to this lab, and so I got rid of it. Dick would never know about it, I thought.

The problem is, it's as though my intervention is having no effect. Just as I was finishing up at the lab and putting on my jacket – the one you love to rub against your perfect skin – Dick beckoned me into his office. He has such annoying habits. This time he was beckoning with one finger and glancing around theatrically. As if anyone would care! Apart from Shirley, they're all immersed in their own secrets. He shut the door behind us. He didn't offer me a seat, and he didn't sit down. Since Dick always sits down, I suddenly realised there was trouble.

He asked me what I'd done yesterday morning.

In the lab, I exaggerate my mother's accent. She'd have been furious with me. She'd think I was sending her up. I wave my hands around because they expect it of a foreigner. She was too elegant to wave her hands.

I explained that I'd gone to the hospital – this lab has had a difficult relationship with the hospital since your father's struggles, so I made my hairbrushing sound like diplomacy – and then I listed my cleaning duties, and how dull they sounded: the loading of the dishwasher, the washing by hand of the irregular glass shapes, the putting away, the sweeping, the folding of linen, the wiping down with bleach, the unloading, the placing of the regular shaped glassware in the oven to dry. Then the ordinary cleaning which Shirley and I never had to do – the vacuuming and mopping of floors, the cleaning of walls, vents and even the doors. Dick's meant to inspect these regularly, but he doesn't.

All the time I could see his questions were leading to something. I fanned myself with the red duster, my badge of office, that I keep in my belt. You can play for time with a red duster.

But he must've believed me because he suddenly told me that Gunther knows someone's stealing the expensive nucleotide bases. The ones I steal.

I gasped, genuinely. How did Gunther get an email through to Dick that I didn't see?

I fanned his face, to hide from him. My forehead was beading with sweat. Am I not the computer expert I thought I was?

I said that maybe the bases hadn't been stolen, merely spilt.

He ignored me.

'When you went to the hospital, you of course locked the door to the car park?' he asked.

I had to think quickly. I decided to admit I might not have locked up. It took him a while to get over that. Then he asked if there were any suspicious signs when I got back.

'Footsteps!' I cried. 'Yes! I heard footsteps!'

'Where?' he asked.

I began to warm to the story of footsteps, it was casting an enchantment over me. I'm finding that for the desperate, lies are like lit corridors enticing us to enter, to go down them looking for something that might become useful. Only afterwards, cast out into the cold again, do I realise that I might not remember my lie. Liars need perfect memories. My imperfect memory may be my undoing.

'I heard footsteps at the door to the car park,' I said. 'Like this.'

I shuffled around his office doing a funny walk.

'Men's footsteps?' he asked.

I said I didn't know. I claimed I'd called out 'Who's there?' and no one seemed to be there. So I thought it was only the wind.

He will find me out. Or my faulty computer skills will. It's only a matter of time.

In fact the lab had been unusually busy. For a start, Abdul brought in from the Mouse Institute a mouse he had to dose with a drug every thirty minutes. He didn't want to go out in the chilly dawn air to the Institute with the bottle. The drug had a radioactive tag. The mouse pissed on the sink. Radioactively. I am only the cleaning lady and know nothing, but I am allowed to know what sinks are supposed to look like. So, vacuum in hand, I said to Abdul (shouting over the re-runs of the football he was watching on TV):

'Excuse me, Abdul, but the sink has gone a funny colour.'

He waited for a goal to be scored before he came to look.

'Should we leave the building?' I asked, and hurried out of the room.

He must have decided on the gross dilution method, because I heard him turning on the hoses full blast. When I came back half an hour later, he was still hosing.

'It's gone down,' he said cheerfully.

'But can't it go up? The –' I wriggled my fingers – 'waves?'

We both stared thoughtfully at the ceiling.

'It's only Sandy's office up there,' he said. 'I don't mind if he goes radioactive.'

Then Frank came in wearing a smart tracksuit that's really his pyjamas to show a dawn customer the stolen cars he sells down in staff parking lot three. He's got two nice models there at the moment, not stolen-looking at all. He'd love to put up balloons and bunting but the doctors would notice. He knows I've noticed.

'Want a car?' he grinned. 'I'll give you a good price.'

'Maybe they'll catch me,' I said, as if anyone would care about that compared to my crimes. I don't know much about his prices because he doesn't run his business by email, only by his new mobile phone.

'It's our funding,' he told me the other day.

He nudged me in the ribs.

'Who can live on our wages, eh?'

The trouble is, I'm not sure how much Frank knows about what I do.

Frank's cars are right beside Dick's window, but Dick's never here at dawn. Besides, he's preoccupied with Jan, who's married to a suspicious man. I'm grateful because it means Dick is less preoccupied with me.

We are all conspirators, if only we knew.

27 February

Today started off just like any other day. I'm up at five am and ready by five-thirty for Laura to come to mind you. She lives across the road and arrives in her pyjamas and dressing gown, face dusty with sleep, almost a child herself though she's finished school. On those mornings when she sleeps in, I run across and tap on her window, my heart in my mouth in case she's resigned. Laura has often resigned.

I lay out your clothes to wear to the Centre, and in hope I lay out hers. She keeps them handy in our linen cupboard, and somehow it's evolved that I wash and iron them, as well as store them. Do you remember her? After I've gone she minds you, which means that she sleeps in front of the TV until the alarm rings, when she wakes you, feeds and dresses you while you contrive to reach past her and play the piano nonstop. Then she takes you to the Centre and brings you back home after lunch.

The first day she worked for us I arrived home to find her on the veranda, about to leave. You were inside the house, screaming.

'I'm resigning,' she shouted at me above your screams. 'Some of those kids stuck food up their noses. One of them stuck some up mine.'

She loves imitating. She staggered around on the veranda, imitating someone sticking what seemed to be a very long carrot up her nose.

'I'm not going to put up with that every day,' she said. 'Yuk.'

I knew no one else who'd do her job, no one who wouldn't start asking questions about me. As Laura will, one day.

'How about more money?' I suggested.

'Your kid was the worst,' she burst out. 'She's an idiot!'

She doesn't realise how smart you are.

'Don't call her an idiot!' I began.

But she added, so fast I knew she must've been figuring it out even during my protest:

'Double.'

One day I'll get to like her, I promise that every morning.

This morning by five-forty I knew I'd missed my bus and I'd be late for work and would have to cheat the signing-in book, which is hard if Einstein, the old grey man from the hospital, arrives first. (One of the nurses told me his name is Einstein, but that's a joke, surely.) By five forty-five I was about to run across the road for

Laura. Then her key scraped in the lock and she slouched out of the darkness in her white dressing gown like a sullen ghost.

'Good morning,' I said brightly.

She grunted and threw herself on the sofa and flipped on the TV remote for old re-runs of *I Dream of Jeannie* and *The Saint*. Her happiest mornings are when she catches the theme tune of *Alvin and the Chipmunks* so she can sing along with them in the same annoying little high voice. She knows it irritates me but I can't say anything. I need her.

'Freshly squeezed juice,' I said as I do every day, smiling and putting it on the coffee table and getting a knock in the eye as she reached out for it blindly.

'Brush my hair?' she asked. 'You've only ever done that once.'

I only needed to do it once.

'No time,' I said. I let myself out the door, but I had to keep her happy, so I popped my head back in: 'Be earlier tomorrow and we'll see.'

Even as I began to run, I could hear her snores.

For this I pay her a quarter of my wage.

On the bus I compose speeches to you, so I can put them into this letter. That's where the idea came from to write this. I'd been mumbling on the bus, while people turned to stare.

This morning, despite Laura's sulkiness, I swayed around the corners in unison with the woman beside me, our hands folded like cats' paws on our handbags, her bag neat, mine sagging and dented. Was she composing a speech to her daughter as well?

The man who I thought was my father used to come into my bedroom on the mornings of my birthdays to make a speech. It had that slightly ringing sound that important speeches have, though there was only me to appreciate it, sleepy in the pyjamas I'd grown out of. He'd perch on the mattress which dented under his weight, so I'd fall towards him like a doll. He'd lick his lips and sit erect, suddenly shy with words in his mouth like loyalty and trust and honour. I'd try to wear a listening look, although I was never good at listening, and what with him fumbling and me nodding, together we'd endure a speech which neither of us remembered afterwards.

My darling, I want to say the important things to you, the things that you'll remember for always. But what are they?

1 March

On the bus I scribbled lists of the things I want to tell you. But I keep coming back to one thing: Tell her what a lab is like, so she'll want to be a scientist too.

When I open the lab door its air comes reeling towards me, pent up, imminent with excitement. This lab has always been the only room in my life where everything seems possible.

Even in a deserted lab, there's no stillness. The workbenches are crowded by agar plates, boxes, bottles standing upright on the boxes with taped labels around their necks, calibrated jars with shiny aluminium hoods for lids, plastic jars crammed with unused pipette tips in primary colours of yellow, red and blue, elastic bands ringed handily around the taps at the sink, calculators, boxes of scissors, little picnic Eskys to be filled not with sand-wiches but ice to keep experiments cool, gel loading tips, jars of toothpicks as if we're at a cocktail party, pens and pencils in rain-bow colours peeping through a pair of spectacles lying on an open diary with the results of yesterday's work laboriously tabulated – crossed out – rewritten, a cigarette lighter for the Bunsen burners because matches are stealable but you'd have to be a real thief to steal a lighter.

Lab coats hang in an orderly line along the wall, next to pinned-up holiday photos all askew, and a sombre, worried *Guide to Morphology* with turned-up corners. The shelves are crammed with books, reports and old diaries, and in the breeze that's fol-lowed me in from the street, flyers from take-away pizza shops flutter. On an empty top shelf a pot plant dies, but there's one new, green unfurling leaf that's my triumph. A blue cardigan is slopped over a chair. On the fridge under a poster warning about Hazards, there's an ad for someone's rowing boat which they have drawn, complete with oars. In the culture room beside the lab, there's the life of the silently growing cells.

This morning, like every morning, I heard a can of soft drink rattle into the chute of the vending machine and I knew that Einstein had arrived, and after a cursory look for break-ins, particularly thieves of nucleotide bases, he'd be watching car races on the TV in the grey men's tearoom down the corridor.

I began my work as I always do, unless I get called on for my hairbrushing. On with thick hospital-strength yellow gloves, cautiously pour somebody's lethal mixture down the sink being careful not to splash it, sterilise the pipettes and bottle filters, stack the dishwasher with Petri dishes, bowls, bottles, and swab down benches with bleach – the sodium hypochlorite I use could dissolve a human. I do this in Top Lab as well as Lab Two, so I have to work fast. I leave till later the sweeping, mopping, cleaning up, stacking dirty linen in bags and the putting away of folded clean linen fresh from the laundry. (I do that while the scientists work.) I creep to the TV and turn the volume down so the rising excitement of the commentary won't wake Einstein. I activate the alarm and put on a tape recording of a vacuum cleaner. If all goes well, about six-thirty or so I walk casually, carrying a mop just in case someone's around, to a forgotten courtyard overgrown with lantana – I have to struggle across what seems to be old rusty gardening equipment, as well as something that might be an old monument, I can't tell, it's so overgrown – but at the far side, there's a disused shed. When I first came, I found there an odd assortment of equipment for spying – what had someone been doing? – but fortunately they'd left a bar fridge. Now I've got it going and I use it for my carefully labelled vials of DNA from all the children, and from you, and your father and our ancestors. It's my work shed.

An early-rising scientist opening the door to the car park would hear my tape and think it really was a cleaning lady vacuuming, a noise as comfortingly unremarkable as a mother handling the saucepans in the kitchen when a child comes home from school. None of our scientists are likely to arrive before eight, even eight-thirty. It's the hour when science sleeps, when the scientists who've come in late at night to change a media solution or check a new growth of tissue cells will have gone home to bed at last, and when the early risers are still leaving their tumbled beds and yawning over their coffees. By the time the door first opens, I will have switched off the alarm and the tape and be unstacking the dishwasher and laying out clean equipment for their experiments. I'll be unimportant, invisible, just the cleaning lady.

I take the cultures out of my fridge and begin my secret work.

2 March

Today I grew cells. I examined them. I thought. Sometimes I work so hard that I'm surprised suddenly to see bright oblongs of sunlight on the weeds in the courtyard. Occasionally an insight about the cells comes, almost it seems from outside of me, like a tree shining with light that I'm walking towards. These are the good days, when I'm entering a shining forest of thought.

But my old love for your father, this may be my undoing. When I was daydreaming of being here, all I thought of was how I'd do this work. What I hadn't thought of was how I'd feel. Sometimes, in these rooms where he's been for so long, all my adult life, in fact, sometimes my entire body seems full of him, layers of him inside me. Today when I bent over to wipe a skirting board, I stopped midway through the stoop, caught in a memory of his quick glance, the dear way he breathed, a movement of a muscle on his shy, sweet face.

My darling, some of us are almost helpless about who we love – do you know that already? Some of us can't teach our minds caution, we can't resist. Like me when my father sat on my mattress, we fall helplessly towards the loved one. I remember my astonishment when Shirley told me that people choose who they love. I didn't choose. Your father was exactly the sort of man I shouldn't have loved, and I loved him almost to my death. He was too preoccupied, too remote, too needy. I was too needy as well.

The trouble was, I thought of myself as a spindly young woman with a long nose that no one could ever love. I'd been called Big Nose at school, and even on good days I still saw myself as shaped like a Concorde jet, all of me behind my nose's thrusting. On bad days, I saw myself as a mouse with a squeaky voice.

'Smile when you talk to boys,' my mother had said.

'I can't,' I'd say. 'I have to concentrate.'

'Smile between sentences,' she urged.

She was good at smiling.

But to me, it seemed the hardest achievement, to marshal my thoughts and at the same time to remember to stretch my lips. I only marshalled thoughts. I was guilty that as a daughter of a Parisian model I was a complete failure.

I was surprised that anyone wanted me, let alone him.

3 March

I'm always putting myself in danger because of my mouth. My heart. My foolish, lurching heart. It spills over, it must talk. I must talk.

Today as Laura left, she shouted:

'Your child's driving me around the bend!' A loose bra strap fell down her fat arm as she yelled and it made her angrier. It was almost at her elbow before she tweaked it up. She banged her front gate, stamped down her path and went inside her house. I took you to the park. Not that you like the park. Nor do I. But there might be people in parks to talk to, someone who won't attempt to ferret out my secrets. I found a woman called Grace, a smiling, contented mother. I pretended that I was. You lay on the ground watching ants.

'Your children?' I asked her, stupidly. Four of them were climbing the dark trees the way I longed for you to climb, inhabiting the branches like giant and cranky birds.

You looked at her and looked away, abashed, as if you'd seen too much. You only ever glance. But I think you see more deeply into people than I do.

She nodded, and asked if you were my only child.

Behind me, red swings creaked.

'It's lonely,' I blurted for no reason except that it was true. 'There's no one at home to talk to. There's no choice,' I stumbled on.

She laughed. 'There's always a choice,' she said knowingly.

I wanted her to keep talking so I could find out what she knew about choice. By now my tongue seemed out of my control.

'Choice is easy for some people,' I said. 'Like you.'

I sounded so self-pitying. Maybe I am.

She called to her children. They fell out of the branches and collected around her like an uneven paling fence, protecting her.

'Let's go,' she said to them. She was walking away, I was sure, to noisy dinners with children eating eagerly, their mouths open and sloppy, friendly bathtimes, and then she'd read to them in bed. And all the while a loving and pleasant husband would be waiting to make sweet love with her.

Unexpectedly, she looked over her shoulder at us.

'Let's talk again soon?' she said. I nodded. Perhaps next time we'll really talk.

When we got home, you ran straight to the piano and played for half an hour, something that scrambled to the high notes and swayed there. I am tone deaf, so all I could do was hope that your strange music was beautiful, while I peeled potatoes for your dinner.

But this isn't what I should've written about – my chat with a stranger in a park. I should be writing about the important things. The trouble is, I've never been able to tell what's important and what isn't. Only afterwards.

It's like research, where you could struggle all your life to get to the furthest corner of the universe to research it, and only afterwards be able to say that it wasn't worth doing, that out there was nothing, nothing at all.

4 March

I haven't been entirely honest with you. I am too deep in my research to stop, even if I am found out. I love it too much. I love you, but I love it as well. 'Science is not made of funny feelings,' Gunther said all those years ago, smiling at me and touching my chin as if I was a child like you. Which I was, for him.

But I am still a child, like you are now as I write, except that you're a child because you're twelve, and I'm a child because I want to know this cell I watch every dawn. It's as if you and I are both standing at a door and someone, or something, begins to talk about the world we're on the threshold of knowing – for you, the way adults live; for me, the way this cell lives – and we have to eavesdrop, we have no choice, we can't turn and walk away, we must listen for our very lives, we are helpless in our longing to know. I can't stop listening any more than you could. Every day I stand at the door, eavesdropping, though what the cell tells me I can't make sense of, not yet. Every day I think I'll understand, and at the end of every day I know nothing more. Its secret is always just out of reach, how it behaves with other cells, what relics it retains of the past, what it promises for the future, what it promises for you. For your brain. I do things to gain its attention. I think about it, I get ideas about it. I'm in love with it, the way I'm in love with you. I'm trying to get to know it as I know you.

So science *is* made of funny feelings, and it was for him before the letter in purple ink that came with the research paper. And it sometimes was afterwards when he had his hunches.

That's how it is for me. The cell I love is your cell, with its history of your parents, your grandparents, his parents and all our ancestors. We are our history.

5 March

Too tired to write, and I've been worrying that what I wrote yesterday was just a speech and not from my heart.

6 March

You'll think, now that you're grown up, you have put behind you childish thoughts, like toys. But we carry our childhood curled up inside us, peeping out all the time, just like the Freudians say. I can admit that, despite Gunther.

Looking in the mirror in the Ladies, I was remembering my mother. I am always remembering my mother.

One day she looked over my shoulder into the mirror as I stood brushing my hair. People say that the camera loves some faces, not others. The silver light of mirrors loved my mother. Almost from every direction, the silver light gloated on her. But not on me.

'I worry for you with that face,' she said.

She pulled my chin around, to examine my face more.

'Perhaps the nose will not grow any longer,' she said. 'And my cheekbones? Where did my cheekbones go? You have a nice smile but a girl can't always be smiling.'

She let my face go, to raise her hands to her own hair and puff it up.

'You must do everything young,' she warned. 'In the young, there's always some beauty.'

She pulled down her mouth.

That's when she said:

'I have only one daughter and she looks like a fish.'

No matter how much I tried, I couldn't get close to my mother. I thought it was my fault, that somehow I didn't love her the right way.

She didn't come to your birth. So I took you to another city and we lived there on my savings. Sometimes we came to stay with Shirley, which was hard for her, keeping it a secret at the lab about her visitors. I still didn't want Gunther to know, I didn't want his confusion, or Clara's condescension.

On one of these visits back here, I took you to my mother's. You were fifteen months old but she made a new dress to wear for the occasion and expected us both to notice. She sat far away from us in the living room of my childhood, now ours, in a raffia armchair that had been unravelling for years. There was a gleaming blank white wall behind her – she'd insisted Cuthbert paint the walls white because she thought white set off her colouring. She crossed her old legs to make parallel lines all the way down to her trim ankles, until her death the ex-model from Paree. She pronounced the name of that city as if she'd trodden its catwalks to tumultuous applause. You could almost believe her still, at least from the knees down.

The conversation was stilted. She was waiting for Cuthbert to come home from the shops with a quiche for lunch. She'd depended on him for everything after I'd bolted, and she hoped he'd think of something to say to her daughter with a baby born out of wedlock. Suddenly she rose from her chair, walked across the floor and opened the fridge. Then she shut it, opened it, shut it, opened it, all the time watching you. She was balanced on high heels that set off the cut of her skirt. I was charmed as I'd always been by her elegance. I was unprepared for what she was about to say. But then, I always was.

'She's been smiling at the wall,' she said.

An observation so threateningly ordinary, my heart crunched.

'And at the fridge,' she added. 'She thinks that the wall is a friend, and the fridge is her mother, not you.'

My tears were already glittering in your downy hair as she said:

'I escaped the family curse, and so did you. But your daughter hasn't.'

One of the reasons mothers don't talk is because they think they will be there always, waiting for the moment to talk, which never comes. It never came with my mother. This is my only moment with you, before I am gone.

7 March

I've tested my DNA. I've discovered that one of my genes is mutated, like yours. I might have the same problem as you. It depends on how many mutated genes cause your problem. If it's only this one, why doesn't it disable me? Was your father wrong? Were the psychiatrists right? Did my mother somehow give me what was necessary for living, something that I failed to give you?

As I lie here, I'm thinking: Should I abandon this work? Then I remember your father on TV, shy in his ill-fitting suit, saying the words that changed my life: 'The problem with most discoveries is what to make of them.' He never thought that was a reason not to make discoveries. Only a reason to make more.

8 March

This afternoon I took you back to the park. I hoped Grace would be there so she'd tell me again about choices. But she wasn't, so I walked with you to the river's edge, the same river that runs near our house but snakes into the park and belongs to other people, and there I lost you. I don't know how it happened. I turned my back and I shut my eyes. I can't believe it now, that I lay on the narrow strip of sand and shut my eyes. I imagined cities in the clouds, and mountains and valleys, a land I could wander in, but alone. That's what I must admit to, that I wanted to wander by myself.

Sand blew on my face, a soft shower, a warning. I sat up, squinting. Even then I didn't look around for you, I was too busy wiping sand away. Only afterwards did I peer at the river. Too late. You were gone. Seconds went by, drenched, spellbound by your absence. Perhaps minutes. I let them go by. Freedom washed over me like the river. Then someone crunched by on the sand, a woman's feet. I remembered duty, responsibility, and love, passionate love. My love that tethers me to you. I began screaming:

'My child! My child!'

I screamed my way down to the grey river and scooped it, sieved it through my hands, half expecting to find your body amongst the dark grit, the abandoned sneaker, the skeleton of an umbrella, the lemonade bottle still capped but with beads of moisture inside, the shreds of white mucus that may have been a jelly blubber, the green slime of river weed. You would have crooned over such a collection, hung the river weed around your neck, put on the shoe and hopped with it, flapping. But you weren't there. Perhaps you never would be again. Perhaps I'd never see you again, your skinny, beautiful body. I ran shrieking to every corner of the park, mad, wild, weeping. The earth had swallowed you up. I ran shrieking up the road to home, my heart flying out behind me, a tattered streamer.

I wasn't to know that you'd gone off to the swings, touched them, rocked them, and then suddenly noticed my familiar shape was gone. That's how I think you know me. A familiar shape. You must've begun to yell. That's how you were found, though not by me. A stranger, more caring than your mother, brought you home.

I came racing up the path and saw two people on the veranda. You were safe! There was your dear, slender figure waiting for me, and, beside you, a large male bulk. When you saw me running, still damp and seaweed-slimed, you jumped up in excitement and clapped your hands.

'Now!' he said.

You both barked.

You must've taught him about your barking. For all I know, you'd been barking at him all the way home.

I puffed up the steps, clutching my stomach with its stitches, my heart in its pain. The stranger stopped barking. You didn't. My eyes met his above your sweet rounded head. We could hardly hear each other for the racket you were making. My heart was banging, it was twitching my shirt, I was sure. I knew him! He seemed utterly familiar, this total stranger.

'She was yelling for you.'

'How did you know our house?' I asked.

He paused, as if he was having trouble speaking. He didn't answer the question. All he said was:

'She was lost.' As if I didn't know, as if I wasn't standing there oozing my frantic, stinking search for your lostness, my dread you were gone, my hope that all this torment was over.

Then you stopped barking. Someone's teeth chattered. Perhaps mine. We all listened.

'You've been lost too,' he said. 'But everything's going to be all right now.'

I think that's what he said. I think it was to me.

Because of that, the dam burst inside me and I was throwing myself on you, weeping so loudly I couldn't hear anything else, even you. With you there's little freedom, but without you there'd be no freedom at all. I only stopped weeping when your dress was wet with my tears.

Your eyes were on your dress, anxiously watching the damp stains spreading.

'Gone,' you said suddenly.

I looked up. Your rescuer had left.

9 *March*

That stranger's words have jangled me.

That I've been lost.

That everything's going to be all right.

As if he knew what my life is like!

I'm still wondering how he got you home. Do you know your way back here, after all? Perhaps you looked up and glimpsed our tree. The dog tree guided you.

I took you back to the park this afternoon after work and Grace was there, with a Thermos and the remains of a cake, looking up from a book, shading the sun from her eyes. She waved to me. Behind her, like a backdrop, her children shrieked on the swings.

She poured me a cup of tea.

'Join them,' I told you.

You lay on the grass instead.

'Why won't she go away from you?' Grace asked quietly, so I explained.

Why did you tell people? I can imagine you asking angrily, your eyes flashing. How could you betray me?

I'm always loyal, in case one day you're cured. But explanations must be given. And explanations let me talk. I talked about how well you'd begun, and then, when you were eighteen months old, you began sleeping rather than waking up, and how doctors said you might never get better, and how I said that of course you'd get better, you were just developing slowly, slower than most children. I said nothing to Grace about genes and chromosomes and molecules and nucleotide bases and vials and DNA sequencers in case I sounded like a scientist. And all the time I was speaking fast, because I wanted her to tell me about choosing another way to live.

Instead she told me she was going to Latin classes, despite the children. 'I'm reading Dido and Aeneas in Latin,' she said. 'About love. Its lack.'

One of the children, Jessica, the four-year-old, ran up and twined around her leg like a puppy, saying her name over and over – 'Mum, Mum, Mum' – but Grace talked louder.

'Look at this,' she said. She flicked open her book. 'Your heart is an oak tree, growing out of a rock.'

She glanced at the child's bobbing head.

'Love,' she cried with a laugh that was almost raucous, no doubt because she has so much loving to do.

She looked at me.

'Your life is so purposeful. Doing all that cleaning, for science.'

'How can a heart be like an oak tree?' I asked, to change the subject.

'It needs to stand up to so much,' she said.

She laughed again, and checked the other children, nine-year-old boy twins in grubby jeans, and an older girl, to see if she should call them to defend her from my questions. She twisted her head this way and that, while I looked at her handsome neck with its fine white skin, like the knitting in a silk pullover. She was heavily made up. I could see where the pink of her foundation ended. Why such make-up on her fine white skin?

She caught me staring and turned, but I couldn't wait any longer.

'What choices do I have?' I cried.

She pushed the four-year-old away and pointed to the swings. Jessica ran off.

'About what?' she asked, puzzled.

She ran her finger around the curve of the Thermos cup.

'I don't know what you're talking about,' she said.

'About how to live,' I said desperately.

She started, sat up, and looked anxiously for her children again. Her breathing was fast, worried.

'I hardly know you,' she said.

She wrapped up the cake in its stained, greasy paper and put the Thermos in her bag.

'Have you got a big house?' she asked suddenly.

It was almost hidden behind our jacaranda tree but I pointed it out.

'A waterfront,' she exclaimed.

I'd never thought of the swampy river as a glamorous waterfront.

'The problem is that the house is so big and empty,' I said.

'Don't you know anyone who'd like to share it?' she asked.

So that was the advice. I sighed, crestfallen. It would be impossible to share our house. The person would find out my secret.

But it started a slow slide in me, those words. Such simple words. Perhaps it was also the stranger's words: 'Everything's going to be all right now.'

I was no longer there in the park with Grace, I was imagining someone beside me, speaking, pausing, listening, we're sitting out on the veranda in the softness of evening, there's a frosted bottle of white wine between us, and we have all the time in the world, or at least an evening. The someone and I are utterly familiar; we've teased, flirted, admired. We know about each other's childhoods. We've explored each other's bodies. He knows about my slack stomach, he knows how many fillings are in my teeth, he even knows what I do at the lab. He doesn't mind. He could list my moments of grandeur and meanness, as I could his. Every word is weighted with familiarity as we talk. So what would we talk about? Him – a little. But mainly my secret work. And you. When I run away, we'll all run away together, him, me and you, like children playing a game.

'A lodger,' Grace was saying. 'Advertise for a lodger. Just a little sign in the supermarket.'

'A lodger?' I repeated.

In my mind's eye I imagined the lodger's face, gently outlined by the kitchen light from inside the house as we talk on the veranda. His head is cocked slightly, the better to listen to me.

'Someone patient,' Grace was saying. 'Someone who'd help with Tina. A granny, of course, a kindly older woman.'

She shook the dregs of tea out of her plastic cup and looked at my startled face.

'Not, of course, a man,' she added.

'Of course not,' I said, and shook the dregs of tea from my cup as well.

I need a kindly old woman lodger who'll be a mother to you when I'm gone.

10 March

But this afternoon, dreary with rain and silence, I needed a lodger for me. We were in the top room and you'd been tearing strips off the wallpaper in dog shapes.

'We need a lodger,' I said. It jerked out of me and, once it was said, I couldn't stop. I was pretending you were listening, the way I always have.

'Someone to live in our big, empty house. An old lady. Any kindly old lady, as long as she doesn't know anything about science or my lab.'

I've begun to bring home the vials and they're starting to clutter up our fridge. But Laura will be too lazy to wonder about them.

I watched your long legs, one of them straightening as the strip of wallpaper turned into a tail. You're skinny, all the way up your body. I wondered if your skinniness and your problem are connected by something that causes both. And how I'd test for that.

'We don't like science,' you suddenly said.

I was so astonished at your coherence that I grabbed your arm, momentarily forgetting that you can't bear sudden touch. You flinched, hit yourself as you always do on your other side, to even things up. But you'd said a sentence again! Were you getting better?

'What do you mean?' I asked.

As if you could tell me.

'What?' you shouted, imitating me.

'When you said, "We don't like science", do you know I'm a scientist?' I gabbled.

'What?' you said. 'What?'

Had I been dreaming? I tried to lower my voice. Perhaps my shouting had frightened you.

'Did you say to me, "We don't like science"?'

'What?' you said. 'What? What? What?'

You repeated it till you were hoarse.

It was always like this. Nothing has changed.

So we walked to the shops this afternoon as if it was any ordinary day. At the community noticeboard we stuck up our advertisement amongst the others for second-hand sofas and babysitters. I read it out to you as if you'd understand.

'Wanted: Lodger for the best room in a large house, furnished, with view of tree. Must like children.'

I put in our phone number and address, because you can trust people in Sudlow.

You fingered the shine of the blue Biro, suddenly quiet. For you, it wasn't the words but the ink that was important.

It wasn't until we got home that I remembered I hadn't asked for an old lady.

11 March

There is always the fear that I'll be caught. Shirley doesn't look at me when I go into Lab Two (where she works with Sandy and the students) to collect their glassware, and Frank smiles at me in an over-friendly way, but nothing has gone wrong, not yet. Anyone could catch me out, even Laura.

Laura has taken to chewing bubblegum, bright turquoise, and smelling of children's birthday parties. Every now and then she sticks a finger in her mouth and thoughtfully prises turquoise bits off her teeth.

This morning as I was passing the lounge room on my way out, she asked why I don't have you taught to play the piano properly. Then she prised bubblegum off a side tooth.

'I suppose a teacher would have to come to this dirty house,' she said.

She had her feet up on the sofa, with her shoes on. She'd trodden on newly mown lawn. Bits of grass were falling on the cushions. So I asked her if she'd clean up while you slept. She rolled her eyes up to the blue dawn sky as if only a celestial being could appreciate my stupidity. She poked at her gum, got her tongue inside the wad and stretched it out. It was almost transparent. I saw her pink finger behind it. She checked the gum and put it back into her mouth.

'You know what?' she said. 'The state of this house, Mum doesn't believe you're a cleaner.'

I blushed, even as she moved her feet on the sofa and more grass clippings fell off.

'Plumbers have dripping taps,' I found to say.

My voice, like her chewing gum, was almost transparent.

They're such a grubby lot in the labs, they don't notice. Some walls in the lab are hung with the past I can't bear to touch, the past greys them like cobwebs do. The corridor just outside the swinging doors of the lab, where it's no longer the lab and not yet the hospital, I can't touch. Its past swirls up to me clammily, and I hurry by, eyes averted. Once Dick hailed me from the end of the corridor. I turned, open-mouthed, expecting him to say:

'You haven't cleaned this corridor in weeks. You're sacked.'

But all he said was:

'Could you bring me in a cup of coffee? A strong one? I've got to do the accounts.'

The ghost of our first kiss is there, as we leaned against the wall. We'd been for a drink at the Duke of Wellington and we'd come back for my cells. The first kiss is so tentative, awkward, unknowing, the lips, faces, shoulders, hands, fingers all so unknowing, and then suddenly so sure. The particular body has to learn about another particular body, how to find the right geometry of reaching and bending and loving. It's a slow, specialised learning.

So I cannot disturb the spots, stains, scuffs. Every day I promise myself that one day I will. That one day, it won't hurt to scrub away the memory of our love.

And there's the corner between the sinks. One day I'll be in trouble for that corner. I can only clean it on brave days, and I'm not often brave. It was where she explained her odd result to him, while my heart toiled in jealousy. I lost my way as a scientist that day.

12 March

I think Shirley has noticed the quality of my cleaning. At the end of my shift she was waiting for me out in the car park. Her hands were on her hips.

When I saw her I went over to her. I had to squint into the sun.

'What's wrong?' I asked.

'What are you up to?' she asked.

I tried not to squint, to show her that I would still like to be her friend.

'Like what?' I said.

Then she took my breath away.

'Are you planning to sabotage someone's experiments?' she asked. 'Don't expect me to say nothing if you're trying to compromise our work. You never got your qualifications – are you trying to get back at us all?'

'Your experiments!' I laughed. 'Of course not.'

I moved slightly, so I didn't need to squint any more.

'It's better I tell you nothing,' I said. 'Better for you.'

She turned on her heel and went back into her lab.

I came home to you.

14 March

Yesterday I found Dick hovering near the window that looks out to my little shed. He's not busy enough. So this morning I edited one of his emails to the Board that was waiting in his Drafts box.

Everyone knows Dick McLaughlin is a fool, but I watch him being a calculating fool. He brings to work an important-looking leather briefcase with nothing in it but his lunch (I peep in it when he's out). He calls long, boring meetings during which he deliberates on his favourite subject: when the tearoom fridge should be cleaned out and how many open packets of each person's food should be thrown away and whether an exception should be made for resealable containers such as mustard. It seems to me that the point of a meeting for him is to be able to record that a meeting was held. He could just go and talk to people but he writes long emails instead, always in the passive voice and never daring to use the first person pronoun so he can't be blamed for anything:

'It can be appreciated that if the said containers in the refrigerator remain in place beyond their use-by date, they hold the potential to become offensive at a subsequent date.'

Dick doesn't know how to keep the lab in budget, but he doesn't know the extent of his ignorance. He doesn't guess that every few days I balance his budgets. When he logs in, he thinks it's due to his work that his budgets have come right. I've heard him exclaim:

'Aha – why didn't I see that before?'

He didn't see it because I hadn't been able to put it right until my shift began.

I need his incompetence. If it wasn't for his incompetence, I would've been found out in my first week.

15 March

Since that appalling day in the park, I keep thinking that I've met your rescuer. Somewhere in my past. But where? When?

17 March

I worked but the work goes so slowly.

No one has called in answer to the advertisement.

On the bus I remembered my mother lying on a sofa, our battered old sofa now. Her skirt was flowing down to the floor. She knew about its flow. She knew at any moment how her clothes looked on her. I imagine her mind was crammed with tiny photos of her poses. She'd riffle through them and decide on one, and arrange her dress to suit.

I was sitting on the floor, fingering the hem of her skirt.

'Why did you become just a dressmaker?' I asked. I wanted her to tell me that she hadn't stopped modelling, she could begin again right now, that we could fly in a silver plane back to Paris and be beautiful models together, she in the beautiful gowns she made, and I'd wear the dresses she sewed for me.

But she was deep in her dreams and had forgotten me.

'Sudlow,' she'd finally answer.

Sudlow wasn't a place, it was an explanation for the decline of her brilliant career.

We'd both sigh with such sadness.

I can't explain about her, not yet. But I must, in the tiny space of this letter.

I must, before I leave.

18 March

I studied the cells. I'm getting nowhere. A black mood settled on me.

When I got home this afternoon shame overtook me, that in the advertisement I hadn't said I needed an old lady. It was a thinly disguised advertisement for a lover, not a carer for you. I walked with you to the shops and opened the display case, but I felt someone watching me, the way you can feel someone staring. I didn't look around, I didn't want to be seen, the woman so desperate for love she had to use subterfuges. I pretended that all I wanted to do was straighten the notice, someone who'd happened to see a crooked sign and couldn't bear signs to be crooked. I found another pin lolling at the bottom of the case. When I'd pinned our notice straight and closed the glass door, I let myself look around. Behind me was only the vast floor of the mall, with a faded streamer blowing around it, leaping up, buoyed by a draught, and falling, disappointed.

19 March

I should give up this diary to you, my confessor, and get more sleep. Abdul asked if I ever slept, I seem so busy. The last cleaner didn't seem so rushed off her feet. He nudged me in the ribs as he said it. What does he know?

I think it's just the dark circles under my eyes. But it's become an addiction, this confession to you. It makes up for the talking we can't do.

The real problem is that there isn't enough time between six-thirty and eight to discover how to help you. Making sure which are your problem genes is one thing. Everyone has known since 1990 that in diseases with one mutation, some adult stem cells without the problem mutation could be sent to the problem gene to replace it. It was even done then to a little girl. But you have several mutations, perhaps three. I could send adult stem cell DNA to them all, packaged up in a virus, because viruses will burrow into your cells and release the stem cell DNA to let it do its work. However, I don't know enough about how your adult stem cells work. Do I need to change them genetically in some way? I can't do all this alone. I need someone else. I must employ someone! Dare I? What I'm doing here is so wrong I can't make it much worse.

To conceal my agitation, I took you to the park. Grace was there.

'No one's answered the advertisement, no one wants us,' I told her.

'Be patient, she's out there, waiting for you,' said Grace.

She's so friendly and happy. She was knitting a yellow jumper for the youngest. She was worried she'd run out of wool and that a new batch of wool wouldn't quite match. I wish I could talk to her. But I might implicate her. What if someone noticed us and she later had to answer questions from the police? I've caused enough harm.

In another lifetime I would like to be an ordinary mother in a green park, with no other worries than the matching of yellow wool.

21 March

Today I wrote to Dick as if I were Gunther and overseas, and told him to employ a young graduate student, a special one for some confidential research for three months, with a view to this being extended if the research went well. Our usual students were paid by the universities they'd come from but this one, I told Dick, was to be paid by us. I told him to use the slush funds – when I was manager I set up the slush fund – and said not to tell Accounts that he would be signing her cheques. And of course I signed your father's name.

It fills my nights with awe when I'm not writing to you, the way I write emails as if I'm Gunther. For the sake of this work, I have to pretend I'm the man I've loved – how did I think I could carry this off?

Your father's face never leaves me, and his thoughts still live in me. So it's possible for me to write the emails, but afterwards I tremble. Is this really me, this criminal?

22 March

Dick, annoyingly, wrote back and said that he'd checked with Accounts and they'd said okay, it's unusual but we can fund a graduate student for three months.

Checked with Accounts! Can't he read?

I couldn't resist pointing this out.

'You fool!' I wrote.

It was such fun to call him a fool at last, though in your father's name.

Then I added:

'I will tell her how to set up. She is exclusively under my instructions. All to be in place within a week. And may I remind you – very hush-hush. Send me a shortlist of three.'

27 March

Dick stealthily interviewed only three people today, very early, trying to be very hush-hush. However, he wasn't very hush-hush in front of me. I mopped under their chairs as they sat waiting to speak to him. My favourite had one of those round, friendly, innocent faces, a little chubby and double-chinned, with a long black plait meandering down her back, tendrils escaping but at the plait's end subdued by a simple rubber band. She wore a crumpled brown shirt and an ill-matching green skirt, and lipstick that looked like purple cement – someone who didn't know how to dress, my mother would have said. Didn't know how things are done. She put her feet up to make way for my mop. I warm to people like that. It made her unforbidding, compliant, unsuspecting.

To double-check, I deliberately left the bucket in the corridor just around the corner from Dick's office and watched. They all fell over it. But the girl with the plait turned to me.

'I'm so sorry! Can I clean up the mess?' she said.

She's my girl.

Report of ongoing investigation commissioned by the
Sudlow Hospital Board

Ref: ghp: 261

An unknown party or parties – from here on, I will assume
Arnoux – seems to have been very cognisant not only with
scientific matters, but also computers. I say seems, for I
have recovered from hard disks many emails purportedly
to and from Professor Mueller and Dr Sanderson and Dick
McLaughlin which none of them recognise, so they must
have been written by the other party. This other party took
advantage of the lack of formal identification in emails,
such as letterheads, which conventionally would have
verified the sender. The other party directed, in the name of
Mueller, a considerable expenditure that was used on
private research. A research student was employed, a Skye
Christopoulos, and instructions for her work were sent
purportedly from Mueller, and she reported, she thought to
him, once a week.

Since these letters coincided with the presence in the lab
of Arnoux, I contend the party was Arnoux, to further her
own research at the lab's expense.

2 April

Dick sent his apologies about telling Accounts, and pretended his shortlist of three applicants had come from a longer list. He promised the new worker would start from next week. He didn't seem to know how to end the message. I saw him write something, delete it, go to the toilet, come back putting his comb in his pocket, his hair newly parted, rewrite, delete, have a coffee and rewrite.

He ended up just signing off with his name.

Gunther will come back and find the slush fund gone. But I'll be gone too.

5 April

I wrote back to Dick as if I were Gunther. 'Employ Skye,' I said.

No kindly old woman has answered my advertisement for a lodger. But a man rang, with the voice of the man of my yearnings, the exact tone, and with a charming, almost familiar way of pausing, as if he was searching the depths of his thoughts. He'd be handsome, with a sculptured, high-cheekboned face and blond hair swept back. It was as if the fates were determined to mock me.

'I'm ringing about the ad,' he began.

I could imagine his slightly tanned flesh glowing. Blue eyes, I decided, with gold flecks.

'I'm searching,' he began – confidingly, as if he already knew me – 'for a room,' he added, remembering that we were only talking, after all, about a room.

'But it's not available,' I said.

'Children are not a problem,' he said after we'd both been silent for several seconds. 'I like having children around. I'm a family sort of person. Could we meet and talk?'

'Not about you being a lodger,' I said, clumsy with longing.

'But that's why I'm ringing,' he said, puzzled.

I blushed and was glad he couldn't see me.

'I need a kindly old lady. A motherly sort of person, who'll stay a long time,' I said.

'I'm quite motherly,' he said. 'And I'll stay a long time if you want.'

'I'm sorry,' I said, and hung up quickly.

I kept thinking of him, his blondness, his cheekbones, his tall, slender build, and putting him out of my mind. But he's here even when I'm trying to sleep. He only goes when I write to you.

No one else has rung. When we went to the shops this afternoon I glimpsed the advertisement behind the shine of the glass case, shoppers wheeling their trolleys past it, talking to their children.

10 April

Skye's first day. She smiled at everybody, and nodded. Now the way she smiles so openly is worrying me. Perhaps I needed someone as furtive as me.

Dick led her into the little room that used to be Shirley's powder room. It was still full of the old equipment from those days. I'd offered several times to clean it out, thinking it'd be much handier for me than the shed. She didn't flinch. She put the rubbish into bags, lugged the equipment to Stores without asking anyone for help, swabbed down the walls and mopped the floors.

'Should I help her?' I asked Dick, elaborately unconcerned, even contemplating a yawn.

'No,' said Dick.

He was in one of his officious moods.

'Since you've got time on your hands, bring me a cup of coffee,' he said.

The problem began when she put my emailed instructions up on screen.

Try to understand, my darling. As a researcher, you write instructions that are the distillation of your thoughts of months, of years, all your inspired moments at three in the morning, all your doodles in the margins of newspapers on the bus, your sudden doubts in the bath. The mind's uncertainties, the mind's chaos.

When she went to Stores, she left her door wide open so anyone could've come in and read my instructions. When she returned, Dick wandered in with her. He was sipping a take-away cup of coffee and telling her that any personal foodstuffs she wished to keep in the fridge should be indicated by a waterproof marker pen – so far no one had appropriated green as the colour for their marker pen, he said.

My mop had taken me nearby. I stood up from my skirting board and peeped through a crack in the door. Dick was lolling there, sipping his coffee, still talking about fridges and marker pens, but his eyes were resting on the screen where my instructions were on view. With nothing better to do, he was idly reading them. And she was allowing him to.

Dick always makes little noises under his breath as he reads, almost a humming. But he interrupted himself.

'Oh, what?' I heard him mutter.

'Is something wrong?' she asked.

I heard Dick take refuge in his coffee, gulping it down.

'That old hobbyhorse,' he said about my instructions. 'I heard about this fracas.'

'Hobbyhorse?' she repeated. 'You told me I'd be doing an important aspect of Professor Mueller's research.'

'Of course,' said Dick. 'I'd just forgotten.'

'Mueller did run it by me once. They do that, you know. They run things by me.'

He threw his polystyrene cup into the bin nonchalantly – it missed.

'You're entirely answerable to Professor Mueller,' he said. 'Just email him.'

He turned on his heel, puzzled, wiping his lips with the back of his hand, so preoccupied that he almost bumped into me.

'Be careful,' he said.

13 April

I wrote to Skye protesting that Dick McLaughlin seemed to know all the instructions that I'd sent her in confidence. I finished:

'If you cannot be confidential, you will have to walk. Hush-hush is hush-hush.'

Of course I signed off as your father.

Every dawn when I write as your father, I tremble for hours.

15 April

Skye wrote back apologising, promising she'd be careful from now on.

She'd better be!

Then tonight the phone trilled through the house, a sound so rare it shocked us.

It was the man with the handsome voice again.

'Have you found your –'

there was a long break

'– kindly old lady?'

'I used the wrong words in the advertisement,' I said.

He sighed over the phone, windily, the sort of sigh you expect an apology for.

'I can imagine your house has a big old flowering tree,' he said.

Then he talked about how he'd love to live in a room with a tree outside his window.

'There is a tree,' I said.

'I imagine it has purple flowers,' he said dreamily.

'It has!' I exclaimed.

'I saw it in my mind's eye,' he said. 'I must be meant to have your room.'

I didn't know what to say. I couldn't invite him even to come and look, not when I'm so unsure about my future and when I'll need to escape.

'Being a landlady, you're probably wondering what I do,' he said, again with those curious pauses. He told me that he sings in bars but he's not famous. There'd be no problem with the rent, he'd pay months in advance if I wanted that.

'May I visit tomorrow?' he ended up.

He was very persistent.

I was panicking.

'No,' I said.

'I'm very kindly,' he said. 'As kind as any old lady.'

'I made a mistake,' I said.

'Just for a look?' he asked.

I had forgotten that if anyone responded to the advertisement, they'd want to see the house. All I'd thought was that they'd ease my loneliness. Laura was right. The house was a mess. Newspapers were toppling off tables, chairs, the sideboard, and strewn on the floor were books, shoes, clothes, toys, paper, crayons. The only clear space was in the kitchen, a shrinking circle between the stove, the sink and the fridge. The sofa cover was ripped. Ivy had trailed through the kitchen window, which I could no longer shut. No wonder Laura's mother doesn't think I'm a cleaner.

But I let him persuade me. It was the understanding in his eyes, as I imagined them, that was weakening me – the way they screwed up at the corners, his bony face, his hair that tangled with light. You know how these moments are with men, now. You know, my daughter.

'When would be suitable?' he said, even though he knew that I didn't want him, I'm sure of that.

I stopped, because I didn't know how to speak unless I blurted out the whole history of my life.

'What about the day after tomorrow?' he asked.

'No,' I said. Then: 'All right.'

What's wrong with me, that I'm so persuaded by him? He talks as if his life depends on living in our room.

16 April

At the lab, Skye works differently from how I'd imagined. She plods away, carrying out my instructions so at last there are two of us doing this work. I can only do mine every day for an hour and a half, if that, but she can work whole days at a time. However, she doesn't think for herself, she doesn't think like me, she's just a robot. So I'm still doing most of it. She can't see when she's going up a blind alley. And I can't stop her, until she emails me and tells me what she's doing.

Was this such a good idea?

Here at home I've tidied, swept, cleaned, washed, mended and shopped – like a competent cleaning lady! This afternoon I even sawed our old paling front fence, to level up the rotted ends. You were watching me, imitating the saw's sound.

'E-aw,' you said. 'E-aw, e-aw.' Then you added, between one screech of the saw and the next:

'No man. E-aw.'

'Yes,' I said.

'No man, no man, no man, e-aw,' you said.

'Yes,' I said.

'No man!' you shouted through my sawing of our entire front fence.

I was about to hit you, but you were too puny, too skinny. I threw the saw down instead.

Why do you sometimes seem like my enemy?

When I lay down earlier tonight, trying to sleep, I imagined the love of the handsome blond lodger licking around me, its warmth moving even in the tender spaces between my toes. I have been without love for your lifetime, and beyond your lifetime, for seven months of your gestation.

Then I cried in self-pity for the child I might've had instead, a chubby, teddy bear sort of child with a little trusting hand in the space of my big one. Perhaps you mourn for the mother you should've had, someone like Grace.

Perhaps I should cross that out.

I've just gone into your bedroom and sat on your bed, frantic with guilt that I'd wake you, but frantic with guilt that I'd thought like this. I'm lucky to have you at all. I could so easily be alone like Shirley. In the dim light from the hall, I looked at the delicate length of your backbone and marvelled that I left that space between us, that I didn't hit you.

'I must keep calm,' I said.

As if I haven't said that a million times.

17 April

Skye's first results came. Interesting, but nothing new. But she'll come good, I'm sure.

He was due today.

I came home early with a big bunch of yellow flowers.

Laura looked at them with narrowed eyes.

'Who are they for?' she asked suspiciously.

'Us,' I said.

I told her she could go early. While I was seeing her out, you cut their heads off with your new scissors, so that the vase was full of sticks.

'Pretty,' you said.

I found a saucer and swam the flowers in that, so they were pools of yellow light. Then I dressed you in your best shirt and trousers, though you ripped them off because I'd got the order wrong in my hurry, I'd put the shirt on first rather than the trousers.

'Shh, we're having a visitor,' I said, but you screamed, 'Wrong, wrong, wrong.' The trousers had to be put on first. Then the left sock first, not the right. I kept getting it wrong. You kept crying. It didn't matter. He didn't turn up.

'That's all right,' I told your reddened, blotchy face, but I was really talking to myself. 'He'll come before dinner,' I said, 'the cocktail hour.'

The sun moved around our dog room that was to lure him to me. He didn't come. 'He'll come in the evening,' I told myself.

By the time I'd cleaned you up after dinner, quickly, crankily, so he wouldn't see how you ate, and picked up the newspaper that catches your falling food and put it in the bin, I allowed myself to doubt. I didn't properly admit he wasn't coming until your bed-time. Then I had to say: 'He's changed his mind. He wanted a smart landlady, he could tell I was a fool.' I wanted to hurt some-body as much as I was hurting, so I refused to kiss your dolls.

'I'm too sad,' I said. I went to bed and wept loudly for all those things I'd said to him.

You came in sometime after midnight and said:

'I hear a big river.'

A whole sentence again!

I took you in my arms and held on to you. I hid my face in the sweet smell of your childhood. I took you back to your bed.

Now, as I write sitting up in bed, I glimpse myself in the dressing table mirror, where my mother often stood. My face is swollen with tears.

18 April

I cleaned and then I worked on your cells. Skye worked in her robotic way. I tried to stay calm. Should I email more instructions? But she'd wonder how I knew to intervene.

When I came home I took you to the park again, hoping to see Grace. There were many mothers with their children, but no Grace. Somehow you and I got through the long, sad afternoon.

After dark there was a knock on the door. No one ever knocks on our door, as you might remember. I couldn't find the key for the deadlock, I was racing around the house, looking under newspapers, tipping over the vase of dying sticks in my haste, slipping on the toys you'd scattered on the newly polished floors. I tripped and sprawled at the front door, got up, smoothed myself down, opened it. A fat man stood there.

'Yes?' I demanded, brusque from all my hurrying.

'About the room,' he said.

'But that was yesterday,' I said.

'I lost my courage,' he said. 'May I come in?'

Why did he need courage?

He had a small bag over his shoulder, a cloth bag that seemed heavy. There were a couple of plastic folders sticking out of it, with sheet music showing. He was ugly, bald and fat. I had to restrain myself from looking down the street to see if he wasn't trailing the handsome blond man.

'Why do you need courage?' I asked.

'It's a long story,' he said.

He paused, one of his strange, long pauses.

'I rescued her, remember? I brought her home.'*

The memory of that day came over me in a wave, the heat, grit, my appalling wish for freedom.

I shut the door, blushing. I didn't want to go on with this, I didn't want him. I needed a kindly, capable old lady who could be a mother for you when I'm gone.

We stood there. Neither of us could think of a thing to say.

You looked up from the floor where you'd been poking a leaf through a crack. You got down on all fours. For a moment I thought you were in pain.

'She remembers me,' the fat man said. He threw back his large head and barked at you, a big throaty bark that startled me. You barked back, the same bark, copying him. You both giggled, and kept on barking, little barks, huge growls, whinnies up and down the scale. Caught between you, I hardly knew where to look. I knew you so well, my daughter, I expect anything from you. But I needed a sensible old lady. This was not only a man, but an embarrassing one.

Then you scampered, still on all fours, to the piano.

'May I see the room?' he asked.

I led him up the stairs to the dog room, but all the time my mind played tricks. I wanted to blurt: But you're not who I was expecting, you're not him, not the one.

He stood in the middle of the floor, staring. I wondered at what. I moved so I could see where he was looking. I had forgotten about all the dog shapes you'd torn into the wallpaper. But he only seemed to be watching the play of light and shadow of the tree's waving.

'You knew we had a jacaranda because you saw it when you brought her home!' I said.

---

* From this letter, the scribbled note, and from stories he told Grace and Laura, I pieced together what must have happened. He must have been watching the house for a couple of years after Eva had left the lab. When she didn't return, he'd given up, assuming she was living in another city. And then discovered her. Maybe it wasn't chance. Maybe he willed it. – T.

'I'm sorry, he said. 'I was desperate to be here. I'll never trick you again.'

'It's not a good way to start,' I said.

He fell silent. His toes splayed under his weight. There were frills of fat on either side of the bones. He looked to be the sort who always wore sandals. He was so fat, even in winter he'd be hot. He would've collected a wardrobe to cope with heat. He would be like a shaggy dog in the tropics. Elasticised waistbands on trousers, loose shirts, a headband. Sometimes he'd probably wear loud blue shirts in tropical island patterns, as if he could hear the lilt and sway of a distant ukulele. I'd have to think of some way to get rid of him.

'We didn't decide about your rent,' I said. 'I should have mentioned. It's quite big.'

I named an unreasonable sum.

His eyelids didn't flicker.

'No problem,' he said absent-mindedly.

I'd manage better with his rent money. I'd be able to buy you things so you'd be set up well when I leave.

He put down his small bag, pushed the door shut behind us, threw his weight down on the chair, gazed up at the window dappled by moonlight, and said:

'At last. Everything's going to be all right.'

Only after a minute did he remember me standing behind him. And his manners. He got up to speak to me, his body so wide and lumpy that it left the chair reluctantly, in sections.

'I'll take the room,' he said.

I was still arguing in my mind that, right now, rounding the corner, there'd be a slim, handsome man following him, coming up the street, I'd hear the clang of the gate any second.

'No,' I said.

'Your child likes me already,' he said.

I felt my resistance quiver.

'You'll hardly know I'm here,' he said.

He seemed very anxious to please.

'A month,' he pleaded. 'It's a good policy, isn't it, to try something for a month?'

He said this in an experienced way, as if he'd lived his life a month at a time. So I nodded. I'll think of a way to get rid of him within a month.

And if I have to run before then?

'When do you want to move in, to begin your month?' I said.

His constant smile broke into a laugh. His belly flopped with mirth. He saw my glare. He nodded at his small bag, and explained the joke.

'I have,' he said.

So he'd been determined to move in, whatever the room was like. He cocked his ear.

'It's your child playing that extraordinary music?'

Despite his size, he bounded down to see you bent over the keyboard, entirely engrossed in the sounds your fingers made.

'No sheet music,' he said in surprise. 'She plays it by heart?'

We stood there surrounded by your music.

'She's using half-steps and perfect fourths like Béla Bartók used, but it's not Bartók. Where did she learn this?'

I shrugged and explained that you'd always played my mother's old piano.

'But who's the composer?' he asked.

'No one,' I answered. 'Well, her.'

His name is Owen.

19 April

I forgot to warn Laura!

When I came home she was waiting angrily for me outside on the front veranda and you were inside sitting on the dog room stairs and moaning. I apologised to Laura, let her go and returned to sit down on a step with you. I put my ear to your mouth.

I made out: 'Dog room, dog room, dog room.'

You were mourning the loss of the room.

Then, 'O, O, O, O.'

So you know his name is Owen? You don't know Laura's name, often you don't know my name, but you know him?

Owen's door opened.

'Come up. Peel some dogs?' he said to you, beckoning and acting as if he was peeling.

You looked at him, bloated, red-faced, overjoyed. Then you nodded, stood and sped up the stairs. I held out my hand to stop you.

'It's okay. I was just going out to sing,' he said.

He'll only be in our lives a month.

24 April

Skye sent me her results. They were disappointing. I rammed jars into the dishwasher and broke one and I had to fish out all the broken glass, bit by patient bit.

'I don't want him! I don't want Skye,' I said to myself. 'I'll tell him this afternoon that I've changed my mind.'

But he was out all afternoon. Then, this evening, he came in and ran to the toilet. When he flushed it, I was there in the shadows in the hall. But so were you, waiting for him. He strode towards you. You grabbed at his hand.

'Me,' you said.

'I'm singing at the Roo Bar,' he told you, smiling. He struck a pose and sang a note.

You laughed at him, delighted. He struggled with our deadlocked door, slammed it behind him and stepped out into the release of the evening.

You shouted at the slammed door and hit it with your fists.

'Me,' you shouted again.

1 May

Some days in the lab my mop leads and I follow. Go and clean the Ladies again, it says. So I go, and find Jan putting on eyeshadow for a tryst with Dick. She leaves, sighing. Now the mop leads me to the coldroom, just outside it, so I can check if Dick is waiting for Jan. He's not there yet. It's as if the mop knows what's going on, and I follow.

This morning I didn't work on your cells. When I was in Lab Two, I went through Sandy's diaries, thinking that, after what Shirley had told me, I might find something extra to incriminate him if I need to. I thought I was being smart. But instead, as I turned the pages, I was overcome by the past. Suddenly I remembered your father protesting at my scribble in the lab diary.

No one ever seemed to look in the diary I shared with Shirley so I allowed myself to jot down things. I scribbled about the blue light that poured into the lab at dusk from distant hills, making ordinary things mysterious, so even the workbenches and the test tubes were hazy with colour. The next week when I was bored, I told the diary about the silence in the lab, so profound when Shirley had left for the night and I could work alone, that I felt wrapped around by the white silence of angels' wings. After that, all sorts of things came tumbling into the diary, unstoppable, irrelevant, just for me. One day I told it about Gunther.

He found it. I'd been hiding up the back of the lab because my lab coat was torn, and the diary was open in his hands, its pages as white and vulnerable as a bird.

He'd found the line where I'd described his buttocks. 'Defeated buttocks', I'd dared to say. He told me later that he'd fallen in love with me, with the way my face – not me but my face – asked him where his life was going, and how could it possibly keep going the way it should if I wasn't there with him.

Plodding Skye is still following my instructions to the letter. Stupid girl! And stupid me, for choosing her, and not setting up properly. I sent her new instructions, knowing that she'll probably follow these to the letter as well.

3 May

Skye sent new results, which promise nothing.

Owen was practising his scales in the dog room when I came home, and you were on the stairs listening. The scales sounded like the wind. Then you imitated him on the piano, the same beat, the same mood. He laughed and opened his door. He sang from the top step and, way below, you played as his accompanist. You clapped each other afterwards.

He has a screechy voice, not deep the way men should sing. A screechy, weird voice. I asked him why he sang so high. He says he's a counter-tenor.

'Not everyone's cup of tea,' he said.

He laughed. Good-humoured, amused laughter. He spread out his hands and laughed, and all his body laughed too. It seems a long time since anyone laughed in this house.

But his singing is not my cup of tea.

5 May

I was late this afternoon again, and expected Laura's wrath. (The bus was caught in a traffic jam. A newly made statue of Samuel Craven Sudlow, the city's founder, was being unveiled in the main street – he was a plump nineteenth-century man with an optimistic and benevolent smile.)

But Laura was humming in the bathroom. She opened the bathroom door when she heard me arrive.

'He's gone out,' she called. 'A woman came in a new car and picked him up.'

She was peering into the bathroom mirror, examining her lipstick, holding it up in the air like a torch.

'So?' I said. 'Probably his mother.'

'Hah!' said Laura. 'She wouldn't have been more than twenty-two. He didn't look so bad, in a suit. He said he'd be back this afternoon.'

She pulled away from the mirror, sliding her lips against each other so they were red and shiny.

'Do you want me to stay? You could put your feet up.'

I asked her how much, and she looked cunning. She redid her lipstick and said overtime was double the hourly rate. But when I told her I couldn't afford it, her hand jerked on her lipstick.

'Now the line's all wrong,' she said accusingly.

I dismissed her.

He's not her type. And too old. He's my age, for goodness' sake! But not my type.

8 May

If I can't cure you, there's no point in all this risk.

Yet every morning, I fall in love with the process itself. It tugs at my imagination all the time, when I'm stacking the glassware into the dishwasher, waiting in a queue, waiting for you to finish cleaning your teeth (tonight it took you forty minutes, with me shouting at you to put the brush down), waiting for the bus. Then a thought drags all the chaos into a pattern. And after the pattern, there's silence. That's what I long for, the particular silence that happens after hard thinking. It's almost like prayer.

I don't want to put my discoveries about this cell into someone else's head, the way that Descartes did, or Moses, or Jesus. I don't want to convert anyone, or change the way other people think. My struggle is not to do with other people, it's about how to see this tiny cell, how to see beyond the conventional ways of seeing, how to go beyond what questions are considered possible, what experiments useful, what explanations acceptable.

Admit it, I say to myself: in my heart I hope to understand what no one else has ever understood. No one in the history of the world.

But of course I want to find your cure as well. Why I work at the lab is for you.

When I finished my shift, Shirley was waiting for me again in the car park.

'Get in my car,' she said. 'I want to talk.'

I tried to say that I was in a hurry to get back to you, but I didn't dare. I feared she'd found out something about Skye. So we sat in her little red car. She looked straight ahead. She didn't seem to know how to begin.

'I've figured out what you're up to,' she finally said.

Her crimson lips were grim.

I folded my arms.

'All I'm doing is cleaning,' I said.

'Are you here because of Sandy?' she asked unexpectedly.

'Sandy?' I yelped.

'You always hated him,' she said. There were tears glittering in her eyes. 'I lost faith in him too, but I wouldn't want to destroy him.'

'I hated him for Gunther's sake,' I said, softened by her tears. 'Sandy thwarted him.'

'So are you trying to get back at him? Maybe you're spying on him?' she asked.

'Why would I?'

'Because of what I told you about him. I shouldn't have said it. I regret so many things . . . I thought I could confide in you, but I gave you ammunition.'

She looked around at me at last, her face twisted in pain.

'When I said that about his results. That they were too good. About his cheating. And the contamination – it was you who contaminated everything, wasn't it? Is that why you came? To hurt Sandy because of what I said?'

'No,' I said.

I began to open the car door.

'Has Gunther put you up to this?'

'Gunther doesn't know I'm here,' I said.

'Tell me,' she said. 'We were friends once. I've been good to you. If you don't tell me –'

'I'll say one thing,' I said, on the asphalt now but still holding the door open. 'I'm not here for Sandy. I'm not here for Gunther. I'm here for Tina.'

I slammed the door.

'That doesn't explain anything,' she cried. 'You won't get away with this.'

12 May

Skye's results showed nothing.

Tonight you wouldn't get out of the bath for three hours, no matter how much I reasoned, pleaded, threatened, yelled. I tried to pull you out but my hands slipped on your wetness. You're too heavy for me now. Then I tried to pull out the brown plug from under you, but you sat on it.

'I'm in the sea. On a little brown spot!' you screamed again and again.

'No, no,' I shouted.

It doesn't matter, it doesn't matter, I told myself. But something shifted in me. I stopped being a caring mother. Do I have the madness of my ancestors? I got a knife from the kitchen. It's hard to write this down but, yes, I got a knife. I'd been calling you for almost three hours and all I could think of was a knife. I went into the bathroom, stalking like a villain in a horror movie. You stayed where you were, wide-eyed. I left, I threw the knife down onto the floor as if it was your stomach. Then I lay on the sofa and screamed. After a while I got up to see if you were still alive despite my murderous thoughts. You'd floated all your dolls, those dolls you've never played with. Their hair was sodden, they were face-down, drowning.

I shut the door on you to shut you out of my mind. But I found myself standing outside the bathroom door, listening to whether there was another splash from the bath. And then I saw it, the absurdity of acting like a stalker, the absurdity of trying to reason with you. How long would I keep trying to reason with a child who can barely speak? What did it matter in the long run whether you got out of the bath now or at midnight? Would I still be doing this in another twelve years? Trying to force a grown-up Tina to get out of the bath? I doubled up with laughter at the thought, laughter at my own despair. I sank into a chair, whooping in paroxysms of laughter.

'Shut up!' you shouted, but that sent me into another fit of giggles. The chair seemed to be giving way, like my life. I allowed myself to roll on the floor with the absurdity of it all. I must've fallen asleep. Suddenly I heard a key turn in the front door lock. I struggled awake.

'Anything up?' Owen was hovering above me, gazing at my crumpled face near his toes. I am, after all, a mother, a landlady, and a respectable cleaning lady, even though my body seemed to have lost its dexterity. I levered it into a sitting position. I looked around for my glasses, my hands making the motions of a blind person. Owen handed them to me. Every light in the house was on.

His hand went towards the knife which was glittering where I'd thrown it. We both blinked at it. I found my voice. 'I was going to . . .' I began, then despair and hilarity came over me again, that incongruous mixture, and I was shrieking with laughter. I gasped for breath.

'I was going to . . .' I began, then I was laughing again, doubling up, chortling and giggling while he waited.

'Murder,' I got out at last.

He didn't laugh, this stranger.

I stopped laughing. 'I was going to murder her.'

There was a terrible silence.

I was aching with spent laughter, all my muscles in my stomach seemed stretched. I struggled to get up. Owen saw it and held out his hand. I leaned on it to get up. For a moment I felt I must tell him the real travesty of my life, my life which was surely bigger than listening at a bathroom door to see if a child was splashing. It was just a matter of words to tell him, just a matter of saying – what would I say? Surely there were words in the world enough to tell him what I'd done with my work, my real work.

I sat heavily on the sofa.

'What's she been up to?' he asked, his voice steady, without criticism, but without sympathy either.

'She wouldn't get off the plug,' I said.

Then I realised that you might be silent because you'd drowned! I'd fallen asleep while you were in the bath! I leaped up, but right at that moment you peeped out from the bathroom doorway, your little round elf face, younger looking than your years.

'Just like a kid,' he said to me, but smiling at you.

14 May

With him here, I feel a new sort of peace. And in this peace, I've thought of another ruse to help you.

Last night a new website appeared on the Internet, apparently set up by an old and anonymous scientist who was retiring but wanted to bequeath to interested researchers the knowledge he'd amassed over many years on a particular – and for a long time unfashionable – line of research on autism. Not that he expected ways of thinking to change in the near future, but just in case anyone else out there was stumbling along the same trail as him, he didn't want them to waste their time.

He set out his theory on the website, suggesting a link between autism and three specific genes which may be the cause of the trouble. He described his research methods and experiments, which were difficult but more or less reproducible. Only more or less, because few things are causally related in a straightforward way. Every experiment is chaotic, the data is usually chaotic. People think that science is a clear progression from one truth to another, but that's only because scientific papers pretend it. He'd never taken short cuts, never faked data.

How could I fake data, not knowing the answer? Only this blind groping.

I even posted a photo of an old and anonymous scientist. The photo I used was the only one I have of my real father, your grandfather, a young sailor, windswept and fearless on the deck of his ship. It's as if your grandfather is helping us. Besides, I took after him. People might notice, if they peered. The same dominating nose, the same thin, pale face. That's why I have a face like a fish. My sailor father ironically with a face like a fish. He seemed only a child in the photo, a child in a uniform, just five or six years older than you are as I write. I tried to say a prayer for his forgiveness, but the words dried in my mouth.

The knowledge I posted was my own. I wouldn't want anyone to waste time going in directions I know to be dead ends. After all, I may soon be caught.

I included an email address, and I'll check the In-box from time to time.

Tomorrow I must tell you about him.

Now, I'm falling asleep.

16 May

A frustrating morning, again.

With cells, you are constantly waiting, and then you may wait twenty seconds too long.

Or, startled by the call of a bird or a creak of a door, you may drop everything, weeks of patient work, weeks of thought and hope, all rolling on the floor to smash in glittering pools of silence.

That's what happened this morning.

But I'm putting off telling you about the past. You need me to tell you, so that you know who you are.

First, I have to explain my mother, your grandmother. Today, thinking I can't go another night without admitting it to you, I went back in my mind to my schooldays. I was swabbing down the benches in the lab but remembering myself crouching on a playground bench, with the girls all laughing, their wide mouths saying that my mother had never modelled dresses in Paris. That all she'd ever been was a dressmaker. She was a liar. And so vain, she'd been jealous of the models and thought she could do better. She thought she should've been up there on the catwalks. She'd never been on a catwalk.

They said this just after the man I thought was my father had left us. He'd told someone's father in the pub that my mother was a fake. It turned out that he wasn't my real father at all, just a man she'd met when she was indecently huge with me.

The scorn of the girls covered me like a spiderweb, it clung to me, I couldn't get free of it.

'You're telling lies, lies, lies,' I shouted. I ran out of the schoolyard.

The asphalt pounded my feet. I didn't stop until I was home in my bedroom. I covered my head with my quilt.

'What's wrong?' my mother asked.

I could tell her nothing.

That night, twisting in my silent, narrow bed, I swore that no one would ever laugh at me again. I never went back to school. Eventually I got a job in the lab, this lab, this place of truth.

One day, rummaging – as I told you, I was always rummaging in drawers and cupboards, the whites of my eyes like ghosts as I whirled when my mother came into the room – that's the day I found the wedding dress and the christening dress. But I also found a photo of a man who looked like me. It was the photo of the sailor.

Before you were born I traced the man I used to call my father. It was difficult to find him. I dared not ask my mother where he was.

He was past retirement age but still working, a spindly, chirpy man with a trimmed moustache and a limp. He was shorter than me, I discovered in astonishment as he shook my hand too hard outside a cafe instead of hugging me. I'd forgotten his limp, I'd forgotten he would've aged. I recognised him so little, it was almost as if I'd dreamed him. I peered at him. He didn't look like me.

He seemed reluctant to meet my eyes. He kept looking at his watch. He'd always been a salesman, a good one, he said, and now he sold insurance. In fact he had five appointments today, he added.

'When did you stop being a sailor?' I asked.

'Sailing? I've never gone to sea, never liked the sea,' he said.

I didn't pursue this, though my heart was pounding.

'Why did you leave Mum?' I blurted too early in the conversation.

'You're going to criticise me? I need another coffee,' he said, and signalled to the waitress, who wouldn't be hailed despite his finger-clicking, so he had to limp into the kitchen and, against the noise of machines, mime tipping a cup into his uplifted mouth with its carefully clipped fringe of grey moustache. He accompanied the

waitress to the machine, chatting eagerly, to try to keep away from
me, I suppose, and he walked with her again as she carried his coffee to our table. He kept her at our table as long as he could.

'If I was ten years younger . . .' he said. He drank rapidly so I
feared for the heat on his tongue. But finally his cup was empty.

'I took your mother in,' he said. 'Men I knew in Sudlow said it
was noble of me. And it was. She was an imposter. She was always
claiming she'd been a mannequin back in France.'

'So she was always a dressmaker?' I asked.

'Of course,' he said.

I was puzzled what it meant, to take my mother in. I asked him.

'Other men wouldn't have,' he said, not understanding my confusion. 'But she had a charming foreign accent, like in the movies,
and she was pale and beautiful, and not showing much, not then.
By the time she was, I felt implicated. There was nothing to do but
marry. Then you came along.'

I clung to the side of the table, which rocked. The espresso
machine screamed.

'So you're not my father,' I said.

He laughed.

'Not even a relative,' he said. 'Think of me as someone kind you
once knew.'

'There's a photo of a sailor,' I said.

He laughed again.

'That's what you were getting at!' he said. 'I know the photo. She
showed me when she first met me. That sailor was your father. Just
a slip of a lad. He'd made her pregnant when he had shore leave in
Paris. She begged, borrowed or stole the money to come out here to
look for him. To Sydney. I happened to be in Sydney, so she found
me instead. More than that, you'll have to ask your mother. She'd
never tell me anything, not even his name. She's a strange woman –
there's no emotion in her that I could ever see, after the first few
weeks. But one night – she's a bit of a drinker, did you know that?
One night, we'd had some friends around – my mates and some of
her customers, we'd been celebrating your thirteenth birthday and
you'd gone to bed – when everyone had gone, she had a few more

cognacs. Then she told me that she'd wanted to be a model in France, but the fashion houses all rejected her despite her face and her figure. It turned out that she had a twist in her spine, a little raised part on her lower back, which I'd never noticed. But when she bent over forward and showed me, I could just make out the horizontal bones of her rib cage which had twisted out of place. "You wouldn't see it on a catwalk," she'd argued, and she was right, you wouldn't have. But the houses could pick and choose and your mother was just another pretty face. Her family had been too poor to get her treated, they couldn't afford the correcting corset, she said. So she never got to being a model. I felt for her, I know what it's like when your dreams won't come true. But the thing was, the next day, she'd forgotten she'd told me, and she wouldn't admit it again and she wouldn't admit it to you. I'd say, "But you weren't a model because of the hump on your back." And she'd say I was insulting her and even deny there was a hump. She kept telling the lie.'

I struggled against the memory of the nightgown, green and majestic as the ocean moving slowly against sand, tugging it away. I struggled with the memory of my real father's childish face. They were probably both very young. I tried to think of my unknown father loving her in a pale green nightgown and conceiving me.

'She only wore it once,' I blurted.

'What?' he asked.

'Sorry,' I said.

I never told my mother about this meeting. We kept pretending, my mother and I. We pretended until her last breath that she'd been a model in Paris, and that I thought my stepfather was my father. I pretend it to myself still, in a confused way. I've let you share my confusion. And perhaps this lie that shaped her life and mine will no longer be important by the time you read this, like a picture once traced on a misty window, but now fading and dribbling into the light. Perhaps no one will care whether she was a model or a seamstress, or that my father was not my father. Or that I have gone about saving you in this strange way.

I don't condemn my mother, as I hope you won't condemn me. My mother's lies taught me a greater truth: that there are layers of what might be, and what might be again.

18 May

To leave you will be to die.

But I'll take your cells in my vials. Will your cells be company enough?

When I was young I learned in the lab that we are made up of millions of machines, because of the theories of an English physician centuries ago, when the new machines promised heaven. We are a clever system of pumps and valves, he said. Then machines didn't bring heaven, just a war, and the story changed: inside our cells we are a consummate strategist in a secret chamber directing the movement of a great army along telegraph wires, we are like a great general who makes a point of keeping every single soldier in his army meticulously informed of his schemes. But then the war was over and there was no more talk of soldiers, and machines were the new hope again, so we became millions of molecules that worked like machines.

Then the stories gendered cells – there were his and her cells, like bathroom towels. There were leader cells and servant cells and daughter cells, manager cells and drone cells and housekeeping cells – there were whole societies of cells.

If I was ever to be a scientist, I had to agree. I imagined the old powerhouse near us, the one that's now a shopping mall. Every time I moved my feet on the sheets of my narrow bed in my mother's house, I made myself think of how I moved thousands of sub-microscopic cranes and chutes and conveyor belts in a Sudlow of cells.

But I never really agreed. One night when I was tipping out my solutions, I looked up out the window at the black sky drenched with stars and I thought rebellious thoughts:

If I'd come from Saturn, I'd look at a chair and probably see not a chair but a pattern of photons. And when I looked into the microscope, what would I have made of the movements inside cells? Would I have seen pulleys and switches? Do I only see machines because humans have made machines? Is this why we made machines? Did we make copies of what's inside us, but huge? To give birth to ourselves?

But what is a machine? And what does 'make' mean?

There are questions a scientist can't ask, thoughts I mustn't think. Sandy, for all his cheating, taught me that.

There is one thing that seems more than a metaphor to me. A molecule knows what's wanted of it by touching other molecules.

Inside our cells, we're touchers. In our cells, we don't use our eyes, or our minds. We touch.

So what hope do the lonely have?

It will be my undoing, this craving. What I must think of, all I must think of, is your cells.

No one has emailed me about the posting on the Internet. Doesn't anyone care?

19 May

The phone bleated all afternoon. The calls are always for him. He seems in great demand with his singing. They echo through the spaces that used to be ours.

All those silent years with you, no one rang me. No one knew my number. There was no one to know. Now we listen to the phone through the afternoon, Owen upstairs in our room, you and me downstairs running to grab the phone, remembering, stopping, heads cocked like dogs. We hear his message machine click on, then his recorded message, then the callers. One woman particularly annoys me. 'I love your work,' she always says. His *work*. Not his voice, not his performance. His work. What man could resist that? What woman? She makes his singing into a vocation. I know nothing about his vocation, I have no time.

These days your piano shrieks like the ringing of a phone. I suddenly know that his kindness could replace me in your love. And isn't that what I wanted – except that I wanted to be replaced by a little old lady?

20 May

Skye's results continue to be unremarkable.

'Love it all,' I used to tell Clara. 'Love the tedium.'

But perhaps my hunch is wrong. Perhaps this is all in vain.

23 May

When he went out this afternoon to his bar again, I crept up to his room. It was, after all, our room. I told myself I just wanted to stand in it for a while and watch the jacaranda paw the window-pane. The phone was ringing, then the answering machine clicked on. It was eerie, standing at the doorway to his empty room with a voice echoing through it, the woman arranging to meet him in town, no doubt his girlfriend.

'What?' you shouted, on the top step. 'What, what, what?'

'I'm looking for dirty cups,' I lied.

You ran up behind me. 'No,' I said, but you pushed me aside – you're so strong now – and darted across to the wallpaper.

'Tail,' you shouted, and began tearing.

'No,' I said, but just for a moment I sat down on his unmade bed. I pulled the sheets over my legs and they billowed softly, like a whisper, a caress. On an impulse I kicked my shoes off, and tucked my bare feet into the caress.

24 May

I took you to the park. Just as we left, the phone rang again, this time an aggrieved voice asking him why he didn't turn up to a gig at the Rive Gauche Cafe. As she hung up, she left a phone number, but her anger muddled her and she left ours. I exploded with mocking laughter. You copied me.

'He doesn't turn up at his gigs,' I grumbled to Grace in the park. 'All that racket, and he doesn't pick up the phone. It makes them angry too.'

It was a grey day, the rain swooping darkly across the park like stormy waves on a beach. Her children were crouched under the black pools of shadowy trees, but every now and then one of them would run shouting into the rain and back, laughing and dripping. You were a lone silent figure in red, ranging close by, hoping one of them would look up and call your name – you wanted to play with them! Are you getting better?

'Lots of women fans?' Grace said.

'They couldn't be lovers,' I said. 'If he rolled on them, he'd squash them. There's a main girlfriend. She rings repeatedly. She loves – wait for it – his *work*.'

'You're jealous,' she said.

'I have no time to be jealous, what with . . .'

I petered out.

'I'm not going to feel responsible,' she said. 'I suggested a kindly old lady.'

'He'll be gone soon,' I promised.

'Wasn't it going to be just a month?' she asked.

I laughed. I couldn't begin to explain my mistake about the handsome blond man and what's happened since.

Only to you.

Grace had bruises on both arms, just above the elbows, as if someone had gripped her from behind. When she pulled her cardigan off in the sun, the sleeves of her blouse didn't quite cover them.

I didn't know how to ask her what had happened. I'm not good at these things. 'What happened to you?' That's all I had to say. But I always expect dark secrets, like my own. When no one has dark secrets, only me.

1 June

I've had to throw away many of my cultures again. How could I make such a mistake?

It was that morning when I lost faith.

One of the many mornings.

6 June

Today Dick called me in.

'We may have to give you your marching orders,' he said. 'Because of your cleaning. I can't believe this has happened when I run such a tight ship.'

'What did I do wrong?' I asked.

'Remember how when you came, we'd battled with contamination? Now it's happened again. One of the scientists has complained. Their cultures don't correlate with the incubation time. We suspect the glassware.'

But I wash everything four times, just as I'd agreed with him I would. I told him that.

'I told you to wash it six times,' he said.

He hadn't, but I said penitently I'd wash everything six times from now on.

'A tiny speck could alter the way a culture grows, whether it grows, what it grows, what happens in this lab,' said Dick. 'We could both be out of a job!'

'How many have complained?' I thought to ask.

'One,' said Dick. 'So far.'

'Who?' I demanded.

He's like me, too weak to resist.

'Skye,' he said.

At least it wasn't Shirley.

7 June

I didn't research this morning. I just cleaned.

12 June

But she won't give up!

I logged in to find an email from Skye complaining, she thought, to Gunther!

'Francoise Arnoux does not seem to do much cleaning,' she said.

How dare she! And she complained that Francoise comes into her room and spies on her results! I'm supposed to be a spy sent from another lab to see what her hush-hush work is all about!

14 June

I wrote to her saying that I happen to remember the woman Francoise. She worked for me in my earlier days, I said, and I knew that she had fallen on hard times.

I told Skye that she'd watched too many thrillers:

'No lab in the world would use a cleaning lady as a spy. Science has standards. Concentrate exclusively on your designated work. We race against time.'

I signed it as your father.

Deep in the night when I wake in my lonely bed and switch on the light to check the alarm clock, and switch it off, and turn over, tormented, and give up and pour a cup of tea and write this, I know I will overstep the mark one day. You have to be so careful of marks, my darling. They are such fine, fine lines.

15 June

I have barely glanced at that viper, that round-faced smiling viper. But I think she is chastened. I hope.

18 June

I'm struggling with a grander plan than just employing Skye, but I don't have the courage. Where can I get the courage?

The lab almost gave it to me today, like it did when I was young, when I felt so alive though it was past dinnertime and the others had long gone home, throwing me their goodbyes as they slammed the door behind them. I would sit there on my stool, looking at the experiments even though I was only a technician and the experiments weren't mine. Everything in the lab would ask questions. What had Tony, or Mark, or one of the others overlooked? What had they thought of too narrowly? Where was their blindness?

I got courage from it. I felt my mind move. Argument seemed the best way to make my mind move. Otherwise, it slept like a dog in front of the fire, masterless.

In the mornings, even when I clean, my eyes rest on the surfaces of the apparatus, like a mother on the future of her sleeping child, getting courage. But not enough.

24 June

On the fourth phone call of the afternoon, I marched upstairs. You watched me, warily, from the bottom step. I knocked on his door. He opened it, in his dressing gown – in the afternoon! But he's an artiste, of course.

'Hello,' he said.

Behind him, the young woman's voice was fluting on the answering machine.

'You still haven't returned my call,' she said.

I was rescued by the voice.

'We have to talk about your month,' I said. 'It's long gone.'

'Come in,' he said. He looked beyond me down the stairs.

'You too,' he said to you, beckoning.

You ran up the stairs, sped past us, and hesitated at the wall-paper you'd shredded.

He touched my arm, to encourage me to enter. He's a toucher. But it was such a childlike, trusting gesture that I allowed myself to be led, a long walk, though of course it was only five or six steps, while the young woman spoke into his machine. Time had slowed because of his touch. I tried to argue with myself: Look at his neck – there are rolls of fat! But my mind argued back: He's large but he walks with dignity. He probably walks onto a stage like this.

We reached his bed and he sat down and companionably pat-ted it, indicating that I was to sit beside him. Something deep inside me lurched. I was back in a bedroom with Gunther, your father, as if love carves such a pattern in us that we must come to it again and again in different ways. We belong to love itself, not to a particular person – or so it seemed to me right then.

'She wants to manage me,' he said, tipping his head in the direction of the answering machine. 'She keeps offering gigs I don't want to do – like cruise ships to the islands, and staying there and performing at the clubs, and performing on another cruise on the way back. When I don't want to leave here.'

The branches of the jacaranda knocked on the windowpane and swung away. You made some sound, I don't know, a twitch, a scratch, something that reminded me you were there, as if I could forget you. You stood watching me, watching the man and your mother sitting on his bed. I'm sure you know how fragile your mother is, how tempted to blurt everything at last.

You smiled an acknowledgment of us, of what it is to be a woman with the imprint of a man's hand still warm on her skin. Or perhaps all you were thinking about was the wallpaper. You turned back to it, and slowly, deliberately, began to tear the shape of another dog.

'You're so fond of here?' I asked.

'Sudlow's where my heart is,' he said.

If we lay down together, his thigh would be a ribbon of warmth against mine. His body against mine, from toe to lips, would be a song of warmth. And afterwards, we'd talk.

But I must resist this. I must resist a man who's only in our life a short while. I'm a mother not a woman, and a criminal at that.

One of his shoulders was bared, and it was rounded and smooth and yearningly young against the window light. With difficulty I shifted my gaze from him to the familiar room, now unfamiliar. A book with handwriting was open on the little table where I used to put the computer. Next to it was a pile of sheet music. His pillows stood upright on his bed against the wall, dented from the shape of his head. My hand nudged some more writing of his in a notebook open on the bedcover.

'What are you writing?' I asked.

'I'm looking over my memoirs,' he said. 'This is a big moment for me,' he added suddenly. His mouth was lopsided when he grinned. It was as if he was struggling emotionally with something huge. I felt his breath on my arm. It was an effort to look up and meet his eyes.

'What do you mean?' I asked.

'Do you feel – as if we've known each other for a long, long time?' he said.

I couldn't think of how to answer. He comes out with such unexpected things. But I found something to say.

'Would you like to eat in sometimes at night? With me and Tina?'

He looked surprised, began to speak in that strange way of his, and stopped.

'They feed me at the bar,' he said at last. 'Instead of wages.'

So he doesn't want that closeness.

'Yes,' I said, 'of course. Besides, Tina and I eat early because we have to go to bed early. You would've noticed that I leave for work at dawn . . .'

My voice was thick and not quite obeying me.

'Sorry,' he said. 'I didn't mean to sound . . .' His voice trailed off into a stutter.

I'd made him uncomfortable with my offer.

'Not at all,' I said, also blushing and incoherent, in the way that discomfort can be infectious. I was stumbling towards the door, trying to walk steadily across the floor of our room, now his.

'I didn't mean –' he called behind me.

I was clutching on to the doorframe.

'Of course,' I said. 'Come on,' I called to you. For once you obeyed me, and followed.

'Tonight –' his voice came to me when I was on the first step going down. I stopped, resisting the impulse to go back into the room. I stood still.

'Tonight, could I have dinner with you? I'm staying in, learning a new song.'

'Yes,' I said. 'I'll put it on a tray.'

I began walking down the stairs.

'You don't have to go to any trouble,' he said, his voice floating down.

'It's no trouble,' I said. 'We wouldn't want to disturb you.'

I made spaghetti for you and a separate dinner for him and me, a curry. But I burnt the curry. And all night I blushed in the dark for my foolishness.

I have to be ready to run at any moment.

25 June

On my replica plates I smudged cells all over one of the most sensitive antibiotics, so I had to throw it away. And Skye's results still show nothing.

But I cleaned the lab well.

26 June

This afternoon someone had picked white flowers from the daisy bush down the back yard and put them in a glass on the table.

I was almost too scared to ask who'd done it.

'Thank you, Laura,' I said eventually.

'Them?' she said, wrinkling her nose. She flicked her finger scornfully against them, so that one toppled out of the glass. It lay forlorn, dripping.

'Aren't they weeds?' she said. 'Why don't you have real flowers? You can buy them in all the shops.'

She didn't put it back, but I did.

Suddenly I was laughing and singing through the afternoon all because of a bunch of white daisies on a shining wooden table.

By the time you and I had our lonely dinner, I feared they weren't for me. And at three in the morning, I'm groaning in my bed again like the girl I once was.

You're a young woman thinking that women older than you never squirm at three in the morning. But we are always young.

28 June

This morning I did very little but clean. Then the hospital rang. They had a new autistic child for assessment. I visited him, and brushed his hair. I took a few hairs back with fresh follicles, and used the DNA sequencer. I began my real work again.

On the bus home, my knees pressed together tensely under my cleaning lady's uniform, I watched rain streak against the windows and told myself that one day I might be able to help other autistic children. You, and many others. On the bus I felt like a brave crusader.

But then, just after I'd got home, Laura went to the toilet and left her bag on the table for a minute. You and I sat down with fruit drinks, as if we were any mother and her daughter.

Not for long.

You began screaming about her bag.

'Take it off, take it off,' you screamed.

'But there's plenty of room,' I said, reassuring, calm. 'It's a big table. Big enough for you and me and Laura's handbag.'

At moments like this, something goes hard and bright in me. I want to resist your strangeness so we're like any ordinary family, not this one.

You ran away outside. I hoped that was the end of it. But no, you were running back with my raincoat, still wet from the rain. You threw it over Laura's bag, to hide it. 'The bag will fall,' I warned, trying to keep my voice reasonable, even though my heart was banging.

Is this how the affliction is coming out in me? That I won't give in, that I won't simply lift a bag off a table to humour a child?

'What's Laura going to think?' I said. 'You can't do that to other people's things.'

'Off, off,' you kept shouting.

'I know what to do,' I said in my falsely reasonable voice while you tugged at the coat to make it cover her bag. I took the bag off the table and put it on a chair. But that wasn't good enough for you and you covered it again with my coat, which slipped off in its wetness, and this time you pushed Laura's bag off the chair onto the floor. Everything rolled out – pencils, a make-up bag, lipsticks, mascara, an orange, old bus tickets, a Scratchie, a key ring.

Then I broke down.

'Look what you've done,' I shouted. 'Idiot! Idiot!'

I slammed the bag, now empty, back on the table, my face flaming.

'You'll just have to put up with it there,' I shouted.

You ran screaming into your room, and slammed the door over and over again.

Laura came in as I scrabbled on the floor, picking up her make-up.

'I'm sorry,' I said. 'I didn't mean to look at your private things.'

She ignored me.

'You mustn't call her an idiot,' she said.

We stared at each other.

'She isn't an idiot,' said Laura.

What sort of scientist am I?

I've lost my courage, though only my courage can make you well.

29 June

More results from Skye that show nothing. My work shows nothing of interest either.

In bed at one in the morning, when there was no sound in the house, it came to me: the email back in February from Gunther to Dick about the bases. It could have been by post! Gunther could have written a letter! They might all be writing old-fashioned letters to each other with old-fashioned stamps!

I sat upright in the dark.

I said aloud:

'They might speak to each other on the old-fashioned phone!'

You turned, your bed creaked.

'Mum!' you called.

'It's all right,' I called back. 'Go back to sleep. Everything's going to be all right now.'

One day I'll be caught. Till then, all I can do is keep thinking.

30 June

You came into the kitchen wordless, holding your hairbrush. You followed me to the fridge, to the bench, to the sink, thrusting the hairbrush at me while I cleared away butter, bread, peanut butter, jam – all the dollops and smears and mess of Laura's breakfast, still there in the afternoon.

'What do you want?' I asked you.

When I turned this way, you were there, the brush poking me; when I turned that way, you were still there. I flushed with fury at your wordlessness. You choose not to use words, you choose silence, I think at these terrible times.

'Say what you want,' I prompted, though I knew what it was.

'Say it!' I insisted, all apparent reasonableness while inside I raged. You knew that I raged. Your eyes were ringed with brown shadows, they seemed untethered by your mind. And my rage came out in a flood.

'Use words!' I shouted at you.

You poked the brush at me one more time, this time almost into my shouting mouth, and I wanted to murder you again over a hairbrush – how I lusted to murder you. I whipped my hand out and slapped you. Then I knew the enormity of what I'd done. I'd slapped my child, my autistic child. Just your bottom, surely it didn't hurt on your bottom. But you were screeching with terror at my wild, black face and you ran behind the table, waiting for me to chase you, to kill you. Then you leaned over the table again poking the hairbrush out, and now I knew you were goading me.

'Talk,' I shouted. 'You've got a tongue in your head. Can't you use it?'

My anger boiled over.

'Idiot!' I shouted again.

Am I as mad as my mother?

Owen was at the door.

'Anything up?' he asked.

He'd caught me open-mouthed. I shut my mouth.

'Not at all,' I said. 'Nothing's up.'

He was in his dressing gown again. You stood there, caught in motion, brush out-thrust. I stood there, 'idiot' drying on my lips.

'Want me to do your hair?' he asked you, gesturing. 'It seems like your mum is busy.'

You didn't move. Perhaps you didn't understand. I have never been sure how much you understand.

'I used to plait my mother's hair,' he added. 'Or help her wind it around her head, and put a pin in it. Like this.'

We both watched him as he swirled his fat hand around his own fluffy hair. His dressing gown gaped to show his chest, the tender skin below his arms, the gentle lines around his neck; he was almost naked to his waist. I sat down suddenly at the table, a wet plate in my lap, the tea towel hanging between my legs. I burst into sobs. You came over, curious, and put out your hand to test the wetness of my tears. Then you ran across the room for tissues, you ran back and jabbed them into my face, and examined them afterwards. Your face, absorbed, was so close to mine I could see the pores in your fresh skin. Your eyes were on what you were doing, the mopping. They were not on my heart, they are so seldom on my heart.

'What's a plait?' you asked him, suddenly coherent.

You said a whole sentence again!

'Want me to show you?' he asked you, holding out his hand for the brush.

You were mesmerised by him, you turned your back obediently to him when he adjusted the angle of your head, he gathered up your wispy hair and you turned again when he asked, you were smiling, holding out your clips, holding out a rubber band. I watched his hands, large but deft, the fingers, the backs of his hands brown-furred, like all of him. We are both falling in love with him.

2 July

I cleaned. I did very little of my own work.

Tonight I was cruel again – how much of my cruelty do you remember?

I shouted again because you'd smeared toothpaste on the bathroom walls. I didn't slap you but you went to bed and screamed:

'Out! Out!'

I sat at the kitchen table and buried my head in my arms.

He came down the stairs.

'Like to go out for an ice-cream?' he said to me. 'Ice-cream might fix it.'

'No,' I said.

But I nodded when he inclined his head in the direction of your room.

He went down the hall and asked if you'd go to the ice-cream shop with him to advise him which ice-cream to eat. And you could have one too. Tiramisu with chocolate, English trifle with raspberry, lemon with lime, orange with chocolate bits, or caramel swirl?

You listened.

'I'm an idiot,' you told him.

I flinched. You'd spoken a sentence again, but what a terrible sentence!

'I never take idiots to ice-cream shops,' he said. 'That's why I need you. Come on.'

You lay still for a moment, considering. Then you swung your legs onto the floor and followed him out the door, red-faced, tear-swollen, still hiccupping with sobs, barefooted. You looked at me rebelliously.

I tried a kindly smile.

'We'll scare all the dogs,' he told you as you left together. He barked, to show you.

You roared with laughter mixed still with an occasional hiccup.

So I stood in the cool garden and listened to your progress up the street, barking at the dogs, setting off barks around the neighbourhood. You did the same coming back. Women opened screen doors, startling the night with a little leap of light that cruelly picked out the loose skin of their old arms. They peered up and down the street for a pack of marauding dogs but they only found a fat man and a young girl licking ice-cream. I was glad of the cool touch on my hot face of a monstera leaf.

You walked in proudly. He kissed you goodnight, and went upstairs. On the landing he turned around.

'I love you,' he called down. You looked up, radiant with him.

He's becoming necessary.

Tonight I checked my website. There was nothing. Why had I imagined there would be? Why would anyone else in the world be interested in my obsession?

3 July

This afternoon at home, I came into the kitchen to find Owen boiling the kettle.

'Like a cuppa?' he asked.

He was looking at the kettle as if he was asking it, not me.

'Sure,' I said.

He leaned on the bench. I wiped down the draining board. We were avoiding each other's eyes, watching the kettle begin its slow song. In your bedroom you were imitating the kettle. I heard him draw in his breath, hesitate, listen.

'She's got perfect pitch,' he said.

We both listened. Your voice was fluting out of you.

He drew in a breath again.

'Real conversations aren't like the ones I have in my head,' he said suddenly, his voice jerking out of him. 'I rehearse them but they veer away from what I hoped would happen. Talking's sometimes like a foreign language I'm blundering about in. I wish conversations were written down beforehand, the way songs –'

He stopped.

'I was clumsy. About dinner. I could see it in your face. Your face . . .' He trailed away.

The kettle screamed. You echoed the kettle's note again and held it. And while I was busying myself with tea leaves, measuring them and ladling them into the pot, he said in his slow, hesitant way:

'You took me by surprise. Could I change what I said about dinner? Could I have dinner with you both sometimes?'

He paused, his breath full of unsaid words.

Then he added:

'It's what I've always wanted.'

He left suddenly, without drinking his cup of tea.

I flung up the kitchen window and for the first time I noticed it's winter, though it's still so warm, it's a winter of contradictions as it often is in Sudlow. Flowers puff perfume at my worried face, but trees huddle together for company against grey skies.

'Always' is a bit excessive for someone who's only known me two months.

Time must be dragging for him. Being here must seem 'always' to him.

4 July

Today Skye's latest results are due. Her three months are almost up. Will I keep her on?

5 July

He's been away for days, it seems. Of course he goes away. He'll be singing somewhere. Maybe he's agreed to her cruise after all.

Tonight, I ran you a bath and you sat in it barking to your washer, making a snout with your hand, opening and closing and twisting it underneath the wet washer, and I felt chilled.

'Talk to me,' I demanded.

You looked at your washer.

'Talk to me,' you said to it.

His room hung above me. I left you in the bath and crept upstairs, and all around me was the sense of him, his shoes comfortably worn and pigeon-toed under his bed, his chocolate bar unwrapped on his desk, a half-eaten packet of biscuits clamped shut with a peg, his chair piled with old newspapers, his pillows slumped against the wall where he'd sat to read, *War and Peace* upside down and open on a chair. I sat on his bed, the bumps already worn to his shape. Then I saw, beyond the bed, that he'd laid out his tracksuits on the floor, his yellow one that he keeps for best, and a dark green one. The arms of the yellow one were angled perhaps to sing a high note. But the arms and legs of the green one were splayed open, as if he was doing a joyful jump in the shape of a star.

I kicked my shoes off, leaned back on his pillows, and then dragged them down and lay where he'd slept on the rumpled sheets. The quietness of his room enveloped me, the sheets and the peeping sound of a cricket outside, and the trustingly quiet house. Then the cricket stopped and there was no sound but the slight scratch of the jacaranda branches on the window glass. I pulled his sheet over my head so I was muffled in it. It smelled like the muskiness of Gunther. Do all men smell like Gunther?

I tell myself for the millionth time that I had to leave your father when I was pregnant. I'd become less of a scientist day by day all the time I was the lab manager. Every life has its stretches of death, almost a rehearsal. Yours will too. For some people, it lasts only for months, for others it lasts for years, as it did for me. I didn't know what to do otherwise, only to hang on and wait. I'm not sure what I was waiting for. Him to return to being the great immunologist he'd been before the past had reared up and waylaid him. Or maybe Clara. That's what I was waiting for. Her. A reason to bolt.

Am I always finding a reason to bolt?

I woke startled by a car's headlights on the road below. The car stopped right outside our house. I must get out of his bed, out of his room. I'd left you in the bath again, you might've drowned, you might be dead. I ran to the door, remembered his bed, ran back to straighten it, ran back to the door. There was a laugh from the street, a hot, young laugh, the sort of laugh only beautiful women have. I ran to the window. He'd just got out of a newly parked car, and so had the driver. I watched her get back in. She had long legs, bared to the thigh. Twenty-two-year-old legs. She slammed the car door. He headed towards our gate. It clicked. I was out the door and halfway down the stairs before his key was properly in the lock.

We greeted each other in the hall.

'Bathtime,' I said, nodding towards the bathroom, and laughing with the pleasure of him in my hall, in my house, as if I hadn't abandoned you to the bath again. He nodded and walked up the stairs. He didn't look back at me. I flung open the bathroom door. You were propped up against the back of the bath, dozing in the quiet water.

I'm gentle with you then.

6 July

But now I have courage. Lying in his bed has given it to me.

I wrote an email to Sandy as if I was Gunther, telling him I needed help with my work. Could he see his way to directing four students to assist me for three months? I added that the work was of course out of his area, but, after all, the students had originally come to Sudlow because of my immunology reputation – anyway, I was only requesting that he allocate and brief the students. Shirley could supervise, surely.

Of course I signed your father's name.

7 July

I wait. I work. I think. This afternoon while you rustled paper in your room I dragged the kitchen table to under the window, and tried to write to you. I gazed out at the two white gum trees in our neighbour's yard – are those trees still there? – in the afternoons the shadow of their leaves dapple our walls with light. I eked out my fifth cup of tea for the day – it was already cold, the milk I'd poured into it was a circle of white feathers on the tea's surface. When I finished drinking it, I wished I could read my fortune in the leaves. I tried to write to you. I couldn't write a word.

In the middle of the night, all I can write is this.

9 July

I'm still waiting. I'm so anxious I find I haven't outgrown my own need for a mother. This afternoon when you were sitting quietly on the sofa twiddling a leaf, I leaned my head on your shoulder, shut my eyes and imagined that you and I had been playing in a big green paddock out on a farm beyond Sudlow, and we'd shouted and laughed until our stomachs were sore. Then, in my daydream, someone called us both in to dinner, a warm, home-baked pie that smelled of grease and flour and salt.

'Off,' you shouted at my heavy, middle-aged head.

10 July

Skye's contract is up. I became your father again and wrote to her, thanking her for her application and hard work, dismissing her, and wishing her well in whatever path she took in her career from now on. Your father was never good at platitudes like that. I felt guilty, not for letting her go, but for misrepresenting his dear, blunt nature.

12 July

The reply today from Sandy was as I feared. That he's racing to complete his own results for publication, and that his students would find it disruptive to be moved from their inquiries. He would of course be happy to help in the future, but not now.

I replied immediately. In brief, I said that if he didn't help me, I'd expose him. I'd been amassing evidence, I said. I mentioned questionable numbers of mice, special antibodies supposedly spilt in a refrigerator when a researcher came to check how he achieved his results, and valuable research time funded by the hospital Board but spent instead on high finance deals.

14 July

Success, my darling!

He'll help. He'll divert and help supervise four students on my work for three months. They'll begin in two weeks.

It's all in the interests of collegial loyalty, he said. Of course!

Even if I'm not there in three months, even if I'm only around for a few more weeks, at least they should make better progress than Skye.

I thanked him and attached instructions, stressing that the work was highly confidential.

This is sweet revenge for the way he betrayed and thwarted your father. But first and foremost, it's for you.

Report of ongoing investigation commissioned by the
Sudlow Hospital Board

Ref: ghp: 261

Now we come to the most daring of the emails purportedly
sent by Gunther Mueller, but this time to Sanderson. In
these emails, it appeared that Sanderson was blackmailed
into supplying four of his students for a period of three
months to work under his supervision on the unknown
party's work. When I questioned him, he explained that he
succumbed not because he feared exposure of faulty
protocol, but because of Mueller's 'emotionality'. He
explained that Mueller had begun on this 'hobbyhorse'
almost twenty years ago and become so overwrought that
police intervention was needed. It seemed to Sanderson
that if Mueller was imagining Sanderson could be
blackmailed, then Mueller was becoming 'overwrought'
again. It also must be remembered, as Sanderson has
pointed out, that he originally headhunted Mueller, and has
always felt, in his own words, 'responsible' for him. He
presented Mueller to the hospital Board, as you would
remember. 'I agreed in the interests of collegiality,' he said.
'In other words, I believed that it was worth assisting him
for three months in the interests of keeping the peace.'

Mueller again says he has no cognisance of this
correspondence, although he does state that in an earlier
phase of his life he was eager to pursue research in roughly
the same area as that required by the author of the emails,
though he says that he would have gone about such
research in a very different way. He wanted the Board to
be told that 'while the unknown party has behaved in the
most irregular, illegal and possibly criminal way, his/her
research has its merits and could, if properly pursued,
provide the breakthrough that this lab has long hoped for'.

Sanderson, to the contrary, told me that he couldn't
imagine any lab anywhere that would be interested.

27 July

Today the young scientists, under the guidance of Sandy and Shirley, began working for me. For us, my darling.

When I arrived at the lab, I found a note from Dick telling me to set out equipment in Lab Two. There followed a list which I wanted to question, but what would a cleaning lady know?

I followed Dick's instructions exactly, with neat piles on the benches of Lab Two. I checked the list one last time, obsessively. I hovered fussily, flicking a feather duster over lab notes on the shelves.

'How did you feel?' I imagine you asking me, I imagine the hospital Board's lawyers asking me if I don't escape. I felt as remote and detached as any criminal must. As if I was a traveller, setting out on a momentous trip and surprised to find myself calmly standing in a bus shelter looking up bus schedules.

It was hard to walk out of Lab Two. Finally, I put the list, all ticked off, on Dick's desk. I only had time to do half an hour's work on your cells, and even then I had to clean very fast to make up for my dithering. Afterwards, I found myself back near Lab Two. It's normal for me to go in towards the end of my shift to pick up dirty glassware, avoiding Shirley – I try to time it with her trip to the cafe for morning tea – but today I couldn't keep away, now that my dream was coming true.

I still wouldn't have walked in if it hadn't been for Dick. He found me on my knees cleaning the skirting boards.

'Something up this morning?' he said from right behind me.

'No, nothing,' I yelped. 'Why?'

'You forgot my coffee and biscuits,' he said.

When I couldn't contain myself a moment longer, I got a ladder and walked towards Lab Two. By this time I was so self-conscious, I almost knocked on the door. That would have made people notice. Instead I pushed it open and barged in.

'Light bulb test,' I called softly and no one turned around. All was as it should be. Four students were sitting in a circle on their high stools, holding cups of coffee, talking quietly to Sandy. Shirley was listening and scribbling a projected tabulation of possible results. Of our research, my darling, yours and mine. She assiduously avoided my eyes.

'So we must be entirely generous with our results,' Sandy was saying to them. 'But only between ourselves. Not with anyone outside. And that means absolutely no one.'

I propped up my ladder. It opened with a squeak. No one looked around.

The students were nodding earnestly in unison.

'What will we say we're investigating, when people ask?' said a young man with thick glasses and a placating sort of chin. I knew he'd been the most deeply involved in Sandy's experiments up till now.

'That you're assisting me. And Shirley, of course,' said Sandy. 'And that you don't know the history of the particular cells.'

'This phenomenon is a significant mutation, isn't it?' asked a girl sitting next to the boy. She had frizzy hair, untidy eyebrows and her mouth moved prettily. 'An extraordinarily extensive mutation, I suppose,' she added. 'That's why it causes the problem.'

I wanted to shout, 'Exactly, exactly!' It was a good thing that all they could see of me, if they happened to look up, was my stockinged legs on the ladder.

'You're right,' said Sandy. He explained – adequately – that evolution occurs all the time because there's so much redundancy, but that usually the changes are small and silent, less than fifty per cent of the protein structure.

'This is more than that,' he added. 'Much more. We don't know how much.'

That's the point, I thought to myself, high up on the ladder, tapping the light bulb.

'I suppose that's the point,' said the frizzy-haired girl as if she was reading my mind. I stopped tapping and looked down, but she wasn't aware of me, none of them were. She was blowing her breath on her coffee to cool it.

'Why have we only twelve weeks?' she asked. 'If the work is so hush-hush and important?'

Sandy paused.

'It's certainly not donkey work. The work of real scientists, not mere technicians.'

But the frizzy-haired girl was not so easily flattered.

'Shouldn't we have whatever time we need?' she asked.

'We're not sure how much time it's worth,' said Sandy. 'It's a bit, shall we say, out on a limb. It isn't why you were sent to Sudlow.'

The frizzy-haired girl was irrepressible. She leaned forward to him.

'The others will have as much time as they need,' she said.

Sandy jerked in his chair.

'What others?' he asked.

'The other labs. The ones we'll be racing.'

When Sandy said nothing, she went on:

'Aren't we doing it because of what's on the Internet? That old man's site – the old scientist who was once a sailor?'

'What?' asked Sandy.

'There are several groups following up his research, doing what we're doing. One group in Japan, two in America, another in England. And no one can contact him to check out his data! That's what's funny, don't you think? He's left an email address, but messages bounce back. His ideas are really interesting, but he's like my grandfather on a computer – he's even made a mess of typing in his email address!'

She's seen my site on the Internet!

I was just getting the globe out of the socket – there was nothing wrong with it, but I needed to justify my lengthy stay up the ladder – when I lost my grip. The globe slipped. It bounced on the top step. I caught it.

'You don't know about his website?' she asked Sandy.

'Of course I do,' he said, too quickly. He paused. 'That's why we're having a crack at it. Now, let's get going. As usual, first we make up a batch of cells.'

They all stood and clustered around the benches. I went to the cupboard to check for spare light bulbs.

On the way, I collided with Shirley. We both pretended not to notice, even though we'd almost fallen over each other. I picked up my ladder and left the room. My hands were shaking. How could I have forgotten to check my posting? The few times I had, there'd been no hits. I'd put it up in such despair. It'd seemed a futile gesture. And then I'd got distracted by love.

On the bus home back to you, I was still distracted, so deep in thought that I missed our stop and had to walk home more than a kilometre. I made good use of it, still thinking, though Laura was angry when I arrived.

'It's all right for some people!' she shouted at me as she rushed out the door. 'Who don't have any calls on their time! This is the afternoon when I always wash my hair!'

As soon as you'd allow me to, I checked the website. My darling, there are many of us trying to find your cure. It's not just me in Sudlow, it's not just the reluctant Sandy and Shirley and their students, it's scientists in Japan and America and England.

No one asked the old man for his credentials. They're too interested in the work which he'd been directing to want to know about him. They wanted details of how he was going about this work, what he knows so far, what his immediate plans are for future work.

Tomorrow I will begin to answer them.

3 August

My email to the lab in Japan has taken all night to write. Luckily, England has asked similar questions, and so has America.

4 August

I kept writing the emails.

5 August

He was out again tonight. I crept up to his room. It's not that I want him. I want a man to hide in, a man's smell, a man's breath, a man's sweat. Not particularly Owen's, I'm sure of that. Just a man's, to bring me closer to Gunther, to how I felt in our early days when the world seemed full of possibilities that sprung from being with him. I opened his drawers and smiled at the way he rolls his socks into innocent balls. I found his sarongs, I opened his wardrobe, I smelled his shoes. Then I got into his man's bed.

And there, I suddenly noticed that it was raining. It was because I was on the upper storey, that's all. Or was it? I could almost hear the earth drinking rain, as if I'd become a beetle. I could hear the crunching and whirring and fluttering of tiny things in the earth, even here at the top of the house. I feel, I still feel in a curious way that I've been reborn.

6 August

I try not to look at the frizzy-haired girl. I know she shares my passion. She works with complete concentration. Her name is Madeline. I tried to breathe love onto Madeline as I collected her dirty glassware.

I made a promise to myself on the bus. I'll ration myself when I go to his room. Not tonight. Tomorrow night. I'll wait until tomorrow night.

Buses are fine places to make resolutions.

I worked again on the emails, and then I sent them.

16 August

I still do my work in the little shed. I don't want to stop, though I have two scientists, four students and labs across the world helping me.

I'm behaving like Laura. Before I left work to come home, I went to the Ladies. I outlined my lips in crimson. More foundation until my skin glowed, darker outlines on the eyes, blacker eyebrows. I brushed my hair so it framed my face. But I always hear my mother, her disappointment in me.

17 August

I took it easy this morning, because the world is working for me.
For us.

Dick met me in the corridor outside the broom cupboard.

'Lab Two,' he said.

'Lab Two?' I repeated, speaking fast, so it came out like a yelp.
Breathe slower, take your time, I said to myself.

'Don't clean it,' he said. 'They're being funny. They don't want
anyone in there.'

'Why?' I cried.

He shushed me.

'It's all hush-hush. So don't go in there. I don't want any accu-
sations. They think they can clean for themselves. Imagine that!
Hush-hush becomes wormy-germy!'

'Whose order?' I asked.

It was Shirley's. She thinks that the cleaning staff are becoming
intrusive.

I'm the only cleaning staff.

28 August

I got home early and he was sitting on our sofa, a glass of beer
beside him, reading to you. You were doing a handstand on one of
the armchairs, your trousers sliding down to your bruised and
knobbly knees, your face determined and red. You screamed when
I came in.

'Go away,' you shouted.

You ran away.

'I took over from Laura and gave her an early mark,' said
Owen, as easily as if he'd sat on our sofa all his life.

I could hear you rampaging in your bedroom, pulling at drawers. You often did this when you were agitated, throwing out the
clothes I'd washed, rushing to the garden, bringing in spilling
handfuls of leaves and dirt and putting them inside your drawers
instead.

'Lunch is on,' he said.

I followed him into the kitchen as if it wasn't our house but his. The benches were bare and sparkling, the dishes piled neatly, there weren't any plates with toast crumbs or knives clumped with butter. Red and green vegetables were already cut.

'Laura's done this?' I asked, astonished.

'Me. I'm cooking lunch for you,' he said. 'I hope you don't mind. I like cooking.'

He began cutting carrots into slants, not circles. He seems an experienced cook.

'A stir-fry,' he said, as if it was all that mattered, what he was making for lunch.

'I believe in an angled slice. It allows the heat to work better.'

'Who's coming to lunch?' I asked.

'Just us,' he said. 'We'll be able to talk. At last.'

It was odd, sharing the kitchen of my childhood like lovers. My mother's kitchen. Why was she always so distant? Was it because she didn't want me to know who she really was?

I panicked about the vials in the fridge. I opened the door but they looked undisturbed – I'd hidden them in old cardboard juice containers, sealed them all with waterproof tape and written 'Don't touch', always using the same green waterproof marker. Even Dick would have approved.

'Those are Tina's,' I told Owen. 'Never open them. She gets very upset if they're moved.'

'No worries,' he said.

I went into my room and took off my cleaning lady uniform and put on a silky pale blue dress that I hadn't worn since Gunther. I clasped my hair back with a blue clip of yours that you won't wear – you always shout 'It's itchy!'

He served our lunch. There was something he wanted to say, I could tell. Perhaps he wants to leave, I feared.

He began to tell me shyly about his performances, that often he can scarcely make himself heard, that sometimes the microphone seems his only audience. I kept nodding, almost as shy as him.

But you ran out and pulled at the tablecloth from under the

plates and wouldn't let it go, though I tried to prise your fingers off.

'Please, darling,' I hissed.

I would have slapped you but for his eyes on me.

'Let her have it,' he said.

'Yes,' I said, forcing a smile.

After all, it was your genes, not your wilfulness. So we cleared the plates off, and gave you the cloth.

You took your clip out of my hair so it fell around my face.

'Darling!' I remonstrated with your genes.

You wore the tablecloth like a ghost and howled at my side until the wine spilt, a red stain on my blue silkiness like blood. Then I'm afraid I stood and shouted:

'Animal! Little animal!'

'She's tired,' he laughed, as if it was endearing, your nonsense and my rage, and the red stain spreading, and the wet silk clinging to my thighs.

He picked you up and carried you off for a game of barking dogs. I heard him croon real music, not his usual scales. He has a good voice after all. So that's what she calls his *work*.

Out on the veranda I swore that one day I would be free of you, free of my mother, free of my grandmother, her mother, her mother, those ghosts of my family, and your father's family. I would be free to be like Owen's girlfriend, to stand at a bar and listen to him sing.

2 September

Today I found a real email to Dick from Gunther, saying that 'further complaints' had reached him about the 'pilfering of resources'. He complained about Sandy handing these problems over to him, but finished:

'I am winding up here and will return soon.'

What will I do about Sandy and the four students? And how will I hide my heart from Gunther? Am I still in love with him? I cannot hide my heart.

Owen was away again this evening, singing in another bar. I allowed myself my addiction. While you were in your bath, I crept up the stairs and lay in his bed. It smelled of the biscuits he eats but I pretended Gunther was with me. I drowsed, comforted. Then I crept down the stairs, back to you.

The trouble is, I can't get over your father. I was burdened with my love of him, and when I left him, I was burdened with the loss of him. Only you distracted me from the full weight of my loss.

As you're doing now, though it's the middle of the night.

3 September

I made an attempt to stop Gunther coming – though I long for him to be back, how I long for him. I wrote to him saying I'd put hospital security onto the job. There was no need for him to return. Of course I signed it Dick.

4 September

Gunther wrote back that he'd give hospital security a fortnight and then he'd start taking action. He was surprised security hadn't already been alerted. He added crankily that heads would roll if protocol had been breached.

I accomplished nothing today. I long to talk it all over with someone. With Owen.

But anyone I talked to, I'd implicate.

5 September

I sat on the floor in a pool of pink sunset through the skylight, putting on my sneakers, planning to take you to the park, hoping to see Grace. After all, that's why I made friends with her – though how I can begin to explain my life, I don't know. Grace who knows how to live as I have never known.

You were playing the piano, as usual. I heard Owen in his room. There was his tread on the stairs. As if he heard my thoughts, he came down, each step clumping. He had on his yellow tracksuit, for best. He's a terrible dresser, but of course those things don't matter. Unexpectedly, he dropped to his knees, watching me and the sky, smiling.

'Do you think we could have that talk?' he said.

'What about?' I asked. I almost yelped. Did he suspect I'd been going into his room? Were we intruding too much into his life, Tina and me?

I kept putting on my shoes, head down, hair falling over my face.

'There's so much going on, we never seem to have time to talk,' he said.

I got up.

'A quick cup of tea?' I asked.

'Yes,' he said. 'She's using some colourful scales,' he said of you. 'The Phrygian before, and now she's into the Dorian,' I think he said.

He laughed at my blank face.

'Old church modes,' he said. 'How does she know them? It's as if she's lived before.'

I was about to scoff at such unscientific talk and then I remembered that I'm not a scientist.

'Maybe she's the ghost of – who was that composer?' I asked.

I felt absurdly happy, talking to him.

'Bartók,' I think he said. Yes, I've just checked back through this letter. He thought you make up music that sounds like Bartók's.

I walked to the kitchen, whistling. My mother always told me not to whistle, but it puts a bridge over silences, so I whistled as I planned: I'll tell him the whole story when I fill the kettle. When it boils. When the tea is brewing. When I pour it into the cups. So by slow degrees, I told him nothing. And he told me nothing either, though I fear he has a lot to tell.

We went to the park, you and me, but I didn't see Grace. All I saw were fluffy clouds racing across the sky, and you rolling in the grass.

I needed to talk to her calmness, her happy life.

6 September

I emailed hospital security as though I was Gunther, but I made it very casual. I've often read their emails. They are very keen on canasta. There's a big canasta competition on. I asked them to investigate a small matter of pilfering when they had time. I knew that they wouldn't have time for a while.

Nevertheless, I brought in an Esky to carry away the rest of the vials from the fridge in my little shed. If anyone saw me, I was ready to say that after my shift I was going to the fish markets. I packed them in, all carefully labelled with each child's name. I brought them home and put them with the others in our fridge. I labelled the Esky with your name and added 'Keep out.'

On the way home in the bus, I happened to see Grace. Not at the park but in the city, just opposite the apartment where I used to live. Your father used to visit me there. We sometimes sat on my little balcony and looked out at the church opposite, and laughed because next door to it was an old disused office block that was really a brothel, and no one seemed to care. It was an odd place for her to be, standing outside that brothel.

With her was a man, a seedy-looking, rather intimidating man and – it was difficult to be sure, just looking out of a bus – but he seemed to be ordering her out. Grace looked oddly glamorous. She's a handsome woman and normally dresses, well, like a mother, but now she was dressed garishly. I called out the window to her. She glanced up, frowning. By that time the traffic had moved and the bus rumbled away from her. I watched her walking down the street, and I suddenly knew that she had as many troubles as me.

Selfishly, I don't want her to have troubles. I want to tell her mine.

7 September

Security didn't come in today. But Frank did. He leaned familiarly on the sink while I was handwashing the odd-shaped glassware.

'There's an international canasta competition on and security are winning,' he said.

I put a dripping flask on the rack. He's never sought me out before.

'That's nice,' I said uncertainly.

He leaned his handsome face close.

'They're doing too well to cause trouble about petty pilfering,' he said.

He stood upright.

'Besides, they've all got teenage sons who need cars. I gave them good deals. Got rid of half my fleet.'

His eyebrows went up and down, really fast.

'That's nice,' I said again.

'It'll keep them off our backs for a while,' he said.

He paused, watched me work.

'Maybe you should buy a car from me too. You wouldn't have to rely on that bus any more. It'd be good for everybody.'

He walked away.

That's when I bought the purple Gemini with the mag wheels. I'm sure you don't remember it. It wouldn't have lasted long. When Owen commented, I told him that it was a bargain I couldn't refuse. I knew the floor was rusted through, but if it keeps things calm for a while, it'll be good for everybody.

8 September

I feel lost, but I'm not daring to do my work every morning for you.

Tonight Owen stood at the doorway to the kitchen while I cooked dinner and you played the piano. I was clawing at a pumpkin's orange heart.

'You're preoccupied?' he asked.

'Just work worries,' I said.

'I thought you had the ideal worry-free job,' he said.

He poured us both a glass of wine and I put down the knife and clinked glasses with him. He leaned easily against the bench, his fat body rippling.

'What, did you forget to clean the verdigris around some tap?' he said.

I smiled, sipped the glass of wine, forced the pumpkin pieces apart with the flat of the knife. Yellow seeds dropped on the bench. I threw all the meat into the hot oil, and it hissed at us. He watched me silently. I finished off my glass of wine. The pause between us lengthened, making it difficult for me.

'Don't burn it,' he warned.

The pan had gone black.

'I'm in terrible trouble,' I said.

'Do you want me to take over?' he said of the cooking.

'Yes,' I said. I sank into a chair.

He busied himself and I didn't watch. The wine had loosened my tears. I turned my head away so that he couldn't see.

'Do your scientists see what's in the world?' he asked softly. 'Or do they just see a mirror of their own minds?'

He surprised me into a laugh. How often I've asked that of myself.

'I'm just a cleaner,' I said.

'Tomorrow,' he said, 'I'll bring home a take-away. My favourite, a shepherd's pie. You like shepherd's pie?'

Then you rushed in, and all conversation stopped.

But I wouldn't have been able to talk to him. Not really.

9 September

I didn't do any work except clean. But at least Lab Two was hard at it. Security didn't come. And when I got home, he was out. There was no shepherd's pie for dinner.

When you were having your bath, I went up to his room. The jacaranda flowers are out. I stayed to watch them pawing at the window in the breeze, that's all I did. I didn't dare do more. I feared that everything was about to change, just when the jacaranda had bloomed.

This letter is taking too much of my sleeping time. But I fear not talking. And, worst of all, I fear you not knowing who I am. Anyway, what better thing is there for me to do at two in the morning?

Above our roof, the seagulls circle again, cawing wisely at the foolish stream of light from my bedlamp.

He hasn't come home.

When he was out I went up to his room again. I thought I'd better do something adult, in case you followed me. You seem to notice more than you used to. You might notice me. So I pulled over his memoir as if I was legitimately reading it.

You came up and played with his shoes, stacking them on top of each other like blocks. I kept reading his memoir. What had he ever done to write about? His handwriting is awful and the pages are full of doodles, hundreds of them in blue, red and green fountain pens, like the absent-minded scribble of a pallid monk as he contemplated how he'd illustrate a medieval manuscript. I turned the page to more doodles, this time in scarlet, but they all festooned into one word: Eva.

I stared at my name. The room was very still, with only the sound of the wind outside and you restacking the shoes after your first pile fell over. I skimmed pages, but I couldn't see my name again. He seemed to have written a story about an old man who lived in a house crammed with plastic bags. Nothing to do with me.

Except my name. As if his thoughts turn to me, as mine do to him.

11 September

Security still hasn't come. But America has written back, deeply interested. Someone there has been following a hunch like mine, but he's not so far advanced. I'll write again.

Owen came in humming tonight. I rushed down the hall like any mother would with my hand over my mouth to indicate silence, and pointed frantically to your room.

'Sorry,' he mouthed, and crept along the hall with me.

'I'm sorry about last night,' he said when he could talk. 'The manager sacked me. He said that my singing is keeping the crowds away. Not to mention my clothes.'

He showed me a take-away carton.

'The shepherd's pie, one night late,' he said.

I could smell beer on his breath. He sat down at the table and began to eat without any preliminaries, a fast eater, pushing food into his mouth with great energy and concentration. Even the air around him seemed intense with his energy.

But I could barely eat. I was playing with the food, guilty, wondering if I'd left anything in his room, a tissue perhaps. I'd been in his bed again. Did I straighten out the sheets? Did I leave his memoir as I'd found it?

He cleaned his plate, wiping a hunk of bread around the gravy slops. He leaned forward and watched me so hungrily that I offered him half of my food. He accepted.

'We still haven't had our talk,' he said. 'My life is a surprise to me,' he added. 'I wasn't expecting things to turn out like they have. As well as they have.'

Then, his tongue loosened by the beer, he began to talk, about science, of all things.

'Do you think science is irresponsible?' he asked, and when I said nothing, he added:

'Because science is not negotiable. The assumptions are irretrievably in place. That makes for a very limited picture. And scientists use metaphors, that blind them. You can see the biases in ordinary language, but they get hidden in metaphors.'

He talked about the way that the human egg used to be seen as passive and the sperm as an active, self-propelled penetrator – but now that society has changed, the egg has been discovered to be grasping sperm and dragging it in.

I wanted to point out that the metaphors also help us to see, but he was still talking.

He laughed. He must be one of those people who, when they're with scientists, try to talk science to show off. But he doesn't know I'm a scientist!

'I read science books,' he said, trying to explain where his knowledge comes from. He mentioned that back in his flat – I didn't know he had a flat! – he has a huge library. Perhaps it's so huge there's not enough room for him to sleep. Anyway, I was going to protest that he'd never been inside a lab, but he didn't stop, he was now on the subject of frogs, saying that frogs can only see what moves. That's true – if you put a dead bug in front of a frog, the frog can't see it.

'So frogs could never build a civilisation,' he finished grandly. 'But we're like frogs,' he went on. 'Our eyes only notice change. Yet we stake everything on what we see. As if seeing with our eyes is all there is.'

Is this what he's been waiting to tell me? That he knows a lot of science?

'What do you do up there in your room all day?' I asked him.

'Practise. Read. Think. Wait. Eat biscuits,' he said.

'Wait for what?' I asked, but you yelled then at the noise we were making.

'I'm talking to your mother and I'm just up to the important part,' he yelled back, but he dropped into silence. I went to sleep still hungry.

What is it he wants to say?

12 September

Security came today, interviewing everyone. Dick assisted them, officiously and anxiously.

'I run a tight ship,' he kept telling them. I almost expected him to open the food fridge, to prove that all the yoghurts were well within their use-by dates. 'Whoever's doing it, it must be an extraordinarily subtle operation,' he said.

Shirley was interviewed. She looked only at them, never at me.

13 September

Still no one's thought to interview me. Yet.

I will run. I always knew I would run, some day soon. That's why I'm writing to you.

14 September

This morning you woke as I was gulping my morning cup of tea. I hurried in, anxious, checking my watch as soon as I switched on the light. You screamed. I had to switch it off, warn you, then switch it on. Laura was almost due, my bus was almost due.

'Goodbye, darling,' I said, my voice edged with impatience.

'Wait!' you shouted.

You reached down to the floor and picked up a sheet and poked it in my face, between my lips and my steaming cup of tea. I read Jessica, Steve, Karen and Tom – a list of the names of Grace's children. You'd given each of them a number of knocks they'd have to do on your door so you'd know who was knocking. A sort of code.

'Who worked this out and wrote it down?' I asked, more of myself than you, and not expecting any answer.

'Laura,' you answered.

I sat down on the bed in astonishment that you'd answered. I tried to act as if it was normal, that you and I should be having a conversation like any ordinary mother and daughter.

'Laura!' I exclaimed. You'd never said her name before, as far as I know. And you'd noticed the names of Grace's children. So you'd noticed the children.

But I continued as if nothing exceptional had happened:

'Are you expecting them all to visit today?'

You knocked to show me.

It was so astonishing, I didn't look at my watch. I was even willing Laura not to arrive. 'Okay,' I said, running out the door, suddenly a child myself.

I stood outside with the list. I tried out the first name on the list: 'Steve four knocks and one beat'. I knocked four times, paused one beat, knocked four times again.

'Jessica's knock. Jessica, you come in,' you said.

I didn't tell you there was a mistake. I walked in and said, 'Hello, Tina,' and you said, 'Hello, Jessica,' and we laughed together. I was as thrilled as if you'd won the Nobel Prize.

I heard our front gate, and Laura's tread on the veranda. 'I must go,' I said, disentangling myself from your arms as thin as sticks. I gulped the rest of my tea.

'Take it to the bus stop,' you said.

Like any ordinary child. No, not like that. Like my friend.

'Leave it at the stop,' you said. 'You don't like that cup anyway.'

Laura had opened the door and was halfway into your room.

'Does she?' you asked Laura, as if we were having a perfectly normal conversation.

'Why are you hanging around?' Laura asked me. 'You'll have missed your bus.'

I went to work late, rejoicing.

I was so deep in thought, I missed my stop coming home again. I expected Laura's anger, but she was smiling sweetly, asking me to iron her best dress.

'It's part of the deal,' she said.

You were banging on the piano, just one note, again and again.

As I heated up the iron, I wondered whether, now that your talking was emerging, your musicality was retreating. I'd have to ask Owen, but it doesn't seem to me as musical as before.

I flattened out the flounces and sleeves of Laura's dress.

'I don't know how to do this,' she said suddenly, watching me.

'What?' I asked.

'Iron,' she said. 'My mother never shows me anything. She's too busy with the other kids.'

'Practice would help,' I said.

She left but she stayed on the back veranda, twisting a handkerchief so I knew that the conversation was going to continue.

'You've got some spare room,' she said. 'Can I move in? You won't have to pay me then, and I'd be Tina's big sister. It's nicer here than my house. I'd help out,' she said as she saw my surprise. 'Learn to do my own ironing. Maybe yours. Get some practice in for when I'm on my own. Cook, maybe. I'd even clean up. And Tina's getting easier.'

'You think so?' I shouted in joy.

'She's talking now. And what she's playing on the piano,' she said, 'I couldn't find anything in it before but now it actually sounds like something.'

15 September

For days the lab has been utterly silent. No preoccupied talk. And then someone sneezed many times and everyone giggled as if it was the funniest thing they'd ever heard.

You didn't say a word yesterday afternoon. It was as if your brilliance in the morning was a dream. The dream all this work is for.

In fact, you hit me.

25 September

Another email from the lab in America. They haven't been able to reproduce my results, but they are very interested. Would I (the old man) be willing to come out of retirement and work with them?

I didn't dare answer. I didn't know how to.

30 September

Laura's moved in. She has the bedroom I had as a child, the little room out the back. You visit her all the time. Every dawn I find you asleep in her bed, your arm thrown around her. Are you feeling love for her, I wonder?

What do you remember of these days? Do you remember me?

5 October

After all my loneliness, and just when I feel I'll have to bolt any day, everything changes.

Last night there was a knock on the door, and the sound of many feet.

'Who is it?' I called.

Owen was out and the front veranda was in darkness.

'Me,' called a woman's voice. Grace's.

'Us,' she added.

Laura ran out in her white nightie, dragging her bedcover, you trailing behind. I switched on the light and opened the door. You ran out, leaning against me, breathing hard. Grace was there with her children in pyjamas, crumpled and stained, their uplifted faces pale and anxious.

'I hoped you wouldn't mind,' she said.

You began to scream about your door and the notice on it. At least, you called: 'Door, door!' over and over, and I knew that you wanted them to read the notice Laura had written for you, and to knock on your bedroom door in code so you could guess who it was.

But Grace's face showed that this was no time for games. She had to shout over you.

'Can we stay the night? We'll go tomorrow, but can we stay? There's nowhere else to go.'

'Of course,' I said, awed by her distress, since she'd always been so calm.

'Come inside. Come into the lounge room.'

I wanted to hear what had happened but I had to take you into your bedroom, and massage you. I sent Laura to her bedroom to go back to sleep.

'Tomorrow,' I kept saying to you. 'The children will play with you tomorrow.'

I don't know if you understood me. You cried and we wrestled. It must've taken half an hour before you slumped asleep.

Grace creaked open your door.

'Can I feed my kids?' she whispered. 'Open some tins from your cupboard?'

'Of course,' I said. She pulled the door to behind her.

By the time I came out, Grace's children were eating. They were downcast and silent.

'I've used up all your bread,' Grace said.

She told me that three days ago her husband had brought home his mistress, and she was pregnant. He wanted her to live with them.

'I said it was either the mistress or me,' Grace said. 'He chose the mistress. We've had a lot of fights in the last couple of months, and I didn't think things would get any better with a mistress there. So we left.'

She had no money. She'd been trying to get work, she said, so that she could pay for somewhere to stay. I thought of her in front of the brothel, but surely she wouldn't go there for work? I said nothing. Two of the children began crying.

'Let's talk more later,' I said. I found sheets and pillows for them, and put them in the guest room my mother and Cuthbert had built for the stream of visitors they'd never had.

After all the children were asleep, Grace and I had cocoa.

'If the children can be kind to Tina, stay here,' I said. 'As long as you like.'

Her face softened with relief.

'If I'm not around would you help with Tina?' I asked. I caught her startled eye and added: 'You know, what with work and such, I'm a busy cleaning lady.'

'We'll all be just one big family!' she cried.

So she is my solution, after all.

Now, in my quiet bedroom, I'm wondering whether, when you and Laura made that sign about knocking, you somehow understood that they were in trouble. In your rapid glances, did you guess that they would need to come to us?

I will think of you whooping with laughter while they knock on your door, using your code. I will think of you shouting, 'Jessica – that's Jessica!' and 'Steve – that's Steve!'

My darling, I will always be with you. When I have to leave, I'll always be thinking of you, your genes, your cure. Your life has given my life purpose.

6 October

You seem delighted with your new company. I looked along the table we've joined together for dinner, the children behaving just as I'd envisaged, giggling with their mouths full of food, and I wonder if I could undo it all and be allowed to stay.

Over the washing up, Owen said to Grace:

'I might've known you once. Did you have silver hair?'

We looked at Grace's mousy hair.

'Not yet,' she laughed.

'Did you have another name?' he asked.

'No,' she said. I saw her blushing, and wondered why.

He was persistent.

'Were you ever called Charlene?'

'Charlene?' Her voice almost trilled. She laughed, and said of course she'd never been Charlene. She'd only ever been Grace.

'There was a Charlene long ago. I never met her but she changed my life,' said Owen.

Grace's face moved as if she wished she'd said yes, and might still do, if Owen asked her again. But he didn't.

8 October

An email from Gunther to Dick. The words are imprinted on my brain:

'Winding things up here. By the way, please try to locate Clara. Rumour has it she's working at a university in Sydney. Perhaps we could celebrate Christmas together.'

I didn't intervene, though jealousy was weakening every bone in my body. Why ever didn't I tell him about you? 'I've had your child. She's beautiful.' That's all I had to say. But I didn't. Perhaps I knew it was over with him. That what he'd given me at first, he'd never give me again.

Forgive me, my darling.

Dick began emailing to search for Clara. I let the emails through. I've done enough damage.

9 October

Run?

I don't want to run.

Even the light in the lab was sad today, the colour of the grey car park, the grey sky. Yet the lab is home. Perhaps I've never really accepted my home with you. My mother's home.

In the late afternoon I was chopping vegetables for dinner and thinking about staying, thinking about being caught. Chop: the police would come here. You would remember it always, your mother led away. We'd be looking over our shoulders at each other, our necks screwed around, our eyes trying to swallow each other.

Chop: Dick would be there, saying, 'I can't believe how I trusted her.'

Chop: hacking. Apart from everything else, they'd jail me for hacking.

Chop: the sirens, the raised voices, the eyes on you, pitying you. Particularly the eyes. You hate eyes.

I am a criminal who took over a lab.

10 October

I've become foolish for this man. I'm just about to leave forever, and still I was listening for his step down the path. I kept running to look out the window. But no, it was a father hurrying home to his wife, a woman clipping by on high heels, a child carrying a skateboard – never him.

Grace, Laura and the other children had gone shopping. You were pounding the piano. I didn't want to go out, I wanted to wait. In case he came home. He didn't come home.

I went up to his room, I lay on his sheets, I kissed his sheets, and wept. Then the gate clicked. Our gate. A key in the lock. His key.

I swung my legs onto the floor. The front door creaked open too soon. 'Eva,' he called. I sat still. You kept hammering the piano. 'Hello, Tina,' he shouted. 'Where's Mum?'

'Maybe she's out,' said a voice, a girl's voice, a long-legged, blonde voice.

He called me again.

'She wouldn't go out and leave Tina alone,' he said. 'Anyway, come in.'

He was walking down the hall and she was following him.

'You okay, Tina?' he called out.

'Hello, Owen,' you called.

'I've brought a friend,' he said to you.

It was too late to leave his room. I bounded across the floor, half tripping, and pulled open the wardrobe and crouched inside it. Do you remember, you'd sometimes hide there and I'd find you with your face pressed against my old dresses, the grand ones of silk and satin and velvet, the ones my mother made me all those years ago? But they'd gone, of course. It was his wardrobe now. I hid my hot face amongst his clothes and they caressed me.

'Do you want to come upstairs?' he asked her. 'Or would you rather stay down there? I'll just be a minute.'

I wriggled his shoes aside and pulled the door to.

'I'll come up,' the girl's voice said.

Their footsteps came up the stairs, his heavy, hers light, the high heels tip-tipping. He threw open his door. I took a deep breath of mothballs and tried to hold it.

'Look at that tree!' she said.

He was walking towards the wardrobe.

There was a plomp. She must've sat on his bed.

'It needs a good trim, it does. Or they should get rid of it.'

He opened the wardrobe door. The open door was throwing a shaft of light on my back!

He paused, shuffled his feet, took hold of a shirt above me, and the hangers swung all the way down the rod, clanging on the sides and the top of the wardrobe. I didn't dare look up. The light changed. He was shutting the door.

'Not that shirt,' she said.

'It's comfortable,' he said.

'I suppose it'll do – put it on,' she said.

There was silence. He was probably putting on the shirt. I heard her walking over to him.

'As long as you wear it open, and with a scarf, with an Ascot knot maybe, a little puffed up. Have you got a scarf?'

'No,' he said.

'Let me check your ties,' she said. 'Are they hanging up in there?'

He clicked the wardrobe door shut.

'I don't want to wear a tie,' he said.

'But you've got to look right for this performance,' she said.

'Forget the tie,' he said.

They argued, but he kept repeating that he didn't want to. He didn't even know if he wanted to do the performance, he said. I could tell it was an important performance that she'd set up, but he was determined not to open the wardrobe door.

'Let's go,' he said.

He walked out of the room. She had to follow him. Just as they walked down the hall, you yelled.

'What, Tina?' Owen asked.

So you bellowed:

'Mum's hiding in your room!'

'Funny little thing!' said the girl.

Are you getting better?

11 October

Tonight I praised him for the way he understands you.

He nodded. 'Of course. She murmurs to me,' he said. 'Like you used to,' he added.

I didn't have a chance to ask what he meant because the children were pounding around the house and hiding from each other, shrieking with laughter. You had to join in. 'Me, me, me!' you called, and raced off in the wrong direction. I didn't thank him about the wardrobe. I didn't know how to.

12 October

I asked Sandy to email me with progress, even though it was a little earlier than the three months we'd agreed to. He emailed back with very, very interesting progress, not that he realised it. Of course he thought he was emailing Gunther.

About six-thirty in the morning, the air-conditioning in the lab died. I wrenched open the windows. I stood while the cold air poured around my face like dark water, as if I was a rock and it was chiselling me into a new shape. If only it could chisel out a new curvature in my mind, perhaps I could solve this puzzle of you.

I crossed to Lab Two despite the prohibition. I can't do anything to stop their work, I can't hide it from Gunther. I wonder what Gunther will make of it, if he makes anything of it at all. But at least I have their progress report.

As I turned the corridor into the lab, the dawn light was like red curtains unfurling across the sky. I tried to take comfort from the beauty of its glow. I tried to tell myself that one day none of this sadness would matter. Then I paused. There was a chink of light under Lab Two's door.

An excuse started in my throat. I'll say that I've come for some equipment, some Petri dishes, we're short of Petri dishes down our end, I'll say.

Then I thought of you. It would be remembered that I'd walked into Lab Two, despite the prohibition, on one of my last mornings. I turned away.

When the sun was properly up, I heard footsteps. Madeline was walking to her car. She'd been working all night. From my window, she was just a rounded head while her coat billowed and swayed. She unlocked the door of her car, climbed in, slammed it, started the engine. It growled immediately. Her coat had caught in the door. I watched her, thinking that she'd be one of my last memories, the way she'd left, preoccupied, after working all night on your cure. The edge of her coat was caught in the car door but she was unaware of it. She drove off. I watched her go out the hospital gates, the edge of her coat still protruding.

I walked across to Lab Two. But I passed Einstein and he was awake now, though still lounging on the sofa. He lifted his hand to me and I returned the wave. I walked on right around the hospital, past night nurses finishing their shifts, past a tired orderly rolling a clanking bank of trolleys, past two doctors leaning on their cars and talking. I walked back to where I started, and all I'd got was chilly fingertips.

Shirley stopped me just as I was finishing my shift. She caught me near the security guard's office. She held a meat pie from the cafe. Steam was rising from its white paper bag.

'I want to check something with you,' she called out. 'But come into the shade. My fair skin . . .'

We moved away from the office and stood in the shade of the hospital.

'Do you know what you're doing?' she asked enigmatically.

'Do you?' I asked.

'I'm guessing,' she said.

We gazed at each other, and then we both looked down at the steam rising from her pie.

'Are you going to tell?' I asked.

'What?' she said. 'What can I tell?'

When I looked up, her eyes were smiling.

Suddenly all the years, all our tension, fell away, and I was her young assistant again.

'I don't know what you're doing, or how you're doing it, and if they –'

her eyes indicated the lab –

'if they can't protect themselves from you, it's not my place to do it.'

She laughed sadly. 'I owe them nothing. Especially Sandy. Mind you,' she added, looking levelly at me, 'I owe you nothing either.'

'I owe you a lot,' I said. 'You were very kind to me when I needed a friend. So kind to me and Tina.'

There was a pause. A loading truck reversed by us. We waited for it to leave.

'It means a lot to me, you saying that,' she said.

There was another pause. I was about to turn and go, but she said:

'The past few months have shown that I don't know much about you after all these years, but I know one thing. Whatever you're up to, you're not doing it like the others, you're doing something crazy, something that's a huge gamble.'

She threw her head back.

'Something real. I think I'm going to be proud of you,' she said.

She waved to Abdul and Frank, who were heading towards the cafe.

'They'll wonder why you're talking to the cleaning lady,' I said.

'Just promise me one thing,' she said. 'When Gunther comes back, hell will break out. The moment he appears, you'll have to go. Go away. Go a long way. In fact, why don't you go to one of those overseas labs that's so interested in your website?'

Then she pushed the corner of her pie out of the paper bag, bit into it despite the steam, and turned towards the lab.

Report of ongoing investigation commissioned by the
Sudlow Hospital Board

Ref: ghp: 261

The apparent Sanderson–Mueller correspondence was
concluded just two days before Arnoux left. Of course, this
timing could be another coincidence.

Sanderson has reported that one of the students was
sufficiently impressed by the line of research to successfully
apply to continue it when she returned to her home
university. 'But we're all easily impressed when we're
young,' he said.

I must add that in the recovery of the hard disk, many
personal items appeared in the letters that seemed to have
no connection with a lab – to wit, car sales, financial deals,
and love letters between members of staff. I have details of
these, and am happy to submit them if required.

In summary it appears that both laboratories were
subject to a hoax masterminded by an ingenious party or
parties who used the climate of negligence to further
particular and eccentric ends. I would argue that the
evidence seems to point to the person known as Arnoux,
but this evidence is circumstantial. Also circumstantial is
the evidence that could point to Arnoux and Chatworth
being one and the same.

I would have been greatly assisted in my investigations
if I could have questioned the third long-term staff member,
Shirley Thompson, but she disappeared a short time after the
departure of Arnoux/Chatworth. However, Dr Sanderson
has informed me that he holds her in the highest esteem.
He contends that her disappearance is not connected in any
way to the disruption in the lab, but to a great personal
distress that she had concealed for more than a decade,
namely a broken love affair. He declined to name the
partner in this love affair.

I have been asked to give an opinion as to whether the

Board should take this matter further. I would recommend against it because exposure of the negligent management practices, and other disclosures that directly implicate a prominent member of the Board, would only lead to general embarrassment.

---

* I'm sure you know that Charles Sanderson was accused of scientific fraud and convicted of insider trading, perjury, obstruction of justice and bank fraud in 2003. (His estranged wife brought it all to the police's attention.) However, his lawyers and the Board members of the Samuel Craven Sudlow Hospital claimed that he was the victim of a vindictive wife and circumstantial evidence. He served part of a five-year jail sentence but was let out on parole early because he was regarded as a model prisoner. – T.

15 October

Tonight when I was washing up for all of us – you were trying to play Monopoly with the others and, to my delight, screeching with laughter – Owen came into the kitchen. I didn't know he was there until he spoke, I didn't know he was in the house. He'd been watching me, I don't know for how long.

'We haven't had our talk yet,' he said.

'What is this talk we're to have?' I asked, trying to keep my voice light.

'Are you in love with somebody?' he asked.

The question was so sudden my heart crunched. It was as if he'd reached in and fingered it.

'Besides Tina,' he added.

'Why?' I asked.

'There's a completeness about you,' he said.

'Oh, no,' I said, 'I'm very incomplete, I'm really the most incomplete person . . . if only you knew . . .' And then, I was bending over the sink with the wasted years of my foolish, dogged love for Gunther.

'Yes,' I said. I sat down with the weight of it.

'Gunther was my great love,' I told him. 'I worked for him. He was how I learned about love, I learned to love a particular shape, size, feel, smell, and nobody else quite fits it. It's a hopeless, stupid love.'

He sat down opposite me, but I couldn't meet his eyes.

'Will you go back to him?' he asked.

'He's with someone else now,' I said. 'And he's Tina's father but he doesn't know about Tina.'

And then I hurtled on:

'He's about to come back to the lab where I clean. And he doesn't know I work there or what I've done. And he mightn't recognise me. Or, on the other hand, he might. And I don't know –'

I was on the point of telling him about this letter I so desperately want you to read. But that would mean telling him about my coming disgrace, and about the lab. I stopped, and there was a pause in the room as if it was holding its breath. But he kept sitting on the chair as if he was prepared to sit there for years, as if there was nothing else on his mind but my problems. His head was on one side, listening to me, and that was such sweetness to me, that he listened intently. No one, it seemed, has ever listened like he does. It seemed like an original act, the very kindest act of being human, that he listened. His listening makes me want to search the corners of my heart to examine if leaving is what I should do after all.

Then he told me that he'd loved me for a long time, in fact for most of his life, and he hadn't dared to speak until he found me hiding in his wardrobe. He told me this very quickly because we'd be interrupted. Then he caressed my face.

'But you've only known me a few months,' I said.

'What you don't realise is –' he began.

Then we were interrupted. You screamed for me and I had to go to you, and by the time I came back to the kitchen, he was no longer there. So I don't know what it is that I don't know.

16 October

So you see, love comes at the wrong time, like most things do. You probably know that already.

The memory of his stroking hand came to me as soon as I woke. It was still dark, a deeper darkness this morning, a confiding darkness. I packed a few clothes. I hid the bag in my wardrobe. Then I ran for the bus. It was late today.

Dick hurried into the lab an hour early, a tie looped around his neck like a scarf. He made a list of what he had to do. He went through all his old emails and deleted the love letters to Jan. He cleared his desk, and inspected my cleaning at last, and said it wasn't nearly good enough and ordered a spring cleaning of Top Lab – but not Lab Two. He personally cleaned out the food fridge, even Frank's unopened bottle of chutney. He cleaned out his briefcase, the apple cores and screwed-up theatre tickets, as if he expected Gunther to check it.

With the memory of Owen's caress, suddenly I was able to clean everything. Ajax on the walls I haven't touched before. Pine-O-Clean on Clara's stretch of bench that I've neglected. Oddly enough, there was no pain.

In the shed, I destroyed the evidence of my work. I scrambled all my emails off Dick's hard disk. The repair people will say that his computer seems to have been affected by a power surge. I stole the floppy back-up he throws into his top drawer. I did all this while Dick was having an early lunch.

Sandy came in. I hadn't seen him since the day he started the students off on our cells.

'Some people are lucky, leaving early,' he said. He even held the door open for me to go through. He's in such a good mood, he's probably sold shares in the trial of his new drug for a fortune.

Before I got on the bus, I bought a bigger Esky for all the vials.

Owen met me at the bus stop. It was raining. 'I was worried you'd get wet,' he said.

Surprisingly, he didn't ask about the Esky, which was good, because it would've been difficult to explain away. He held his raincoat up above our heads like a tent. It hid our hug though the Esky came between us at first, and I had to put it down on the footpath.

Suddenly I knew I could hold someone again, someone who was not your father. It seemed a chaste hug, as if we were measuring the length, width, warmth and kindness of each other's bodies. His seemed very kind.

Gunther got on his plane from London tonight, two hours ago. I have to decide what to do. I think I've decided.

17 October

Dick called me into his office while he was on the phone. He put his hand over the receiver.

'A final spruce-up today,' he said.

'Is tomorrow special?' I asked.

'Business as usual,' he said.

'Oh, hello,' he said into the phone. It was a difficult phone call about an email I'd composed to keep him busy.

Today my mop took me around and around Dick's office. I knew he was worrying that he'd be found out for something he hasn't done but should've done, or that he has done but shouldn't have. He's so muddled, anything is possible.

He shouted for me. I opened his door and popped my smiling face around it.

'You keep banging your mop on my wall!' he shouted. 'Can't you see I'm stressed?'

When I looked out the window, the sky was immense, as if we're nothing.

My mop kept taking me to the Ladies. I propped it against the white tiled wall, and amongst the sighing of the cisterns I looked at my face. My face like a fish. Every hour I found another wrinkle.

I got older through the long morning.

Tonight Owen wasn't home. On my last night! Everyone else was watching TV. I went up to his room, buried my face in his pillow and cried until you called for me.

All night I've charted Gunther's long flight above oceans and deserts and cities and villages, my mind a little lit-up map with the plane moving like a slow, slow arrow across it.

18 October

I stood at the hallstand mirror in the dawn light, brushing my hair. There was a creak on the stairs. I glanced up. Owen was coming down in his sarong, barefooted.

'You've seemed so worried, and last night I had to sing in a bar,' he said. 'So I wanted to see you before you went to work.'

He walked towards me. I turned halfway to meet him. His face was soft, smiling, gentle. His steps seemed to slow down, so that as he crossed from the stairs to me, he seemed to move through light, or perhaps I was the one moving through light. I panicked. I turned back to the mirror where for a moment we swam as if we weren't real, only reflections.

'I can smell your fear,' he said. 'Are you afraid?'

I said yes, because of the warmth of his hands. It didn't seem dangerous to admit to fear.

'Of him?' he asked. 'Are you frightened of him?'

I said no. I allowed myself to lean slightly on his bulk as he searched my face in the mirror. What I leaned against seemed solid, strong, permanent.

'I can't imagine what you'd be afraid of,' he said. 'I think you've come into your power.'

Then he held me close to his large body and for the first time I realised that he has long arms, arms that seem to enfold me so I can lean away from him and still be held. He nuzzled the back of my neck. I told myself that it was fine that he should kiss the back of my neck, it won't hurt him later when he remembers, I can give in to the softness of his lips on the back of my neck. Whereas it might be dangerous if he kissed my face. I might be moved. I might fall in love. And he might too, and I wouldn't want to hurt him, he's too dear. The kissing of my neck went on and on, so sweet, the mouthing of his lips on my neck. He lifted my hair to find all the places on my neck I've never been kissed, the dark, secret places where Gunther's lips never went. I was in a swoon from his lips. Then he paused and I wanted to cry out in disappointment. But I pulled myself away.

I told him we shouldn't kiss.

'But I'll be here for you tonight,' he said into my hair. 'In fact, I'll ask Laura to make dinner for everyone and I'll take you out to my bar. You can hear me sing. There's a special song I've been planning to sing to you. A favourite of mine, all my life.'

He mentioned a composer. Handel, I think.

He turned my face towards him and examined me anxiously.

'I still have to make that confession,' he said.

I nodded, and for a moment his face was very close to mine, so that the air between us was as soft as his skin must be. His eyes seemed as gentle as light.

'If something happens to me –' I began.

'Like what?' he asked, drawing back, fearful.

So I told him about this letter, and where it would be, and that it was for you. 'For when she's older, for when she's loved someone. But there's a lot I have to accomplish for her to be able to read it,' I said.

I wanted to say that I knew I could trust him with you, but I couldn't speak any more.

'I couldn't bear losing you,' he said. 'Not again.'

He said 'not again', I'm sure.

'I'm not actually a proper cleaning lady,' I said.

'I know,' he began.

And then it was too late to find out what he knows because my mother's house was full of children, and Tom ran out to wake you, to play your game of knock-knock. I pulled myself away from him.

'I must go,' I said. 'I'll miss my bus.'

'Just a minute,' he said. 'I'm going to sing for you right now. I'm going to sing my song.'

I was already halfway out the door.

'Your song?' I flung over my shoulder.

He burst into song, following me out to the veranda, switching on the light mid-note.

'It's about freedom,' he said, descending from some high note to interrupt himself, and then he breathed into the next phrase, his chest building and deflating like bellows.

'The bus,' I reminded him, but he didn't stop singing. As if he'd know about freedom! I know all about freedom, and not having freedom. More than him, more than anyone.

But he kept singing about freedom as if he knew all about it, singing in Italian, I think, something grand and magnificent that followed me all the way up the street, past the dewy letterboxes and the sleeping cars. A window was thrown up here, a door creaked open there. Faces peered out, and someone swore. But his voice kept singing.

I turned at the corner. He was watching me, still afloat in his song about freedom, a fat man in a sarong standing in a pool of light on our veranda. I could no longer hear him but he didn't know that, or perhaps he didn't care. I could tell he was at some particularly passionate part of the song because his long arms, those arms that had held me so protectively, were lifting out from his body with the swell of music, they were lifting like an opera singer's arms do, up, up, now bent at the elbows and curved towards heaven. He seemed to be holding the song in his arms, cradling it. Then it struck me that he wasn't free at all, it was as if he was only a marionette being controlled by strings from somewhere above him, maybe from the gutters around the roof, or maybe from heaven. As if I am. I stopped walking then. There's a little paling fence around the end house. I found myself clutching its dampness. Dew ran down my fingers. I didn't know which way to go. I longed to go back. I nearly did. To him, to you.

Maybe they'd let me out of prison after two or three years. But I'd never be trusted in a lab again.

Then the bus came and decided it for me, all lit up like a beacon and rumbling busily through the roundabout, heralding an ordinary day, like any other. I ran for it. That's how I made the decision in the end, because the bus happened to come, right at that moment. If it had been late – I don't know.

Instead of doing my secret work, I wrote this.

Through the morning I could make no plans. All I could see in my mind's eye was a long, straight, dusty road, white edged by dead grasses. It wound up over a mountain. I climbed the mountain. There was another mountain, and another. I had to climb them because it was too late to turn back. I didn't know where the road ended. If it ended.

My mop kept taking me to the windows.

At eleven-thirty, a taxi swept into the car park.

'Taxi!' I shouted.

'It'll be him,' Dick said. 'He said he'd come straight here, to get things sorted out.' He began to knot his tie.

Shirley had left Lab Two and was suddenly there beside me, breathing with me but not looking at me. It wasn't cold, but our breathing was making two circles of mist on the windowpane, side by side. The passenger was paying the driver.

'Is it him?' called Dick.

A walking stick was thrust out of the back door of the taxi.

'Is it?' called Dick. He came over to stand with us at the window. Shirley said nothing.

'Of course, you've never met him,' Dick said to me. 'He left just before you started.'

The walking stick wobbled under the weight of a hand. A man with a suitcase emerged, a man much smaller than I remembered, much slighter, older, bent. I used to swell with importance whenever I looked at him, that this great scientist belonged to me. But where that feeling once was, there was a gap, a silence.

'It's him,' breathed Shirley to me at last, as if I wouldn't know.

Dick hurried away from the window to call everyone.

'He's here! Shirley, will you get everyone?'

Shirley touched the small of my back as she turned to do as Dick had asked.

'Go,' she said to me.

Before Gunther got to the car park door, I was hurrying through the hospital. I came home and packed all the vials from the fridge into the big Esky.

No one's here. You're at the park, my darling, trying to play with the children.

Goodbye, my love.

Professor Mueller,

I never knew I had a mother till the phone rang. The phone was always ringing in our house and I hated the noise. But this time it was dawn and I was the only one up. I did what I shouldn't have done – I grabbed the receiver and slammed it down so the caller would go away. The phone rang again. This time I listened to someone crying. 'I'm your mother,' the crying voice kept saying. That's how Owen found me, sitting on the floor listening to a voice. I remember repeating her words to him: 'I'm your mother.'

He took the receiver, listened for himself, pushed me gently out of the room and talked into the phone. Then everyone was awake and in the living room, dishevelled in their pyjamas and opening the fridge and shaking out cornflakes into bowls and arguing about who should go around to the shop for milk, and would the shop be open. In all this confusion, I didn't think any more about the voice on the phone until Owen came into the room. He was hugging me and saying that it was my mother at last, my mother had found my cure, and that he and I were to fly immediately to a clinic in America that would treat me by the method she'd invented.

Everyone burst out arguing even though their mouths were full, especially Grace, who'd become very particular about talking with food in your mouth. Grace said I didn't need treatment any more, and so did my friend Laura. Grace said I was just eccentric. I'd had lots of psychotherapy, the sort you'd disapprove of. I'd started talking to my family and stopped talking to the piano. I couldn't go to school, though, and I couldn't read or write. I remember letters looked just like sticks thrown down at random on the ground. Often I couldn't follow what people said, and I could never understand their feelings. And I was very bad about phones – all noises, in fact, except music. But Owen insisted. My mother had given her life to finding this cure, he said.

He added something that I didn't understand then, but I do now that I've read his memoir: on the phone he'd confessed to her.

We flew to America the very next day, Owen and me, with Owen saying all the way, Keep calm, we must keep calm. He wasn't keeping calm at all. When we got to the clinic, my mother wasn't there, and he believed his confession had frightened her away. Of all people, who should come and shake our hands but Shirley. I didn't recognise her, of course, but later I found out that my mother had sent for her so they could work together. Shirley said she'd be doing the therapy because my mother didn't trust herself, she was afraid that her emotion would ruin her life's work. She would meet us afterwards.

The treatment and the check-ups lasted a month. That's how little time my mother's lifework took to accomplish my cure. On the last day, Shirley told us that we were to meet my mother in the centre of the city, at a fountain. We went there and waited and waited, watching the water leap in the sunshine and fall back again, but she didn't turn up. She must've lost her courage, said Owen.

He was determined to find her, and arranged for me to fly back to Sudlow with an escort. Shirley said she didn't know where my mother was, but her face said something else. That was the thing that changed first for me. People's faces seemed to talk even when their voices were silent.

Back at home, I found I could do things that seemed impossible before. I could follow what people said, even instructions when I wanted to. I learned to read, and eventually I got a job in a library clearing away the books people had read, and setting out more books so they'd want to read them as well. I always loved organising things.

I was twenty-two by then. But Owen hadn't got back yet, and he still hasn't. He's found my mother, and now they live together. We've spoken on the phone. She tells me that she was always in love with you but she loves Owen, and that's sufficient, she says. Now she wants to come home, with him.

It took us a while to go to Owen's old apartment, but one day we had to, it was a way of being near him. He'd told us on the phone we'd find something that would surprise us. We'd known nothing about his apartment till then. He's such a big, hearty, kind man, not at all like the pale, creeping spy you'd probably imagine from his memoir. There we found his peephole, and his huge, messy library and next door all the furniture just as he described. (Apparently, once he moved into our house, he'd told the old lawyer to leave both apartments just as they were, like a museum.) He'd taken his memoir back there with my mother's letter and folded them around each other and put them under his mattress, so they were part of each other, a marriage of manuscripts, Grace said. I had to read it all there and then, sitting on what I was soon to find out was my mother's bed. I'm afraid I couldn't wait for my first love affair, as my mother had wanted.

I'm sending you this because I want you to use your reputation to enable my mother to come back and work again. Her misdeeds were a long time ago and her work has achieved so much – at least for me, and perhaps for many autistic children. And I'm sending it because I thought if you saw all the details of how it happened, you'd believe that I'm your daughter. I'm enclosing her red beads, to prompt your memory.

Tina

15 November 2010

Tina,

I've read it and I'll take action. I'm sending back the diaries but I'll keep the beads. Thanks for them.

Your father, Gunther.

Historical Notes

Hans Asperger, the real-life hero of this story, was a paediatrician in Austria who noticed a constellation of symptoms in apparently unlike but disturbed boys brought to his practice, and then to his school, over the decade before he published his groundbreaking paper 'Die Autistischen Psychopathen im Kindesalter' in 1944. In this paper he described four boys, none of whom is Gunther. He had high hopes for 'his children', as he grew to call them, and whether or not he deliberately overstated in his paper his belief in their normal, even brilliant futures to try to protect them from extermination in those terrible days of the Nazi regime is a matter of conjecture.

Asperger noted that his children all had a close relative who could at least be called odd, while never blaming these relatives. Because nearly all his children were boys, Asperger suggested a 'sex-linked mode of inheritance' for the autistic condition – and used the term 'autism'.

Asperger's paper was lost to English speakers for four decades. It is both an irony and a tragedy for autism sufferers and their families that this loss was probably because, despite the doctor's defiance of the Nazis, Asperger and his paper had the misfortune to be associated with the Nazi era. When it was eventually translated into English by Uta Frith in 1992, it explained a phenomenon that had puzzled thousands of doctors, families and patients. Asperger's Syndrome has now, in Australia at least, become quite a familiar diagnosis, and it has been extended, with different symptoms, to include girls. At the time of writing, it is considered to be part of the autism spectrum.

Asperger's was a particularly useful definition of autism because it was so wide, including severe cases as well as those that 'shaded into normality'.

Leo Kanner, working contemporaneously but independently of Asperger in America, described a much smaller and more limited group of children with what are now regarded as 'classic' autistic features. He coined the term 'early infantile autism' in 1944. Sadly, Kanner's article was published in America at a time when theories about parental causes of mental disturbance were seizing the popular imagination there, without the benefit of Asperger's insights about the genetic nature of the condition.

Kanner weighed in on both sides of the blaming debate, even publishing in the same year an article on the destructiveness of mothers of autistic childen, calling them 'refrigerator' mothers, as well as a book in which he sought to relieve the guilt of mothers of autistic children. He continued taking both sides all his life – but he was joined in parent-blaming by other much publicised experts, such as Bruno Bettelheim.

Bettelheim had been a prisoner in a Nazi concentration camp and believed that autistic children had been mistreated by their mothers in the same way that Nazi prisoners had been mistreated by their guards. They'd withdrawn from reality into despair.

Since autism, as Kanner defined it, was a debilitating condition, very often children were considered incurable and sent to homes to die. In fact Kanner advocated that the children should be sent away so that they would be separated from their poisonous parents.

The parent-blaming hysteria has had terrible consequences that still mark many families living today. It hijacked the possibility of effective biological research for treatment – or at least amelioration of the condition – for at least two generations. It caused untold and unnecessary guilt, grief and misery to many innocent families. But worst of all, it must have been responsible for the slow deaths of hundreds – probably thousands – of children who were sent away to die.

A C K N O W L E D G M E N T S

For the scientists' dialogue, I drew heavily on:

An Imagined World by Jane Goodfield, Harper & Row, New York,
   1981

Im/Partial Science by Bonnie Spanier, Indiana University Press,
   Bloomington, 1995

Darwin's Black Box by Michael J. Behe, Simon & Schuster, New York,
   1996

The Making of Memory by Steven Rose, Bantam, London, 1992

Autism and Childhood Psychosis by Frances Tustin, Karnac Books,
   London, 1995

The Golem: What You Should Know About Science by Harry Collins
   and Trevor Pinch, Cambridge University Press, Cambridge, 1998

*Madness on the Couch: Blaming the Victim in the Heyday of
   Psycholanalysis* by Edward Dolnick, Simon & Schuster, New York,
   1998

*It Ain't Necessarily So: The Dream of the Human Genome and Other
   Illusions* by Richard Lewontin, Granta, London, 2000; and also his
   earlier work, *The Doctrine of DNA: Biology as Ideology*, Penguin,
   London, 1991

428 THE SECRET CURE

428 THE SECRET CURE

The Eighth Day of Creation by Horace Freeland Judson, expanded
edition, Plainview, CSHL Press, New York, 1996

I also referred to:
The Seven Daughters of Eve by Bryan Sykes, Corgi, Great Britain, 2001
Rosalind Franklin: The Dark Lady of DNA by Brenda Maddox,
HarperCollins, London, 2002
Women in Science by Vivian Gornick, Simon & Schuster, New York,
1990
Nobody Nowhere by Donna Williams, Doubleday, London, 1992
Autism and Asperger Syndrome, edited by Uta Frith, Cambridge
University Press, Cambridge, 1992
Intellectual Suppression: Australian Case Histories, edited by Brian
Martin, Angus & Robertson, Sydney, 1986
*Developmental Disorders of the Frontostriatal System:
Neuropsychological, Neuropsychiatric and Evolutionary Perspectives*,
by John L. Bradshaw, Psychology Press, Philadelphia, 2000
The Politics of Objectivity by Randall Albury, Deakin University Press,
Victoria, 1983
The Lives of a Cell by Lewis Thomas, Viking, New York, 1974
The Birth of Molecular Biology by Michel Morange, Harvard
University Press, Cambridge, Massachusetts, 1998
*Infantile Autism: The Syndrome and its Implications for a Neural
Theory of Behaviour* by Bernard Rimlard, Appleton-Century-Crofts,
New York, 1964
The Third Reich by Michael Berwick, Putnam, New York, 1972
In the Name of Eugenics: Genetics and the Uses of Human Hereditary
by Daniel J. Kevles, Knoft, Harvard, 1985

I consulted:
'Y is it so' by Deborah Smith in the *Sydney Morning Herald*,
25 November 2000
'The Geek Syndrome' by Steve Silberman in *Wired Magazine*, Issue 9.12,
December 2001
'Unquiet Grave for Nazi Victims' by Kate Connolly, *The Guardian*,
29 April 2002

'Scientific Fraud and Defamation' in *The Health Report with Norman Swann*, Radio National, 17 August 1998

This work wouldn't have been possible without the help of many scientific advisers – especially Peter Jamieson and Nicky Buller, who were unstinting in their help with encouragement, information, anecdotes and research material. Lorel Colgin in her 2001 course 'Hot Topics in Bioscience' with Continuing Education, Sydney University, deepened my understanding of DNA research. I'd also like to thank Uta Frith for her kind encouragement, and also Robyn Barker, Norma Tracey, Tamara Sztynda, Mike Woolfe, Robyn Williams and Lawrence Bartak for their scientific advice. Norman Swann and Brian Martin advised me about scientific fraud. Rebecca Roubin corrected the scientific details of the last draft, and Teena Caithness, then of the Autism Association of NSW, was pivotal in suggesting to me the possible role of Hans Asperger's paper during the time of the Nazis in Austria.

My thanks also to the Australian Society of Authors for including me in its mentorship programme; the Literature Fund of the Australia Council for a one-year fellowship; at the University of New South Wales, Professor Merilyn Sleigh of the Faculty of Life Sciences permitted me to observe its laboratories, and Professor Hans Coster inspired me with his view of science; and at the University of Technology, Sydney, the Writing Programme in the Department of Humanites and Social Sciences gave my research much-needed support.

I must acknowledge the help of Oliver Edwards-Neil and Lotta Sundstrom for their translation of a paper about Hans Asperger, Kitty Graham for her translation of Handel's song, Eva Rebhun, Louise Dolan, Sue Britton, Jose Borghino and Annie Coussins for their suggestions and inspiration, and Bonnie Spanier, whose book *Im/Partial Science* set me on this search; she also suggested my first reading list.

The novel went through many drafts, one or all of which were read and commented on by Glenda Adams and Graham Williams of the University of Technology, Sydney, Jane Gleeson-White, and Anne Brewster of the University of New South Wales. I valued greatly the suggestions made by my mentors Debra Adelaide, and Peter Bishop of Varuna, the Writers' Centre. Gordon Graham read every word. My heart-felt thanks to my patient editors Sarina Rowell and Jo Jarrah (whose insights inspired a whole new draft), my publisher Nikki Christer, and my agent Lyn Tranter who always urged me on when I lost heart.